Veil Dawn

Lydia Page

Published by Lydia Page, 2024.

This is a work of fiction. Similarities to real people, places, or events are entirely coincidental.

VEIL DAWN

First edition. November 8, 2024.

Copyright © 2024 Lydia Page.

ISBN: 979-8227543684

Written by Lydia Page.

Chapter 1: The Storm and the Sword

The rain drenches us both, but he stands unshaken, the water dripping from his brow barely a hindrance. I can't read him—not fully. His eyes, a glacial blue that seem immune to the warmth of anything human, flicker with something close to amusement. I raise my sword, every inch of its weight pulsing through my arms as if demanding the kind of ruthlessness I'm still uncertain I possess. He tilts his head, that smirk never faltering. It's not arrogance; it's something worse. A challenge. An unspoken taunt. Like he's seen every fear I've buried, every flaw I've ever pretended wasn't there.

We move in sync, circling one another, each footstep an echo, bouncing off the wet cobblestones beneath us. I hear the distant clap of thunder, the lightning casting sharp shadows across his face. He lunges, and I parry instinctively, the metallic clash ringing out, breaking the rhythm of the storm. For a moment, I wonder if this entire fight is just an elaborate game for him, something to stave off boredom. His gaze flickers again, the faintest trace of satisfaction. I try to hide my frustration, not letting him see how he's unnerving me.

And then he does something unexpected. He pauses, sword lowered just a fraction, and extends a hand toward me, palm open, the rain beading off his fingertips. I freeze, not understanding. "Truce?" His voice is low, a murmur that feels more like a dare than a request. I hesitate, glancing between his hand and his face, the wariness digging deep into my bones. Every instinct tells me to refuse, to keep my guard up. But there's a glint in his eye that promises more than this fight, something unspoken but magnetic, and against my better judgment, I lower my blade.

I take his hand, and it's shockingly warm, grounding in a way I hadn't expected. We're strangers, barely more than adversaries, but his grip is steady, pulling me to my feet, drawing me into his sphere as if we've done this a thousand times before. The rain falls harder, washing away the blood and grime as we turn, moving as one down the narrow alleyway that winds through the heart of the city. This place is a maze of secrets, each shadow hiding something dangerous or forgotten, and he leads the way as if he knows every corner intimately. I keep my sword raised, a cautious step behind him, but he doesn't seem to care. We pass under stone arches, past doorways that whisper with voices just out of reach, and I can't help but wonder if I've made a grave mistake.

It's not until we reach a dimly lit staircase that he pauses, glancing back at me with an expression that's almost—no, it can't be—curious. "You don't trust me," he says, half amused, half resigned, and I want to laugh. "You wield that sword like it's an extension of yourself, yet you hesitate. Why?"

"I don't make it a habit to trust strange men who look at me like I'm some kind of puzzle," I retort, the bite in my voice sharp enough to cut. He grins, unabashed, and for a moment, I'm struck by how effortlessly he absorbs every jab, every insult, as if they're compliments. It's infuriating.

"I could say the same about you," he replies, his tone soft but probing, and something flickers in his eyes—an understanding, almost. It's the first genuine thing I've seen from him. Before I can respond, he turns, descending the staircase in silence, leaving me to follow or risk being swallowed by the shadows creeping up the alleyway.

We step into a vast underground chamber, the flickering torchlight casting strange shapes across the stone walls. The air is thick, stifling, each breath tasting of damp earth and secrets older than memory. He moves with ease through the darkness, as if he belongs here, his every step confident. I feel like an intruder, my senses on high alert, every sound amplified in the stillness. Somewhere in the distance, a soft murmur of voices echoes through the tunnels, a reminder that we're not alone, that we're walking straight into something far more dangerous than any sword fight.

He glances back, eyes scanning my face as if searching for cracks in my resolve. "There's a reason I brought you here," he says, his voice barely a whisper, but it carries a weight that makes me stop. "There are forces at work in this city, alliances that shift like the tide, and you're right in the middle of it."

"You're assuming I want to be," I reply, my words clipped, the unease growing in my chest. He only nods, a glimmer of understanding in his gaze.

"Perhaps not. But sometimes the storm finds us, whether we're ready or not."

There's something about the way he says it, the way he seems almost resigned to the chaos that lies ahead, that makes me see him differently. For all his arrogance, his knowing smirks and sharp remarks, there's a vulnerability there, buried deep beneath the surface. I don't trust him, not by a long shot, but there's a part of me—a part I hate to admit—that wants to understand him, to peel back the layers and see what lies beneath.

As we move deeper into the underground, the voices grow louder, indistinct but menacing, and I feel his hand brush against mine, a silent reassurance. I want to pull away, to pretend I don't need his help, but the truth is, I'm not sure I'd make it through this labyrinth without him. The city may be a familiar place, but down here, everything feels different, every shadow a threat, every corner hiding something sinister.

We reach a door, heavy and reinforced, and he pauses, his hand on the handle, his gaze meeting mine. There's a challenge there, a question he doesn't need to ask. I nod, a silent acceptance, and as he pushes the door open, I feel a surge of something I can't quite name—fear, excitement, maybe even hope. Whatever lies ahead, I know one thing: there's no going back.

The room we step into is cavernous, swallowing sound, so quiet that I can hear my own heartbeat pulsing in my ears. Torches line the walls, casting erratic shadows that twist and curl over ancient stone. Somewhere in the distance, the faintest hum of voices fills the air, low and steady, like the heartbeat of the city itself. I glance over at him, but he's already moving, his focus sharp, like he's slipping into a role he knows all too well.

It's unsettling, really. How this man can shift so easily between roles: the cocky opponent, the reluctant ally, and now, something darker. There's a certainty in his stride that tells me he's been here before, and perhaps that should make me feel safer. It doesn't. It only reminds me that I'm the outsider here, following him through an underworld I barely understand.

I almost wish he'd talk, fill the space with something—anything—that would ease the tension. But he seems content to move in silence, the air thick with words unspoken. So, naturally, I break the quiet. "Do you always lure strangers into damp, shadowy cellars, or is that something you reserve just for me?"

He looks over his shoulder, and there's a glint in his eye—a flash of something I can't place. "Only the ones who look like they could kill me if they wanted to." He says it so calmly, so unbothered, that I'm left standing there, torn between laughing and rolling my eyes. Before I can decide, he gestures for me to follow him through a narrow archway, and I have no choice but to fall in line.

The corridor narrows, the ceiling lowering to a point where I feel like I need to duck, though he moves easily, even with his height. I catch the scent of something earthy and old, the kind of smell that clings to places forgotten by time. Dust tickles my throat, and I resist the urge to cough, unwilling to break the silence again. We reach a small, dimly lit room, its walls covered in faded tapestries that look like they've seen centuries pass.

He pauses in the doorway, his hand resting against the rough stone, his eyes scanning the room as though expecting something to jump out at him. "Wait here," he says, his tone leaving no room for argument. Without another word, he slips inside, disappearing behind a heavy curtain in the corner, leaving me alone.

I shift my weight, the unease creeping up my spine as I scan the room, searching for anything that might make this place feel less ominous. There's a chill in the air, the kind that settles into your bones and stays there, and I can't shake the feeling that I'm being watched. I take a step forward, curious despite myself, and brush my fingers along the edge of one of the tapestries. The fabric feels brittle, delicate under my touch, and I wonder how much history these walls have seen.

I'm still lost in thought when he returns, his expression unreadable. His gaze flickers to my hand on the tapestry, and for a moment, I think I see something soften in his eyes. But it's gone just as quickly, replaced by the familiar guardedness I'm beginning to recognize. He steps closer, his voice low. "There's someone you need to meet."

"Someone?" I raise an eyebrow, crossing my arms. "And here I thought this was just a romantic evening stroll through the city's most depressing basement."

He smirks, and I almost hate the way it makes me feel like I've won some small, invisible victory. "If this is your idea of romance, I can't imagine what your last date looked like."

Before I can come up with a retort, he's leading me down yet another corridor, this one even narrower than the last. The walls here are rougher, unfinished, as though the builders simply gave up halfway through. The flickering light from the torches creates eerie patterns, and I have to fight the urge to keep looking over my shoulder, half expecting to see a shadow trailing us.

We stop in front of a large wooden door, its surface scratched and battered, as if it's held back a thousand secrets—or perhaps people who've tried to leave. He places his hand on the door, hesitating for the first time since we began this strange journey. His expression hardens, and he looks back at me, his face shadowed but unmistakably intense. "What you see in here... it might change things. For both of us."

I don't know what he expects me to say. That I'm ready? That I trust him? Neither would be true. But I nod anyway, steeling myself, not wanting him to see the uncertainty flickering in my eyes. He pushes the door open, and we step inside.

The room is dimly lit, smoky, and crowded with figures that shift and whisper in the shadows. The scent of incense clings to the air, mingling with the faint smell of something metallic, something sharp. A figure stands at the center, cloaked and hooded, their face hidden in shadow, and I feel his hand brush against my arm, a subtle warning.

"Ah," says a voice from the darkness, smooth and unsettlingly familiar, as though I've heard it in a dream. "So, this is the one who's caused such a stir."

The figure steps forward, and I catch a glint of something silver at their throat—a pendant, shaped like a twisted coil of metal, gleaming in the torchlight. The figure's eyes, dark and piercing, lock onto mine, and I feel an unexplainable shiver run through me. It's as if they're looking straight through me, peeling back every layer I've carefully constructed, leaving me exposed.

I glance at him, hoping for some kind of explanation, but he's watching the figure with an expression I can't decipher. There's something like respect, maybe even fear, in his eyes—a vulnerability I hadn't expected. He takes a step forward, lowering his head slightly, and I realize this isn't just any encounter. This is something far bigger than I'd been prepared for.

"Is this the one?" the figure asks, their voice carrying a note of amusement, as if they find the entire situation terribly entertaining.

He nods, his jaw set, and for the first time, I see a hint of uncertainty in his gaze. "Yes. This is her."

The figure laughs, a sound that echoes off the walls, hollow and unsettling. "Good. Then we have much to discuss."

There's a weight to those words, a finality that makes my pulse quicken. The figure reaches out, their hand hovering just above mine, and I feel a strange warmth radiating from them, a power that feels ancient and unyielding. I don't know what they see in me, what they're expecting, but I can't bring myself to look away.

In that moment, I realize that whatever path I've just stepped onto, there's no turning back. The city above, the storm, even the fight—all of it fades, leaving only this room, these strangers, and the feeling that I've crossed a line I didn't know existed. And, against all logic, I want to know what lies on the other side.

The figure's hand hovers near mine, the air between us humming with a strange, unspoken energy. I'm acutely aware of how exposed I feel, standing under their gaze, every instinct screaming at me to turn, to leave, to run as far from here as possible. But I don't. My fingers curl into fists, steadying myself. There's a dark thrill in the danger, in the way this cloaked stranger seems to know things about me I haven't even admitted to myself. I hold their gaze, refusing to flinch.

"You're braver than he lets on," the figure murmurs, their eyes flicking briefly to my companion, whose expression has settled into a practiced mask of indifference. I know it's a performance; I'd seen the hint of unease in him earlier, a tension that even he couldn't hide. There's something he hasn't told me, and it gnaws at me, a nagging itch in the back of my mind.

I can't resist pressing. "Is that why I'm here? Because you think I'm brave?" The words are half-sarcastic, but my heart hammers as I speak them. I know there's something else at play, something neither of them are willing to say.

The figure's smile is slight, almost imperceptible. "Not just brave. Useful." They pause, letting the word linger between us, and I feel a chill run down my spine. "You're here because you have something we need."

There's a beat of silence, and I glance at him, hoping for some kind of reassurance, a sign that he knows what's happening. But he avoids my gaze, jaw clenched, eyes fixed on some invisible point just over my shoulder. It's an answer in itself. Whatever is happening here, he knew it was coming. He'd known all along.

My voice is steadier than I feel. "So, what is it you think I have?"

The figure's eyes gleam, amusement glinting in the depths of their shadowed face. "Courage, of course. And a blade sharp enough to cut through a very stubborn knot."

I glance down at the sword still in my hand, feeling its weight, its strange familiarity. "What kind of knot?"

The figure's laugh is soft, barely more than a breath. "Ah, but that's what you're here to discover, isn't it?"

I open my mouth to press further, but they turn, their cloak whispering against the stone floor as they glide to a small, iron-bound chest in the corner. They lift the lid with a creak, withdrawing a small bundle wrapped in dark cloth, which they cradle with a gentleness that seems out of place in this foreboding room. They glance at me, something almost resembling reverence in their gaze.

"Take it," they say, holding it out toward me. "It will show you the path forward."

I hesitate, feeling the weight of their words settle like stones in my stomach. My hand reaches out, almost of its own accord, and I grasp the bundle, feeling an immediate warmth seep through the fabric. I glance up, but the figure's gaze has shifted, unreadable and distant.

"What am I supposed to do with this?" I ask, hoping for some hint, some sliver of understanding.

Their voice is soft, almost regretful. "That's for you to discover."

I glance at him, hoping for some kind of answer, but he's watching me with a curious mix of apprehension and anticipation, as though I'm the one who's supposed to understand all of this. Frustration flares in me, but before I can speak, the figure gives a small nod toward the door. "Go. Before it's too late."

The sense of urgency in their voice sends a fresh wave of adrenaline through me, and I don't hesitate this time. I turn, clutching the bundle tightly, and move toward the door. He follows, his steps quick, matching my pace as we weave through the twisting corridors, back the way we came.

The silence between us is heavy, charged with questions neither of us seem willing to ask. My mind races, trying to piece together the fragments of this strange encounter, the weight of the bundle in my hands growing heavier with every step. Finally, I break the silence, unable to keep the tension bottled any longer.

"You knew, didn't you? You knew what they wanted from me."

He glances over, his expression unreadable, but there's something raw in his eyes, something almost vulnerable. "I suspected. But knowing and seeing are two very different things."

I let out a harsh laugh, the frustration bubbling over. "So, what, I'm just supposed to go along with whatever cryptic quest they've set up for me? Carry around this—" I hold up the bundle, "—this whatever-it-is, and trust that it's all part of some grand plan?"

He stops, turning to face me fully, his gaze intense. "You can turn back if you want. Walk away, forget any of this ever happened. No one's forcing you to stay."

The words hang between us, daring me to choose the easy path, the safe path. And maybe I should. Maybe I should leave this underground labyrinth, toss the bundle into the nearest river, and return to whatever semblance of a normal life I can piece together. But there's a fire in me now, a curiosity that won't let go, a pull that's stronger than fear.

I narrow my eyes, meeting his gaze with a defiance I didn't know I possessed. "No one's forcing me. But you know I'm not going anywhere."

He nods, a faint smirk tugging at the corner of his mouth, and I feel a flicker of satisfaction, knowing I've called his bluff. We continue walking, the silence less tense now, almost companionable, though the weight of what lies ahead presses down on both of us.

As we near the exit, I catch the first hint of fresh air, a relief after the thick, stale atmosphere of the tunnels. I quicken my pace, eager to break free from the oppressive walls, but before I can take another step, he grabs my arm, pulling me back sharply.

"Wait."

His tone is low, urgent, and the hairs on the back of my neck prickle. I turn, about to ask what's wrong, but the answer is already there, lurking in the shadows at the end of the corridor.

A figure stands silhouetted in the dim light, cloaked in darkness, watching us with an intensity that makes my skin crawl. They're close enough that I can make out the glint of a weapon in their hand, the faintest shift of movement as they step forward, blocking our path.

He tightens his grip on my arm, his voice barely a whisper. "Stay behind me."

I don't argue, instinctively lowering myself into a defensive stance, my hand tightening around the hilt of my sword. The figure steps closer, their face hidden in shadow, and I feel the weight of the bundle in my hands, a reminder of the responsibility I never asked for, the danger I'm now neck-deep in.

The figure stops, their voice cutting through the silence, smooth and sinister. "Did you really think it would be that easy?"

My pulse quickens, my body tensing, ready for whatever comes next. The stranger's gaze fixes on me, cold and unyielding, and in that moment, I know that whatever happens here, nothing will be the same.

And then, without warning, they lunge.

Chapter 2: The Velvet Secret

I clutched the rusted iron torch bracket on the wall, breathing in the earthy scent of damp stone and stale air. The flickering light from Damian's torch carved shifting shadows on the walls, revealing carvings of figures twisted in silent agony, relics of an era none of us were meant to remember. I glanced at him, jaw clenched, lips twisted into that devil-may-care smile that had me grinding my teeth. He was taller than I'd initially realized, the slant of his shoulders broader, filling the narrow space with an easy confidence. Even with his unruly dark hair and a face that looked like it had never known a single misstep, he was out of place here—no, we both were.

"Careful," he murmured as he noticed me studying him. "Stare any longer, and you might learn my darkest secrets."

"Careful," I mimicked, voice dipping low. "Pry too much, and you'll find out I've got no time for arrogant know-it-alls."

He laughed softly, the sound echoing down the tunnel like a melody, low and haunting. He didn't respond, just continued moving forward, his torch revealing more crumbling stones and the occasional glint of old metal embedded in the walls. The air grew colder with each step, and a shiver crawled up my spine that I tried to dismiss as nothing but the chill.

I hated him a little more with each stride. He wasn't supposed to be here, and he certainly wasn't supposed to know about the Velvet Charm. The amulet was mine to find, mine to leverage. A shot at rewriting history, at taking back something I'd lost. And here he was, playing some mysterious partner, his eyes darting over every detail of the catacombs like he knew them better than I did.

"So, how did you even know about the Velvet Charm?" I tried to sound casual, but my voice betrayed me, an edge that had him glancing over his shoulder, eyebrow arched. He knew he had the upper hand, and damn if he wasn't about to exploit it.

"A man doesn't reveal his sources, darling," he replied, adding that smirk I was already beginning to loathe. "And it's not the kind of knowledge that you come across in casual conversation. This isn't a weekend treasure hunt for the curious."

"I'm well aware," I snapped, kicking a loose stone with more force than I meant to. It skittered down the uneven path, clinking against the ground before falling silent. "And I'm not curious, either. I'm committed."

"Committed to what, exactly?" he asked, his voice surprisingly soft, almost too soft for someone who had no right asking questions.

I hesitated. The truth danced at the back of my throat, bitter and jagged. But I didn't owe him that part of me, not when he was still just another obstacle to my goal. Still, I couldn't deny the sting of his question or how close he'd gotten to something I'd buried deep.

"To things you don't get to know," I muttered, hoping that would end the conversation.

He shrugged, apparently content to let it go. For now. But his silence felt heavier than any more words he could have thrown my way, thickening the air between us as we wound deeper into the catacombs. The stones here were older, the carvings more elaborate. One depicted a woman holding an orb, her eyes wide with terror as shadows clawed at her from all sides.

Damian slowed beside me, studying it with an intensity that caught me off guard. He ran his fingers lightly over the woman's face, a fleeting gentleness in his expression that didn't fit with the cocky, unflappable persona he wore like armor.

"It's said the Velvet Charm isn't just an artifact," he said softly, his voice barely more than a whisper. "It's a key. A key to doors we're not meant to open."

My heart hammered, each beat pulsing in my ears. I didn't want to admit it, but the legends around the Velvet Charm had always been more than just myth to me. They had been lifelines, paths to a redemption I didn't know if I even deserved. And yet, here was Damian, voicing the thing I'd barely dared to believe in myself.

"And what about you?" I challenged, forcing myself to hold his gaze. "You think it's a key, too?"

He leaned against the wall, tilting his head in that infuriatingly casual way. "I think it's whatever we need it to be."

"And what do you need it to be?"

The question surprised him—I could tell by the flicker in his eyes, there and gone. But he recovered quickly, a glint of humor flashing across his face.

"Maybe I just need it to pay my rent," he quipped.

I snorted, rolling my eyes, but there was a tension now, an unspoken understanding that we both knew wasn't really a joke. He was here because, like me, he had something to fight for, something too raw and too personal to hand over easily. I could almost respect that. Almost.

But respect didn't mean trust, and as much as I wanted to ignore it, the truth was clawing at the back of my mind: we needed each other, whether I liked it or not. Alone, I'd have to rely on nothing but fading maps and half-remembered tales. With Damian, though...he knew these tunnels, these histories, as if he'd lived them himself.

"So, truce?" he offered, reaching out a hand that I stared at with pure suspicion.

I raised an eyebrow, crossing my arms. "Not a chance."

He laughed, withdrawing his hand but nodding, as if he expected no less. "Suit yourself. Just don't get lost."

The path narrowed again, forcing us closer together. The walls seemed to press in, the darkness tightening around us. In the silence, I became all too aware of Damian's steady breathing, of the warmth of him standing close enough to brush against my shoulder. I hated that I noticed it, hated even more that I felt something other than annoyance, something uncomfortably close to relief.

The darkness shifted, and for a moment, I thought I saw movement up ahead—a shadow darting out of sight, too quick for me to catch. I froze, instinctively grabbing Damian's arm.

"What was that?" I whispered, the words barely audible.

"Nothing good," he replied, his voice calm but his hand moving to the dagger strapped to his belt.

And in that breath of silence, with nothing but the oppressive darkness around us and the unsettling feeling that we were no longer alone, I felt it—an unspoken alliance threading between us, fragile but real.

The silence in the catacombs felt like a living thing, pressing in on us with a damp, oppressive weight. Shadows curled around the edges of our torchlight, playing tricks with my vision, whispering promises of dead ends and dangers lurking just out of sight. I took another careful step forward, only to have Damian halt suddenly, his hand shooting up to stop me.

"What now?" I hissed, trying to keep my voice low but firm. I couldn't help the irritation that crept in; he'd barely said a useful thing since we started, and I wasn't in the mood for more of his cryptic nonsense.

"Shh," he murmured, tilting his head like he was listening for something. His jaw tightened, and I had a sinking feeling that maybe he wasn't just trying to be mysterious. "Do you hear that?"

I strained my ears, but there was only the faint drip of water from some hidden source and the occasional scratch of rats skittering along the stones. I shook my head. "All I hear is the sound of you wasting time."

He flashed me a quick, humorless grin. "Trust me, if we don't take this seriously, time won't be the only thing wasted down here."

There it was again, that hint of something darker lurking beneath his arrogance. Against my better judgment, I let him lead, watching as he scanned each shadow, every uneven stone. My chest tightened with every step; I couldn't help but wonder how much he truly knew. And more disturbingly, how much he wasn't telling me.

We turned a corner, and the tunnel opened up into a cavernous chamber that took my breath away. It was magnificent, in the eerie, haunting way only something ancient could be. Columns lined the walls, carved from stone that shimmered faintly, as if touched by starlight. Crumbling frescoes adorned the walls, depicting strange symbols I couldn't quite make out, half-hidden by layers of grime and decay.

Damian moved forward slowly, reverence in his every step. He reached a hand out, tracing the outline of one of the symbols, and I could see his face soften, a faraway look in his eyes. I was seized by an urge to know what he was seeing, what ghosts he was communing with here in the belly of the earth.

"Do you even know what any of that means?" I asked, trying to sound casual but unable to keep the curiosity from my voice.

He let out a long breath, fingers lingering on the stone as if it were the skin of a lover. "Maybe I do. Maybe I don't." He turned, catching the look on my face, and his smirk softened. "History's just a story we tell ourselves, isn't it? And I'm quite good at telling stories."

"Just not at sharing them, apparently," I shot back, folding my arms and raising an eyebrow. He wasn't getting off that easily.

He chuckled, the sound low and dark. "There's more truth in secrets than in stories, wouldn't you say?" He leaned in close, his voice a mere whisper. "I'd rather hold onto the truth than scatter it carelessly. Especially down here."

I opened my mouth to argue, but the torchlight flickered, casting strange shapes on the walls. For a moment, I could've sworn I saw movement—a fleeting figure darting just beyond the reach of the light. I tensed, glancing around, but everything was still again, silent and watchful.

Damian must have noticed my reaction because his gaze sharpened, torch raised higher as he scanned the darkness. "We're not alone," he muttered, more to himself than to me.

I tried to laugh, but it came out strained. "What, you think the ghosts are restless?"

"Maybe," he said, his tone dead serious. "Or maybe someone's been keeping an eye on us since we entered."

A chill crept up my spine. I wanted to brush off his words, but the way he said it, so matter-of-fact, left me with no room for doubt. We might have been the only living souls in this place, but that didn't mean we were alone. The darkness here felt alive, watching, waiting.

"You're not going to tell me you actually believe in this haunted catacomb nonsense, are you?" I forced a laugh, though it sounded hollow even to me. "I mean, I didn't peg you as superstitious."

His gaze slid over to me, a little too piercing for comfort. "It's not about superstition. It's about survival. Sometimes, it's the things you can't see that are the most dangerous."

For once, I had no retort. His words settled over me like a heavy fog, filling the spaces where my bravado usually lived. I swallowed, trying to push down the uneasy feeling growing in my chest. But as we moved deeper into the chamber, the weight of his words clung to me, a constant reminder of how little I understood this place—or him.

We edged further in, each step a gamble in the flickering light. And then I saw it: at the far end of the chamber, partially hidden by the shadow of a crumbling column, lay a pedestal, worn but unmistakably ancient. And on it rested something that made my heart stop.

It was a pendant, or rather, what was left of one. A shimmering amulet shaped like an eye, set with a single dark stone that seemed to drink in the light, pulling it into an unfathomable void. This had to be it—the Velvet Charm.

I felt Damian stiffen beside me, and I knew he saw it too. He reached out a hand as if to touch it, but I grabbed his arm, my fingers digging into his sleeve. "Wait," I breathed, barely able to keep my voice steady. "What if it's... you know, cursed?"

He glanced down at me, amused. "I thought you didn't believe in curses?"

"Doesn't mean I'm stupid," I muttered. But my gaze stayed on the amulet, mesmerized by the way it seemed to pulse in the torchlight, a dark heartbeat in the depths of the stone. "What if... what if touching it does something? Something bad?"

He smirked, though there was no mockery in it this time, just something darker, more complex. "The Velvet Charm isn't a bedtime story, and it's not some object for the faint-hearted. It's power, pure and simple. And power, as I'm sure you know, doesn't come without a cost."

The way he said it, like he was speaking from experience, sent a shiver down my spine. But I couldn't back down now, not when I was so close. Whatever danger the amulet held, whatever secrets lay within it, I needed to know. I had come too far, risked too much to walk away empty-handed.

Ignoring the voice in my head screaming at me to stop, I reached out, fingers trembling as they hovered over the surface of the amulet. For a split second, my hand brushed against Damian's, and I felt a jolt—not from the amulet but from him, from the tension simmering between us that neither of us wanted to acknowledge.

He withdrew his hand, but his eyes remained fixed on me, daring me to go through with it. My heart thundered as I inched closer, fingers brushing against the cool, smooth surface of the stone. And just as I made contact, the chamber seemed to shudder, a low rumble that made dust fall from the ceiling and sent a wave of foreboding rolling through me.

The air thickened, turning suffocatingly heavy, and I felt a strange pull, as if the amulet were reaching inside me, searching, assessing. My stomach twisted, and I wanted to pull away, but something kept me rooted there, my hand fused to the stone, bound to it in a way I couldn't explain.

And Damian's face, usually so unreadable, was now alight with something almost like fear.

The ground beneath us trembled, subtle at first, then a sharper jolt that made me gasp and snap my hand back from the amulet. Dust showered down from the ceiling, the entire chamber seeming to shudder like it was alive and about to exhale. I shot a look at Damian, hoping he'd be the calm one, but even he seemed rattled, his usual smirk nowhere in sight.

"Well, that was…ominous," he muttered, his hand hovering protectively near his belt where a dagger gleamed in its sheath. The pulse of danger in the air was palpable, thick and electric, and I suddenly regretted every brave or stupid decision that had led me to this moment.

"Ominous?" I echoed, my voice tight as I fought to keep my panic in check. "That's how you're going to describe the possibility of being buried alive in an ancient tomb?"

He shrugged, a shadow of his old bravado flickering back. "What else would you call it?"

I opened my mouth to argue, but a deep groaning sound reverberated through the chamber, drowning out any witty retort I might have had. The walls, once imposing and immovable, seemed to flex, and cracks snaked along the floor, winding their way toward us like the veins of some ancient, malevolent creature. Instinct took over, and I grabbed Damian's arm, pulling him back as a massive stone slab crashed down where we'd just been standing. The noise echoed, deafening, and for a moment, the air felt full of nothing but the weight of our own breath.

"Still think it's a cute little story?" I whispered, my hand still clutching his sleeve, our faces mere inches apart. I could feel his pulse under my fingertips, and it struck me how human he suddenly seemed, stripped of his smugness and mystery. Just as scared as I was.

"Not exactly the romantic evening I'd planned," he replied, a forced smirk twisting his lips. But I could see the tension in his jaw, the way his gaze flickered around the chamber, assessing every shadow, every possible escape route. We were trapped here, and he knew it as well as I did.

The silence that followed was heavy, expectant. I watched as he took a step back, his eyes narrowing as he studied the amulet still sitting innocently on its pedestal. I could see the wheels turning in his mind, the calculation, the weighing of risks. It was maddening how quickly he could go from vulnerable to detached, as if he'd simply decided to shut off any fear, any emotion, in favor of cold, unfeeling strategy.

"Don't," I warned, reading the intention in his stance.

His gaze snapped to mine, steely and challenging. "And why not?"

"Because," I replied, trying to keep my voice steady, "whatever just happened, it's because of that thing. You touch it again, and who knows what else it'll unleash."

"That's the thing, though," he said, tilting his head thoughtfully. "We're already here. Whatever forces are at play, we're part of them now. The question is, are we going to just sit back and wait, or are we going to take control of the situation?"

"'Take control?'" I scoffed, glancing around at the disintegrating walls. "Are you hearing yourself? There's no controlling this. It's ancient magic, Damian, the kind that doesn't care about our plans or our cleverness."

His eyes softened, just for a heartbeat, before that icy resolve slipped back over his face. "Maybe. But if you're right, then what's our other option? Walk away empty-handed?"

I wanted to scream at him, to tell him that survival was more valuable than whatever prize he was after. But the look in his eyes, fierce and unrelenting, made me hesitate. There was something deeper driving him, something raw and desperate. And even as a part of me resented him for dragging me into this madness, another part—one I didn't want to acknowledge—understood him.

He took a step toward the pedestal, his fingers grazing the air just above the amulet. I reached out instinctively, grabbing his hand, feeling the roughness of his skin, the warmth that contradicted his icy demeanor.

"Damian," I said, my voice barely above a whisper. "If you touch that thing, there's no going back. You don't get to rewrite history without consequence."

He turned, meeting my gaze with an intensity that stole the air from my lungs. "Maybe I don't want to go back."

His words hung between us, charged and electric. But before I could respond, the amulet seemed to pulse, a faint glow emanating from its dark center, casting an eerie light over Damian's face. I felt an inexplicable pull, something inside me reaching out to the amulet, an ache that defied reason or logic. And judging by the expression on Damian's face, he felt it too.

Then, all at once, the light intensified, flooding the chamber in an ethereal glow. The ground trembled again, more violently this time, and I stumbled, my grip on Damian's hand the only thing keeping me from falling. The air grew thick, oppressive, as if the very walls were leaning in, listening, waiting for us to make our choice.

"We have to leave," I gasped, pulling at his arm, desperate to drag him back to safety. But he remained rooted, transfixed by the amulet, his eyes glazed with a strange mixture of awe and determination.

"It's calling to us," he murmured, his voice distant. "Don't you feel it?"

I did, and that terrified me. There was something seductive in the pull, a promise that was both exhilarating and damning. I could feel it threading through my veins, igniting a fierce longing for power, for control. For the chance to change everything. But I forced myself to shake off the feeling, to cling to the part of me that remembered why we had come here in the first place—and the dangers that came with it.

"Damian, please," I pleaded, my voice breaking. "This isn't what we came for. We need to leave before it's too late."

But he didn't move. Instead, he reached out, his fingers brushing against the surface of the amulet with a reverence that was almost painful to watch. And the moment he made contact, the light surged, blinding and searing, as if it were feeding off his touch, his desires.

The ground split beneath us, a jagged crack snaking through the stone, spreading outward with a violent force. I screamed, stumbling back as the floor began to crumble, revealing a chasm so deep that the bottom was lost in darkness. The light from the amulet shot upward, twisting and spiraling like a living thing, filling the chamber with an unholy glow.

And then, in the chaos, I felt something cold and solid grip my wrist, pulling me back just as the floor gave way beneath my feet. I looked up, heart pounding, to see Damian staring down at me, his face pale but determined.

"We're not finished here," he said, his voice steady despite the madness erupting around us. "Not until we know what it wants."

"What it wants?" I echoed, panic clawing at my throat. "This isn't some game, Damian! This thing—it's alive. It's dangerous."

"Exactly," he replied, a dark glint in his eyes. "And we're the ones who woke it up. So we're the ones who need to figure out what happens next."

His words, his grip, the unyielding determination in his gaze—all of it felt like a noose tightening around me, binding me to this moment, this madness. And as the light from the amulet surged, casting twisted shadows that seemed to dance with malevolent glee, I knew there was no easy way out.

But before I could respond, a chilling voice echoed through the chamber, as if the walls themselves were speaking, each word dripping with ancient malice.

"You sought me," the voice intoned, low and resonant, filling the air with an icy dread. "Now... face the price."

Chapter 3: Mirrors and Masks

My eyes linger on the glint of candlelight bouncing off the intricate web of mirrors surrounding us, each one holding an uncanny reflection that seems just slightly wrong. Shadows flicker at odd angles, stretching and contorting as if they're mocking our movements, or perhaps hinting at secrets we'd rather keep hidden. Damian's reflection catches my attention first. He's standing just behind me, his figure outlined in sharp contrast against the dim room, every inch of him dark and stormy, as though he's made of midnight itself. In the mirror's fractured light, he almost looks like a stranger—someone dangerous, someone who could shatter me just as easily as the glass between us.

But it's his eyes that unnerve me the most. They're the same stormy gray I've seen a thousand times, yet here they glint with something sharper, something predatory. I shift my gaze away, only to meet my own reflection in the next mirror, and I'm no better off. This version of me is somehow taller, poised, self-assured, and the look in her eyes is equal parts fierce and unfeeling. I'm half-tempted to press a hand to the glass, to test if this creature is real, and not some darker facet lurking within me. I feel Damian move closer, a subtle shift that sends my pulse racing.

"I hate this room," I mutter, half to myself, trying to break the spell. My voice sounds too loud, bouncing back at me in whispers from a dozen different reflections.

"Feeling a bit... exposed, are we?" Damian's voice carries a hint of amusement, the faintest curl of a smirk at the corner of his mouth. He leans in, close enough that I can feel his breath against my shoulder, warm and unsettlingly comforting.

"Amused, are you?" I reply, trying to keep my tone light, but the tremor betrays me. This place is supposed to be an empty hall in a long-abandoned mansion, and yet every part of it feels alive, watching, judging. I can't shake the feeling that someone—or something—wants us here. And not to play nice.

I glance at him, catching his smirk in the glass, and see a flicker of something softer than his usual brooding distance. But there's no time for that. Not here. We're not supposed to be vulnerable in a room haunted by reflections of who we might become if we're not careful.

With a roll of my eyes, I slip out of his reach, focusing on the cold, creeping dread pooling in the pit of my stomach. "The Velvet Charm's supposed to be hidden somewhere in here, right? Any idea where?"

"Somewhere," he replies, shrugging in a way that's infuriatingly casual, like we're on a leisurely scavenger hunt instead of caught in the middle of the Crimson Society's stronghold. "But I'd be careful. Rumor has it this room has… a mind of its own."

"Oh, how convenient." I keep my voice flat, but my fingers twitch, aching for something solid to hold on to. "Did that little 'rumor' mention how we might escape?"

He chuckles, low and throaty, and there's something dangerously thrilling in the sound, like he enjoys seeing me squirm. "Not in so many words, but there might be… a price. This place only gives what it takes in return."

The air turns colder, thick with something more than just damp and decay. I swallow, feeling the weight of his words sink in. This isn't just a room of mirrors—it's a trap designed to unravel you piece by piece, to strip away layers until there's nothing left but the barest slivers of truth, and the lies you wish you could hold onto.

A shiver prickles down my spine, and for once, it's not because of him. "So, what exactly are we supposed to give up?"

He doesn't answer, just watches me, his expression unreadable. For once, the teasing edge is gone, replaced by something darker, something almost… sad. He looks away, and I follow his gaze to the mirror beside us, where a faint glimmer catches my eye.

My pulse quickens as I step closer. It's almost hidden, a faint etching on the glass itself, delicate lines curving into an intricate pattern that could easily be overlooked. The Velvet Charm. It has to be. But the more I stare at it, the more it twists and changes, like it's testing me, daring me to look deeper.

As I reach out to touch it, Damian's hand closes over mine, stopping me. The contact is electric, sending an unwelcome thrill up my arm. I meet his gaze, and the look in his eyes is more warning than anything else.

"Careful," he murmurs, barely more than a whisper. "Once you touch it, there's no going back."

My breath hitches, a flood of memories and warnings rushing to the surface. The Crimson Society, with their whispered promises and deadly threats, the reason we're both here, bound together by mutual distrust and some twisted sense of loyalty neither of us wants to acknowledge. I know he's right, but something inside me rebels. I didn't come all this way to walk away now.

"What's the worst that could happen?" I reply, my voice steadier than I feel.

Damian sighs, his fingers still holding mine in place, but there's a flicker of admiration in his gaze. "Why do I get the feeling that's going to be your last question one of these days?"

"Because I like to keep things interesting," I counter, raising an eyebrow. And just like that, the tension between us shifts, turning warm, almost inviting. I don't dare acknowledge it, though. Not here. Not with everything at stake.

But the spell breaks as a sudden noise shatters the silence—a harsh, scraping sound, metal against stone. We both freeze, instincts sharpening as the air grows colder, sharper, laced with danger. Damian's hand slips from mine, and just like that, the fragile moment between us is gone, replaced by the cold reality that we're not alone.

I swallow, stepping back, every nerve on edge. In the mirrors around us, shadows stretch and deepen, moving like they're alive, like they're watching. And for a second, I'm not sure if I'm looking at my reflection anymore, or something else entirely, something darker and far more dangerous.

Damian pulls a dagger from his belt, his expression unreadable as he steps into the shadows. I hold my breath, hands clenched, as a cold whisper curls through the room, echoing in a voice I almost recognize—a voice promising secrets and lies, power and ruin, if only we'd reach out and take them.

The room seems to breathe, the silence laced with something predatory as shadows curl into the corners, stretching with a life of their own. The Crimson Society must be close, lurking somewhere beyond the reach of the candlelight that sputters in defiance. Damian moves with calculated calm, his expression hardening as he surveys the room, and I almost admire the way he can flick that switch, sliding from sardonic to lethal in a blink.

"We should move," he whispers, voice barely a thread of sound. "They won't wait forever to see if we make the first mistake."

"And what's that supposed to mean?" I mutter, though I'm already scanning for an exit, or at the very least, something to throw if we're ambushed. My reflection catches my eye again, and this time she's sneering at me, lips curled in a way that makes me wonder if she thinks I'm brave or just plain reckless. I've never been fond of mirrors, and this room is definitely reinforcing the aversion.

"It means," Damian murmurs, taking a step closer, "that they'll make the room feel as claustrophobic as possible until we start making decisions we can't take back. They've done this before."

A chill prickles down my spine. "So, we're the lab rats, I suppose?"

"If you like metaphors that make you sound helpless, sure." He smirks, though his eyes are anything but amused. "But I'd prefer to think of us as the unpredictable variables."

"Oh, so now I'm unpredictable?" I scoff, eyeing him with as much disdain as I can muster. "You're the one who just about signed us up for a lifetime membership to this shadowy club without so much as a warning."

His brow arches, gaze flickering with something unreadable. "Believe it or not, I'm not exactly a fan of memberships. I'd rather be the... freelancer type. A little riskier, but you know—more freedom."

"Oh, of course, because you're just a poster boy for personal freedom," I mutter, though there's a part of me—an infuriating part—that's oddly charmed. "So, Mr. Free Spirit, what exactly are we risking right now?"

He hesitates, glancing into one of the mirrors, and there's a flicker of vulnerability that I almost miss. Almost.

"We're risking becoming who they want us to be," he says softly, barely loud enough for me to hear. "People shaped by fear and ambition, people willing to lose everything to be more powerful, more... useful."

His words linger, sinking into the quiet, heavy with unspoken meaning. It's strange, but I feel like he's baring a truth neither of us really wanted to acknowledge, and for a second, I see a side of him I don't quite understand—a side that makes me think he's more familiar with the Crimson Society's ways than he's letting on.

But before I can probe further, a soft rustling interrupts us, a whisper of movement that feels like a cold hand grazing my skin. We both freeze, and I see Damian's jaw tighten as he grips the hilt of his dagger, a silent warning to stay alert. I don't need telling twice. Whatever's coming, it's not just a figment of the mirrors.

I brace myself, every nerve on edge, as something slithers into the dim light. At first, I think it's a shadow, but then I realize it's a figure cloaked in dark, tattered robes, moving with an unnatural grace that sends a jolt of terror through me. The figure stops just beyond the candlelight, head tilting as if appraising us.

"Unexpected visitors in the hall of mirrors," a voice rasps, more like a hiss than anything human. "You do know that those who enter here rarely leave unchanged... if they leave at all."

Damian shifts subtly, positioning himself between me and the figure, his voice smooth but laced with a threat. "We're just passing through, thanks. No need to go all dramatic."

The figure's laugh is a low, chilling rumble. "Passing through? Oh, no, you came here for a reason, didn't you?" The shadowed face turns to me, and I feel a strange tug, like it's seeing straight through me. "You seek the Velvet Charm. And perhaps... something more?"

I swallow, forcing myself to meet its gaze. "And if we are? Are you here to play cryptic guide, or just to spook us?"

The figure chuckles, amused. "A little of both, perhaps. But mostly, I'm here to remind you that nothing in this room is as it seems, least of all your own reflections." Its gaze flicks to Damian, lingering, and a smirk forms beneath the hood. "Especially him."

I glance at Damian, who's gone perfectly still, his expression unreadable. But I can feel the tension radiating from him, a coil wound so tightly I'm half afraid he'll snap. Whatever this creature is, it knows something—something I suspect Damian would rather keep hidden.

I'm about to press him, to demand answers while we still have the chance, when the figure steps forward, holding out a hand. A small, dark object dangles from its fingers—a tarnished silver locket, shaped like a heart but twisted, warped, as though it's been burned. The Velvet Charm.

"This," the figure murmurs, "is what you seek. But be warned: it comes at a price, one neither of you may wish to pay."

I reach for it, but Damian's hand catches mine, holding me back, his grip firm but careful. His eyes are locked on mine, and there's a desperate intensity there I've never seen before.

"Don't," he says, his voice low and urgent. "Once you take it, there's no going back. No undoing whatever it reveals."

I pull my hand free, bristling at his interference. "And since when did you decide what I can and can't handle?"

He shakes his head, a dark look passing over his face. "You have no idea what you're inviting in, what this charm really holds. It's not just a trinket—it's a piece of a curse, a piece of their power. If you take it, you'll be bound to them in ways you can't even imagine."

The figure watches us, silent, patient, as though enjoying the spectacle. But there's something almost hungry in its gaze, like it's waiting to see what we'll choose. And as much as I hate to admit it, Damian's words echo in my mind, weighing on my decision. The Velvet Charm gleams in the dim light, a beautiful, twisted thing, and it calls to me, promising power and answers and danger all at once.

But the price... is it one I'm willing to pay?

I feel the weight of Damian's stare, the way his hand hovers just close enough to stop me, and there's an odd comfort in it, despite the simmering tension between us. He's protecting me, even if I don't want him to. Even if I don't need him to.

The figure's laugh breaks the silence, low and mocking. "Ah, the dilemma of choice. How... poetic."

With a breath I didn't realize I'd been holding, I reach out, fingers brushing the locket, and feel a jolt run through me, cold and electric, like a spark from a storm.

The moment my fingers brush the locket, it's as if I've tapped into a current, a shock of cold that shoots up my arm, sharp and unforgiving. The world spins, the mirrored room tilting and stretching, warping until I can't tell what's real. Damian reaches for me, but his hand doesn't quite make it, his face distorted by the glass, his expression slipping between rage and desperation. The figure in the shadows watches with an eerie calm, as though it's seen a thousand souls fall into the same trap, and the spectacle has long since ceased to surprise it.

My vision blurs, but I can still see Damian, still hear his voice as it cuts through the strange, muffled silence. "Let go of it. Now."

I know he's right. I can feel the Velvet Charm's pull, the raw, irresistible tug that's winding itself around me like tendrils of ice. But I can't let go. Something deep and visceral holds me in place, like the locket has anchored itself to my bones, to some hidden part of me I barely understand.

Damian's voice grows sharper, cutting through the fog in my mind. "If you take this, you don't get to walk away. You don't get to choose who you are anymore."

His words slice through, igniting a spark of defiance. I yank my hand free, stumbling back, breathless and unsteady. The locket slips from my grasp and dangles again from the shadowed figure's hand, but its pull lingers, haunting me. I feel its absence like a wound, a dark ache beneath my skin.

"Such restraint," the figure murmurs, its voice curling around the words with dark amusement. "And here I thought you were ready for true power. Perhaps I was mistaken."

"Or perhaps I just don't take kindly to creepy sales pitches," I snap, though my heart is pounding, my voice barely holding steady. Damian steps up beside me, his face hard and unreadable, and for a moment, I hate how calm he looks, as if he's known all along what would happen. As if he's been waiting for me to fail.

The figure tilts its head, watching us with that same hungry interest. "You think you can leave without paying? You came here uninvited, seeking what isn't yours, and now you want to simply… walk away?"

I bite back a retort, glancing at Damian, but his gaze is locked on the figure, his expression dark and unreadable.

"Leave her out of this," he says, his voice low, cold as ice. "She didn't ask for your power, your 'price.' She just came along for the show."

The figure's laugh is a soft, mocking sound, echoing around us. "So gallant, Damian. But I believe you misunderstand. She came with her own intentions, her own desires. And the Charm... it knows. It always knows."

There's a heavy silence, and I feel a chill creep up my spine as I glance at Damian, suddenly aware of a hundred questions I've never asked. What does he know about this place? About the Crimson Society? And more disturbingly, what does he know about me?

His eyes meet mine, and for a fleeting moment, there's something raw there, something that slips past his usual mask. But before I can decipher it, he turns back to the figure, his tone sharp.

"Enough games. If you want a price, take it from me. I'll pay for both of us."

A shock runs through me at his words. I open my mouth to protest, but the figure raises a skeletal hand, silencing me with a simple gesture.

"Oh, you'll pay, Damian," it says, voice dripping with satisfaction. "You've already paid more than you know. And now, perhaps, it's time to collect."

The air grows colder, pressing down with a weight that's almost tangible. My skin prickles as the mirrors begin to shift again, each one showing a different fragment of reality, of possible futures and memories. I catch a glimpse of Damian in one—a version of him I don't recognize, eyes hard and merciless, his smile twisted into something cruel. In another, I see myself, standing alone in a desolate field, clutching the locket like it's the only thing I have left.

The figure's laugh echoes, filling the space, and I realize with a sickening jolt that it's manipulating the mirrors, showing us versions of ourselves that we could become. Or perhaps... that we already are, deep down.

"Enough!" I shout, the sound slicing through the eerie silence. "Stop playing games and tell us what you want."

The figure pauses, as if considering my words, and then its gaze shifts to me, a slow, unsettling movement that makes me feel like I'm standing on the edge of a cliff.

"What I want," it says softly, almost gently, "is to see how far you're willing to go. The Velvet Charm is yours, should you take it. But know that it will demand... everything."

Damian's hand closes around mine, his grip firm, grounding me. I can feel the tension in him, the silent warning, but I can't look away from the figure, from the twisted beauty of the locket it dangles before me.

"Why do you care?" I ask, my voice barely above a whisper. "What does it matter to you what we do with this... charm?"

The figure chuckles, a low, chilling sound. "Because power is an addiction, my dear, and once tasted, it rarely lets go. The Crimson Society exists for those who understand that simple truth... and for those willing to embrace it, no matter the cost."

Damian pulls me back, his voice urgent. "We're leaving. Now."

But the room seems to shift, the walls closing in, mirrors twisting around us until there's no clear way out. I feel a surge of panic, but I force it down, focusing on Damian's grip, on the steady presence beside me. We've survived this long, survived worse than some haunted hall of mirrors. We can make it out.

The figure's voice follows us, soft and taunting. "Run if you must, but you'll be back. They always come back. Power calls to the soul, and once it has tasted its own reflection, it craves more."

I take a shaky breath, tightening my hold on Damian's hand. The room spins, the mirrors blurring until they're nothing but shadows, and I feel the pull of the Velvet Charm, lingering, haunting, a whisper at the edge of my mind.

But as we stumble toward the door, I hear one final sound—a soft click, like a lock sliding into place. I glance over my shoulder, and in the mirror, I see the locket dangling, gleaming in the dark, calling to me.

And as the door slams shut behind us, I realize, with a sinking dread, that the real trap has only just begun.

Chapter 4: Crimson Shadows

The air around us sizzles with the tang of burnt metal and magic, thick enough that I can almost taste it. We're racing through the twisting corridors, echoes of our footsteps swallowed by the endless stone. The walls are alive with shadows—long, tapering things that lunge and retreat with every flicker of torchlight, as if the darkness itself conspires with our pursuers. Damian's hand around mine is the only steady thing in this shifting nightmare, though I can feel the slight tremor in his fingers, and his breath, too fast, betrays the calm he wears like a second skin.

I don't need to look back to know they're close. The Crimson Society has a way of letting you know they're coming without ever really showing themselves. Cloaks blend into the walls, figures slipping in and out of sight like fish beneath black water. Once, I glimpse a gloved hand stretch toward me, fingertips glowing with a dark light that turns the stone walls red before I yank myself out of reach, pressing forward with Damian's hand pulling me like a lifeline.

"Is this—" I barely get the words out between gasps. "Is this all part of the plan?"

Damian's answering laugh is sharp and tight. "Do you see me looking like a man with a plan?"

We dart into a narrow alcove, flattening ourselves against the wall as a trio of crimson-robed figures passes us by. I can feel Damian's breath against my ear, shallow and a little too loud, but somehow it doesn't feel out of place. If anything, the desperation suits him.

"This way," he whispers, his eyes meeting mine with something new—fear, maybe. Or recognition. Either way, it's not comforting.

But we don't have time to figure it out. They're circling back, their spells humming in the air, a heartbeat of power thrumming against my skin. I grip Damian's hand harder, and he lets out a strangled noise that might be a protest, but I don't stop. I don't dare.

There's a door up ahead—half-hidden behind a crumbling statue with a face worn away by time and neglect. The door is wood, rotting and veined with greenish moss, the kind that's seen centuries come and go without anyone ever giving it a second glance. I pull Damian toward it, my gut twisting with an inexplicable certainty that this is our way out. Or at least a way to survive a few more breaths.

"What are you—" Damian starts, but I push the door, and it swings open with a groan loud enough to wake the dead.

Behind us, the torches flicker as the Crimson Society draws nearer. There's no time to wonder why this door exists or why it opens so easily; there's only the cold darkness on the other side, and the instinctive knowledge that we don't have any other choice. I yank Damian through, and he stumbles in, still clutching my hand like he's afraid to let go.

The door slams shut behind us, and with it, the air goes heavy, thick, and still. It's the kind of silence that presses down on you, a silence too deep for comfort, like stepping into a world where sound has been outlawed. I fumble in the dark, my fingers brushing the damp, gritty walls as I try to get my bearings.

"We're in a tunnel," I whisper, as if the realization might change something. "An old one."

"Convenient, don't you think?" Damian's voice is cold now, his fingers slipping away from mine. I can't see his face, but I can feel his suspicion. It radiates from him like the heat from a dying fire. "An old, hidden tunnel that you just happened to find. Care to explain?"

There's a challenge in his tone, but I don't rise to it. I can't. Not now. My mind is whirling too fast, filled with fragmented memories of another time, another place, echoes of voices that don't belong to the present. This tunnel—it feels like something out of a dream I've forgotten, a memory that refuses to settle into place.

But Damian doesn't need to know that. Not yet.

"I just... knew," I say, feeling the words slip out awkwardly, as if they're as unsure as I am. "Would you rather stay here and ask questions or keep moving?"

A moment of silence, and then he lets out a low, reluctant sigh. "Fine. But don't think I'm letting this go."

There's a small thrill of victory at his concession, but it's dampened by the fact that he's right. There's no logical explanation for why I know this tunnel. No way to explain why the intricate carvings on the walls feel familiar under my fingertips, why the air here smells like an old, forgotten place that once held secrets too heavy to carry.

We press forward, each step crunching softly in the dark. The walls narrow around us, forcing us closer together, and I can feel Damian's eyes on me even when I can't see him. I want to tell him to stop looking at me like that, like he's unraveling some puzzle, but I don't dare break the silence again. Not while we're still so close to whatever's lurking behind us.

The tunnel slopes downward, and the air grows colder, sharper, until each breath feels like an icy stab in my lungs. Somewhere far ahead, there's a faint glimmer of light, the kind that doesn't belong in a place like this. It's soft and silvery, casting a faint, eerie glow that dances over the stone, turning the shadows into moving things that seem to watch us with silent eyes.

Damian's pace quickens, and I struggle to keep up, feeling his frustration in every tense movement. He's afraid, but he won't admit it—not to me, not to himself. But I can see the way his shoulders stiffen, the way his jaw tightens every time he glances back, as if expecting to see those red-robed figures creeping up behind us.

"Do you know where we're going?" I ask, my voice barely a whisper.

He doesn't answer, just gives me a look that says more than words ever could. I bite back a retort, swallowing my pride and following him into the unknown. There's no point in arguing—not when every second counts, and every step could be our last.

The light grows brighter, and I can make out the faint outlines of what lies ahead: another door, this one heavy and ancient, carved with symbols that seem to pulse in the dim glow. It feels like something out of a story, a place that shouldn't exist in reality, and yet here we are, standing on its threshold.

"Only one way to find out what's on the other side," Damian mutters, his voice a thin thread in the dark.

I reach out, my hand trembling slightly as I touch the door. And for a moment, just a moment, I swear I feel something stir beneath my fingertips—something old and powerful, something that knows more about me than I know about myself.

The door resists, heavy under my hand, as if testing whether I have the right to open it. My fingers press harder, nails digging into the old wood, and just when I think it might not give, it swings inward with a low, shivering creak that echoes down the tunnel behind us. I throw a glance over my shoulder, half-expecting to see the shadowed figures closing in, but all I see is Damian, close and watchful, like he's searching for a flicker of explanation in my eyes. There's something in his gaze I don't want to unravel—not here, not now, with survival so uncertain.

We step inside, and the air shifts, warmer, charged with an energy that prickles over my skin. It's a vast, cavernous space, bathed in the soft, surreal light of floating orbs suspended high above. They hang like captive stars, glowing a hazy silver that turns the stone walls into something almost alive, patterns shifting and swirling as though they breathe. The effect is strange and beautiful and just on the edge of terrifying.

"What is this place?" Damian's voice is low, almost reverent, as he stares around, clearly as mystified as I am.

I shake my head. "I don't know, but I think we're alone." The words feel flimsy, like an offering to some unseen force that could snatch them back at any second. "At least, for now."

He lets out a humorless laugh. "Alone isn't exactly comforting coming from you."

I choose to ignore his dig, mostly because it's fair, and partly because my attention is caught by the carvings stretching across the walls. They're intricate and dizzying, spirals and lines converging into shapes that tug at something buried deep in my memory. Symbols that don't quite make sense but feel weighted with importance. I trace one of them lightly with my fingertip, and a flicker of warmth travels up my arm, as if the stone is alive, humming with something both ancient and strangely familiar.

"You're not telling me everything," Damian says, watching me with that scrutinizing gaze again, the one that sees too much and yet understands too little.

I let my hand drop, focusing on him as if he might tether me back to something solid. "We're stuck here together, Damian. Believe me, if I had anything worth telling, I would. But this…" I wave a hand around the cavernous room, feeling the weight of words I can't explain. "This place—it's as much a mystery to me as it is to you."

He doesn't look convinced, but he also doesn't press further. Instead, he takes a cautious step toward me, his expression softened by something that almost looks like curiosity. "I believe you," he murmurs. And for a moment, there's a fragile truce between us, a quiet understanding that maybe, just maybe, neither of us knows what's happening—and that maybe, that's enough.

But the moment is short-lived. The air pulses, a faint vibration rippling through the room, sending the silver orbs swaying slightly above us. I brace myself, feeling a prickling unease settle between my shoulder blades. Damian's hand hovers near his belt, fingers twitching toward the hilt of his blade as his eyes dart around the room. There's a faint scraping sound, barely audible, but it's enough to snap us both to attention.

"Tell me you heard that," I whisper, my voice so soft it's barely more than a breath.

He nods, his jaw clenched, every muscle in his body coiled like a spring. "We're not alone." His words are barely out when a figure steps out from the shadows, cloaked and faceless, moving with a fluid grace that sends a chill racing down my spine.

I take a step back, feeling Damian's hand steady against my shoulder as we both watch the figure approach. They stop a few paces away, silent and unmoving, like a living shadow, and for a long moment, none of us speak. Then, in a voice that's deep and resonant, they say, "You've trespassed into sacred ground. There is a price."

The words hang heavy in the air, and my throat feels tight, my mind racing through a hundred possible answers, none of which seem like they'll save us. But Damian, of course, remains unfazed. He steps forward, his face set in that infuriating look of defiance he wears like a second skin.

"We're not here by choice," he says, his voice cold and commanding. "We were driven here. Tell us what this place is, and maybe we can settle on that price."

The figure tilts their head, as if considering his words. "This place was never meant for your kind. You walk paths meant only for those bound by blood and magic, and neither of you carries the mark."

I swallow, my heart pounding as I realize what they mean. "Then why did the door open?" I ask, surprised by the strength in my own voice. "Why did it let us in?"

A silence stretches, the figure's head still cocked, as if considering. "Sometimes doors open for reasons beyond understanding. Sometimes they open to trap those who believe they are cleverer than fate."

Damian's grip on my shoulder tightens, a silent warning. "We mean no disrespect. We're only looking for a way out."

"Out?" The figure's laugh is a low, rolling sound, humorless and cold. "The way out lies through the heart of the maze. But beware, traveler—only those who know themselves can find the path."

Damian lets out a frustrated sigh. "I've had enough riddles. Just point us in the right direction, and we'll be out of your way."

The figure remains silent, but they raise one hand, pointing to an arched doorway on the far side of the room, half-concealed by shadows. It's narrow and ominous, carved with the same swirling patterns that cover the walls. I don't need to see Damian's face to know he's thinking the same thing I am—this isn't going to be as simple as finding an exit.

"Thank you," I manage, though the words feel hollow as I force them out. The figure doesn't respond, just melts back into the shadows, vanishing as suddenly as they appeared.

We stand there, staring at the doorway, and Damian lets out a low breath. "So, a maze. Could be worse."

"Could it?" I shoot back, unable to keep the tremor out of my voice. "We're in a room that just told us it's meant to trap people. And now we're supposed to trust it'll show us the way out?"

Damian shrugs, giving me that infuriating grin that seems completely inappropriate in a life-or-death situation. "Got a better idea?"

I hate that I don't. So, with a reluctant nod, I step forward, feeling the weight of the room's unblinking gaze on us as we make our way to the doorway. Every step feels heavier, as if the air itself is thickening, trying to hold us back. But I push on, Damian close behind, his presence somehow both reassuring and maddening.

We reach the entrance to the maze, the archway looming over us, and I hesitate, glancing back one last time at the strange, star-lit chamber. There's a part of me that wants to ask, to demand answers, but I know it's pointless. Whatever rules this place plays by, they're not ours.

Damian reaches out, nudging me forward with a look that's half-impatience, half-encouragement. "After you."

I roll my eyes but take the first step, crossing the threshold into the unknown. And as I do, a shiver runs down my spine—a feeling that we're leaving more than just a room behind.

The maze swallows us whole, a winding labyrinth of stone walls rising high above our heads, twisted and damp, like the ribs of some ancient beast. Each passageway feels narrower than the last, forcing us to sidle through shadows that cling like smoke, leaving us no room to breathe. Every turn is a risk, every shadow a silent threat. And even as we press forward, I can feel Damian's gaze darting over me, sharp and unreadable, as if I'm some riddle he's determined to crack before the walls close in around us.

The silence here isn't the ordinary kind—it has a density, a weight that presses down on us, making it hard to tell if the faint whispers are our imaginations or something lurking just out of sight. My nerves are a taut wire, each step an exercise in pretending I'm not one breath away from breaking.

"What do you think lives in a place like this?" Damian's voice cuts through the silence, low and sardonic, a feeble attempt to chip away at the tension.

I cast him a wary glance, trying to ignore the eerie shadows that seem to stretch and shift along the walls. "Considering our luck? Probably something with teeth. Big, sharp ones. And likely fond of... trespassers."

He smirks, that dangerous spark of humor returning to his eyes. "Good thing I've got a way with dangerous creatures, then."

"Sure you do," I murmur, quickening my pace just enough that he has to catch up, the faintest thrill of triumph warming my insides. Let him stew in his own bravado—if I can keep us moving fast enough, he won't have time to question how I knew to find that door or why the strange symbols on the walls make sense to me in a way they shouldn't. That's a confrontation for another day, another maze. Hopefully one without impending doom around every corner.

We turn yet another sharp corner, and the path narrows further, barely wide enough for us to slip through one at a time. The stones are slick underfoot, covered in a thin layer of something that might be moss but feels wrong, too alive, like the maze itself is holding its breath, waiting. I reach out to steady myself, my hand brushing the wall, and pull it back with a shudder, fingertips tingling with a strange, electric sensation.

Damian notices, of course, because he doesn't miss anything, especially when it involves me. He steps closer, brows furrowing as he studies me, too close for comfort. "You all right? Look like you've seen a ghost."

"Only one? I think I've seen a whole family reunion's worth since we stepped in here," I mutter, trying for humor to mask the truth, but it lands flat, even to my ears. There's something wrong with this place, a wrongness that settles in my bones and whispers things I don't want to hear.

We push on, neither of us willing to be the first to break, and the silence thickens, the faint, inexplicable whispers growing louder, their meanings just out of reach. A faint light glimmers up ahead, pale and flickering, and we exchange a glance—unspoken agreement that, like it or not, we're going to find out what lies beyond.

The passage widens, opening into a cavernous chamber, and I have to stifle a gasp. It's... beautiful, in a way that sets my skin crawling. Crystals hang from the ceiling, shimmering with an unnatural light, casting strange, fractured reflections across the walls.

Pools of water dot the floor, perfectly still, each one reflecting the crystal light in unsettlingly vibrant colors. They're arranged in a precise, almost ritualistic pattern, one that feels calculated, ancient, and deeply ominous.

Damian steps closer to one of the pools, crouching down to examine it. "Looks harmless enough," he murmurs, though his expression is anything but convinced.

I kneel beside him, staring down into the water, and my breath catches. The surface isn't just reflecting light—it's showing something else entirely. Scenes flash across the water, fractured images of places and people I don't recognize. A dark forest bathed in moonlight, a stone temple half-swallowed by mist, a pair of hands reaching for each other and then pulling apart, fingers slipping away in silence. The visions swirl and fade before I can make sense of them, leaving only a faint ache in my chest, a memory I can't place.

"Do you see that?" I whisper, afraid to break whatever spell has settled over us.

Damian nods, his jaw clenched, and for the first time, I see genuine uncertainty in his eyes. "This place—it's meant to show us something," he says, almost to himself. "But why?"

The question hangs in the air, and I have no answer. All I know is that these images, these fragments—they feel as if they're reaching out to me, trying to remind me of something just beyond the edge of memory. Something important, something I've forgotten.

Suddenly, the water ripples, and a new image appears, clearer than the others. A cloaked figure, face obscured, standing in a darkened room, a blade held to their side. They turn, and for an instant, I could swear they're looking straight at me. I freeze, my heart hammering as the figure raises their hand, and I catch a glimpse of a mark on their wrist—a symbol, one of the very ones carved into the walls.

I pull back, the shock of recognition like a blow to the chest. Damian catches my reaction, his gaze sharpening. "You know that mark."

It's not a question. And he's not wrong. I nod, the truth bubbling up before I can stop it. "It was on the door we passed through. I think…" I swallow, the words sticking in my throat. "I think it's connected to this place, to everything we're seeing."

He studies me, a look of dawning understanding mingled with something else—something close to fear. "So, you're not just a stranger to this place. You're bound to it."

I don't answer, because I don't know. All I know is that something here is calling to me, something I don't want to answer but can't ignore. The silence stretches between us, heavy with questions neither of us is ready to voice, and I look back at the pool, half-expecting the vision to have changed.

Instead, the water remains still, showing only my own reflection. But my eyes—they're different. Darker, haunted, as if some shadow lies just beneath the surface, waiting to emerge.

"Let's get out of here," I say, my voice shaking. "We're wasting time."

Damian doesn't argue, though his eyes linger on the water a second longer than necessary. When he rises, there's a new wariness in his stance, a subtle shift that makes it clear—he's seeing me in a different light, one that makes my skin prickle with a mixture of discomfort and strange excitement.

We leave the chamber, stepping back into the maze, and I can't shake the feeling that something's changed, that each turn is leading us closer to something I may not want to find. The maze seems darker, the walls pressing in, as if aware of the truth I'm beginning to uncover.

Then, from somewhere far off, a soft, eerie laughter echoes, chilling my blood. It's a sound that shouldn't exist, a sound that feels as ancient as the maze itself. Damian freezes, his hand on his blade, his gaze locked on mine. "Tell me that's just my imagination," he says, voice tight.

But I can't. Because I hear it too, and it's getting closer. The laughter twists through the air, low and mocking, as if it knows something I don't, something it's eager to reveal. And as we stand there, paralyzed in the suffocating dark, I realize that whatever's waiting for us in the heart of this maze has been waiting a very long time.

Chapter 5: Ash and Ashen Hearts

Damian leans against the splintered wall of the outpost, his silhouette outlined by the faint glow of the waning moon filtering through cracked windows. His face is a study in shadows, jaw clenched, eyes flashing under his furrowed brows. He exudes danger, the kind that doesn't need an announcement. I shift uncomfortably in my seat, wrapping my arms around myself to block out the chill. The temperature isn't the only thing making my skin prickle.

"Are you going to tell me who you're really working for, or am I just supposed to keep guessing?" I ask, trying to sound casual, though there's an unmistakable bite in my words. I hate being in the dark, hate the secrets curling in on themselves like smoke in his gaze. My life—messy as it is—has at least been straightforward until now. But Damian seems to exist solely to disrupt things, a dark current lurking just beneath a deceptively calm surface.

He smirks, that infuriating, practiced expression that speaks volumes while revealing nothing. "Trust me, you don't want to know."

I narrow my eyes, leaning forward just a bit. "Maybe I do."

There's a long silence as he looks at me, really looks at me, like he's weighing something about me he hasn't dared before. His hand drifts to the medallion around his neck—a small, carved silver charm in the shape of a wolf's head. I've never seen him take it off or let anyone touch it. He fingers it as if it's the last thing tethering him to this world, grounding him in a way I can't quite understand.

"The Velvet Charm has its uses," he murmurs, almost to himself, before letting out a breath and raising his gaze to mine. "It's not for me. Not really. It's... it's for balance, in a way." He stops, grimacing at his own words. "Or at least, that's the line I'm supposed to believe."

"Balance?" I scoff, trying to keep my tone even as curiosity digs its claws in deeper. "Are you really expecting me to buy that? What, is there some secret society lurking out there, playing moral referee?"

His half-smile returns, but this time, it falters just enough for me to see a crack in his confidence. "Let's just say... I owe someone. And they think the Velvet Charm can restore what was lost."

I feel the weight of his words, the chill that accompanies them. There's something darker, something heavy and unspoken, and it hangs between us like a ghost. Suddenly, I'm struck by the thought that maybe Damian has as many chains holding him down as I do, even if his are gilded with secrets instead of iron.

I fold my arms tighter, forcing a lightness into my tone that I don't feel. "And how exactly do I fit into your master plan to right all these cosmic wrongs?"

He laughs, short and mirthless, a sound that feels like gravel under my skin. "You don't. Not really. You were just... convenient." His eyes linger on me, softening for a fraction of a second. "But then, you make things difficult, don't you?"

"Is that supposed to be a compliment?" I arch an eyebrow, even though the sting of his words still echoes in my chest. Convenient. As if I'm some tool he happened to pick up along the way.

For a moment, I think I see regret flicker across his face, but it's gone as quickly as it came, replaced by his familiar mask of indifference. He shrugs. "Take it however you want."

The silence stretches between us, taut as a bowstring. I don't trust him—not as far as I could throw him—but there's something about the way he stands, the way he talks, that makes me feel like I'm teetering on the edge of something far bigger and darker than I ever imagined. And against my better judgment, I find myself wanting to reach out, to peel back the layers and see what lies beneath.

"What if I don't want to be a convenient asset in your grand scheme?" I ask, my voice softer now, almost contemplative. "What if I want... something else?"

He tilts his head, a glint of intrigue sparking in his gaze. "And what would that be?"

I bite my lip, suddenly unsure. I want freedom, sure, but not the kind he offers, tangled in webs of deception and dangerous alliances. No, I want something that feels real, solid—something I can hold onto without it slipping through my fingers.

"Honestly, I don't know," I admit, feeling exposed in a way I haven't felt in a long time. I expect him to mock me or brush off my vulnerability, but instead, he surprises me.

"Neither do I," he murmurs, his voice barely above a whisper.

It's such a small admission, but it feels monumental. He shifts, casting a fleeting glance toward the door as if he's calculating the time he has left here before the next mission pulls him away. I can feel the distance growing between us, and I suddenly have the irrational urge to close it, to say something that will keep him tethered here, just for a little longer.

"Stay," I say impulsively, the word slipping out before I can think better of it.

His eyes meet mine, unreadable. He looks like he wants to laugh, to tell me how naive I am for even suggesting it. But then he does something unexpected. He takes a step closer, his voice low and rough.

"Be careful what you wish for."

There's a challenge in his gaze, a spark that's equal parts danger and invitation. I feel the air grow thick between us, my heart pounding loud enough to drown out every rational thought. And in that moment, the absurdity of it all—him, me, the secrets and half-truths and shadows lurking between us—feels like a bridge we might just be bold enough to cross.

"Maybe I like a little risk," I reply, my voice barely a whisper, each word hanging heavy with the weight of unspoken possibilities.

A chill wind slips through the cracked windows, carrying with it the faint scent of damp earth and something metallic. It stirs the dust in the abandoned room, making shadows dance along the walls. Damian's face is partially obscured, but I can feel his eyes on me, calculating, like he's piecing together a puzzle he can't quite solve. The weight of his attention makes my skin tingle, and I try to shake it off, burying my unease beneath a mask of indifference.

"Let's say I believe you," I start, folding my arms. "About this 'balance' nonsense. What exactly do you plan to do with the Velvet Charm when you get it? Return it to its rightful owner? Destroy it?" I arch an eyebrow, adding just enough sarcasm to keep my question from sounding too genuine.

He shifts, crossing his arms, the barest hint of amusement flickering in his gaze. "Oh, you think I have some grand plan? Hate to break it to you, but this is more of a... freelance gig."

"Freelance gig?" I scoff, unable to mask my disbelief. "You talk about balance and yet you make it sound like a side job you picked up because you were bored on a Tuesday."

He chuckles, a low sound that rumbles in the small, empty space between us. "Maybe I was. Or maybe I'm just very good at pretending not to care." He leans forward, his voice dropping, and there's a mischievous glint in his eyes. "But if you'd like, I can tell you a very dramatic story about honor and duty and impossible choices. Would that help you sleep better?"

I roll my eyes, though a reluctant smile tugs at my lips. "Oh, I'd love nothing more than to hear you spin some grand tale, but I think we both know you'd rather keep your secrets under lock and key." I pause, letting my gaze wander over him. "Convenient, isn't it?"

His expression hardens, that brief moment of levity disappearing as quickly as it arrived. "Secrets are necessary. If you knew everything about me, you'd be running in the opposite direction."

"Who says I'm not already running?" I counter, though my voice softens. The words ring hollow, a bluff neither of us buys. Because if I were really running, I wouldn't be here, sitting in the cold shadows with a man who feels like a storm held at bay. I wouldn't be caught in the pull of his gaze, wondering what lies beneath the anger and the evasions, the charm and the danger.

He's silent, and for a moment, I think he might leave it at that, retreat back into the shadows and give me the space to collect my own thoughts. But instead, he reaches into his coat pocket and pulls out a small, worn notebook. It's leather-bound, edges frayed, the kind of object that carries the weight of memories pressed between the pages.

He hesitates, then hands it to me. "Take a look if you're so curious."

I blink, caught off guard. "You're actually... letting me see this?"

He smirks, though it lacks his usual confidence. "What's the point of a secret if there's no one left to share it with?"

I flip open the notebook, my fingers brushing over the delicate, careful handwriting inside. The words are messy but deliberate, as if each one has been considered, then etched in place with a pen pressed a little too hard. My eyes skim the first page, expecting to see something incriminating, maybe names or dates that will reveal the answers he's refused to give. But instead, I find poems, fragments of thought scattered like breadcrumbs. Some are dark, edged with sorrow, while others are laced with humor and a surprising amount of heart.

"This... is poetry?" I glance up at him, half expecting him to laugh it off, to tell me it's a decoy, a joke. But he just watches me, his gaze steady, unflinching.

"What, surprised I know how to write?" His voice is light, teasing, but I can tell he's waiting for my reaction.

"No, I just..." I trail off, feeling unsteady, like I've stepped into a part of him that's raw and vulnerable in a way I wasn't prepared for. "I didn't expect this."

He shrugs, an attempt to play off the vulnerability, but there's a tightness in his jaw that betrays him. "Guess I have a softer side. Don't get used to it."

I can't help the smile that breaks through. "Wouldn't dream of it. Wouldn't want to tarnish that reputation of yours."

His mouth twitches, but he doesn't respond, just lets me continue reading. And as I do, the words blur together, each one laced with a haunting beauty that resonates deep within me. I feel like I'm seeing pieces of him he's kept hidden, shadows of a life he rarely lets bleed through his sharp edges and biting wit. I can sense the weight he carries, the scars hidden beneath his smooth facade, and something shifts in me, an uncomfortable warmth blossoming in my chest.

When I finally close the notebook, I hand it back, not quite able to meet his eyes. "You're... surprising, I'll give you that."

"I'll take that as a compliment," he murmurs, slipping the notebook back into his pocket with an ease that makes me wonder how long he's carried it, how many times he's held it like a lifeline in the dark.

We sit in silence for a moment, each lost in our own thoughts. I want to ask him more, pry into the shadows he so carefully guards, but I can feel the line drawn between us, thin but solid. Trust is a dangerous thing, a fragile thread that can snap with the slightest misstep.

Instead, I focus on the outpost around us, the walls scarred with bullet holes, remnants of battles long past. There's a sadness to the place, a heaviness that feels like it's seeped into the very bones of the structure. And for the first time, I wonder if Damian feels it too, if he's been haunted by the same ghosts, caught in the same endless struggle.

"So," I say, breaking the quiet, "where do we go from here?"

He leans back, eyes narrowing as he looks out the window at the dim city lights flickering in the distance. "That depends. Are you willing to keep going, even if it means walking through fire?"

There's a challenge in his tone, a dare that stirs something fierce in me. Maybe it's reckless, maybe it's foolish, but for once, I don't want to play it safe. I don't want to retreat into the comfort of solitude, of self-preservation. I want to see where this path leads, even if it means facing the unknown with only a sliver of trust to guide me.

I meet his gaze, a slow, defiant smile spreading across my lips. "I think I can handle the heat."

The silence between us grows, heavy as the shadows that fill the room, and the longer it stretches, the harder it becomes to break. Damian leans back against the cracked wall, his gaze distant as if the conversation has already drifted far behind him. I can feel that familiar, sinking tug of uncertainty, a whisper that maybe this was all a mistake. I don't like the feeling, so I shove it down, bury it under a wry smile and an arched eyebrow.

"Do you have any idea how insufferable you are?" I ask, tilting my head. It's a half-hearted barb, but he turns his attention back to me, and there's a spark of humor in his eyes that makes me feel like we're both a little less alone in this mess.

"Insufferable?" he repeats, crossing his arms over his chest in mock offense. "Now, that's uncalled for. I prefer 'enigmatic.' Or maybe even 'mysterious and brooding'—but insufferable? That stings."

"Is that right?" I lean forward, meeting his gaze, refusing to be intimidated by the amusement lurking there. "I could probably come up with worse. In fact, I have an entire list somewhere, if you'd like me to retrieve it."

He raises an eyebrow. "You keep a list? How very organized of you."

"Believe me, it's a short list, but only because I'm running out of synonyms for 'impossible,'" I shoot back. A small, proud part of me notes that the faintest twitch of a smile touches his lips, though he tries to mask it with a casual shrug.

"So I'm impossible," he says, pretending to mull it over. "But you're still here. That either makes you very determined... or very foolish."

I'm quiet, thrown by the way he looks at me, as if he's peeling back the layers of sarcasm to search for something buried deeper. And then, almost without thinking, I say, "Maybe it's both."

His smile fades, replaced by something serious and contemplative, and for a moment, the mask slips again. The vulnerable version of him, the one with fragments of poetry hidden in a battered notebook, hovers just out of reach. The urge to close the space between us, to ask the questions I'm not sure I want answers to, surges like an itch I can't scratch.

But before I can give in to that impulse, a loud creak echoes through the outpost, sharp and intrusive. I straighten, heart pounding, and Damian's hand moves instinctively toward his waist, where he's stashed a small, lethal-looking knife. His gaze hardens, the playful spark in his eyes vanishing as he scans the shadows.

"Did you hear that?" I whisper, more out of habit than necessity, given that we're the only ones here.

He nods, putting a finger to his lips in a signal to stay quiet. I press myself against the wall, pulse quickening, and strain to listen. The creak comes again, followed by a shuffling sound, then silence. My skin prickles as I glance at Damian, whose entire demeanor has shifted to something cold and alert.

"Wait here," he murmurs, his voice low and steady. He slips out of the room before I can protest, leaving me alone with nothing but the thick, oppressive quiet and the distant sound of his footsteps.

As soon as he disappears, the shadows in the outpost seem to press in closer, as though they're alive, pulsing in rhythm with my racing heartbeat. I tell myself to stay put, to trust that he knows what he's doing. But a minute passes, then another, and the silence grows heavier, more unsettling. My instincts scream at me to go after him, to make sure he hasn't walked headfirst into some unseen trap.

I push off the wall, my resolve hardening. Fine. I'll wait—just outside the door, close enough to intervene if necessary. Peering around the corner, I catch a glimpse of his silhouette further down the corridor, moving with deliberate caution toward a half-open door. The faint outline of something—or someone—shifts on the other side of it, and my stomach clenches.

Before I can blink, there's a flash of movement, too fast to track. A figure leaps from the shadows, lunging toward Damian. He's faster, sidestepping with a quick, fluid motion, his knife flashing in his hand. They grapple, the stranger's low growl filling the narrow corridor as Damian twists his arm and slams him against the wall. I can barely make out the intruder's face, but there's a look of wild desperation in his eyes, and I feel a cold, creeping dread slink down my spine.

The stranger struggles, letting out a strangled laugh. "You're too late, you know. You think you're clever, skulking around in the shadows like this. But you have no idea what you're meddling with."

Damian tightens his grip, his jaw clenched, muscles taut. "Then enlighten me."

The intruder sneers, his voice low and scornful. "The Velvet Charm isn't a relic—it's a warning. And you've already sealed your fate by seeking it out."

The words hang in the air, twisting like a curse, and I feel the urge to step forward, to ask a thousand questions that crowd into my mind. But something holds me back, a nagging instinct that warns me not to reveal myself just yet.

Damian's voice is ice-cold, every word calculated. "I don't believe in fate. And neither should you."

The stranger lets out a rasping laugh that echoes in the corridor, like nails scraping across metal. "Oh, but fate believes in you. It's woven its threads around you so tightly that you can't even feel them anymore. Go ahead, fight it. You'll only pull the noose tighter."

Before Damian can respond, the man jerks his head, something sharp and vicious glinting in his eyes. And then, in a swift, brutal motion, he breaks free, shoving Damian back and disappearing down the hall, vanishing into the shadows with a speed that leaves me breathless.

Damian recovers quickly, already sprinting after him, but a voice in the back of my mind whispers that the stranger's words weren't empty threats. They were a promise, a dark omen woven into our lives whether we wanted it or not.

I hesitate, watching Damian's form vanish around a corner, and a heavy, unfamiliar weight settles in my chest. The outpost feels colder, the darkness pressing in tighter as if it's closing around me, drawing me toward something I can't see but can feel deep in my bones.

Then, out of nowhere, there's a sound—a low, pulsing hum. It vibrates through the air, growing louder, more insistent, until it drowns out everything else. I turn, following the sound to a small alcove hidden in the shadows, where something faintly glows with an eerie, pulsating light.

The Velvet Charm.

The air thickens around it, shimmering with a strange, electric energy that makes my skin crawl. It lies nestled in the darkness, innocent and deadly all at once, like a trap waiting to be sprung. My hand trembles as I reach toward it, curiosity and dread tangling in my chest. But before my fingers can brush its surface, a hand grips my shoulder, yanking me back.

I whirl around, my breath catching in my throat as I stare into Damian's fierce, unyielding gaze. His jaw is tight, his eyes blazing with a warning I've never seen before. And in a voice barely above a whisper, he says, "Don't touch it. Not unless you're ready to face everything you can't take back."

Chapter 6: Whispers of War

My breath plumed in the chill of the morning as we slipped through the trees toward the village. I could feel him at my side, moving as silent as a shadow, though occasionally his cloak snagged on a branch or a damp leaf slapped across his face. It should have been a comfort that he was there, that we weren't walking into the fray alone. But the air between us simmered with a tension sharp enough to sting, born from a thousand unspoken words and a single secret that sat heavy as iron in my chest.

The first wisps of smoke caught on the breeze, an acrid warning before we could see the fire. I quickened my pace, the rough ground biting through my boots. We hadn't even gotten close enough to hear the screams, yet my blood raced as if I could feel them tearing at the air. Somewhere, in the hollow place I kept quiet even from myself, I knew this kind of destruction too well. The helplessness, the rage—it was a rhythm I'd come to recognize with cruel clarity. I tightened my jaw and kept moving.

We broke through the edge of the forest, and the village sprawled before us, humble, nestled close to the mountainside, defenseless. The Crimson Society had already worked its way through the southern quarter, and here and there, flames licked at rooftops, the thick wooden beams hissing and snapping as the fire took them. People ran in frenzied paths, clutching bundles, pulling children, or staggering under the weight of whatever they could carry.

Without a word, he surged ahead, his hand lifting to shape a spell even as his foot hit the ground. For a man so polished in his clipped tone and cold restraint, his magic was a raw thing. It spilled out like he couldn't hold it back, arcs of crackling light that carved into the ground and lit up the space in front of us, halting the Crimson Society's soldiers in their tracks. I hung back for a heartbeat, caught in the sick thrill of watching him wield his power so freely, so openly.

But then, one of the soldiers broke away, a flash of red slicing through the air, and my instinct kicked in.

I closed my eyes, just for a breath, and reached for the thing I kept hidden, the power I'd sworn never to use. My fingers tingled, alive with the energy that flowed through me in a rush, as familiar as breathing, as forbidden as the thoughts that came to me in the dark. I flung it toward the soldier, and a barrier snapped into place between him and an elderly woman clutching a crying child to her chest. I knew what she'd see: a shimmer, almost invisible, like a heat wave in the air. But I could feel the weight of it, every bit as solid as the fear churning in my stomach.

He turned, just for a second, and our eyes met. I didn't know what I expected—anger, maybe, or judgment. But his gaze softened, not in pity, but in a way that saw more than I wanted him to. He knew. Somehow, he knew exactly what that power meant, what it cost to summon it. And in that split second, we were bound by a thread of understanding, thin and fraught but real.

"Are you going to stand there all day?" he called, voice low and sharp as a blade. "Or do you want to give me a hand?"

The moment snapped, and I forced myself to focus, hurling another pulse of energy at a group of soldiers that had turned their attention to us. They didn't even flinch, moving forward in eerie, synchronized steps, undeterred by the heat pressing against them. The Crimson Society trained their people well, disciplined them into fearlessness. Or maybe it was just that they feared the Society more than they feared us. Either way, it set a prickle along the back of my neck.

"I'm working on it," I muttered, pouring my focus into fortifying the shield around the villagers. I could feel it thinning, slipping through my fingers with every heartbeat. The sheer pressure of it was beginning to throb through my temples, and I had to clench my jaw to stay grounded. He, on the other hand, barely looked winded. His magic flared, wild and bright, a weapon born of years of training, shaped with brutal efficiency.

"Cover the west side," he ordered, voice taut with a frustration I didn't dare question. He was the one with the experience, after all. My power—strange and volatile, born of something I couldn't name—was a blunter tool, hard to control, harder to hide. But I trusted him, just enough to let him lead, and as I fell back toward the western edge of the village, I felt the air around me shift. Shadows stirred, flickering at the edge of my vision.

A soldier lunged from the darkness, red cloak swirling like blood in water, and before I had time to react, he was close enough to see the madness in his eyes, a fervor that bordered on hunger. But then he froze, his gaze sliding up to something behind me. I didn't need to look to know it was him. Even his presence held power, an aura that rippled like a warning. I spared the briefest glance over my shoulder, and his mouth quirked up in a faint, humorless smile. He enjoyed it, this dance between life and death, the game of it.

"You're really not going to do anything about him?" I asked, half exasperated, half daring. He shrugged, still smiling, and I scowled, snapping my wrist as the shield rippled outward, slamming into the soldier with a force that left him crumpled in the dust.

"Well, I had it under control," he drawled, but there was something warm in his tone, a thread of approval that caught me off guard. I didn't want his approval, not really, but that didn't stop my pulse from skipping at the hint of it.

As we fought side by side, his magic flaring like lightning, my own power a dark, steady pulse beneath it, the lines between ally and enemy began to blur. The Crimson Society fell back, retreating into the shadows as the villagers clung to what little remained of their homes. And as the last soldier vanished into the night, I caught his gaze one final time, the question unspoken between us.

It was too easy to forget the scars beneath his sharp smiles, the history hidden in the hard lines of his face. Just as it was too easy for him to see through my carefully crafted mask, to find the pieces of myself I tried so desperately to keep hidden.

The night deepened as the last embers of the fire flickered, leaving a haze of smoke and ash settling over the village. I could still taste it on my tongue, bitter as regret. The villagers were beginning to gather in small groups, some leaning on each other, some quietly sifting through what little they'd managed to salvage. Their whispered reassurances drifted through the cool night air, but it did little to quiet the hum of adrenaline still pulsing through me.

I could feel him hovering nearby, his presence like a second shadow, watching me with that infuriating look of half-amused patience, as if he were waiting for me to stumble. Or waiting for me to explain. But I wasn't about to offer anything. Not after tonight. The way he'd looked at me, that flicker of knowing, of understanding—no, I'd learned enough about him to recognize that look, the way he could see right through my thin walls. I was still reeling from the slip, from the power I'd let loose without a second thought. It had been reckless, unwise. I could still feel it humming beneath my skin, like a secret I'd betrayed.

He moved closer, and I forced myself to keep my face calm, my eyes steady, as if he hadn't caught a glimpse of the part of me I worked so hard to keep buried. His gaze, sharp and heavy, settled on me.

"Going to pretend like nothing happened?" His tone was light, teasing, but there was an edge to it, a thread of something serious. He studied me, his eyes flicking over my face like he was cataloging every twitch, every slip of expression.

"Nothing did," I said, and I could hear the lie in my own voice, brittle and thin. He raised an eyebrow, unbothered by my denial, and for once I wished he'd just let it go. But he didn't. Instead, he tilted his head, like he was piecing together a puzzle.

"That was...impressive," he said finally, his tone shifting, becoming something closer to sincere. I braced myself, knowing there was more. "Also a bit terrifying, if I'm being honest. You've been holding back, haven't you?"

I shrugged, feigning nonchalance, but the words had already hit their mark. Holding back. It wasn't as if I'd been hiding for the sake of some grand reveal. No, it was self-preservation, plain and simple. Because once you let people see that kind of power, once they knew what you could do...well, it tended to complicate things. It had, more than once.

"Everyone has secrets," I replied, trying to match his casual tone. But he wasn't buying it. He leaned in closer, his eyes narrowing slightly, and the shift in his expression—soft, calculating—set my heart pounding.

"Maybe," he murmured, as if he were humoring me. "But yours have teeth."

I glanced away, feeling the heat rise in my cheeks. His words lingered in the air between us, sharp and unrelenting, and for a moment, I was sure he could hear the frantic beat of my heart, the way it hammered against my ribs.

"You're one to talk," I shot back, aiming for deflection. "I'm not the one tossing around sorcery like it's a parlor trick." I raised an eyebrow, hoping my challenge would take the focus off me. But he only smiled, an infuriating little smirk that made me want to shove him—or maybe kiss him, if I could bring myself to admit it.

"Oh, I think we both know there's a difference," he replied smoothly, and his gaze was so intense, so unblinking, that I had to look away.

Silence settled between us, thick and heavy. I could still hear the villagers murmuring in the background, but it felt distant, unimportant. All I could feel was him, standing too close, his gaze too probing, and the thrum of my own power, still simmering beneath my skin. It made me restless, uneasy.

"Why are you so interested in what I can do?" I asked finally, my voice barely more than a whisper. I hated the way it sounded, vulnerable and raw, like I was asking for something I didn't even know I wanted.

His expression softened, just slightly, and he looked at me in a way that made my heart stutter, like he saw right through the walls I'd spent years building. "Because you're different," he said, and his voice was quieter than I'd ever heard it, almost reverent. "Because you're more powerful than you realize. And because I think—" he hesitated, as if the words were foreign on his tongue, "I think we're more alike than you'd care to admit."

It hit me like a punch to the gut. The way he said it, so sure, so certain, as if he understood something about me that even I didn't fully grasp. I opened my mouth, wanting to argue, to deny it, but the words caught in my throat. Because deep down, I knew he was right.

And that scared me more than anything else.

Before I could respond, a shout cut through the night, pulling us back to reality. A villager was running toward us, her face pale and frantic. "Please," she gasped, clutching at her chest as she struggled to catch her breath. "My son...they took him. They took him!"

The desperation in her voice sliced through my haze of confusion, and I turned to him, the remnants of our conversation forgotten. He was already in motion, his expression hardening, his body tensing with the readiness of someone who had seen this kind of terror before.

"Where did they take him?" he asked, his voice steady, grounding.

The woman pointed toward the hills, her hand trembling. "The Crimson Society. They—he tried to fight them. He wouldn't...he wouldn't let them hurt us." Her voice cracked, and I felt a sick twist in my gut. I didn't have to look at him to know he was feeling the same thing.

He nodded, and before I could question it, he started walking, his steps quick and purposeful. I fell into step beside him, and for once, there was no banter, no snide remarks. Just the silent understanding that we couldn't leave this unfinished.

We moved quickly, slipping through the shadows, our senses alert, every nerve taut. The silence between us wasn't tense—it was necessary, a shared determination to reach the boy, to get him out. And as we walked, I felt the steady beat of something I couldn't quite name, a connection that bound us as surely as any blood tie. It was uncomfortable, unnerving, but it was there.

Ahead of us, a faint glow flickered in the trees, and we both stilled, exchanging a glance. He nodded, signaling for me to follow his lead, and we crept forward, our footsteps soft, our breathing shallow. As we drew closer, I could see the group of soldiers huddled around a small campfire, their shadows twisting and writhing in the firelight. And at the edge of the circle, bound and gagged, was the boy.

A knot of anger tightened in my chest, and I felt my power stir, surging forward, raw and insistent. But before I could act, he placed a hand on my arm, stopping me. His touch was firm, grounding, and I met his gaze, feeling the weight of his silent message: patience.

For once, I listened. And as I watched him slip into the shadows, disappearing into the night, I felt something shift within me, something I wasn't ready to name. But as the Crimson Society's soldiers began to fall, one by one, silent and precise, I knew one thing for certain.

This was only the beginning. And whatever lay ahead, we would face it together.

VEIL DAWN 65

The night was dense and silent as we melted back into the trees, slipping between shadows as we approached the edge of the Crimson Society's camp. The boy's slight figure was huddled on the ground, hands bound behind his back, his face smeared with dirt. I could see the faint glimmer of tears on his cheeks, catching the firelight in a way that made my stomach twist. But he wasn't making a sound, his small body taut and defiant even in captivity. Brave, I thought, though that bravery was laced with fear—a dangerous thing to feel, but perhaps, I knew, even more dangerous to suppress.

Beside me, he gave a barely perceptible nod, his eyes gleaming with a fierce focus. There was a comfort in his steadiness, a grounding calm that made me feel like, for just a moment, maybe we weren't in over our heads. I was still shaking off the rush of power from earlier, my nerves singing with the memory of it, but his quiet control steadied me, reminded me to breathe, to stay in the present.

His voice was a low whisper, barely more than a breath. "We need to take out the guards by the fire without drawing attention. Think you can manage that?"

"Oh, I think I can manage," I replied, matching his tone, a flicker of a grin breaking through. He rolled his eyes, but the corner of his mouth twitched. Even here, surrounded by enemies, he couldn't resist a faint smile. It was ridiculous and maddening—and oddly reassuring.

He moved first, a flash of movement that barely disturbed the night air. He worked like a ghost, silent, precise, his magic weaving subtle distractions and lulling the guards into complacency. A murmur of laughter rose from the group, too easy, too relaxed, just as his magic intended. And that was my opening.

I focused, feeling the warmth of my power unfurl within me, controlled this time, honed. I let it slip into the ground, curling through the earth until it found their feet. With a flick of my fingers, the ground shifted beneath them, throwing them off balance, sending them stumbling and confused.

"What the—" one of them barked, but his voice was cut off as my companion's spell struck, sending the guard slumping to the ground in silence. It was almost too easy. My pulse quickened, every sense heightened as we moved toward the boy, still lying on the ground, his eyes wide as he watched us approach.

"You okay?" I whispered, crouching beside him and feeling for the ropes that held his wrists. He nodded, his face a mixture of fear and awe, and for a moment, I saw myself in his eyes—a flash of the terrified child I'd once been, clinging to any hope of escape. I worked quickly, loosening the knots, until the ropes fell away and he rubbed at his chafed wrists.

"Thank you," he whispered, his voice hoarse. I smiled at him, trying to make it reassuring, though I wasn't sure it did much. My companion nudged me, his gaze shifting back to the campfire, where the last guard was stirring.

"Time to go," he muttered, his hand firm on my shoulder as he nudged me forward. But just as we turned, a flash of red appeared at the far edge of the clearing. More guards, too many to slip past unnoticed.

"Did you really think it'd be that easy?" A voice drifted over to us, calm and oily, laced with the kind of confidence that made my stomach turn. The man who stepped forward wore the Crimson Society's insignia with a smug pride, his eyes gleaming with a sick delight as he surveyed us.

The boy stiffened, his small fingers digging into my arm. My companion shifted, his body tense beside me, and I could feel the weight of his power, simmering just below the surface. He was ready to unleash it, consequences be damned.

The leader tilted his head, his gaze flickering between the two of us, as if he were deciding which of us would pose more of a challenge. He settled on my companion, a slow, almost patronizing smile curving his lips.

"We know what you're looking for," he sneered. "And we know you won't find it here. The Velvet Charm is well out of your reach, and so is this boy."

I felt my companion's anger coil beside me, a restrained force that I could almost see, could feel thrumming in the air. He took a single step forward, his voice low and dangerous. "Let us go. Or you'll regret it."

The man laughed, a harsh, brittle sound that grated against my nerves. "Oh, I don't think so. In fact, I was hoping you'd put up a fight. It's been a while since we've had a challenge worth our time."

I was about to retort, to demand he let us go, when I felt it—a pulse, a tremor of energy beneath my feet, growing stronger with every heartbeat. My companion glanced at me, his eyes dark with worry. Whatever was coming, it wasn't just the guards or their leader. This was something else, something deeper, a force that felt ancient and unyielding, like the earth itself was rising up against us.

The guards began to advance, their footsteps synchronized, their movements unnaturally stiff. I recognized it for what it was—a binding spell, one meant to strip them of their will, to turn them into tools, mere weapons for the Crimson Society to wield. The sight of it chilled me, a reminder of just how ruthless the Society could be.

Without waiting for permission, I reached for my power again, feeling it rise within me, raw and untamed. But just as I was about to let it loose, my companion grabbed my hand, his grip firm, his gaze sharp.

"Careful," he murmured, his voice barely a whisper. "This is different. They're waiting for you to use it."

I met his gaze, searching for any sign that he was wrong, that I could risk it. But his eyes held a certainty that was hard to argue with. I forced myself to take a breath, to reel my power back in, even as every instinct screamed at me to unleash it, to tear through the guards and leave nothing in our wake.

The leader watched us, a glint of satisfaction in his eyes, as if he could sense my restraint, as if he knew just how much it cost me to hold back.

"Oh, what's the matter?" he taunted, his voice dripping with mock sympathy. "Afraid to show us what you really are? Or are you just too weak?"

I clenched my jaw, biting back the retort that burned on my tongue. But my companion squeezed my hand, a silent reminder to stay calm, to stay grounded. His voice was low, barely more than a murmur in my ear.

"We'll find another way," he whispered. "But right now, we can't risk it. Not here."

The words settled over me, heavy but reassuring, a tether that held me steady in the face of the storm. I nodded, forcing myself to let go of the power, to let it slip back into the depths where it belonged.

But just as I made the decision, the leader's face twisted into a sneer, and he gestured to his guards. "Take them," he commanded, his voice cold and final. "And if they resist, make them pay."

The guards surged forward, closing in with a terrifying, mechanical precision, and I felt my heart race, panic clawing at the edges of my resolve. My companion moved beside me, his stance shifting, ready to fight, and the boy clung to my side, his small frame trembling.

As the guards closed in, the ground beneath us began to shake, a rumble that grew louder, stronger, until the very air seemed to pulse with it. I glanced at my companion, a question in my eyes, but he looked just as confused as I was.

And then, just as the first guard reached for me, the earth split open beneath our feet.

Chapter 7: Blood of Betrayal

Damian and I staggered through the forest under the weight of exhaustion and triumph. The village lay behind us, still and safe, untouched by the blaze of violence we'd narrowly escaped. The trees, thick and towering, cast cool shadows over our path as we stumbled forward, heads lowered, both of us too spent to speak. I could still feel the heat of flames licking at my skin, the shouts and cries of battle echoing in my ears. There was something intoxicating in our shared silence, as though we could both feel the same electric thrum of survival, of purpose finally realized.

But as we emerged from the forest, stepping onto the narrow path that wound back to the city, I felt something—a prickle at the back of my neck, a chill that had nothing to do with the air. My instincts had served me well over the years, and now they screamed at me to stop. Beside me, Damian halted, his hand already resting on the hilt of his sword. For a moment, the two of us stood frozen, listening, breathing in time with the trees around us, as though the forest itself were holding its breath.

Then she stepped out from the shadows, graceful as a cat and twice as deadly. Her eyes, a piercing shade of emerald, settled on Damian, and her lips curled into a smile that was as dangerous as any weapon. She wore a cloak as dark as night, her hair falling like a cascade of silk around her shoulders, framing a face that could have belonged to a queen or a conqueror—or perhaps both. My pulse quickened, and I clenched my fists, instinctively stepping closer to Damian.

"Well, well, Damian. It's been too long," she purred, her voice dripping with mock warmth, like honey laced with poison. "I wondered if you'd made it out of that last little 'situation' alive."

Damian's hand remained on his sword, but I could see the flicker of something—hesitation, maybe even regret—flash across his face.

It was gone in an instant, replaced by the stony mask I'd come to recognize as his only real defense. He didn't respond, didn't even acknowledge her presence, but she took his silence as an invitation to continue.

"Come now, don't be rude. You owe me at least that much." Her gaze shifted, resting on me, and I felt the weight of her scrutiny, sharp and assessing, as though she were peeling back layers of skin to see the vulnerable heart underneath. "And you must be the latest one he's lured into his web. A bit scrawny for his taste, aren't you?"

I narrowed my eyes, my jaw tightening. "You don't know anything about me," I shot back, refusing to let her see the spark of doubt that her words ignited. It was ridiculous, of course. I knew Damian better than that. Didn't I?

Her laughter was soft, almost musical, but it held an edge that made my skin crawl. "Oh, I know more than you think, darling." She turned her attention back to Damian, her smile widening. "Shall I tell her, then? Or will you finally admit what you really are?"

I felt Damian tense beside me, his knuckles white as he gripped his sword. He hadn't moved, hadn't said a word, but his silence spoke volumes. There was a secret here, something dark and twisted, hidden beneath his charm and his easy, teasing smiles. I'd sensed it before, that hint of something dangerous lurking just beneath the surface, but I'd ignored it, brushed it off as nothing more than the scars of his past.

"Corinne, this is beneath you," he said at last, his voice low and steady, though I could hear the strain beneath his words. "Whatever grudge you have against me, it's over. I don't owe you anything."

Corinne's eyes flashed, and I saw a hint of fury in her gaze, raw and unfiltered. "Oh, but you do, Damian. You owe me your loyalty. You owe me the truth." She took a step closer, her voice dropping to a whisper that sent a shiver down my spine. "Tell her, Damian. Tell her what you did. Tell her how you betrayed me. Tell her about the blood on your hands."

A chill settled over me, colder than any blade. Damian's face was unreadable, his eyes fixed on Corinne as though he could will her into silence, but it was too late. The words were out there, hanging between us like a dark cloud, and I felt the ground shift beneath my feet.

I looked at him, searching his face for any sign of denial, of protest, but he remained silent, his expression guarded. "Is it true?" I asked, my voice barely more than a whisper. "Did you... betray her?"

For the first time, I saw something flicker in his gaze—a hint of vulnerability, of pain, quickly masked by that familiar arrogance. He looked away, his jaw clenched, and I felt a pang of something I couldn't quite name. Betrayal, maybe, or disappointment. I'd trusted him, believed in him, and now... now I wasn't so sure.

"I did what I had to do," he said at last, his voice hard, unyielding. "Corinne made her choices. She knew the risks."

Corinne laughed again, a harsh, bitter sound that cut through the air like a knife. "Oh, don't flatter yourself, Damian. You were nothing but a pawn, a tool to be used and discarded. And now... now you're just a shadow of the man you once were."

Her words hit their mark, and I saw the flash of anger in his eyes, the tightly controlled fury that simmered just beneath the surface. But he didn't respond, didn't give her the satisfaction of a reaction. Instead, he turned to me, his gaze steady, unwavering.

"I won't lie to you," he said, his voice low and serious. "I've done things I'm not proud of. I've made mistakes. But I'm not that man anymore."

I wanted to believe him, wanted to trust in the man I'd come to know, the man who'd saved me more times than I could count. But Corinne's words lingered, her accusations like a poison seeping into my thoughts, casting doubt over everything I'd thought I knew.

"You don't have to believe me," he continued, his gaze intense, almost pleading. "But I swear to you, I'm telling the truth. Corinne... she's twisting things. She wants to tear us apart, to turn you against me. Don't let her win."

Corinne's laughter echoed around us, mocking, triumphant, as she watched us with a satisfied smile. She knew, as well as I did, that the damage was done, that the seeds of doubt had already taken root. And as I looked at Damian, standing there with that same defiant arrogance, I felt my heart twist with a mix of anger and something else, something deeper, something I didn't dare name.

The forest seemed to close in around us, the shadows deepening, and I felt a chill settle over me. For the first time, I wondered if I was fighting a losing battle, if Damian was beyond saving—or if, in trying to save him, I'd only end up losing myself.

I stared at him, words jammed in my throat, feeling as if the ground beneath me had vanished. Corinne's eyes sparkled with dark amusement as she leaned against a tree, watching us like a cat playing with cornered prey. Her smile, sharp as a blade, curved up as she sensed my hesitation.

"Damian, you never told her, did you?" she drawled, each word dripping with venomous glee. "What a shame. And here I thought you'd changed."

Damian's shoulders tightened, and he gave her a look that could have frozen fire. "Corinne, if you're here for revenge, get in line," he said, voice steady but rough around the edges. "But don't think you can drag her into this."

"Oh, darling," Corinne practically purred, savoring the tension like it was fine wine. "She's already in it. Whether she knows it or not, she's part of this whole mess now. And you know as well as I do that she deserves to hear everything."

My heart thumped in my chest, loud and erratic. Every instinct screamed at me to turn around, to leave them here to hash out their tangled past and whatever twisted history they shared. But I was rooted to the spot, unable to tear my gaze from the scene unfolding before me.

"Fine," I said, lifting my chin, daring them both to try and push me out of this. "I'm not going anywhere. So, what's the truth? What is it that he's not telling me?"

Damian clenched his jaw, and for a moment, I saw something raw and unguarded in his expression. His shoulders slumped, just a fraction, but enough for Corinne to seize the opportunity. She moved closer to me, her smile softening as though we were sharing some private joke, though her eyes remained as calculating as ever.

"He didn't tell you that he used to be one of us, did he?" she said, her voice a whisper meant to cut. "He was one of the Society's finest—until he got squeamish, decided he was too good for the work we did. Turned on his own people. On me."

My gaze darted back to Damian, who looked away, jaw tight. The silence stretched, heavy and bitter, until finally, he met my eyes.

"It's true," he said, his voice low, like gravel. "I was... involved. But it wasn't what I thought it was. The Society—they promised protection, order. But all they wanted was control. They used people like pawns, didn't care about the lives they destroyed."

Corinne scoffed, crossing her arms. "Oh, listen to him—now he's the hero, the misunderstood saint who couldn't bear to do the dirty work." Her eyes narrowed, glinting like the edge of a knife. "But he enjoyed it, in the beginning. The thrill, the power. Don't let him fool you into thinking he's innocent. He's got just as much blood on his hands as I do."

I took a step back, feeling the air shift between us, the weight of their shared history pressing down on me. The man I'd trusted, fought beside—suddenly, he seemed a stranger, haunted by shadows I hadn't seen before.

"Damian," I whispered, searching his face for some kind of explanation. "Is it true?"

He hesitated, a flicker of pain crossing his face. "I was young, reckless. I didn't realize how far they'd go, how much they'd take from me. When I finally saw what they were, I got out."

"But you didn't get out clean, did you?" Corinne's voice was as sweet as poison, her gaze cold and unrelenting. "Tell her about what you left behind, the people you betrayed to save your own skin."

Damian's face tightened, his eyes darkening. "I didn't betray anyone," he said, each word clipped, as though he was trying to convince himself as much as me. "I made a choice. I chose a different path."

"A different path," Corinne repeated, laughing without humor. "Is that what you tell yourself? That you walked away with some noble cause?" She shook her head, looking at me as if I were a fool. "The Society doesn't just let people walk away. They make sure there's a price for everything. And he paid it—at least, he let others pay it for him."

My fists clenched at my sides. I wanted to shout, to demand answers, to shake Damian until he admitted whatever he was hiding. But instead, I forced myself to take a deep breath, to look him in the eye and ask the question that had been gnawing at me since Corinne had first appeared.

"Damian, did you really leave people behind? Did you let them... suffer for your choices?"

For a moment, he looked at me with such an intense sadness that I felt my heart twist in my chest. "I did what I had to do to survive," he said, his voice barely more than a whisper. "I thought... I thought if I could get out, if I could find a way to stop them, then maybe it would be worth it. But the truth is, I don't know if it ever will be."

Corinne's smile widened, triumphant. "See? Even he doesn't believe in his own redemption. And now you're tangled up in his mess, just like the rest of us."

I took a step back, letting the words sink in. The weight of them, the truth of them, settled over me like a heavy cloak. I'd thought I knew Damian, thought I understood the man who had fought beside me, who had stood by my side when no one else would. But now... now I wasn't sure if I'd ever really known him at all.

"Why did you come back, Damian?" I asked, my voice trembling with anger and something else I couldn't name. "Why did you come to me, bring me into this, if you knew what you'd done? If you knew they were still after you?"

He looked at me, his eyes full of regret. "Because I thought I could make things right," he said, his voice barely a whisper. "Because I thought maybe... maybe this time, I could actually save someone."

Corinne laughed, the sound harsh and mocking. "Oh, how noble of you. Trying to redeem yourself by dragging someone else down with you. Classic Damian."

I felt the anger rise in my chest, hot and fierce, a fire I hadn't realized was there. "Enough," I said, my voice steady. "I don't know what kind of games you're playing, Corinne, but I'm not going to be a pawn in this."

She tilted her head, looking at me with a mix of amusement and curiosity. "You think you're not already part of the game? Darling, you're in this deeper than you realize."

I ignored her, turning back to Damian. "You told me you wanted to help me, that we were in this together. But how can I trust you when you're keeping secrets? When you're hiding this whole other side of yourself?"

He opened his mouth to respond, but before he could say a word, Corinne stepped forward, her gaze icy. "Oh, he'll say anything to keep you close. That's what he does—he draws people in, makes them believe he's something he's not. And then, when it suits him, he'll leave you behind, just like he left me. Just like he left everyone who ever trusted him."

I felt my stomach twist, her words like a dagger twisting in my chest. But I refused to let her see the doubt, the hurt that was gnawing at me. I took a deep breath, squaring my shoulders, and looked Damian in the eye.

"If you want me to trust you," I said, my voice firm, "then you have to tell me the truth. All of it. No more half-truths, no more secrets. Because if you can't do that... then I can't be a part of this."

Damian's face softened, his expression one of remorse. He looked down, taking a steadying breath, and then finally, he nodded. "You're right. You deserve the truth. And I promise—I'll tell you everything. No more secrets."

Corinne's smile faded, a flicker of something unreadable crossing her face. For the first time, I saw a shadow of doubt in her gaze, as though she hadn't expected him to be willing to open up.

Damian took a long breath, his shoulders rising and falling as if he could somehow shrug off the weight of Corinne's accusations. His face held a fragility I hadn't seen before, the kind that only appeared when masks were abandoned, when truths were raw and jagged and too sharp to handle without injury.

"I never wanted you to be part of this," he said, his voice hushed and deliberate. "The past I left... it should have stayed buried. But life doesn't give second chances that easily, does it?" His gaze shifted to Corinne, his expression hardening. "And some people can't seem to leave well enough alone."

"Don't flatter yourself," Corinne retorted, crossing her arms and tilting her head with a venomous smile. "You think I chased you down for old times' sake? Please. I'm here because you owe me. And because you're about to ruin everything we worked for." She took a step closer, her voice dropping to a hiss. "You think you can save her?

Protect her from them? The Crimson Society will swallow you both whole, and they won't leave a trace."

I opened my mouth to object, but Damian shot me a look that silenced me, a subtle shake of his head that said this wasn't the time. His eyes softened when they met mine, and I saw a flicker of something in his gaze—apology, maybe, or regret for the tangled mess we now found ourselves in.

"What do you want, Corinne?" he asked, his tone dangerously calm. "Because if it's revenge, there are easier ways to get it than ambushing us in the woods."

Corinne's smile was as cold as the moonlight filtering through the trees. "Revenge is such a crude word, Damian. No, I want something far more interesting. I want you to come back."

The silence that followed was dense and suffocating, pressing down on us like a vice. Damian's face twisted, a look of mingled disbelief and disgust flashing in his eyes. "You must be joking."

"Oh, I'm dead serious," Corinne said smoothly, her gaze unwavering. "The Society is stronger than ever, and they need someone like you. They need your skills, your... charm. And besides, think of all the chaos we could unleash together."

Damian laughed, a bitter sound that held no humor. "You mean, all the chaos you could unleash with me as your pawn."

Corinne shrugged, unbothered by his scorn. "Call it what you want. But think about it—returning to the Society would give you power, control. You wouldn't have to keep running, hiding like a fugitive. They'd welcome you back with open arms."

Damian shook his head slowly, a strange sadness flickering in his eyes. "And they'd do the same to her as they did to everyone who tried to leave." His voice softened, and I could feel the pain underlying his words, a sorrow that had etched itself deep into his soul. "No. I won't go back. Not for you, not for them. And certainly not at the expense of someone I care about."

Corinne's smile faded, her expression hardening. "Care about?" Her voice dripped with contempt, and she shot me a look filled with scorn. "Oh, please. Don't tell me you've actually grown a conscience over this one. How... tedious." She raised her chin, her eyes blazing with renewed fury. "Let me remind you, Damian, of the cost of betrayal. The Society doesn't forgive easily, and they've already noticed your... indiscretions."

A chill slid down my spine, and I forced myself to meet Corinne's gaze, refusing to let her see the fear simmering just below the surface. "You think you can scare me with vague threats?" I asked, managing to keep my voice steady, even if my heart was pounding in my chest. "The Society may be powerful, but they don't own everyone."

"Oh, how adorable," Corinne said, her smile returning, crueler than ever. "Bravery from someone who has no idea what they're up against. I almost envy your naivety."

Damian's hand drifted toward his sword, his face darkening with anger. "Leave her out of this, Corinne. Whatever you came here to settle, settle it with me."

"Fine." She pulled a small dagger from beneath her cloak, twisting it between her fingers, the blade glinting in the faint moonlight. "Then here's my offer: you come back willingly, and she walks away. Simple as that. No blood, no mess. Just you and me, back where we belong."

The words hung in the air, sinister and seductive. I looked at Damian, a knot forming in my stomach. If he accepted, I would be safe, free from the Society's clutches. But I knew it would destroy him. The cost of going back, of surrendering to Corinne's dark influence, was something he might never recover from.

Damian's jaw clenched, his eyes filled with a storm of emotions, each one flashing across his face too quickly to catch. His gaze flicked to me, and I saw the resignation there, the sense that he was preparing to make a sacrifice, to do something he'd regret for the rest of his life.

"No," I said, stepping forward before he could speak, surprising even myself. "This isn't his choice alone. If he goes back to them, it's only because you're forcing him, not because he wants to. And I won't let you do that."

Corinne's eyes narrowed, her grip on the dagger tightening. "Oh, you won't let me? What do you think you can do, girl?" She laughed, a dark, bitter sound. "You're nothing compared to what he used to be. Nothing compared to what I am."

"Maybe," I said, feeling a strange surge of defiance, a fierce determination that steadied my nerves. "But I know he's not the man you remember. And if you force him into this, it'll only end one way—badly, for all of us."

Damian looked at me, his expression softened, a mix of gratitude and something else I couldn't quite name. "She's right, Corinne," he said, his voice low but firm. "I'm not going back. Not for you, not for anyone."

Corinne's eyes flashed with rage, her lips twisting into a snarl. "So be it," she spat, her voice venomous. "But don't think this is over. The Society will come for both of you, and when they do, you'll beg me for mercy."

She turned sharply, disappearing into the shadows as swiftly as she'd appeared, leaving only the rustling of leaves and the lingering chill of her threat in the air. I released a breath I hadn't realized I was holding, my heart still pounding as I turned to Damian.

"Is it true?" I asked, my voice barely a whisper. "Will they come after us?"

He hesitated, his eyes haunted. "Yes," he said quietly, each word laced with regret. "They won't stop until they have what they want. The Society... they don't let go."

I swallowed hard, feeling the weight of his words settle over me. I'd known, on some level, that we were facing powerful enemies, but hearing it spoken aloud made it all too real.

"We'll deal with them," I said, forcing a note of determination into my voice. "Whatever it takes."

But Damian didn't look convinced. His gaze drifted to the darkened path where Corinne had vanished, a frown etched deep into his brow. "They're not like the others we've faced. The Society doesn't fight fair. They'll use every weakness, every fear... everything that matters to us."

A cold dread washed over me, and I felt the beginnings of panic stirring in my chest. "What do you mean?"

He turned to me, his expression grim, and I saw the fear in his eyes—the same fear I felt clawing at my insides. "They'll find a way to make us betray each other," he whispered, his voice hollow. "That's what they do. They turn allies into enemies, trust into ashes."

The words hit me like a physical blow, stealing the breath from my lungs. And as I looked into Damian's eyes, I saw the horrifying truth reflected there: the Society wouldn't just come after us. They would tear us apart, turn us against each other until there was nothing left but betrayal.

In the silence that followed, the forest seemed to hold its breath, and I felt the weight of an unspoken question hang between us—a question I didn't want to ask, but knew I couldn't avoid.

What would we be willing to sacrifice to survive?

Chapter 8: The Thief's Heart

The Silver Night Market is a labyrinth of shadow and light, where narrow alleyways twist through stalls that seem to sprout from darkness itself, lit by flickering lanterns strung high above. The lanterns cast glimmers over everything—jewels sparkling like dewdrops, potions that bubble with mysterious colors, fabrics woven with silver thread—and I'm captivated by the sheer magic of it. Yet beneath the surface charm, an undercurrent of danger thrums, a silent warning in the way strangers' eyes flick over us, appraising, calculating.

Damian moves beside me, his usual playful energy tempered, his jaw set in a hard line. I reach out, brushing my fingers against his arm, but he barely responds, only a subtle twitch of his muscles under my touch. Corinne's words linger like smoke, poisoning the air between us. I don't know exactly what she told him, but whatever it was, it's cracked open something inside him, something he's desperately trying to hide. The Damian I know would have thrown a flirtatious smile my way, murmured a joke to lighten the tension, maybe even tugged me into one of these shadowed corners for a stolen kiss. But tonight, his charm is buried under layers of icy restraint, and it stings more than I want to admit.

Ahead, the market narrows, and I sense a faint shift in the air, a cold shiver down my spine. This is the part of the Silver Night where rules bend, where only those who know how to keep their secrets survive. We're here for one reason: to find the thief who holds the key to the Velvet Charm. No one else has managed to find it, and we're hoping this thief might at least give us a direction, if not the answer itself.

A flicker of movement catches my eye—a slender figure with a sharp, predatory grace slipping through the crowd. I watch, intrigued, as he weaves effortlessly past the stall keepers, his hands moving in a delicate, practiced rhythm. He barely brushes a sleeve, and yet somehow, when he moves on, rings, trinkets, small purses seem to have vanished from sight. The thief. There's a calculated, effortless confidence to his movements, the kind that comes from a life lived on the edge of shadows.

Damian's eyes narrow, and without a word, he steps forward, his hand on the hilt of his blade. But I touch his arm again, stopping him with a look. Damian hesitates, then sighs, loosening his grip but not his gaze.

As if sensing our approach, the thief spins around, one brow lifting in mock surprise. "Ah, the lovers," he says, his voice low and smooth, with a hint of an accent I can't quite place. He looks between us, his eyes gleaming with a wicked intelligence. "What brings you two to my corner of the night?"

"We're here to talk," I say, keeping my voice calm, steady. "About the Velvet Charm."

The thief's smirk widens. "Ah, everyone's favorite myth," he purrs. "Priceless, powerful, and entirely unattainable. Isn't that the allure?" He leans in, close enough that I can see the flash of a scar on his cheek, almost hidden by the fall of his hair. "But you're serious, aren't you? You actually think you can find it."

Damian steps forward, tension rippling through his frame. "You know where it is," he says, a statement more than a question, his voice barely above a whisper.

The thief laughs softly, but there's no mirth in it. "Maybe I do, maybe I don't." He tilts his head, studying us with an interest that feels unsettling, like he's dissecting us, peeling back layers we've tried to keep hidden. "But if I did, do you know what it would cost?"

My stomach twists, and I can feel Damian tense beside me. "What do you mean?"

The thief's gaze turns sharp, his voice dropping to a near whisper. "The Velvet Charm demands a sacrifice," he says, each word dropping like a stone into a still pond. "Not just any sacrifice. It needs something...personal. Precious." He pauses, his gaze flicking to Damian, a glint of curiosity in his eyes. "Something you're willing to lose."

Damian's mask cracks, just for an instant, but it's enough. I see the fear in his eyes, raw and unguarded, and it catches me off-guard. This is Damian, the man who has laughed in the face of danger, who has challenged foes twice his size without flinching. Seeing him like this, vulnerable and afraid, sends a strange ache through my chest. I want to reach for him, to tell him it'll be alright, but I can't seem to find the words.

The thief watches us, his smirk fading as he reads the tension between us. "The Charm doesn't care about your strength, your bravery, your plans for the future," he murmurs. "It only wants what you love most."

"What if we're willing to make that sacrifice?" I ask, my voice stronger than I feel. "What if we'll do whatever it takes?"

The thief raises an eyebrow, looking between us as if weighing the truth in my words. "Then you're braver—or more foolish—than most." He steps back, his face slipping into shadow. "If you want to find the Charm, start by asking yourselves what you're truly willing to lose." With that, he disappears into the night, leaving us standing alone amidst the hum of the market, the weight of his words settling heavily over us.

For a moment, neither of us speaks. The market bustles around us, but it feels distant, muffled, as if we're caught in a bubble of silence. I glance at Damian, but he won't meet my gaze, his expression hardening into something unreadable.

"Damian," I begin, reaching for him, but he pulls back, his face an unreadable mask.

"Let's go," he says, his voice flat, as if all the warmth has been drained from it. He doesn't wait for me, already pushing through the crowd, his shoulders rigid, his pace brisk.

I follow, my heart pounding with a mix of frustration and hurt. Every step feels heavier, like the ground is pulling me down, rooting me in a despair I can't shake. For the first time since this journey began, I feel as if I'm losing him, as if something vital is slipping through my fingers, no matter how tightly I try to hold on.

And the worst part is, I don't know what to do to stop it.

The alleys leading out of the Silver Night Market twist and turn like veins, pulsing with an energy that matches my own unsettled heart. Every few steps, I hear the scuff of Damian's boots ahead of me, but he's making no effort to wait, his figure an indistinct shadow slipping through the haze of lantern smoke and murmured voices. He's pulling away in more ways than one, and I'm helpless to stop it.

I take a deep breath, tasting the faint spice of incense and the metallic tang of the city air, thick with the scent of burning oil and something deeper, older. It's a place made for secrets and bargains, the kind of place where people vanish into the night and reappear the next morning with promises they never meant to keep. I hate the way it all makes me feel—a little afraid, a little desperate, and very, very alone.

I don't realize I've stopped walking until Damian's voice, colder than the night air, cuts through the din. "Are you coming?"

I bristle at his tone. "I would, if you'd slow down," I snap, refusing to let him get under my skin more than he already has. He stops and turns, and for a moment, I almost expect him to soften, to see the Damian I know—a quick grin, maybe, or at least a sarcastic remark to ease the tension. But there's only a hard line to his mouth, a guardedness in his eyes that's starting to feel more familiar than I'd like.

"If we waste time, he'll vanish," Damian says, nodding back toward the market. "Or did you think he'd leave a forwarding address?"

I bite my lip, swallowing down the sharp response that threatens to slip out. "It's not like that thief was planning to tell us much more, anyway," I mutter, catching up to him. "He enjoyed keeping us in the dark, watching us flounder. He probably would've taken bets on it if he'd had an audience."

Damian snorts, a hollow sound that's close enough to a laugh to make my chest ache. "He wouldn't be wrong," he says, his voice softer, but then he shakes his head, his expression hardening again. "I don't need to be a fool in front of a thief. Or anyone else."

There's something in his tone that stops me short. I can feel the sting of his words, as if he's laying a warning between us—a reminder of the wall he's building, brick by stubborn brick, and he's not about to let me climb over it. For once, I don't argue. I don't press him to talk or try to soften that edge of his. I just nod and keep walking, matching his pace, every step echoing with the silence that's taken root between us.

We turn down another alley, one lined with buildings that loom tall and dark, their windows like the hollow eyes of skulls. It's quieter here, away from the market, and I feel a strange sense of calm settle over me, thick and expectant, like the air before a storm. I glance at Damian, watching as he surveys the shadows, his body tense, his hand resting on the hilt of his blade.

"Are you expecting an ambush?" I ask, half-joking, though I can't shake the prickling sensation creeping up my spine.

He gives me a sidelong glance. "This city's full of surprises," he says dryly, then pauses. "And not the kind you usually want to see twice."

I open my mouth to ask him what he means, but before I can, a voice cuts through the stillness. "Lost in the dark, are we?" It's low and soft, carrying the same sly humor I heard earlier, and I know without looking that the thief has followed us. I whirl around, my pulse spiking as he steps out from the shadows, his face half-hidden beneath his hood, that glint of amusement never far from his eyes.

Damian draws his blade instantly, the steel catching the faintest bit of light, but the thief merely raises his hands, the movement lazy, almost bored. "Now, now," he chides, "is that any way to treat someone who's just here to help?"

"Help?" Damian's voice drips with sarcasm, his grip on the blade steady. "You mean take advantage, mock us, leave us to rot—those are the kind of games you play, right?"

The thief tilts his head, regarding Damian with a mixture of curiosity and mild amusement. "Not all games are meant to be won," he says cryptically, then lets his gaze slide to me, his eyes narrowing in a way that feels uncomfortably perceptive. "But maybe you already knew that."

A shiver runs down my spine, and I resist the urge to glance away, to hide from that knowing stare. "If you know something, tell us," I say, keeping my voice steady. "We don't have time for riddles."

The thief chuckles, a sound that's more shadow than laughter. "Time," he muses, "is exactly what you'll need. And more than a little luck. But if you're so determined to find the Velvet Charm, I suppose there's one last thing I can tell you."

I hold my breath, every muscle tense as I wait for him to continue. He takes a step closer, and for a brief moment, I can smell the faint hint of leather and smoke on him, the scent of someone who's spent a lifetime dancing between light and shadow. "There's a place," he says, his voice barely more than a whisper. "It's hidden, like most things worth finding. An old chapel, long abandoned, past the edges of the city. It was said to be a place of sacrifices. Offerings made in the dead of night. People say that if you're looking for the Velvet Charm, that's where you start."

Damian's eyes narrow, his grip on the blade tightening. "And you just happened to know about this place?"

The thief shrugs, a casual, almost lazy movement. "I know a lot of things. Doesn't mean I go looking for them myself. But you two?" He smirks. "You look like you'd go to the ends of the earth for a chance at something as elusive as the Velvet Charm. Or maybe just for the thrill of it."

Damian scoffs, sheathing his blade with a sharp, decisive motion. "We're not here for thrills," he mutters, though I can hear the edge of something bitter in his tone, something that stings with the weight of half-truths.

The thief's eyes gleam, and he leans in, his voice a soft murmur. "Oh, but you are," he whispers. "Whether you know it or not." He pulls back, his gaze lingering on us both, then with a mocking bow, he vanishes back into the shadows as effortlessly as he appeared.

For a long moment, Damian and I stand there, caught in the wake of his words, the air around us thick with unspoken thoughts and questions that neither of us knows how to ask. I feel Damian's hand brush against mine, a fleeting, hesitant touch, and it's all I can do not to turn and pull him close, to break down whatever wall he's hiding behind and remind him that he doesn't have to carry this alone.

But he lets go, turning away as if the moment never happened, and the ache in my chest only grows. It's maddening, this distance he's keeping, this refusal to let me in. And as we begin walking again, the weight of it presses down on me, as solid and unyielding as stone.

It's then, as we step out of the narrow alley and back into the open night, that I realize just how dangerous this journey is becoming—not just because of the risks we'll face, but because of what we might lose along the way.

The chapel stands at the edge of the city, half-swallowed by the overgrown woods that guard its secrets. What remains of the building is cloaked in ivy, dark and twisting like veins across its crumbling stone walls. Moonlight slips through the gaps in the roof, casting fractured silver patterns across the ground. Every step feels like a transgression, as if the ground itself is whispering secrets I'm not meant to hear. Damian and I have walked in silence since leaving the market, each lost in thoughts we don't dare speak aloud.

I glance at him, hoping for some signal, some word to break this invisible thread of tension, but his expression is shuttered, his jaw set in a way that tells me whatever he's feeling, he has no intention of sharing it. It's maddening, this unyielding stoicism. The thief's words hang between us like smoke, intangible but impossible to ignore. The chapel seems to pull at us, as though the stones themselves are reaching for us, eager to take whatever we've come to leave behind.

Inside, the air is thick and cold, holding the chill of centuries, of lives and promises long past. Our footsteps echo against the stone, a hollow sound that reminds me of the thief's mocking laugh. Damian moves toward the altar at the far end of the room, his face illuminated by a slant of moonlight that makes him look as if he's been carved from the same stone as this place, both beautiful and unyielding.

"This is it, then?" I ask, my voice low, as if afraid to disturb whatever spirits linger here.

He nods, barely glancing at me. "If the thief was telling the truth," he says, running his hand along the edge of the stone altar, "then this is where we'll find it. Or where we'll find...something."

There's a bleakness in his voice that makes me ache, but I push it aside, focusing instead on the task at hand. The altar is worn, chipped at the edges, but its surface gleams faintly under the moonlight, as if some part of it has been polished by a thousand hands, each one leaving a fragment of hope or fear behind. I reach out, feeling the smoothness beneath my fingers, and I shiver. This place hums with power, old and hungry.

"Whatever we're supposed to sacrifice," I murmur, glancing at him, "it's not something easy, is it?"

Damian's eyes meet mine, and for a brief, startling moment, I see the turmoil he's been hiding—a flicker of doubt, fear, even regret. But then he looks away, his face hardening once more, and I wonder if I only imagined it. "Nothing worth having comes without a cost," he says, his tone so cold it feels like a slap. "You knew that when we started this."

I want to argue, to tell him that I didn't know—couldn't have known—just how much it would take. But I can feel the distance between us widening, and I don't want to give him another reason to pull away. Instead, I nod, swallowing down the words that crowd at the back of my throat.

He turns back to the altar, his hands curling into fists as he braces himself against it. For a moment, he looks almost vulnerable, like a man standing on the edge of a cliff, staring down into something vast and unknowable. I want to reach for him, to tell him that he doesn't have to face this alone, but I hesitate, afraid that if I touch him, he'll shatter into pieces that I won't know how to put back together.

"What are you willing to give up?" His voice is so quiet, I almost don't hear him. He doesn't look at me as he speaks, his gaze fixed on some point far beyond the walls of the chapel. "What would you sacrifice for this?"

I open my mouth to respond, but the words catch in my throat. It's not an easy question, and I know it's not one he's asking lightly. For him, this isn't about curiosity or adventure. It's something deeper, something raw and painful, a part of himself he's been guarding with all the strength he can muster. I realize, suddenly, that he's not asking about the Velvet Charm. He's asking about us.

"I don't know," I admit, my voice barely more than a whisper. "I thought I did. But being here, in this place…I'm not so sure anymore."

He closes his eyes, a flicker of something unreadable crossing his face. "Maybe that's the point," he murmurs, as if speaking to himself. "Maybe we're not supposed to know until it's too late."

The silence stretches between us, thick and suffocating, until I can't stand it any longer. I step closer, reaching out to touch his arm. "Damian, whatever happens, you don't have to face it alone."

He flinches, just barely, but enough for me to feel the tension thrumming beneath his skin. He doesn't pull away, though, and for a moment, I allow myself to believe that maybe—just maybe—he might finally let me in.

But then a sound shatters the silence, a soft rustling from the shadows behind the altar. I freeze, my heart pounding as Damian straightens, his hand instinctively going to his blade. The air grows colder, the faint glow of moonlight flickering like a dying candle. Something is here with us, something ancient and unseen.

A figure emerges from the shadows, cloaked in darkness, its face hidden beneath a hood. I feel a jolt of recognition—it's the thief. Or at least, it looks like him, but there's something different about him now, something almost spectral. He stands in the doorway, his gaze fixed on us with a cold, calculating intensity.

"Did you think you could come here without being noticed?" His voice is low and mocking, the same sly tone he used in the market, but with an edge that makes my skin crawl. "The Velvet Charm does not yield to those who merely seek it. You must prove yourselves worthy."

Damian steps forward, his jaw clenched, his blade gleaming in the moonlight. "And how exactly do we do that?"

The thief's smile is chilling, his eyes gleaming with a sinister light. "The sacrifice must be made willingly," he says, his gaze shifting to me. "One of you must give up something precious. Something you hold dearer than life itself."

My heart races, my mind scrambling to make sense of his words. I glance at Damian, seeing the same fear mirrored in his eyes, but he doesn't back down. He meets the thief's gaze, his stance unwavering.

"If that's what it takes," he says, his voice steady, though I can hear the tremor beneath it, "then tell us what to do."

The thief steps closer, his smile widening. "The choice is yours," he says, his tone almost gleeful. "But be warned—once the sacrifice is made, there is no turning back."

He raises a hand, gesturing toward the altar, and a faint glow begins to emanate from the stone, pulsing with a rhythm that feels almost like a heartbeat. I can feel its pull, a magnetic force that draws me closer, even as every instinct screams at me to run. I glance at Damian, seeing the same struggle in his eyes, and for the first time, I wonder if we've come too far, if we've crossed a line that cannot be uncrossed.

Before I can decide, Damian reaches out, his hand hovering over the glowing stone. His face is pale, his eyes wide with something between fear and determination. He glances at me, his gaze lingering for a moment, as if memorizing every detail, every breath.

Then, before I can stop him, he presses his hand against the altar, and a blinding light erupts, swallowing us both in a surge of power that knocks the breath from my lungs.

And then, everything goes dark.

Chapter 9: Veils of Fire

I let the market's noise fade behind us, its chaotic sounds giving way to the eerie silence of the crimson forest looming at the edge of town. Damian's footsteps match mine, steady and measured, and I can feel his eyes on me, cautious yet curious. It's unnerving, really, that mix of mystery and familiarity he exudes—how he always seems to anticipate my next move without a word. But it isn't until the forest swallows us in shadows that I start to wonder if he, too, has secrets he's left unspoken. Not that I can ask. Not now, anyway.

The Crimson Society isn't far behind, and even though Damian's assured me they've lost our trail, I can still sense them. Their leader—no, her name still stings too much to even think—she's closer than I'd like. I never expected her to have climbed so high in the ranks, never thought she'd come to wield the kind of power that could send shivers down my spine from hundreds of paces away. If I'd known, I might have reconsidered, might have kept my distance from the Velvet Charm, that damned relic of tangled fates and promises.

We edge along the forest's perimeter, moving from tree to tree. The bark here is a deep red, and the roots twist out from the ground like gnarled fingers reaching up to drag us down. Every step echoes, and with each one, I'm convinced they'll hear us, that she'll hear us. Damian catches my eye, nodding toward a hidden path leading further into the thick. I hesitate. He leans close, voice low and calm.

"Trust me, it's safer than staying out here."

I raise a brow, feigning nonchalance. "Since when did you become an expert in surviving the Crimson Society?"

He smirks, leaning in a fraction too close. "Since I decided I had a vested interest in keeping you alive."

The look he gives me is smug and soft all at once, an infuriating mix of confidence and something else I can't quite place. But there's no time for that. I swallow whatever retort I might have had and push forward into the path he's chosen. The forest seems to close in around us, the light dimming with every step. The silence is oppressive, pressing down like a weight on my shoulders, but I don't slow down.

Our lead is slim. Too slim, if I'm honest with myself, but I'm not about to let him see me sweat. After all, I've been running from shadows for far longer than he's known me, and I'd rather be the one haunting them than the other way around.

Branches snap behind us, close enough that I almost lose my footing in my haste to turn. Damian catches my elbow, his grip firm, steadying me just as a flicker of flame lights up the dark. It's her. Just as I knew it would be. I force myself to take a breath, my mind racing with a dozen escape plans, half of which involve leaving Damian behind. But his grip on my arm tightens, and I realize, reluctantly, that he's already pieced together the truth.

"Keep moving," he whispers, his tone void of that teasing lilt from earlier. Now it's all business. And for the first time, I glimpse the man behind the mask he's worn so well.

We dive deeper into the trees, his hand never loosening its hold. The forest seems to open up in a way I didn't expect, the path widening to reveal a stretch of abandoned ruins half-buried under a blanket of moss. I can hardly catch my breath as we duck behind the crumbling wall, pressing ourselves close to its cool, damp surface.

She steps into the clearing just moments later, her red cloak flowing like blood down her back, her eyes as sharp as I remember. The memory hits me, unbidden and fierce—a girl with a wicked smile and eyes that held a promise I'd foolishly trusted. Now, she's flanked by two shadowy figures, their faces obscured, their every move synchronized as if they shared a single mind.

"Come out, come out, wherever you are..." Her voice is light, mocking. She knows I'm here. I can feel her enjoying this, the thrill of the hunt.

Damian inches closer, close enough that his breath grazes my ear. "We can't stay here. She'll find us if we wait too long."

I know he's right, but every instinct in me wants to leap out, confront her, demand answers to the questions that have haunted me for years. The answers she stole when she walked away, leaving me with nothing but fractured pieces of a past I can't fully understand. But before I can move, she speaks again.

"The Velvet Charm won't protect you forever, you know." Her words curl through the air, and for a moment, I swear I see a flicker of uncertainty in her gaze. But it's gone as quickly as it came, replaced by that same ruthless confidence.

Damian tugs on my hand, his eyes fierce. "Now or never, sweetheart."

He hardly gives me a moment to think before he's leading me around the far side of the ruins, ducking under low-hanging branches and weaving between trees with a speed that leaves me breathless. The sounds of pursuit are fainter now, but they're still there, an unrelenting beat that reminds me of all the other times I've run, all the other close calls.

Finally, the forest breaks open to reveal a rocky hillside that slopes down into the valley below. Damian glances back, his expression unreadable, before releasing my hand and starting the descent. I follow, stumbling on loose stones and catching myself more than once on sharp rocks. My heart pounds, louder than the footsteps behind us, louder than the frantic thoughts that swirl in my mind.

Just as we reach the bottom, he stops abruptly, turning to face me. "You know this isn't over, right?"

I manage a grim smile. "If it was, I'd be worried. But you...you're still with me, aren't you?"

He doesn't answer, not directly. Instead, he takes my hand again, and in that moment, under the darkening sky and with the memory of her mocking words still fresh in my mind, I realize something that chills me to the core.

The wind slices through the valley, bitter and sharp, as we crouch low beneath a ragged outcrop of rock. My pulse hasn't quite returned to normal, each heartbeat a reminder of how close she came. The past is a beast with claws—never quite as dead as you think. Damian's breathing is slow and controlled beside me, though his gaze darts over the expanse of trees we left behind, watchful, calculated.

"Something tells me," I say, barely more than a whisper, "that you weren't exactly forthcoming about your expertise in all things forest-related."

Damian's lips curve into that maddeningly calm smile of his, the one that makes me question every instinct I have. "Maybe I was holding back a few surprises." He leans his head against the rock, looking up at the darkening sky. "Besides, a man's entitled to a bit of mystery, don't you think?"

"I'd rather mystery and survival be separate hobbies," I mutter, brushing dust from my sleeve and trying not to give away how much his steady presence is starting to feel like something I need. The thought is equal parts infuriating and... something else, something I can't afford to name.

"Well, we're here now," he says, his voice uncharacteristically soft. His gaze meets mine, and for a fleeting moment, I wonder if he's thinking the same thing—if he, too, feels like fate's tightening its grip around us.

A sharp cry cuts through the silence, echoing from the depths of the crimson forest. It's distant, muffled by the thick canopy, but it's enough to make me grip the Velvet Charm instinctively. The polished surface is cold, almost too cold, and a peculiar chill spreads from my hand up my arm. I feel Damian's eyes on me as I clutch the relic, its weight both familiar and foreboding.

"You think it's really as powerful as they say?" he asks, his tone unreadable.

I look down at it, tracing the delicate, intricate patterns etched along its surface. "It's hard to say. It's not exactly the kind of thing that comes with a user manual." I try for a smirk, but it falls flat. Even I can hear the tension lacing my voice.

Damian reaches out, his fingers brushing mine as he wraps his hand around the charm, holding it alongside me. I don't pull away, even though I probably should. There's something strangely comforting in his touch, a warmth that seems to counteract the chill radiating from the charm. For the first time, I allow myself to wonder if he feels the same weight of our fates, tangled up together in this mess of shadows and secrets.

Before I can dwell on it, another sound cuts through the quiet—a rustle, then the soft crunch of footsteps over loose gravel. My body tenses, and Damian's grip tightens on my hand as he glances past me, his expression shifting to something darker, sharper. Without a word, he lets go of the charm and positions himself in front of me, shielding me from whatever's approaching.

The figure that steps out from the treeline is dressed in the muted grays and browns of the Crimson Society's foot soldiers, her face obscured by the low hood. I don't recognize her, but there's a familiarity in her stance, an ease with the shadows that makes my skin prickle.

"Hand it over," she says, her voice calm, almost gentle, though her stance is anything but. Her hand rests on the hilt of a blade at her side, and her eyes—dark, unyielding—flick from Damian to me with a kind of bored indifference that unsettles me more than open malice would.

Damian doesn't flinch. "We're not in a bargaining mood."

Her eyes narrow, just a fraction, but enough to hint at the threat she carries. "Funny," she says, her tone dry, "because I wasn't asking." She draws her blade, a thin, curved weapon that catches the fading light with a sinister gleam. "We can do this the easy way, or—"

She doesn't get to finish. Damian moves before I can even register his intent, stepping forward with a fluidity that's almost frightening, knocking her weapon to the side as he closes the distance between them. I'm not sure if I should feel relief or unease at how easily he handles her, his movements precise and controlled, as if he's done this a thousand times before. There's no hesitation, no mercy in the way he disarms her, pinning her against a tree before she can so much as draw another breath.

I take a step closer, trying to ignore the small voice in my head that's a little too impressed. "You seem oddly comfortable with all this," I say, my voice steady, though my hands are anything but.

Damian glances back, a glint of something unreadable in his gaze. "Let's just say I've had my share of run-ins with people like her."

The woman scowls, her dark eyes narrowing with a hatred that feels all too familiar. "This won't end well for either of you," she hisses. "You think you can just walk away from this? From her?"

Her words slice through the air like a blade, and for a moment, I see a flicker of something in Damian's expression, a crack in the unshakable calm he usually wears. But it's gone as quickly as it appeared, replaced by that maddening composure of his.

"We'll take our chances," he says, releasing his hold on her and stepping back. "Go. Tell her that the Velvet Charm is ours."

She glares at us, but something in his tone must convince her, because she finally turns and disappears into the shadows, leaving us alone once more. The silence settles like a weight over us, and for a moment, I'm not sure whether to thank him or question every choice I've made that's led us here.

Damian brushes a stray leaf from his shoulder, his expression unreadable. "We should keep moving."

I give a curt nod, pretending that my heart isn't still racing, that the last few minutes haven't left me feeling oddly unmoored. We make our way down a narrow trail, the forest thickening around us with each step, the trees seeming to close in as if they're watching, waiting.

Finally, when the tension becomes too much to bear, I break the silence. "So...what's your story, then? You've got all the moves of a Society soldier, but you don't quite fit the mold."

He laughs, a low, quiet sound that feels almost out of place. "I'm not as interesting as you think," he says, though there's a glint in his eyes that suggests otherwise. "Let's just say I have a...complicated history with people who think they can own things that don't belong to them."

I roll my eyes. "Right. Because that's not vague at all."

Damian's smile is wry, though there's a hint of something softer underneath. "Trust me," he says, his voice dropping to a murmur, "there are some things better left unsaid."

I don't know what to make of that, or of him, really. He's like a puzzle with half the pieces missing, each one leading to another mystery rather than a solution. But there's a strange comfort in that uncertainty, a sense that maybe, just maybe, he understands the weight of what I'm carrying.

As the last traces of sunlight fade from the sky, we continue our path into the shadows, our fates intertwined more closely than ever, each step pulling us deeper into the unknown. The Velvet Charm rests heavy in my pocket, a silent reminder of everything I've lost—and everything I stand to lose. And as I glance at Damian, wondering if he's truly friend or foe, one thing becomes painfully, undeniably clear: there's no turning back.

The deeper we go, the thicker the air becomes, like the forest itself is holding its breath. It's an oppressive kind of quiet, the sort that seeps into your bones and makes your instincts scream. Even Damian's usual quips are absent, his gaze fixed on the path ahead, shoulders taut and braced as if he senses something I can't yet see.

A faint mist curls around the roots of the trees, swirling as if disturbed by something unseen. Shadows twist within the fog, their movements almost too fluid to be natural. I catch Damian's gaze, and he gives the slightest shake of his head, as if to tell me not to react. But I can't help it; my fingers twitch, and the Velvet Charm seems to pulse in response, a steady thrum that mirrors the rhythm of my heartbeat.

"Feeling jumpy, are we?" Damian murmurs, his voice low enough that it could almost be mistaken for a sigh.

"Only as jumpy as anyone with half a survival instinct would be," I shoot back, trying to ignore the way the charm hums against my palm. "Or would you prefer I skip into the mist without a care?"

"Oh, don't let me stop you," he says, the corner of his mouth quirking up in that infuriating way. "I'll just watch from a safe distance and take notes."

Despite myself, I almost laugh. Almost. But the sound dies in my throat when a shape emerges from the fog—a figure, tall and slender, cloaked in a shroud of shadows. Its face is obscured, a blank mask where eyes should be, and for a moment, I swear it's looking straight at me. I swallow, my grip tightening on the charm, and out of the corner of my eye, I see Damian tense as well.

"Is it real?" I whisper, not entirely sure if I want the answer.

"If it's not," he replies, his voice edged with the barest hint of unease, "then we're having one very convincing hallucination."

The figure drifts closer, silent and spectral, like a piece of the mist come to life. Every instinct screams at me to run, to bolt back down the path we came from, but I stand rooted to the spot, caught between fear and a strange, inexplicable pull toward the apparition.

Just as it reaches out a hand—if you could even call it that, given its indistinct, smoky form—Damian grabs my arm and pulls me back, breaking the spell. The figure's head tilts, almost as if in disappointment, before it dissipates back into the fog, leaving only a faint chill in the air where it once stood.

"Next time," he says, his voice tight, "how about we don't wait for the ghostly figure to extend an invitation?"

I shake off the lingering sense of dread, forcing a weak smile. "Good advice. I'll add that to my extensive mental notes on how to handle shadow apparitions in the woods."

His mouth twitches, but he says nothing as we press on, moving faster now, the silence between us thicker than the mist. The trees grow closer together, their branches clawing at us as we weave through them, and every so often, I catch glimpses of movement out of the corner of my eye. More shadows, darting just out of reach, as if taunting us.

At last, we stumble into a small clearing, the mist thinning enough that I can finally take a full breath. But the relief is short-lived; at the center of the clearing stands a stone pedestal, worn and cracked, with symbols carved into its surface that glow faintly in the fading light.

"Convenient," Damian says, arching a brow as he eyes the pedestal. "You think this is part of the Crimson Society's décor, or did we stumble onto something even worse?"

I approach the pedestal cautiously, brushing away a layer of moss to reveal a symbol etched deep into the stone—a spiral intertwined with a crescent moon, familiar and yet alien all at once. A chill skates down my spine, and I glance at Damian, who's watching me with a rare look of genuine concern.

"This symbol..." I hesitate, unsure of how to explain the sense of dread creeping through me. "It matches the one on the Velvet Charm."

Damian's expression shifts, his gaze flicking between the pedestal and the charm in my hand. "If this is a trap, it's a damn elaborate one."

Before I can respond, the charm in my hand begins to vibrate, a low, thrumming hum that resonates with the symbols on the pedestal. It feels as though the charm is drawing me in, pulling me closer to the stone, and despite every logical part of my mind screaming at me to stop, I reach out, my fingers hovering just above the pedestal's surface.

Damian's hand clamps down on my wrist, hard enough to pull me back from the edge. "Don't," he says, his voice sharper than I've ever heard it. "This feels wrong. All of it."

He's right, of course. Every instinct tells me to turn back, to leave this place and never look back. But the charm's pull is relentless, like it's alive, like it has its own agenda that neither of us fully understands.

"I can't explain it," I say, struggling to find words that make sense, "but I feel like... like if I don't, something worse will happen. Like this is the only way forward."

He stares at me, something close to fear flickering in his eyes. "And if you're wrong?"

I don't answer. I don't have to. The truth hangs heavy between us—I might very well be wrong, but whatever power the Velvet Charm holds, it's not going to wait for me to make sense of it.

With a steadying breath, I let my fingers brush against the symbols on the pedestal, and the effect is instantaneous. The air crackles with energy, a surge of heat and light that pulses outward, surrounding us in a blinding glow. I hear Damian shout something, but his voice is drowned out by the roar in my ears, the world dissolving into a whirlwind of fire and shadow that twists and writhes around us.

When the light finally fades, we're no longer in the clearing. The forest is gone, replaced by a vast, open field that stretches as far as the eye can see. The sky above is a sickly shade of green, streaked with veins of red lightning that crackle and arc across the horizon. And in the distance, silhouetted against the unnatural sky, stands a figure cloaked in black, waiting.

Damian is beside me, his face pale but resolute, his gaze fixed on the figure ahead. He doesn't speak, and neither do I; words feel useless in the face of whatever awaits us. The Velvet Charm rests heavily in my hand, its surface now warm to the touch, almost pulsing like a heartbeat.

The figure raises a hand, beckoning us forward, and though every part of me screams to turn back, I find myself stepping toward it, drawn by a force I can't explain. Damian follows, his movements tense and guarded, his eyes never leaving the figure.

As we draw closer, I finally make out the features of the face beneath the hood, and a sickening realization settles over me. It's her—the leader of the Crimson Society, the woman who once held my trust and shattered it beyond repair. Her eyes gleam with a cold, merciless light as she watches us, a twisted smile playing at her lips.

"I knew you couldn't resist," she says, her voice a haunting echo that sends shivers down my spine. She holds out her hand, palm open, as if inviting me to place the Velvet Charm into her grasp. "You've brought me exactly what I wanted."

Damian steps forward, putting himself between us, his stance protective, defiant. "You'll have to go through us first," he says, his voice steady but edged with fury.

She laughs, a sound that chills me to my core. "Oh, darling, that was always the plan."

Before either of us can react, a burst of fire erupts from her hand, and everything around us is engulfed in flames.

Chapter 10: The Scarlet Pact

Damian leans back, one hand resting on the worn table between us, his fingers trailing absently over a scratch carved by some forgotten blade. His eyes, a shade of gray that feels as cold and steady as steel, flick to me, gauging my reaction to each word he offers like breadcrumbs in the woods. He speaks in half-truths, a habit I've learned to match, though I know he watches for slips, for cracks. The tavern around us hums with murmurs and the occasional raucous laugh, but our table is a cocoon of tension and intrigue.

The scent here is stale—old ale, burnt tobacco, and something like damp wood, worn into the walls from years of spilled secrets and broken promises. It's the kind of place where everyone minds their own business, where eyes only linger long enough to determine that whatever trouble you're in, it's none of theirs. My fingers drum lightly on the edge of my tankard, the cool metal grounding me as I keep my face relaxed, a mask of mild interest. If I let Damian see how much his words affect me, he might stop talking altogether.

He's telling me about the city—his city, he calls it. He claims to know its every cobblestone, every shadowed alley where the walls close in like lovers who know too much. "Here, loyalty is a currency," he murmurs, his gaze distant. "You pay it out, or you hoard it. But sooner or later, you'll end up broke." There's a bitterness there, a story woven in his words that he doesn't want me to pull on too tightly. I catch the faintest twitch of his jaw, like he's weighing whether to trust me with the rest, and I wonder if he knows how much I'm withholding, too.

My instinct is to reach across the table, bridge this chasm we've spent weeks widening, despite the flickers of connection that slip through. I want to know who he was before he became this man sitting across from me, his edges sharpened by the things he's done, the ghosts he won't name. But trust is a fragile thing in our world, a luxury neither of us can afford. I swallow the impulse, let my fingers still. Let him think I'm as unaffected as the barmaid who brings us another round with barely a glance.

A loud crash by the door pulls me from my thoughts. My heart stumbles as I glance over, recognizing the figure who has entered, his dark coat and the way his eyes scan the room with lethal purpose. One of the Crimson Society's enforcers. He's new to his role, his face young and unlined, but his gaze stops when he sees me, recognition flashing in his eyes. Damian shifts beside me, a tension settling over him like armor. He's ready to fight if he has to, and I know he will, even if he claims to be indifferent to my fate.

I don't move, don't breathe, watching the enforcer's slow, deliberate steps as he approaches. The tavern's other patrons quickly avert their gazes, pretending they see nothing, hear nothing. A woman at the next table over drops her head, the clink of her glass against the wood masking the low mutter of her companion. The walls seem to close in tighter, the air thickening as if even the tavern itself knows a storm is coming.

"Long way from home, aren't you?" The enforcer's voice is deceptively soft, his eyes gleaming with the satisfaction of a cat that's cornered a mouse. I keep my expression steady, meeting his gaze without flinching, though my pulse drums wildly beneath my calm exterior.

Damian clears his throat, his casual air a lie I almost believe. "I think you've got the wrong table," he says, the hint of a smile tugging at the corner of his mouth. His words are gentle, almost playful, but his eyes hold a promise of something far darker. The enforcer's gaze flicks to Damian, sizing him up, deciding how much of a threat this stranger could be.

"Didn't know the Crimson Society had started recruiting babysitters," I say, my voice cold enough to match the look in his eyes. I can feel Damian's approval, his silent encouragement as if to say, that's my girl. The enforcer's lip curls in a smirk, one that's almost mocking but doesn't quite mask the wariness underneath.

"Funny," he says, though there's no humor in his tone. He leans in, his voice a hiss meant only for me. "They've got a job for you, whether you like it or not." His fingers twitch toward his coat pocket, and I catch a glimpse of a folded piece of paper. I know what it means before he even pulls it out. Orders.

My gut twists, a dread coiling tight and hot. Whatever's written on that paper isn't just a task; it's a trap, a game I'm supposed to lose. And the Society is nothing if not efficient at ensuring outcomes. Damian's hand shifts under the table, brushing against mine. A silent reminder. We're in this together, whether I like it or not.

"What's the job?" I ask, though I don't let my curiosity show. I can't afford to give this enforcer any satisfaction, any inkling that he has power here.

The enforcer's smirk widens. He unfolds the paper with slow, deliberate motions, like he's savoring the moment, making sure I see the faint Society seal at the top. Crimson wax, stamped with the silhouette of a dagger. He slides it across the table to me, his eyes glinting with an unspoken threat. My hand itches to shove it back at him, to deny whatever this is, but I force myself to pick it up, the paper cold and rough against my fingertips.

The words are simple but unmistakable. I'm to retrieve a stolen relic, one with power and blood-ties to the Society's oldest families. And my reward, if I can believe such promises, is that they might let me live long enough to enjoy it.

The enforcer waits, an air of patience about him that feels more dangerous than any weapon. The silence stretches, thick and heavy as oil, and it's a battle to keep my fingers from tightening around the slip of paper. I glance at Damian, who looks back at me with that inscrutable gaze he wears like a mask, his mouth quirked in something that could almost pass as a smile, if you didn't know him.

It's a silent dare, a challenge to refuse or to play along. With Damian, you're always being tested, even if you don't know what the prize is.

I turn back to the enforcer, giving him my most unimpressed look. "I don't usually work on demand," I say, my tone as sharp as the dagger tucked in my boot. "Tell your superiors I prefer a proper invitation."

The man doesn't flinch. He leans closer, close enough for me to catch a whiff of cheap cologne and the faint hint of metal—the unmistakable scent of blood and iron. "It's not a request," he says, voice a low growl that cuts through the noise of the tavern like a blade. "Refuse, and you'll find out just how persuasive the Society can be." His eyes flick to Damian, almost as if he's calculating whether my companion is friend, foe, or merely collateral damage.

Damian just shrugs, as if to say he doesn't particularly care how this turns out. His gaze drifts lazily over the enforcer, appraising him with an indifference that's almost insulting. "You see, the thing about making threats," he says, his voice smooth and disarming, "is that it only works if the other party thinks you can follow through. And my friend here is terribly difficult to intimidate."

It's strange how Damian can shift the air around us with a few words, like casting a net that draws me in, tighter and tighter. I could almost laugh at the frustration flickering in the enforcer's eyes. There's a beat, a flicker of indecision, and then he straightens, finally dropping his attempt at intimidation like a failed magic trick. With a sigh, he folds his arms, the calculated menace slipping from his face, replaced with something more exasperated than threatening.

"They told me you'd be difficult," he mutters, rolling his eyes like I'm a petulant child refusing her medicine. "They don't pay me enough for this."

I raise an eyebrow, feigning a casual indifference I don't quite feel. "Must be hard," I say, sympathy dripping from my voice like honey, "having to follow all those orders without a thought of your own. Tell me, what's it like being a trained dog?"

The enforcer's eyes darken, and for a split second, I wonder if I've pushed him too far. But before he can respond, Damian cuts in, his voice cool and sharp. "Perhaps you'd best tell us what exactly the Society wants. You're clearly not here to debate career choices."

The man's jaw clenches, and he digs into his coat pocket, pulling out a second folded slip of paper. He drops it on the table between us, the thin parchment almost mocking in its simplicity. Damian reaches for it, unfolding the note with the same meticulous care he gives everything. His gaze skims over the words, and something shifts in his expression—a flicker, so quick I almost miss it.

"What is it?" I ask, my voice quiet, suddenly wary. I can feel the weight of whatever's written there pressing down on him, settling into the grooves of his expression, though he keeps his face carefully neutral.

He looks up at me, his eyes unreadable. "They want more than a relic," he says, his voice low. "They want us to retrieve something from a place no one has dared enter for years. A vault." His gaze drops back to the note. "They're calling it an 'artifact of unknown origins,' but we both know that's code for something far more dangerous."

The enforcer watches us with a faint smirk, his amusement barely concealed. "You can try to be clever all you like, but it's simple, really. You get the artifact; they don't hunt you down. I'd take the offer if I were you."

"Why not send one of your own?" I ask, turning my full attention back to him. "Surely the Society has more than enough of its own people to risk on something so… dangerous." My words are edged with sarcasm, but the question is real, a crack in their logic that unsettles me.

"Think of it as a trial," he says smoothly, as though the stakes are nothing more than a test of skill. "They want to see what you're made of." He pauses, eyes gleaming with a perverse kind of pleasure. "Consider it an honor."

Damian's hand comes down on my shoulder, his grip firm. I can tell he's trying to signal me to calm down, to keep my temper in check, but the implication in the enforcer's words ignites a slow burn beneath my skin. It's more than a job. It's bait. A trap. And they think I'll walk into it willingly.

"Fine," I say, my voice steady, betraying nothing. I meet the enforcer's gaze, letting him see the fire simmering there. "Tell your masters they'll get what they want." I can feel Damian's silent approval, though he says nothing, just watches me with that unreadable expression as the enforcer gives a slight nod, satisfied.

With a parting glare, the man turns on his heel and strides back toward the door, his shadow stretching across the tavern floor before he disappears into the night. I let out a slow breath, the tension draining from my shoulders, though I can still feel the chill of his words lingering in the air between us.

Damian is watching me, a slight smile tugging at the corner of his mouth. "Well, that was a polite way of agreeing to certain doom," he says, his tone dry. "You really know how to keep things interesting."

"Interesting is just another word for complicated," I reply, my voice softer, a rueful smile on my lips. "Besides, I couldn't exactly let him leave without an answer, could I?"

He chuckles, the sound low and warm. "And here I thought you'd finally learned to play it safe."

"Safe is for people who aren't hunted by the Society," I shoot back, unable to suppress a wry smile.

He leans back, still watching me with that faintly amused expression, like he's seeing a side of me he hadn't expected. "If we're going to do this," he says slowly, "we need to be careful. They're playing a game, one we don't know the rules to. But I don't think they'll expect us to play by our own."

I nod, the fire inside me tempered but not extinguished. There's a thrill in his words, a promise of something more, something dangerous and exhilarating. And for the first time in a long while, I feel the stirrings of excitement, a glimmer of something that feels like hope, reckless though it may be.

"Then let's give them a game they won't forget," I say, lifting my tankard in a mock toast. Damian's eyes gleam as he raises his own, his smile sharp and dangerous, a promise wrapped in a grin.

The cold night presses in as we step outside the tavern, a bitter wind pulling at my coat, snatching away any remnants of warmth from the fire inside. Damian is silent, his face shadowed and thoughtful as he walks beside me. There's a chill in the air, a bite that reminds me of just how little the Society values the lives it toys with. A "trial," they called it. Nothing more than a power play disguised as a test, a leash to remind us of their control. The truth tastes bitter on my tongue, and I keep my head high, unwilling to let the weight of it bow me down.

Damian glances at me, his mouth curving in that half-smile that always seems like it's holding a secret. "Do you think they're watching us now?" he asks, his voice casual, as though he's asking about the weather.

I meet his gaze, shrugging. "Of course they are. They wouldn't send us on this suicide mission without enjoying the show. This is sport for them."

"Then maybe we should give them something to talk about." There's a glint in his eye, a spark of something reckless and wild that both unnerves and thrills me. He's right, though—we're walking on a stage, our every move observed, evaluated. And I refuse to give them the satisfaction of seeing any fear.

"So what's the plan?" I ask, matching his tone with a forced lightness. I know Damian well enough to recognize the shift in him, the way he steps into the persona of the master strategist, calculating ten moves ahead while keeping everyone else in the dark.

He pauses, his gaze drifting toward the distant lights of the city. "We'll need supplies. Information, too. The Society isn't going to hand us a map to this vault, which means we'll have to dig. And I know just the person who might have the answers we need."

I raise an eyebrow. "A friend?"

His laugh is low, edged with irony. "I don't have friends. Not the kind that stay alive, anyway."

I'm not sure whether he's joking, but I don't press him. He turns down a narrow alley, gesturing for me to follow, and I do, drawn by a strange trust I don't entirely understand. We walk in silence, our footsteps echoing off the cold stone walls as the city's heartbeat pulses around us. The night stretches long and quiet, the stars above seeming colder, more distant. I can feel the weight of what lies ahead pressing on us, a dark and inescapable tether.

After what feels like an endless maze of turns, we arrive at a door set back in the shadow of a crumbling building. Damian taps on it in a strange rhythm, one that's unfamiliar but feels deliberate, like a code. A long pause follows, filled only by the faint rustling of the wind, and then the door creaks open, revealing a narrow face, eyes sharp and wary. The man looks us over, his gaze flicking from Damian to me, assessing.

Damian's voice is low, unyielding. "Tell Marius we need a word."

The man studies us, his mouth set in a hard line, but something in Damian's stance must convince him. He steps back, allowing us inside. The space is dimly lit, the walls lined with shelves filled with a mix of relics and curiosities—odd bits of metal, tarnished jewelry, and leather-bound books worn soft with age. It feels like stepping into a forgotten world, a place where secrets have weight and everything is kept under a shroud of dust and silence.

Marius emerges from behind a curtain, his expression somewhere between curiosity and irritation. He's older, his hair graying at the temples, but his eyes are bright, sharp as a blade. He stops when he sees Damian, a hint of recognition darkening his gaze.

"Damian," he says, a trace of reluctance in his tone. "I thought I'd seen the last of you."

"You know I have a habit of showing up uninvited," Damian replies with a smile that doesn't reach his eyes. "But tonight, we need your expertise."

Marius raises an eyebrow, his gaze flicking to me. "And this is…?"

"She's with me." Damian's words are clipped, final, as if that explains everything.

Marius snorts, clearly unimpressed. "Your charm hasn't improved, I see. What do you want?"

"A location," Damian says, cutting to the point. "We're looking for a vault connected to the Crimson Society. One they'd go to great lengths to keep hidden."

Marius's eyes narrow, and he crosses his arms. "The Crimson Society doesn't just hide their vaults—they bury them. And even if I knew what you were asking for, I'm not in the habit of crossing them for a vague promise of… friendship."

"Not friendship," Damian says, his tone sharpening. "Payment. You help us, and I'll make sure you're compensated. The kind of compensation that lets you disappear, should you ever need it."

The room is silent, the air taut as Marius considers the offer. I feel his gaze settle on me again, weighing me, measuring the potential risk against the reward. There's a flicker of something in his eyes—interest, or maybe just greed—and he finally nods.

"There's one place," he says slowly, choosing his words with care. "An old crypt beneath the city. The Society sealed it years ago, but there are whispers that it's more than just a burial site. Rumors of artifacts, relics... powerful things left to rot in the dark."

Damian leans forward, his eyes gleaming with intensity. "Where can we find it?"

Marius hesitates, glancing over his shoulder as if he expects the walls to have ears. "There's a passage through the catacombs. It's hidden, warded—only those who know the old ways can enter." He gives Damian a look, a faint smirk tugging at his lips. "But something tells me you already know that."

Damian's expression is unreadable, a mask of quiet calculation. "I know enough. Thank you, Marius."

As we turn to leave, Marius calls after us, his voice edged with a warning. "Watch yourselves. The Crimson Society isn't the only one guarding those secrets. There are things down there that aren't meant to see the light."

We step back into the alley, the night colder and somehow darker than before. Damian says nothing, his focus set, the lines of his face hard as stone. For once, I don't question him. The weight of Marius's words lingers, a subtle chill that seeps into my bones. I know that whatever waits in that crypt won't be easy to face, that we're playing a game with forces far more powerful than ourselves.

As we make our way through the winding streets, a figure steps out from the shadows, blocking our path. My heart stops, the familiarity of his face a shock that roots me to the ground. He's someone I thought I'd left far behind—a ghost from a past I'd tried to forget.

The man smirks, his eyes locking onto mine with a twisted delight that sends a thrill of fear through me. "Long time no see," he says, his voice smooth and venomous. "Thought you could leave it all behind, didn't you?"

Damian tenses beside me, his hand inching toward his blade. I can feel the unspoken question hanging in the air, the confusion radiating from him as he glances between me and this man who, by all rights, shouldn't be here.

My pulse races, the world narrowing to the three of us. I force myself to keep my voice steady, though my hands tremble at my sides. "What are you doing here?"

He smiles, that cruel, familiar smile. "Oh, you know me. I never could resist a good chase." His eyes gleam, and he steps forward, his voice a low whisper meant only for me. "And this time, I'm not letting you go."

Chapter 11: Tides of Silver

Salt stings the air, sharp and bracing, as waves crash against the hull of the ship, their spray cold and unrelenting, like tiny daggers against my skin. I stand at the railing, fingers wrapped tight around the slick wood, and stare out at the endless gray that surrounds us. The sky and sea blend together, a merciless expanse that pulls at the mind as much as the body. Somewhere beneath these dark waters lies the Isle of Mourning, a speck of land whispered about in taverns and shaded corners, a place that holds answers—or, perhaps, more questions than either of us are ready to face.

Damian is beside me, though he might as well be a ghost, silent and watchful, as though waiting for something to rise out of the sea itself and claim us both. There's a tension in his posture, a hardness in his gaze as he looks out over the water, the set of his shoulders stiff under his dark coat. He's different out here, stripped down by the salt and wind and the constant threat of storms. The man who haunted ballroom floors and wielded words like knives is gone, replaced by someone more raw, more real—and infinitely more dangerous.

I steal glances at him, wondering what it is he's hiding. I know he fears the same legacy that claimed his father, the lure of power that eats at men from the inside out, but there's more to it than that. His secrets linger in the air between us, unsaid but as real as the cold metal of the dagger at my waist. I consider pressing him, demanding answers. Instead, I say nothing, and let the silence stretch.

"Do you believe in fate?" His voice breaks the quiet, low and rough, barely carrying over the rush of the waves.

The question takes me by surprise, but I keep my face blank, staring straight ahead. "Only when it suits me."

His lips quirk in a smirk that doesn't reach his eyes. "Convenient."

I shrug, still not looking at him. "Why believe in something that gives you no control? Fate is just another chain, isn't it? Something to bind you when things go wrong, so you can shrug and say, 'It wasn't my fault.'"

"And yet," he murmurs, "sometimes it feels as though we're pulled toward things—people, places—as though we're part of some larger scheme."

There's a wistfulness in his tone that catches me off guard, a softness I've never heard from him before. "Do you feel that way about the Isle?" I ask, trying to keep my voice steady, as though his answer doesn't matter to me.

He doesn't answer right away, his gaze drifting over the waves. "The Isle has...drawn me for as long as I can remember. My father spoke of it like a ghost, a place of myth and nightmare. And the Velvet Charm...that's the last piece of his puzzle, the last thing he sought before he..." He trails off, and I see his jaw tighten, the pain flickering in his eyes before he shutters it away.

Against my better judgment, I reach out, my fingers grazing his hand where it rests on the railing. The touch is brief, a whisper of warmth that leaves a trail of sparks in its wake. He looks down at our hands, his expression unreadable, and for a moment, I wonder if he'll pull away. But he doesn't. Instead, he lets out a shaky breath, and when he meets my gaze, there's a vulnerability in his eyes that makes my heart stutter.

"I never wanted any of this," he admits, voice barely audible. "I never wanted his legacy, his ghosts. I thought if I ran far enough, I could outrun it all. But here I am, right back where he left off, chasing shadows on a cursed island."

It's strange, hearing him speak like this. The polished, impenetrable Damian I knew is gone, replaced by someone raw, almost...fragile. The realization twists something inside me, a strange mix of pity and understanding. Because I know that feeling—the weight of expectations, the fear of becoming something you despise. In that moment, we're not rivals or allies or anything defined. We're just two people, lost and searching.

"You don't have to follow his path, Damian," I say, the words soft but certain. "You're not bound to his mistakes."

He gives a hollow laugh, shaking his head. "You say that as if I have a choice. But some things are inevitable. Some destinies you don't choose—they choose you."

I want to argue, to tell him he's wrong, that we all have a choice, but the words die on my lips. Because, deep down, I'm not sure I believe it myself. Maybe we're all just playing parts, filling roles set out for us long before we took our first breath. And if that's true, then what hope is there for either of us?

The silence between us thickens, heavy with unsaid things. I can feel the pull of him, the way his presence fills the space around me, as if he's the only solid thing in this vast, shifting world of gray. My heart races, and I have to remind myself to breathe, to keep my head clear. Whatever this is, whatever strange connection binds us, it's dangerous. And I can't afford to let my guard down—not now, when the stakes are higher than ever.

A shout from the lookout snaps me back to reality. Damian and I both turn, our hands slipping from the railing as we look toward the front of the ship. There, rising out of the mist like a specter, is the Isle of Mourning, dark and forbidding, its rocky cliffs shrouded in fog. The sight sends a shiver down my spine, a feeling of dread settling in my stomach.

Damian's gaze hardens as he stares at the island, his jaw set in determination. Whatever doubts or fears he may have had moments ago are gone, replaced by a steely resolve that both frightens and inspires me. I know, in that instant, that there's no turning back. We're committed to this path, bound to the island and the secrets it holds, whether we like it or not.

As the ship draws closer, I feel a strange thrill—a mixture of fear and excitement, anticipation and dread. This is what we've come for, what we've risked everything to find. And yet, as we near the shore, I can't shake the feeling that we're stepping into something far darker, far more dangerous than we could ever have imagined.

And somehow, despite every warning, every instinct screaming at me to turn back, I find myself stepping forward, drawn toward the unknown, toward whatever fate awaits us on the Isle of Mourning.

The wind bites harder as we edge closer to the shore, each gust laced with the promise of something ominous. The Isle looms, a jagged silhouette carved from rock and shadow. Against all better judgment, I feel my heart race, a strange exhilaration rising alongside the dread. Damian stands beside me, a brooding statue with his gaze fixed forward, his profile hard and unreadable. The softness from moments ago is gone, replaced by that familiar, iron determination. Yet I can still feel the faint brush of his fingers, the unexpected warmth lingering against my skin like a secret.

"Does it feel... different?" I ask, my voice barely louder than the wind.

He turns to me, his expression carefully neutral. "Different?"

"You've spent years chasing down every corner of the coast, every half-told rumor, every whispered legend. And now, here we are. Isn't it... I don't know. Strange?"

He huffs a quiet laugh, one that's more bitter than amused. "You make it sound romantic. I'm not sure I'd call it strange."

"Really? Nothing about this feels romantic to you?" I mockingly widen my eyes. "Not even the cursed island? Or the howling wind? Or the way we might very well be swallowed by the sea at any moment?"

His lip twitches, betraying the smallest hint of a smile. "You have a particular way of making death sound appealing."

I flash him a grin, though it feels hollow. "I prefer to think of it as honest marketing."

The ship shudders as we approach the Isle, the creaking of the hull echoing in the eerie quiet that's settled over us. The crew members are moving around with tense precision, whispering to one another and throwing wary glances at the shoreline. It's as though even the sea itself knows better than to encroach too far on this place. I can feel their unease settling over me, a prickling sensation at the back of my neck.

Just as the anchor drops, Damian's hand finds my elbow, his grip firm and steady. "Stay close," he murmurs, voice low and commanding.

I raise an eyebrow, but there's no mockery in his gaze this time. He's deadly serious, and that unfamiliar expression pulls at something deep inside me. For a moment, I feel an odd warmth—a sense of safety, even—as if his presence alone could shield me from whatever waits on that forsaken shore. But the moment is fleeting. I brush his hand off with a smirk that hides the uncomfortable truth: I don't want to be shielded. I want to face this head-on, to conquer it, and if he thinks I need protection... well, he'll have another thing coming.

We disembark in silence, our boots sinking into the wet sand with every step. The air is thick here, almost suffocating, and I can't shake the feeling that the Isle itself is watching us, a silent judge weighing our worth. As we move forward, the landscape unfolds in strange, surreal shapes—sharp rocks jutting from the sand like the broken ribs of some ancient beast, the mist swirling around them in ghostly tendrils. I can hear the distant call of seabirds, their cries lonely and haunting, echoing through the fog.

The path ahead is narrow, winding between towering cliffs and dense thickets of thorny shrubs. Damian moves with purpose, his gaze scanning the surroundings with the precision of someone who's done this a thousand times, and yet, I can see the tension in his shoulders, the slightest hesitation in his steps. He's as wary as I am, maybe more so. Whatever secrets this place holds, he feels them as keenly as I do.

After what feels like hours, we reach the mouth of a cavern, a dark opening in the rock that seems to swallow the light. I glance at Damian, searching his face for any hint of hesitation, but his expression is stone. He moves forward, his hand brushing the cold rock as though grounding himself. The shadows stretch and twist as we step inside, the air growing colder with each step, our breaths forming faint clouds in the dim light.

It's as if we've entered another world entirely, a place where the outside rules no longer apply. The silence is oppressive, thick and heavy, pressing down on us like a physical weight. I can feel my pulse quicken, my instincts screaming at me to turn back, to leave this place and never return. But I push forward, one foot in front of the other, matching Damian's pace. I won't let him see my fear—not here, not now.

"Do you know where we're going?" I ask, keeping my voice low, as if afraid to wake something lurking in the shadows.

He glances back at me, his eyes unreadable in the half-light. "No. But I can feel it."

I snort. "Vague, but encouraging."

He flashes me a look, a small spark of irritation flickering in his gaze. "Do you ever stop talking?"

"Only when I'm dead. And unfortunately for you, that hasn't happened yet."

Despite the tension, I see the faintest hint of a smile tugging at the corner of his mouth. It's a small victory, but I'll take it. In this place, any reminder of life—of warmth and humor—is a welcome reprieve.

As we press deeper into the cave, the walls close in, the passage narrowing until we're forced to move single file, our shoulders brushing the rough stone. The air grows colder still, and I can feel a chill seep into my bones, a damp, biting cold that no cloak could hope to ward off. My hands are trembling, though whether from the cold or something else, I can't be sure.

And then, abruptly, the narrow passage opens up into a vast chamber, the ceiling stretching high above us, lost in shadow. A pool of dark water sits in the center, still and glassy, reflecting the dim light like a black mirror. I catch my breath, staring at the strange, almost otherworldly beauty of it. There's something ancient about this place, something that speaks of secrets long buried, of power waiting to be unleashed.

Damian moves forward, his footsteps eerily quiet on the stone floor. He kneels by the edge of the pool, his gaze intent as he studies the water. I stand back, watching him, a strange mixture of fascination and apprehension swirling within me. There's something dangerous about him here, something that feels... primal. I realize, with a start, that I don't fully know this man—that whatever I thought I understood about him barely scratches the surface.

"What do you see?" I ask, my voice barely above a whisper.

He doesn't look up. "A warning."

The word sends a chill down my spine, and I instinctively step back, my gaze darting around the chamber. The shadows seem to move, to shift and writhe like living things, and I can't shake the feeling that we're not alone. I open my mouth to say something, but the words die on my lips as a low, rumbling sound fills the air, echoing off the stone walls.

Damian rises to his feet, his gaze sharp and focused, his hand instinctively reaching for the dagger at his side. "Stay close," he murmurs, his voice tight with tension.

I don't argue this time. Whatever lies ahead, I'm not about to face it alone.

The rumbling deepens, vibrating through the floor, setting loose dust and tiny pebbles that tumble and scatter in trembling paths toward the pool. I clutch Damian's arm instinctively, a motion I barely notice myself making, though he spares a quick glance down at my hand, one brow raised. There's no smirk, no teasing glint in his eye, just that razor-sharp focus. Whatever calm he possessed a moment ago has dissolved into a wary, bracing intensity, and it unnerves me more than any rumbling ground ever could.

His hand covers mine for just a moment, a silent reassurance, before he steps forward, eyes darting around the dark cavern walls, searching. "It's close," he mutters, almost to himself. "Too close."

"You mean... this thing we're looking for?" My voice sounds small, swallowed by the echoing chamber and dwarfed by the raw, inexplicable presence pressing in on us from all sides.

He doesn't answer, just moves closer to the pool, his gaze sweeping across the water, watching the ripples form, undulate, and vanish again. The pool's surface is dark, glassy, and oddly still for the tension humming through the air. I find myself holding my breath, though I'm not sure if it's the silence or something in Damian's stance that compels it.

Then, without warning, the surface of the pool trembles, as if something is stirring beneath. A flicker of movement—a shadow slipping below, vanishing, then reappearing. I instinctively step back, gripping the dagger at my side with white-knuckled fingers, feeling the hard edge press into my palm. My pulse pounds in my ears.

"Damian, do you see—?"

"Shh." His voice is low, a hiss of warning. He gestures with a quick flick of his hand, and I fall silent, eyes glued to the water. The shadow below grows darker, its form beginning to take shape. I squint, but all I can make out are shifting patterns, a vague, undulating outline that twists and elongates, hovering just beneath the surface.

The rumbling grows louder, and with it, the water begins to roil, waves breaking against the pool's edge. Something is coming. I can feel it, a crawling, prickling sense of dread that worms its way into my bones.

Damian's jaw tightens, and I see his hand twitch toward his weapon. "Whatever happens," he says, his tone sharp and commanding, "stay behind me. Do you understand?"

My immediate instinct is to argue—I've never been one to follow orders, especially his—but the look in his eyes stops me. There's no room for defiance in that gaze, only a fierce, unyielding focus that seems to anchor me, grounding me despite the chaos erupting around us.

Just as the shadow below nears the surface, a loud, splintering crack echoes through the chamber, making us both flinch. A fissure has appeared along the far wall, jagged and thin at first but widening, the stone seeming to split apart like some ancient wound reopening. From the crack seeps a faint, shimmering glow, an ethereal light that pulses faintly, filling the chamber with an eerie radiance.

Damian takes a step back, his expression hardening as he studies the fissure, his eyes darting between it and the pool. "It's... connected," he murmurs, almost to himself.

"What is?"

He doesn't answer, but his hand tightens on the hilt of his dagger. "This isn't a relic," he says, almost to himself. "It's... a gateway."

I stare at him, the words tumbling over each other in my mind. A gateway? A portal to what? I open my mouth to press him, but the water suddenly surges, a wave crashing over the edge of the pool, and from beneath the surface rises a figure, cloaked in dark, dripping robes that cling to its gaunt frame, its face obscured in shadow. It stands motionless at the water's edge, as if waiting.

Every instinct screams at me to run, to put as much distance as possible between myself and this apparition, but my feet refuse to move, locked in place by some primal fear that I can't shake. Damian, however, steps forward, unflinching, his stance wide and ready, his eyes blazing with that fierce determination.

The figure turns its head, its hollow gaze settling on him, and in that instant, the silence thickens, hanging in the air like a leaden weight. Damian meets its stare without flinching, his jaw set, and the tension crackles between them, something unspoken but powerful, a current that I can almost feel in the air.

Then, in a voice that seems to echo from the depths of the earth itself, the figure speaks, its tone low and rough, scraping over my nerves like shards of glass. "You seek what you cannot possess."

The words are a chill, settling over the room, and for a moment, Damian falters. I see his hand clench tighter on his dagger, a flash of hesitation in his gaze. But it's gone as quickly as it appears, replaced by that same stubborn resolve.

"And you guard what you cannot keep," he replies, his voice steady, a challenge simmering beneath his words. "Stand aside."

The figure tilts its head, almost amused, though there's no mirth in that dark gaze. "Bold. Foolish." It extends a bony hand toward the fissure, and the glow intensifies, the air vibrating with a palpable energy that makes the hairs on the back of my neck stand on end.

I step forward, unable to hold back any longer, my voice sharp as I demand, "What is this place? What are you?"

The figure's gaze shifts to me, its expression inscrutable. "I am a keeper, bound to the dark, bound to the secrets your kind cannot know. This place is not for you."

Something in its tone stirs an anger within me, a frustration that surges despite the fear. I feel my hand grip the dagger tighter, and I meet its gaze, refusing to back down. "We didn't come here for permission."

The figure's laugh is a hollow, scraping sound, as if it hasn't been used in centuries. "Then you are more reckless than I imagined. But courage, foolish as it may be, has its rewards." It gestures toward the fissure, the glow flaring brightly, casting the chamber in harsh, shifting shadows. "If you wish to pass, you must pay the price."

A chill settles over me at those words, and I glance at Damian, searching his face for any sign of hesitation. But he's already moving forward, his expression grim, his jaw set. "Name it," he says, his voice steady.

The figure smiles, a grim, twisted expression that sends a shiver through me. "A life must be given," it intones, its gaze shifting between us. "One for the gate, one for the path. You may choose."

The air goes cold, and a dreadful clarity settles over me. One of us must be sacrificed. A life given, just as it demanded. I look at Damian, my heart racing, the weight of his gaze on me heavy and unyielding. The silence stretches, a decision hanging in the balance, and in that instant, I know there's no easy escape.

The figure's smile widens as it watches us, its patience endless, the faint glow of the fissure casting a sickly light across its hollow face. Damian's hand finds mine, his grip warm and steady, his eyes locking with mine in a silent question, a wordless plea.

And in that moment, I realize what he's about to do.

Chapter 12: Shadows in the Sand

The air on the Isle of Mourning is thick and stagnant, the sort of air that clings to your skin, seeping into your lungs with each shallow breath. I've never known silence to be this loud, with every step I take feeling like an intrusion in a place that remembers every footfall. The sand here isn't the soft, sunlit kind that begs for bare feet. It's a gritty, lifeless thing, biting into my soles through worn leather, a dull reminder that this is no ordinary island. It feels more like a place that got stuck halfway between worlds and never managed to pull itself fully into any of them.

We're only a little ways inland, but already the water is barely a glimmer on the horizon. The remnants of some ancient civilization dot the landscape: crooked stone pillars, half-buried statues, and the haunting silhouette of a temple that must've been glorious once, now more ruin than structure. I want to feel awe, to imagine the kind of life that once pulsed here. Instead, all I feel is the itch to turn back and leave this island to whatever spirits haunt it. But turning back isn't an option. Not anymore.

Damian moves beside me, his steps light and deliberate, as if he knows what this place demands. There's a stillness in him that puts me on edge, a quiet intensity in the way he looks at the ruined temple. He's a man of secrets, his eyes always half-shuttered, and though I've traveled with him for weeks now, he remains more mystery than companion. Maybe that's why I'm surprised when his hand finds mine as we set up camp under the broken shadow of the temple walls. His fingers are calloused, rough around the edges, but his touch is soft, a little hesitant, as if he's offering something fragile.

I should pull away. I should keep that distance I've clung to all this time. But tonight, under the pale stars, I don't want to be alone with the darkness pressing in. So, I let his hand rest in mine, let that small point of contact remind me that maybe I don't have to face this place entirely on my own.

Damian's voice breaks the silence, low and almost reverent, a murmur meant for me alone. "Didn't think you'd make it this far, if I'm honest."

I snort, unable to help myself. "What, you thought I'd just drop dead back on the mainland?"

"No," he says, his mouth quirking up in a lopsided grin. "Just figured you'd have better sense than to follow me here. Most people do."

"Well, I've never been known for my sense."

He laughs softly, a sound I haven't heard nearly enough, and for a moment, it's easy to forget the island around us, to let the tension slide away like a weight I hadn't realized I was carrying. I settle beside him, feeling the rough stone beneath me and the chill creeping up from the ground. Damian doesn't say much more, but I can feel him watching me, can almost hear the thoughts churning behind those guarded eyes.

I offer him a piece of my past as a gesture, a token of trust. "When I was younger, I used to think I'd end up in some big city. The kind with lights that drown out the stars, you know?"

He nods, not pressing, just listening, and something in that gentle patience loosens words I hadn't planned to share. "Guess I thought I'd live somewhere that would make me feel... bigger, I suppose. Important."

"Does this feel important enough for you?" His tone is teasing, but there's something deeper in it, a kind of acknowledgment that maybe he feels the same ache for something more.

I shrug, letting the silence wrap around us again. I don't know what this is—not yet, anyway—but it feels real, in a way that all my old dreams never did.

The dawn comes too soon, bringing with it the sharp reminder that whatever peace we found in the night is fleeting. A sound in the distance pulls me from a restless sleep, and when I glance toward the horizon, my heart stutters. A line of red, like a smear of blood across the landscape, cuts through the sands. The Crimson Society. We'd been careful, or at least I thought we had, but it seems that care wasn't enough. They've found us.

Damian's face hardens when he sees them, the tenderness of last night gone, replaced by something steely and unyielding. He's been on the run from them longer than I have, knows better than anyone what they're capable of. And now, because of me, he has one more reason to fight.

I grip his arm, feeling the tension in his muscles. "We have to move. They're too close."

His gaze flickers to mine, a brief moment of vulnerability that's gone almost as soon as it appears. "Running's not going to help us now. They've got us pinned." He pauses, his voice dropping lower. "But we can't let them take us without a fight."

He pulls out a slender dagger, one of those blades so finely crafted that it gleams even in the muted morning light. I've seen him wield it before, watched the way it moves like an extension of him, swift and deadly. I feel a strange comfort in that, knowing he's beside me, knowing that whatever happens, we're in this together.

As the first of the crimson-cloaked figures draws closer, I brace myself, heart pounding. Damian's hand finds mine again, a fleeting touch of reassurance before he steps forward, his body tense and ready. The figures are close enough now that I can make out their faces beneath the hoods—faces cold and unyielding, devoid of any humanity.

"Stay behind me," Damian says, his voice low and steady. There's a finality in it, a promise, as though he's prepared to lay down everything to protect me. And I hate that, because I didn't come here to be saved. I came here to fight.

"Not a chance," I reply, raising my own blade, a defiant grin tugging at my lips. "Let's show them they messed with the wrong people."

He glances at me, surprise flickering in his eyes, followed by something that looks suspiciously like pride. We stand side by side, two against a swarm, but in that moment, I feel invincible. And as the Crimson Society closes in, I know that, for the first time, I'm exactly where I'm supposed to be.

The first figure in crimson steps forward, his face an impassive mask beneath his hood. He's older than I expected, with graying stubble peeking out above a sharp, unmoving jawline. The way he holds his weapon—steady and unbothered—tells me he's done this a thousand times before, cutting down people who dared stand in the way of the Society's cold, unrelenting justice.

Damian's eyes narrow, a flint-like spark in them, as if he's holding back just enough rage to keep himself focused. His body is taut beside me, a coiled spring ready to snap, but his voice is calm as he addresses the man in front of us.

"Looks like you all went to a lot of trouble for two people who don't care much for your rules," he says, his voice laced with something dark and amused. "Should we feel honored?"

The man in crimson tilts his head, studying Damian with a faintly patronizing smile that makes my skin crawl. "It's not about rules, Damian," he replies, the words rolling out in a voice so smooth, it's nearly a whisper. "It's about order. And you, my friend, thrive in chaos."

"Chaos suits me," Damian counters, smirking. "And it keeps life interesting."

I resist the urge to throw a retort at the man myself, but I don't trust myself not to give away the twisting unease in my stomach. So instead, I keep my mouth shut and my grip on my blade tight, taking a step closer to Damian, letting him sense my resolve beside him.

The man in crimson clicks his tongue, glancing over his shoulder as if waiting for something—or someone. There's a tension building in the air, thickening between us, and I can feel it settling in my bones like a heavy mist. He doesn't flinch, doesn't even blink, but then his gaze flicks past us, as if he's looking at the temple behind us, at the shadows creeping along its broken walls.

"What do you think you're protecting here?" he says, his tone dripping with quiet disdain. "This place has been dead for centuries. It's nothing but bones and ashes."

"Maybe that's all it is to you," I speak up, surprising even myself. My voice sounds steady, strong, even though my heart's pounding loud enough to drown out my thoughts. "But I don't think you get to decide what this place means."

The man's eyes settle on me, a brief spark of interest lighting up in them, as if he's only just noticed me for the first time. "Ah," he murmurs, his voice almost a purr. "You must be the reason Damian's been slipping up lately."

Damian lets out a low growl beside me, stepping half in front of me, his body language broadcasting a silent warning. It's as if the words have struck some deep nerve in him, something raw and guarded. I want to tell him it's fine, that I don't care what this man thinks, but the words stick in my throat. Instead, I let Damian take that step forward, the fierce protectiveness in his stance bolstering my own shaky confidence.

The man merely smirks, unfazed. He's in no hurry, enjoying the way he's getting under our skin, unraveling us one barbed word at a time. "Do you think she'll still stand by you when she knows the whole truth?" he taunts, a glint of malice sparking in his eyes. "When she finds out what really brought you here?"

My pulse stumbles, thrown by the weight of his words. I glance at Damian, a question hovering unasked between us, but he doesn't look at me. His jaw is tight, his eyes fixed on the man in crimson as if he's the only person in the world.

"Save your games," Damian says, his voice low and deadly. "If you're here to fight, then stop wasting our time."

The man sighs, a feigned weariness in his posture as he raises his hand, signaling to the rest of the crimson figures. In an instant, the stillness shatters. The cloaks move like a blood-red wave around us, their shadows dancing across the sand as they draw their weapons. The silence breaks into chaos, a blur of motion and sound, and suddenly there's no time to think—only react.

I throw myself into the fray, my blade meeting the closest figure in a clash of metal and sparks. Every strike feels both clumsy and desperate, but I force myself to focus, to keep moving. My body aches from the strain, muscles burning as I fend off blow after blow, each one closer than the last. The crimson cloaks are relentless, pressing in from all sides, and I know it's only a matter of time before they overwhelm us.

Somewhere beside me, I hear Damian fighting, his movements swift and lethal, a deadly dance in the sand. He's stronger than I ever realized, faster, more practiced. But even he can't hold them all off alone. I feel the panic rising, clawing up my throat, and I know that if we don't find some way out of this, we're finished.

Just as the thought crosses my mind, a sudden flash of light blinds me, a blinding burst that leaves spots dancing across my vision. I stagger back, blinking rapidly, and for a brief, disoriented moment, I think it's the end.

But then I realize the light is coming from the temple, spilling out from some hidden crack in the ancient stone. It's as if the building itself is waking up, responding to the violence around it, and the very ground beneath my feet begins to rumble. The figures in crimson falter, just as stunned as I am, their attention shifting to the source of the disturbance.

I don't waste a second. I grab Damian's arm, pulling him toward the temple as the ground quakes beneath us. His face is ashen, eyes wide with something between fear and awe as we stumble through the crumbling archway and into the temple's shadows. Behind us, the Crimson Society regains their focus, their shouts echoing through the air as they scramble to follow.

The light inside the temple is blinding, an ethereal glow that seems to emanate from the walls themselves. I can feel the energy pulsing around us, sharp and electric, filling the air with a charged tension that prickles against my skin. Damian looks at me, his expression a mix of determination and something softer, something like regret.

"Stay close," he says, his voice barely audible over the noise. He tightens his grip on my hand, pulling me deeper into the temple, through a labyrinth of dark hallways that twist and turn in ways that make no sense. It's as if the building itself is shifting around us, guiding us, but toward what, I have no idea.

Behind us, I can hear the Crimson Society, their voices growing louder as they give chase. But with each step we take, the walls seem to close in, the passage narrowing until I can barely breathe. It's a strange sensation, like being pulled underwater, the weight pressing down on me until I feel I might suffocate.

And then, just when I think I can't take another step, we stumble into a vast, open chamber bathed in an eerie, otherworldly glow. The walls are covered in symbols, ancient markings that seem to pulse with their own faint light, illuminating the room in a ghostly hue. At the center of the chamber stands a massive stone altar, its surface worn smooth by time and ritual, and I can feel a strange pull emanating from it, tugging at something deep inside me.

Damian lets go of my hand, stepping forward as if in a trance. I reach out to stop him, to pull him back, but the look on his face stops me cold. There's something in his eyes, something raw and vulnerable that I've never seen before, and for the first time, I realize that he knows exactly what brought us here—and what lies ahead.

The air in the chamber hums, thick with an energy that wraps around me, pressing against my skin like a second layer, damp and unnerving. My eyes flick to Damian, who stands frozen in front of the altar, his face bathed in that strange, otherworldly glow. There's something almost reverent in his gaze, as if he's standing before a relic he'd thought lost forever. He's breathing hard, his chest rising and falling with each breath, his hand hovering just above the altar's surface.

"Damian." My voice sounds smaller than I intend, barely a whisper, but it snaps him out of whatever trance has him locked in place. His eyes dart to me, and for a split second, I see something raw and wounded there, something that feels too intimate to witness.

"They were right," he murmurs, his voice barely louder than a breath. "It's here."

"What's here?" I step closer, feeling the hair on the back of my neck prickling with every inch forward. The symbols carved into the walls seem to pulse in time with my heartbeat, and each step makes me feel like I'm trespassing somewhere I was never meant to see. "What aren't you telling me?"

He hesitates, running a hand through his dark hair, the tension in his shoulders nearly tangible. "This place... it's more than just ruins. The Society—they believe it holds the last fragment of the Divine Key."

The words hang in the air, unfamiliar but ominous, each one a fresh layer of dread settling in my stomach. I don't want to ask, don't want to hear the answer that might make all of this too real, but the question slips out anyway. "And what does the Divine Key do?"

Damian's gaze sharpens, his expression darkening. "It opens a doorway—a path between realms. Whoever holds it can bend the barriers between our world and… other places."

Other places. The words linger, twisting themselves into an unspoken threat that crawls beneath my skin. I want to tell him he's insane, that none of this makes any sense, but the pulsing light in the chamber, the strange hum in the air, tells me otherwise. Something ancient and powerful is stirring here, something beyond either of us.

"But if it's so powerful," I say, struggling to keep the tremor out of my voice, "why would it be left here, in ruins?"

"It wasn't left," Damian says quietly. "It was hidden. Locked away, so it couldn't fall into the wrong hands. And now… now the Society's here to claim it."

The words settle like lead in my chest, and suddenly, the weight of every step we took to get here feels like a mistake, a path I never should have followed. But there's no turning back now. The Crimson Society is outside, closing in, and even if we somehow slip past them, the knowledge of what's here will haunt us forever.

A sharp clang echoes from the hallway behind us, followed by the murmur of voices. Damian's face goes pale, and he grabs my wrist, pulling me toward the shadows of the chamber. "We can't let them take it. If they get their hands on that key, they'll tear apart everything—this island, our world, whatever worlds lie beyond. They'll destroy it all."

His voice is fierce, low, but there's an edge of fear I've never heard from him before, a kind of desperation that tightens my own chest. "So what do we do?" I ask, not sure if I even want the answer. I just know I want to get out of this chamber, out of this island, away from whatever nightmare we've found ourselves in.

Damian's gaze flickers to the altar, his expression hardening. "We take it first."

I stare at him, unable to process what he's just said. "Are you out of your mind? You just said this thing can open doors between realms! We don't even know what that means. For all we know, touching it could tear us apart!"

He hesitates, just a fraction of a second, and I see the conflict in his eyes—the uncertainty, the fear. But then he squares his shoulders, setting his jaw. "If we leave it, they'll find it. If we take it, we might have a chance to stop them." He reaches for my hand, his grip firm and steady. "I won't let anything happen to you. But I can't do this alone."

The sincerity in his voice, the quiet strength, pulls something deep inside me, even though every instinct screams to turn and run. I nod, swallowing back the fear clawing at my throat, and together we move toward the altar, our footsteps soft but deliberate, each one a silent agreement, a binding promise.

Just as we reach the altar, the chamber shudders, a deep, bone-rattling tremor that seems to come from the walls themselves. The symbols flare, casting an eerie light that illuminates the room in harsh, flickering shadows, and I can feel the power radiating from the altar, pulsing like a heartbeat beneath my fingers. Damian reaches forward, his hand brushing the stone, and for a moment, the entire room seems to hold its breath.

Then, with a sound like cracking glass, the altar splits, and a blinding light spills out, filling the chamber with a brilliance that forces me to shield my eyes. When I open them, I see it—a small, delicate object floating just above the altar, encased in a shimmering, translucent sphere. It looks almost innocent, barely bigger than the palm of my hand, a simple key wrought in silver, its surface etched with symbols that seem to shift and dance under the light.

Damian reaches for it, his hand steady, but just as his fingers close around the sphere, the walls tremble again, and a low, guttural sound rips through the chamber, like the howl of something ancient and feral, awakened from a long slumber.

I grab his arm, my voice a strangled whisper. "Damian, what did you do?"

Before he can answer, a figure appears in the doorway—a figure cloaked in crimson, his face obscured by shadows, but I can feel his eyes on us, cold and piercing. He steps forward, his movements slow and deliberate, and with a flick of his wrist, the others follow, fanning out to block every possible escape.

Damian's hand tightens around the sphere, his knuckles white as he pulls me close, his voice barely a whisper in my ear. "We're going to have to fight our way out of this. Are you with me?"

I don't have time to answer. The Crimson Society is upon us, their weapons drawn, gleaming in the eerie light. I brace myself, my heart hammering, the weight of everything pressing down on me, suffocating, but Damian's hand in mine keeps me grounded. He nods, a silent promise that we're in this together, and in that moment, I feel a strange, reckless surge of courage.

The first figure lunges forward, his blade flashing, and I raise my weapon, meeting his attack with a fierceness I didn't know I possessed. The clang of steel fills the chamber, echoing off the walls as we fight, each movement a desperate attempt to survive, to protect the key, to keep the Society from ripping our world apart.

But as I parry a blow and glance toward Damian, I see it—the look in his eyes, a flicker of something almost resigned. A split-second realization hits me, chilling me to the core. He's not just fighting for survival; he's fighting for something more, something he's been hiding all along.

And as the next blow falls, I understand with a sudden, sinking dread that whatever Damian's endgame is, I'm only just beginning to unravel it.

Chapter 13: The Price of Power

The earth trembles beneath us, the ground slick with the remnants of battle. Shadows cast by fires licking up toward the sky flicker across Damian's face, illuminating his sharp cheekbones and clenched jaw in a fiery glow. Blood seeps from a cut above his brow, winding its way down his cheek like a crimson tear. He doesn't notice—or maybe he simply doesn't care. His focus is elsewhere, intense and unwavering, as he stands amidst the remnants of the chaos he created. The air around him is thick with the aftershock of power, a residual hum that makes the hairs on my arms stand on end. It's a feeling both familiar and foreign, a strange cocktail of awe and dread that knots in my stomach.

When he finally turns to look at me, his eyes are shadowed, darker than I've ever seen them, as if something vital has drained out of him, leaving only an empty shell. For a moment, I see a flash of the boy I used to know, the one who'd laugh with reckless abandon, who'd promise to keep me safe no matter what. But now that boy is buried beneath layers of something colder, sharper—something that scares me more than I'd like to admit.

I take a step forward, reaching out instinctively. "Damian—" The name barely escapes my lips before he turns away, his back rigid, shoulders squared. It's a clear dismissal, but I refuse to let it silence me. I step closer, the taste of iron and smoke heavy on my tongue, the acrid scent of charred earth filling my lungs. "Don't shut me out. Not now."

He stiffens, muscles coiling like a spring about to snap. "What do you want from me, huh?" His voice is laced with a bitterness I've never heard from him before, each word sharp enough to cut. "You wanted a hero? I told you, I'm not that."

I take in his disheveled appearance, his clenched fists, the tremor in his hands that he's desperately trying to hide. "I don't want a hero, Damian. I want you. Just... you."

He lets out a harsh laugh, hollow and mirthless. "Me? You wouldn't like what you'd find." He pauses, eyes flickering over the Velvet Charm clutched in his hand, the artifact he fought so hard to obtain. The object pulses faintly, casting a sickly green light, an eerie reminder of the magic it holds, and the toll it's already taken on him.

The Charm, with its intricate patterns etched into obsidian stone, looks almost innocent in his grip, as if it isn't the root of our troubles, as if it hasn't already claimed its pound of flesh. I can feel its pull too, a quiet whisper in the back of my mind, a seductive promise of power that lingers, tempting, taunting. But I know better than to reach for it. I've seen what it does to people, how it warps them from the inside out. It's already taken too much from Damian, stripping him of the warmth and light I used to know. If he holds onto it any longer, I fear he might lose himself completely.

"Give it to me," I say, my voice firmer than I feel. "You don't have to bear this alone."

He regards me, the hardness in his gaze softening for a heartbeat before the mask slips back into place. "No, Liv," he says quietly, voice laced with something that feels like resignation. "I can't. This is my burden. It was always going to be."

"Then let me carry it with you," I whisper, the desperation in my words surprising even myself. "You don't have to be the one to bleed every time. I'm here too."

For a moment, I think he might actually hand it over. His fingers loosen, and his gaze meets mine, raw and vulnerable in a way I rarely see. But then something shifts in his expression, a shadow passing over him, and he pulls back, clutching the Charm tighter.

"This isn't about choice, Liv," he says, voice barely a whisper. "It's about survival. And sometimes, to survive... you have to sacrifice pieces of yourself."

There's a finality in his tone, a resignation that feels like a door slamming shut. My chest tightens, a sinking dread clawing at me, knowing that if he continues down this path, the Damian I know might be lost forever. But I can't force him to trust me, not with something this dangerous, this consuming. All I can do is stand by him, even as he spirals further into the darkness.

The silence stretches between us, thick and suffocating. I take a shaky breath, trying to steady myself. "Damian, I know what it's like to carry something that feels too heavy to bear. But trust me when I say, you don't have to do this alone."

He looks at me then, really looks, as if trying to find something in my face that might sway him, some reason to let me in. But whatever he sees only hardens his resolve. He lets out a long sigh, shoulders slumping ever so slightly, before he speaks again, voice softer this time. "Liv, there's a part of me that wants to let you in. But if I do... if I let you see what this power does to me, I'm afraid you'll never look at me the same way."

I swallow, words of reassurance on the tip of my tongue, but I know better than to offer platitudes. Instead, I step closer, reaching out to touch his hand, my fingers brushing against his skin. He flinches at first, but then his hand relaxes, his grip loosening ever so slightly on the Charm.

"You're wrong," I say softly, hoping he hears the conviction in my voice. "No matter what this does to you, no matter how it changes you, I'll still be here. I'm not going anywhere."

His eyes search mine, as if trying to detect a lie, as if daring me to back down. But I don't. I hold his gaze, unflinching, unwavering, and for the first time, a hint of doubt flickers across his face. It's a small victory, a tiny crack in the armor he's wrapped himself in, but it's enough.

After a long, tense moment, he lets out a breath, the weight of it heavy and resigned. "Maybe one day, you'll understand why I have to do this. But for now... just promise me you'll stay safe."

I want to argue, to tell him that staying safe isn't an option when he's putting himself in danger. But I know that any attempt would only drive him further away. So instead, I nod, swallowing back the fear and frustration that bubbles up inside me.

"Just... promise me," he repeats, eyes pleading, his voice barely more than a whisper.

"I promise," I say, though the words taste bitter on my tongue, knowing that the safety he's asking for comes at a price I'm not sure I'm willing to pay.

Damian stands rigid, his face a mask of indifference, but I can see the subtle tremor in his hand, the barely controlled rage simmering beneath the surface. He doesn't need to say it—he's drowning in the weight of whatever happened on that battlefield. I don't dare break the silence, but my mind races, each unspoken word like a stone piling up between us, creating a wall I don't know how to tear down. All I can do is wait, hoping he'll let me in. But he remains silent, locked inside himself, the Velvet Charm clutched in his hand as if it's the only thing anchoring him to this world.

The tension snaps when he finally speaks, his voice low and brittle. "They don't tell you, you know?" He laughs, a sound so devoid of joy it cuts deeper than any blade. "They don't tell you what it takes, what you have to give up. They make it sound... noble. Like you're doing some great, selfless thing by sacrificing yourself for power. But it's not noble, Liv. It's just... hollow."

I don't know what to say. My hand twitches, an instinct to reach out and offer comfort, but I hold back. He's too raw, like a wounded animal that would sooner bite than accept a gentle touch. "Damian,

I never asked you to be noble. You don't owe anyone that. Least of all me."

He shakes his head, almost as if he's laughing at some private joke I'll never understand. "I think I wanted you to see me that way, though. As someone worth... saving. Worth fighting for."

The vulnerability in his voice shocks me. This is the same Damian who's faced down creatures twice his size, who wields power most can only dream of. Yet here he is, unraveling before me, and all I want to do is pull him back together.

"Damian," I say softly, my voice barely more than a whisper. "You don't have to do this alone. Whatever the Velvet Charm is doing to you, we'll find a way to stop it. Together."

The words hang in the air, heavy with a promise I'm not sure I can keep. But I have to try. I can't stand by and watch him slip further into the darkness without at least fighting for him.

He looks at me then, a strange mixture of hope and despair in his eyes. "You're so stubborn, you know that? It's infuriating."

"Comes with the territory." I offer him a small, lopsided smile, hoping to coax even a fraction of his former self out from behind the layers of pain and power that have trapped him. "Besides, you'd miss me if I wasn't."

He scoffs, but there's a faint flicker of amusement in his gaze. "Don't flatter yourself."

We lapse into silence again, but this time, it's a little less suffocating. I can almost believe we're back to the way things used to be, before the Velvet Charm, before the battles and the blood. But I know better than to trust this fragile peace. Damian may be here beside me, but there's a part of him that's already gone, claimed by the curse of the Charm he clings to like a lifeline.

Out of the corner of my eye, I catch a flicker of movement in the shadows. I tense, reaching instinctively for the knife at my waist, but Damian's hand on my arm stops me.

"It's just them," he murmurs, nodding toward the darkened figures slipping through the trees. His followers, the remnants of those loyal to him, each one touched by the same desperation and darkness that seems to have taken root in him. They keep their distance, watching us with wary eyes, their faces hidden in shadow, but I can feel the weight of their gaze, like a thousand invisible threads binding Damian to them, pulling him deeper into their world of secrets and sacrifice.

I want to scream at them, to tell them to leave him alone, to let him be free. But I know it's pointless. Damian has chosen this path, and for all my stubbornness, I can't force him to turn back.

"Why do you let them follow you?" I ask, my voice tight with frustration I can't quite suppress. "They're only dragging you down."

He doesn't look at me, his gaze fixed on the flickering glow of the campfire in the distance. "They're lost, just like me. They don't have anyone else."

"Neither do you," I say, the words slipping out before I can stop myself. "Not really. Not if you keep shutting me out."

He flinches, the faintest twitch of his jaw, but he doesn't respond. The silence stretches between us, heavy and unyielding, until I feel like I'm drowning in it. I want to reach out, to shake him, to make him see that he doesn't have to carry this alone. But I know it's useless. Damian has built walls around himself, and no matter how hard I try, I can't tear them down.

I don't realize I'm crying until he reaches out, his thumb brushing a stray tear from my cheek. The gentleness of the gesture takes me by surprise, and for a moment, I see a glimpse of the boy he used to be, the one who would have done anything to make me smile. But then the moment passes, and his hand drops back to his side, as if the touch was a mistake he's already regretting.

"Don't cry, Liv," he says, his voice barely more than a whisper. "It doesn't suit you."

The words are meant to comfort, but they only make the ache in my chest worse. I want to scream, to shake him and make him see that he's slipping away from me, that he's disappearing into a darkness I can't pull him out of. But I know it's pointless. Damian is on a path of his own making, and no amount of tears or pleas will bring him back to me.

"Then don't make me cry," I whisper, my voice choked with the weight of everything I can't say. "Stop pushing me away. Stop letting this… this curse consume you."

For a moment, he looks like he might actually listen, like he might finally let me in. But then the walls go back up, and he turns away, his face a mask of cold indifference once more.

"It's too late, Liv," he says, his voice distant and hollow. "Some things can't be undone. Some paths can't be turned back from."

I watch him walk away, his silhouette swallowed by the shadows, and I feel a part of myself shatter. Damian may still be here, but he's already lost to me, claimed by the curse of the Velvet Charm and the power it offers. And no matter how much I want to save him, I know deep down that I can't. Not unless he's willing to save himself.

But as I watch him disappear into the darkness, a spark of defiance flares within me. Maybe I can't save him, but I'll be damned if I let him slip away without a fight. I'll find a way to break the curse, to tear down the walls he's built around himself, even if it means risking everything I have. Because Damian may have given up on himself, but I refuse to give up on him.

I square my shoulders, determination hardening within me like steel.

The fire crackles low as I sit alone, watching the embers flicker in the darkness. Damian has gone, vanished into the night with that determined stride of his, as if he can outpace the shadows creeping into his soul. My fingers curl around the pendant at my neck, a simple thing made of silver, the last gift he gave me before all of this.

Back then, it had felt like a promise. Now, it's a reminder, a weight I can't put down. I trace the cool metal, as if somehow it might anchor me, keep me grounded in the middle of this strange, relentless world we've found ourselves in.

The quiet stretches on, broken only by the occasional crackle of the dying fire. The others—the followers, the remnants of those loyal to him—hover just out of sight, moving like shadows at the edge of my vision. I know they're watching me, silent as ghosts, their loyalty to Damian unwavering, even as he retreats further from all of us. I can't help but wonder if they see what I see, if they understand the cost of the power he's taken on. Or maybe they're drawn to it, captivated by the raw, terrifying strength he wields so effortlessly now.

A twig snaps behind me, and I whirl around, heart hammering in my chest. But it's only Rian, one of Damian's closest followers, his face partially obscured by the flickering light. His gaze is sharp, assessing, and I can't shake the feeling that he's measuring me somehow, calculating my place in this strange order they've built around Damian.

"You're still here," he says, voice low and devoid of any particular warmth.

"Obviously," I reply, forcing a calm I don't feel. "Not all of us disappear into the night when things get hard."

A faint smile plays at the corners of his mouth, though it doesn't reach his eyes. "You don't understand him. Not really."

The words sting, even though I know he's wrong—or at least, I want him to be wrong. "Maybe not. But I understand enough."

He takes a step closer, the firelight casting eerie shadows across his face. "He's chosen a path most can't follow. Power like his... it doesn't come without sacrifice. You think you're ready to walk that same road?"

I square my shoulders, meeting his gaze head-on. "If you're trying to scare me, it's not working."

Rian chuckles, a dry, humorless sound. "I'm not trying to scare you. Just warning you. You don't know what he's carrying, what he's given up for the Velvet Charm."

"And you do?"

He doesn't answer, just watches me with that calculating gaze, and I feel an unsettling mix of pity and contempt radiating from him. As if he's already written me off, decided that I'm just another piece in a game I can't possibly understand.

"Stay out of it, if you know what's good for you," he says finally, his tone dismissive. "Damian has his path, and you... well, you're just a distraction."

The words sting deeper than I want to admit, but I force myself to stay calm, to keep my voice steady. "If that's true, then why am I still here? Why hasn't he sent me away?"

Rian's expression darkens, and for a moment, I see a flash of something—fear, maybe, or resentment. "Because he's not thinking clearly. The Charm... it twists things, makes you see what isn't there. It's dangerous for him. Dangerous for you."

He steps back into the shadows, leaving me alone by the fire, his words lingering in the night air like a bitter aftertaste. I sit there, silent, the weight of his warning settling over me. Part of me wants to dismiss it, to believe that Rian is just trying to scare me off. But deep down, I know he's right. The Velvet Charm is changing Damian, twisting him into someone I barely recognize, and if I don't do something soon, I might lose him completely.

I don't know how long I sit there, lost in thought, but eventually, I hear footsteps approaching. I turn, heart leaping, only to see Calla, another of Damian's followers, her expression unreadable as she stops a few feet away from me.

"Rian was harsh with you," she says, her voice softer than his, though there's a guardedness to her words.

I nod, not trusting myself to speak, afraid my voice might betray the fear creeping up my spine.

She glances around, as if making sure we're alone, then leans in, her voice barely more than a whisper. "You should leave. While you still can. Damian is... not who he used to be. The power, the Charm—it's changing him."

Her words echo Rian's, but there's a kindness in her tone that makes them harder to brush off. I can see the worry in her eyes, the same fear that's been gnawing at me since I first saw the darkness creeping into Damian.

"He needs me," I say, more to convince myself than her.

She shakes her head, a sad smile tugging at her lips. "Maybe he did, once. But now... I think he needs something none of us can give him."

The fire crackles between us, the light casting strange shadows on her face. For a moment, I consider her words, the possibility that I might not be enough to pull Damian back from the edge. But then I remember the way he looked at me earlier, the vulnerability in his gaze, the way his hand lingered on mine as if I were the only tether keeping him grounded.

"I'm not giving up on him," I say firmly, my voice steady. "Not yet."

Calla studies me for a long moment, then nods, a resigned look in her eyes. "Then I hope, for both your sakes, you're right."

She disappears into the shadows, leaving me alone once more. The night stretches on, silent and still, as I sit by the fire, my mind racing. I know that staying by Damian's side is dangerous, that the Velvet Charm is a curse none of us fully understand. But I also know that I can't walk away—not now, not when he's spiraling into darkness.

I stand, determination settling over me like armor. If I can't pull him back, then I'll find someone who can. There are legends, stories whispered around fires just like this one, of those who've faced curses like the Velvet Charm and lived to tell the tale. If there's even a chance, a sliver of hope, then I have to try.

Just as I turn to head into the forest, a chill runs down my spine, and I freeze, a prickling sense of dread washing over me. The fire sputters, casting long, twisted shadows across the ground, and I hear a faint whisper, so soft I almost think I've imagined it.

"Liv..."

The voice is unmistakable—Damian's, low and urgent, but there's something off, a strange hollowness to it that sends a shiver down my spine. I scan the darkness, heart pounding, but there's no sign of him. The whisper comes again, fainter this time, as if it's slipping away.

I break into a run, following the sound, my feet pounding against the forest floor as I push through the darkness, branches clawing at my skin, the cold biting into me. But the voice keeps fading, drifting further and further away, until it's little more than a ghostly echo.

And then, just as I think I've lost it, I see him—Damian, standing alone in a small clearing, his back to me, his shoulders hunched. Relief floods through me, but as I step closer, the sense of dread intensifies. There's something wrong, something terribly, impossibly wrong.

"Damian," I whisper, reaching out, but he doesn't turn. His body is rigid, unmoving, as if he's frozen in place. And then, slowly, he lifts his head, his gaze locking onto something in the shadows.

A faint, otherworldly glow pulses in the darkness beyond, and a voice—not Damian's—echoes through the clearing, cold and chilling, carrying a warning that makes my blood run cold.

"You were warned, Liv. This is what happens to those who meddle in powers beyond their reach."

And in that moment, I realize—too late—that the fight for Damian's soul has only just begun.

Chapter 14: The Broken Crown

Rain lashed against the broken stone walls, each drop a drumbeat against the ancient relic of a kingdom that had faded to little more than folklore. The castle loomed in the darkness, its jagged towers and shattered battlements casting long, ominous shadows under the slivers of moonlight that pierced through the storm clouds. I hugged my coat tighter, feeling the damp cold seep into my bones as I followed Damian into the heart of the ruin.

The place had once been magnificent, I could tell, even in its decay. Massive tapestries clung to the walls, tattered but regal, the colors dulled by years of neglect but hints of their once-royal hues still visible under the grime. The floors, though cracked and scattered with debris, bore intricate designs carved by artisans long gone. Every detail whispered of forgotten splendor, tales of long-gone queens and kings, whispered promises of peace that had never come to pass. I couldn't help but feel small here, swallowed up by history and shadows.

Damian moved ahead of me, his silhouette stark against the dim light filtering through a massive, broken window. He stopped, head bowed, shoulders slumped as if bearing the weight of every ghost that lingered in this forsaken place. The Velvet Charm glinted in his hand, an object deceptively simple—a circlet of gleaming silver, unremarkable save for the single blood-red gem set into its center. In the low light, the gem pulsed faintly, like the beat of a heart, as if the crown itself was alive, longing, perhaps, to taste glory once more.

"Do you know what this really is?" His voice was barely above a whisper, yet it seemed to echo through the empty hall. I could feel the tension radiating off him, a wire pulled tight, ready to snap. Damian had always been enigmatic, but now, here in the depths of this shattered castle, he seemed almost like a stranger to me.

"A crown?" I ventured, though I knew that was only part of the story. Everything about the Velvet Charm, from the legends that had haunted our childhood stories to the ruthless desire in people's eyes when they spoke of it, hinted at something much darker.

He laughed softly, a humorless sound that sent a shiver down my spine. "Not just a crown. This... this was supposed to be a symbol. Something pure. A promise forged in metal." He raised it, and I watched as he stared into the gem, almost mesmerized. "They made it to bring peace between kingdoms, to end centuries of bloodshed. They said whoever wore it would have the power to bind nations, to unite even the bitterest of enemies."

"And yet here we are," I replied, my voice tinged with bitterness. "Running for our lives because of it."

"Because people corrupted it," he snapped, his tone harsh. "Greed, fear... They tore it apart from the inside out. What was supposed to bring peace became a weapon, something twisted, something to be feared." He took a step closer, holding the crown out to me. "And now, somehow, I'm supposed to believe that all of this can be undone. That peace can be restored if someone makes... if I make the ultimate sacrifice."

The words hung between us, a bitter, impossible truth. I felt the cold ache of realization settle in my chest, heavy and unrelenting. Damian's eyes met mine, and I saw the decision there, hard and unyielding. He'd already made up his mind, his fate intertwined with that of the Velvet Charm in a way that terrified me. But more than that, I saw the sorrow buried beneath the resolve, the weight of responsibility he was carrying alone.

"There has to be another way," I said, though my voice sounded weak, like I didn't even believe it myself. "We can't have come this far, survived this much, only for you to..."

"To die?" He cut me off, his voice barely a murmur. "It's the only way, don't you see? This crown—this relic—it's poison. Every hand that has touched it has been cursed. If destroying it means ending that curse, then so be it." He looked away, his fingers tightening around the crown as if he could squeeze the darkness out of it by sheer will alone.

"No," I said, stepping closer, the desperation in my voice surprising even me. "No, you're wrong. You're stronger than that, Damian. You've already proven you're better than the people who ruined it. You don't have to do this alone. I—"

"You think I want to do this alone?" His voice cracked, the admission slipping out before he could catch it. He turned to me, his face shadowed and raw. "I've lived my whole life fighting this... this curse, trying to resist the pull of power that everyone else gave into. And now, finally, I have a way to end it, to make sure no one else has to suffer because of this damn thing."

"But you'll suffer," I whispered, and for a moment, my voice seemed to be the only sound in the room. Even the storm outside seemed to hold its breath.

He looked at me, his eyes dark and unyielding. "Better me than the rest of the world."

There was a finality in his words that left me reeling, a certainty that both terrified and infuriated me. I wanted to grab him, shake him, force him to see that he was more than just a pawn in this ancient curse. But before I could say anything, he turned away, his gaze drifting to the broken window, his jaw clenched in silent agony.

"If you do this," I said, my voice barely more than a whisper, "you're just another casualty. Just another sacrifice in a long line of lives lost to this cursed thing. You're better than that, Damian. We're better than that."

He didn't answer, but I saw his hand falter, his grip loosening on the crown. The silence stretched between us, a fragile bridge connecting two souls caught in a web of fate and fury. And in that silence, I felt it—the aching, impossible hope that maybe, just maybe, we could find another way.

The storm outside raged on, but here, in the heart of this forgotten castle, a quiet battle raged between us—a battle not just for a crown, but for a future, for a chance to break free from the chains that bound us to a history we hadn't chosen. And in that moment, I made a promise to myself: I would not lose Damian to the darkness, not if there was still a chance to save him, to save us both.

A sudden crash sounded from above, the sharp crack of splintering wood echoing through the desolate corridors. Both of us froze, our breaths mingling in the damp, cold air. Damian's eyes flicked to mine, a silent warning passing between us. We weren't alone. The realization settled in my stomach like a stone.

Damian slipped into the shadows by the wall, his hand reaching instinctively for the dagger at his belt, while I pressed myself against the frigid stone, every muscle tense. The Velvet Charm glinted faintly in his other hand, betraying our hiding spot with its dim, sinister glow. I wished he would hide it, stuff it into his coat or shove it in a pocket, anything to stop that eerie red light from flickering through the gloom. But the crown seemed to resist being concealed, as if it demanded to be seen.

A pair of voices floated down the hall, harsh whispers laced with urgency. Whoever they were, they sounded close enough to touch. I could feel my heartbeat in my throat, a rapid, panicked drumbeat that I was certain they'd hear. I chanced a glance at Damian, who gave a single, sharp nod, signaling that we'd wait until they passed.

"Look at this place," one of them muttered, his voice heavy with disdain. "You'd think a king's palace would have more to it than cracked stone and rat nests."

"Quiet, you fool," the other snapped. "It's not the palace itself that matters. It's what's hidden here."

Another flash of lightning illuminated the hall, and for an instant, I caught a glimpse of their faces—hardened, scarred, eyes sharp as blades. Mercenaries, hired muscle sent by the very people who'd twisted the Velvet Charm's purpose. I swallowed, my throat dry. We had to find a way out, but Damian's grip on my arm kept me rooted in place.

"They say it's here," the first voice continued, his tone hushed and reverent. "The Velvet Charm, just waiting to be reclaimed. Can you imagine the power it would give us? No more scrabbling for scraps. No more taking orders from idiots in silk robes."

"We're not here to dream about power," the second man growled, his patience clearly thinning. "We find the crown, we bring it back. We don't mess this up."

The footsteps moved closer, and I felt Damian's hand tighten on my arm, his signal to stay hidden. My pulse hammered as their shadows stretched along the floor, dark tendrils creeping closer to where we crouched.

But just as the pair reached our hiding spot, a sudden gust of wind slammed a nearby door, rattling the entire hall. They spun toward the noise, weapons drawn, and in that instant, Damian acted. He lunged, knocking one to the ground with a swift, brutal motion that left no room for hesitation. I didn't even think—I grabbed a loose stone from the floor and threw myself at the other one, bringing it down hard against his arm. He cursed, swinging wildly, but I ducked, moving instinctively, dodging blows like my life depended on it.

Which, I supposed, it did.

"Run!" Damian's voice snapped through the air as he yanked me to my feet, and without a second thought, I tore down the hall, my heart racing. I could hear the mercenaries shouting behind us, recovering faster than I'd hoped.

We sprinted through the maze of corridors, the castle a confusing labyrinth of twisted halls and crumbling staircases. Every shadow felt like it was reaching for me, the stone walls pressing in, as if the castle itself wanted to trap us within its forgotten secrets. I could hear Damian's labored breathing beside me, his hand gripping mine as he pulled me along, his determination burning as bright as the red glow of the crown.

Finally, we burst through a doorway into an open chamber, the vast expanse of the ruined throne room looming before us. High above, the ceiling had crumbled away, leaving only a jagged hole that framed the storm-torn sky. Rain poured down, drenching us instantly, and I shivered, my clothes sticking to my skin. Damian didn't stop, his gaze fixed on the massive throne at the far end of the room, a grim, towering seat carved from obsidian and stone.

"Damian," I gasped, pulling against his grip, trying to get him to stop, to think. "We can't—there's no escape here!"

But he didn't seem to hear me, his eyes locked on the throne as if in a trance. It was then that I realized he wasn't just running. He had a plan, a last, desperate gamble that I wasn't privy to.

He released my hand, striding toward the throne with grim purpose, the Velvet Charm in his hand gleaming like a beacon. I stood rooted to the spot, watching in helpless horror as he approached the seat of ancient kings, the seat of the very power he'd spent his life resisting. Every instinct screamed for me to run to him, to stop him, but something kept me still, a dark fear that I would only make things worse if I intervened.

He held the crown high, letting the storm's light catch on its sinister beauty, and his voice rang out, clear and defiant. "If you want it," he shouted, his words echoing through the chamber, "come and take it!"

The shadows at the edges of the room seemed to shift, the air thickening with an unnatural chill. My skin prickled with dread as

I realized he wasn't just calling out to the mercenaries still chasing us. No, Damian was calling something older, something darker, something that had been waiting in the forgotten corners of this castle for centuries.

"Damian, stop!" I cried, my voice swallowed by the storm, but he didn't turn back. He was already too far gone, his fate bound to the crown, to the shattered remnants of a kingdom that had been lost to time.

A low, haunting laugh echoed through the hall, and I froze, my blood turning to ice. Out of the shadows stepped a figure cloaked in tattered robes, their face hidden beneath a hood, but their eyes... their eyes gleamed with an unnatural light, a cruel amusement that made my stomach churn. They took a step forward, and the rain seemed to fall slower, as if the very air had thickened in their presence.

"Ah, the Velvet Charm," the figure murmured, their voice smooth and chilling. "You've brought it to me at last."

Damian stood his ground, holding the crown between them like a shield. "If you want it," he repeated, his voice steely, "then take it. But know that it's a curse as much as it is a crown. It will devour you as it devoured all who came before."

The figure chuckled, a sound that echoed off the ruined walls. "Oh, I know the price," they said softly. "But what are a few souls compared to the power of a kingdom reborn?"

In that moment, I understood Damian's gamble. He hadn't brought the crown here to give it up—he'd brought it here to destroy it, to end the cycle once and for all. But as he raised the crown, ready to cast it into the rain-soaked darkness, the figure lunged, faster than I could comprehend. They seized his wrist, their grip like iron, and the world seemed to freeze around us.

The air thickened, an invisible force pressing down on the room, and I felt my breath catch. Damian's arm was frozen mid-motion, his fingers clenched around the Velvet Charm, while the shadowy figure's grip tightened around his wrist, each knuckle sharp under their skin like bone claws. Every instinct screamed at me to move, to pull him away, but I was rooted to the spot, held captive by that same chilling power. Rain poured in through the shattered ceiling, each drop striking the stone floor like the beat of a war drum.

"You don't understand what you're playing with, do you?" the figure murmured, tilting their head just enough for me to catch the glint of hollow eyes beneath the hood. Their voice was low, rich with a mocking kind of amusement that twisted something in my gut. "You thought a few words and good intentions would be enough to destroy it?"

Damian gritted his teeth, struggling against the iron hold, but he didn't look away. "Maybe it's not enough. But I'm still going to try."

The figure's laugh was soft, but it rippled through the chamber, stirring shadows that clung to the walls like smoke. "Oh, you brave little fool," they purred. "Every king, every warrior, every sorcerer who has ever touched the Velvet Charm thought the same thing. That they could control it. That their intentions were pure enough to withstand its call." They leaned in, their breath cold against Damian's cheek. "And every one of them was wrong."

I could see the strain on Damian's face, the flicker of doubt that crept into his gaze despite his iron resolve. He'd been fighting this battle alone for so long, bearing the weight of every choice, every consequence, every death that had ever come from that cursed crown. And now, in the dim light of the castle, facing the embodiment of all he'd ever feared, I saw his shoulders sag, just for a moment, under the crushing burden of it all.

But before I could let my own fear take hold, he looked up, his gaze finding mine, a fierce defiance sparking back to life. "It's not just my intentions," he said, his voice barely more than a whisper, "it's hers." His eyes flashed, filled with a desperation so raw it felt like a physical blow. "It's our choice. Together."

My heart stumbled, his words slicing through the thick, pressing dread like a blade. I didn't know what he meant, what he expected me to do, but somehow, I understood. I took a step forward, pushing past the trembling terror that tried to tether me back, and reached out, my fingers brushing the freezing metal of the Velvet Charm. The moment my skin touched it, a pulse of something ancient and dark shot through me, every nerve buzzing as if charged with fire.

The shadowed figure hissed, their hold on Damian faltering as if my touch had broken some invisible chain. The room trembled, the very walls seeming to groan in protest as I held on, feeling the crown's terrible power coursing through me, an endless torrent of memories and emotions and something darker, something twisted. It whispered promises, its voice rich and silky, seeping into my thoughts like honeyed poison, tempting me to take it, to claim it for myself, to wield its power in the name of every injustice I'd ever faced.

But beneath that pull, I felt Damian's hand over mine, steady and warm, an anchor that pulled me back to myself. I gripped the crown tighter, feeling the weight of his trust, his faith, a belief in me that ran deeper than words.

"No," I whispered, my voice trembling but resolute. "You don't get to win. Not like this."

The figure's eyes flashed with fury, and they released Damian's wrist, lunging forward with a speed that stole my breath. But before they could reach me, Damian moved, stepping in front of me, his arm flinging out to shield me. I heard the sickening thud of impact, felt the air shift as the force of the blow pushed him back against me, nearly knocking us both to the ground. I clutched the crown, the only weapon I had, and met the figure's gaze, daring them to come closer.

They halted, their face twisted with a mixture of rage and something that almost looked like fear. "You think you can defy me?" they spat, their voice scraping through the silence like a blade. "You, who barely understands the first thing about power?"

"Maybe," I shot back, my voice steadier than I felt, "but we're willing to try."

For a heartbeat, they were still, their gaze fixed on us with a dark intensity that made my skin prickle. And then, with a sneer, they stepped back, their form blurring at the edges like smoke in the wind. "Very well," they said, their voice soft, but laced with menace. "You think you're worthy? Then prove it."

Before I could process what was happening, they raised a hand, and I felt a searing pain course through my chest, as if something had taken hold of my heart and was squeezing it with ruthless force. My vision blurred, and I stumbled, my knees buckling under the onslaught. Damian caught me, his arms wrapping around me as he whispered my name, his voice tight with fear.

"You can't fight it alone," I managed to gasp, the words barely audible over the roaring in my ears. "We... we have to do this together."

He nodded, his face pale but determined, and with a shuddering breath, he placed his hand over mine on the crown. The moment his skin touched the metal, a burst of light shot from the Velvet Charm, blinding and fierce, illuminating the room in a searing blaze that forced the figure to stagger back, shielding their eyes. The power coursing through us was relentless, an unyielding tide that threatened to sweep us under, but together, we held on, refusing to let go.

The light grew brighter, hotter, filling every corner of the throne room, and I felt something give, a shift in the air as if the very walls were breaking apart. The figure screamed, their voice warped with rage and desperation, but I held on, feeling Damian's strength flowing into me, grounding me, anchoring us both as we pushed against the darkness that threatened to consume us.

And then, just as suddenly as it had begun, the light vanished, plunging the room back into darkness. I staggered, the silence pressing down on me, and for a heart-stopping moment, I thought we had failed, that the figure had won, that we'd been swallowed whole by the very power we'd sought to destroy.

But when I looked up, I saw Damian still standing beside me, his face drawn and weary, but alive. The Velvet Charm lay in our hands, dull and lifeless, as if the power that had once driven it had finally been extinguished. I felt a wave of relief, so fierce it nearly brought me to my knees, and I turned to Damian, ready to speak, to let him know we'd made it through.

But the words caught in my throat as I saw the figure standing just beyond him, their gaze fixed on the crown in our hands, their expression a mixture of fury and something else, something that twisted my stomach with dread. They raised their hand, and before I could scream, before I could warn him, a blade of pure darkness formed in their palm, sharp as night, and they drove it straight through Damian's back.

Chapter 15: Veins of Gold

The castle's heart isn't like any part I've seen before. It's hidden, nearly forgotten, wedged between walls that feel centuries old and stone steps that crumble beneath our weight. Here, the air is thick and damp, with a metallic tang that makes my lungs burn, like I'm breathing in ages of history all at once. Damian moves ahead of me, his footsteps steady, but even he looks hesitant. Every flicker of his torch casts shadows that seem to cling to us, the light almost afraid to chase them away.

His voice, low and rough, is barely more than a whisper. "You can feel it, can't you? The magic... it's not dead."

I don't need him to tell me. The walls almost pulse, their veins of gold glowing faintly in the dim light, stretching like sinews through stone. They snake and curve, flowing down the walls in fractured patterns, like lightning caught and frozen mid-strike. This place feels alive, as though it's holding its breath, waiting. The thought sends a shiver through me, and I force myself to step closer, reaching out to press my hand against the wall. Cold. Unyielding. And yet, I can feel it—a faint hum beneath the surface, like a heartbeat slowed to a whisper.

"Why here?" I ask, not really expecting an answer. "What makes this spot different?"

Damian glances over his shoulder, a smirk twitching at the corner of his mouth, though his eyes are all shadow. "Not sure. Maybe it's because this is the last place anyone would think to look."

I let out a bitter laugh. "Yeah, because no one in their right mind would want to be down here."

He just shrugs, and that smirk of his only deepens, like he's amused by my discomfort. "Sometimes, the places we least want to go are the ones that hold what we need most." He steps back, motioning to a section of wall, his fingers tracing the outline of the golden veins. "Look closer. It's here, beneath all of this."

Together, we set to work. Digging, scraping. The rough stone grates against my fingertips, and soon enough, my hands are raw and bloody. The castle seems determined to keep its secrets, resisting every effort to pull it apart. But as each layer falls away, I feel something shift. It's subtle, like a change in the air, a new note in the song of silence. This isn't just stone; this is something more.

Damian's shoulder brushes against mine as he leans closer, his breath warm on my neck. There's a brief, strange comfort in the proximity, in his solid presence beside me as we tear into the wall. Then, suddenly, my fingers hit something cold and smooth, a texture so unlike the stone around it that I pause, heart pounding.

"I think I found it," I say, my voice barely more than a breath.

Together, we pry it free—a piece of the crown, gleaming in the dim torchlight, a sliver of gold that practically hums with power. It's surprisingly light, almost weightless, yet it pulses with an energy that makes the hairs on the back of my neck stand on end. Damian's hand covers mine, his fingers curling over mine around the artifact, and for a moment, we're caught in the same rhythm, our breaths mingling in the cool, damp air.

He glances at me, and there's something unguarded in his eyes that I've never seen before, a softness that almost makes me forget where we are. But the moment shatters as a low chuckle echoes from the shadows behind us, dark and taunting, sliding over my skin like ice.

We both freeze. Damian's fingers tense around mine, but he doesn't let go. We turn together, the torch casting a flickering glow across the walls, stretching our shadows long and distorted. And then he steps forward—a figure cloaked in darkness, his face hidden, but his presence unmistakable.

"Well, well," the voice drawls, slick as oil and twice as cold. "Didn't expect to find you two down here, digging through ancient stones like rats."

Damian shifts, his body angled protectively in front of me, though his voice is steady, almost mocking. "Funny, I didn't realize we'd need permission to look around our own castle."

The figure laughs again, and the sound sends a shiver through me, the kind of laugh that speaks of knowledge, of secrets kept for far too long. He steps closer, and the light catches a glint of gold beneath his cloak—a crest, familiar and ominous, marking him as one of the high council's agents. Of course. They'd sent someone to watch us, to make sure we didn't get too close to anything they didn't want us finding.

I grit my teeth, a pulse of anger mixing with the fear twisting in my gut. "If you think you can just stroll in here and claim this for yourselves—"

"Oh, but we can, my dear." He draws out the words, savoring each one like it's a piece of some exquisite, rare fruit. "You see, the council has rights to all magical artifacts discovered within this kingdom. That little trinket belongs to us." He stretches out a hand, fingers curled like claws.

But before I can respond, Damian steps forward, his stance brimming with a quiet, simmering fury I've never seen in him before. "If you want it, you'll have to take it from us."

The man's smile doesn't falter, but there's a flicker of something in his eyes, a hesitation. "Brave words for someone standing on ground that's about to collapse," he murmurs, his gaze drifting up to the ceiling.

I don't even have time to process the warning before I hear the creak of stone, a low rumble that vibrates beneath my feet. Damian grabs my hand, his grip tight, and suddenly, we're running, the artifact pressed between us, the weight of it like a promise, a pulse that urges us forward. The ground shifts and trembles beneath us, cracks snaking along the walls as pieces of stone begin to rain down.

The only thing I can focus on is the pressure of Damian's hand in mine, the way his fingers curl around mine like an anchor. We don't stop, don't look back, even as the tunnel collapses behind us in a cacophony of dust and rubble.

The air thickens as we lurch forward, a surge of adrenaline blurring my vision as we navigate the trembling corridors. Dust rises in choking clouds, mixing with the taste of damp stone and bitter earth. Damian's grip on my hand is unrelenting, steadying me even as my legs strain to keep up. My lungs burn, a hot reminder of how deep we are, and how the weight of the entire castle looms above us, pressing down.

A loud crash echoes behind us, and I steal a glance over my shoulder. The passage we came through has vanished beneath a pile of rocks and debris, sealing off any retreat. It feels like a cruel joke—surviving long enough to find the artifact only to be buried alive for the trouble. But Damian doesn't falter, doesn't even glance back. His face is set, his jaw tight, as if he's already calculating every step between us and freedom.

He turns sharply, pulling me into a narrow side passage I hadn't even noticed. Here, the veins of gold in the stone seem almost alive, shimmering as they snake along the walls. They cast an eerie light, just enough for us to see each other's faces. Damian's eyes meet mine, and I catch a flash of something fierce, almost reckless.

"This way," he mutters, his voice low and rough, barely audible above the rumble of collapsing stone.

"Are you sure?" I whisper back, swallowing against the dry panic clawing its way up my throat.

"Not at all," he replies, flashing a grin that is entirely too calm for the situation. "But it's better than staying put, isn't it?"

With a tight nod, I follow him, my pulse pounding in my ears. The golden veins grow thicker here, practically wrapping around the walls like roots digging deeper, as though the castle itself is aware of us, guiding us—or perhaps trapping us. Each step we take, the faint hum of magic grows stronger, vibrating through my fingertips as they graze the rough stone for balance.

Then, abruptly, Damian stops, his shoulders tense as he tilts his head to listen. I hold my breath, straining to hear whatever has caught his attention, and there it is—the faint echo of footsteps, unhurried, purposeful, coming from somewhere just ahead. My heart sinks. Whoever that figure was, he's not content to let us slip away so easily.

Damian's hand tightens on mine, a silent warning, and we press ourselves against the cold wall, blending into the shadows. The footsteps draw closer, each one a steady beat, like the ticking of a clock winding down. The golden veins cast faint patterns across our faces, and I can see the same defiance in Damian's eyes that I feel stirring in my own chest.

As the figure rounds the corner, his face is finally illuminated—a man with a hawk-like gaze and a faint sneer that seems permanently etched into his sharp features. He's dressed in the dark, severe robes of the council, his hands clasped behind his back as if he has all the time in the world.

"Well, you've certainly made quite the mess," he remarks, glancing at the crumbling walls and the narrow passage. His tone is mild, almost bored, but there's an edge to it, a coiled menace that makes my skin prickle.

Damian steps forward, a protective wall between me and the council agent. "Funny, I thought the council preferred to do its spying from a distance," he says, his voice sharp as a blade.

The man's smile is all teeth. "Ah, but when a pair of troublemakers starts digging up relics best left undisturbed, exceptions must be made. You didn't really think we'd let you walk out of here with that, did you?" His gaze slides to the golden fragment clutched in my hand, and I tighten my grip on it instinctively.

"I didn't realize relics could be claimed by people who didn't even know they existed," I snap, my voice surprisingly steady. "And as far as I'm concerned, this belongs to the castle. To the people it was meant for."

The man's smile doesn't falter, but there's a glint in his eye now, a spark of irritation. "Oh, my dear, you're amusing, truly," he drawls, taking a step closer. "But let me clarify something. The council has rights to all powerful artifacts, no matter where they're found. The power in that fragment is too valuable to fall into... shall we say... untrained hands."

Damian shifts his stance, and I can feel the tension radiating off him, his body coiled and ready. "Then you'll just have to take it from us," he says, his voice like steel.

The man's gaze narrows, and for a split second, I see a flicker of uncertainty. He hadn't expected us to stand our ground. But the hesitation is gone as quickly as it appeared, replaced by a predatory gleam as he raises one hand, fingers curling in a gesture that sends a chill down my spine.

The walls around us shudder, and I feel the fragment in my hand pulse in response, as though it's alive, aware, reaching out. There's a sharp tug in my chest, and without thinking, I press the fragment against the golden veins running through the wall. The reaction is immediate—a bright, blinding surge of light that floods the narrow passage, filling every corner, every crevice.

The council agent stumbles back, his face twisted in shock, as the light swirls and coils, wrapping around Damian and me like a shield. It's warm, fierce, and I can feel it sinking into my skin, filling me with a strength that I didn't know I had.

Damian's hand finds mine again, and he squeezes it tightly, his expression both surprised and triumphant. "Whatever you just did, don't stop," he murmurs, his voice a mix of awe and exhilaration.

"I didn't exactly plan it," I whisper back, unable to tear my gaze away from the light. It feels like the castle itself is coming alive, pouring its energy into us, lending us its strength.

The council agent lets out a snarl of frustration, his composure shattered as he raises both hands, sending a wave of dark energy crashing toward us. But the light around us flares brighter, absorbing the attack with a faint shimmer before it fades, leaving only the faintest trace of ash on the ground.

"You can't fight the castle," I say, surprised by the certainty in my voice. "It's not yours to control."

For the first time, I see real fear in his eyes. He takes a step back, his gaze darting between us and the golden veins now pulsing steadily along the walls. He knows, just as we do, that he's lost.

The council agent's face contorts with fury, the calm façade stripped away as he realizes the castle itself has turned against him. Damian keeps his hand tightly around mine, grounding me as the light pulses in rhythm with my racing heart. Every beat feels like a promise, a surge of power I can barely control but somehow understand on an instinctive level. This castle has secrets, and in this moment, it's as if I'm part of them, woven into its walls, its ancient magic.

The agent's hands twitch as he prepares to launch another wave of dark energy, his face twisted in desperate determination. But before he can act, Damian steps forward, blocking me from view, his voice hard and clear.

"Enough." The single word echoes off the stone walls, laced with authority I hadn't realized he possessed. Damian's grip on my hand tightens, and I can feel the tension humming through his body. He's not just a figure from my past or an accomplice in this mad quest;

he's part of this castle's legacy, its heartbeat. And he's not backing down.

The agent's expression shifts, a sneer replacing the fear. "Do you really think you have control here?" His eyes flick toward the golden fragment clutched in my hand, his gaze hungry. "You have no idea what kind of power you're dealing with. That artifact belongs to us. It's been ours from the beginning."

Damian laughs, sharp and defiant. "Funny, I don't recall you lifting a finger to uncover it. Seems to me, the castle has other ideas."

I can feel a smirk forming, despite the tension coiling in my chest. "And anyway," I add, feigning nonchalance, "we're not the ones skulking around dark tunnels in borrowed robes, hoping to steal what's already been claimed."

His face flushes an ugly red, and he takes a step closer, the shadows clinging to him like a second skin. But before he can speak, the ground shudders, a deep, ominous tremor that ripples through the stone beneath us. It feels as if the castle itself is angry, its patience worn thin.

The agent glances down, his confidence wavering, and I see a flicker of uncertainty pass over his face. The golden veins in the walls glow brighter, pulsating in time with the tremors, and a faint hum fills the air, growing louder until it's almost a roar. I clutch the fragment tighter, feeling its warmth seep into my skin, like it's anchoring me to this place.

Then, as if on cue, a narrow crack appears in the wall behind the agent, spreading like a spiderweb. It widens with a groan, chunks of stone tumbling to the ground, and the air is suddenly filled with dust and the sharp scent of ancient earth. Damian and I exchange a glance, each of us realizing the same thing—the castle is opening up, revealing something hidden within its depths.

The agent turns, momentarily distracted by the gaping fissure behind him. Damian uses the distraction to tug me forward, and we sidestep around the man, our movements swift and silent as we edge toward the newly revealed passageway. It's narrow and unwelcoming, but there's a glow emanating from its depths, faint and golden, calling to us.

"Going somewhere?" the agent sneers, his attention snapping back to us.

Damian grins, the kind of reckless, defiant grin that makes my heart skip a beat. "Oh, just to see what else the castle has in store for us," he replies, his tone as casual as if we're discussing the weather.

With a flick of his wrist, the agent hurls a bolt of dark energy in our direction, the shadows twisting and writhing as they shoot toward us. I barely have time to react, but the fragment in my hand flares to life, casting a shield of light that deflects the attack. The energy dissipates into wisps of smoke, and I feel a rush of exhilaration as I realize the artifact is responding to me, protecting us.

"Nice try," I say, my voice steady despite the wild thumping of my heart. "But it seems like the castle has other plans."

Damian and I exchange a nod, unspoken understanding passing between us, and together we step into the narrow passageway, leaving the agent behind. The walls close in around us, the golden veins casting an otherworldly glow that illuminates the path ahead. The air is thick, charged with a power that feels both exhilarating and dangerous, and every step takes us deeper into the unknown.

The passage winds and twists, the ceiling low and the floor uneven, as if this part of the castle was carved out of the rock itself, hidden away for centuries. I keep my hand on the wall for balance, feeling the thrum of energy beneath my fingertips. It's like the castle is alive, guiding us, showing us the way.

Finally, the passage opens into a cavernous chamber, and my breath catches in my throat. The walls are lined with veins of gold so thick and bright they cast a warm, pulsing light over everything, illuminating a raised dais in the center of the room. And there, resting on a pedestal carved from the stone itself, is the crown.

It's more beautiful than I could have imagined, crafted from gold so pure it seems to glow from within. Intricate patterns are etched into its surface, swirling and twisting like the veins in the walls, and at its center sits a single gemstone, a deep, dark blue that sparkles with hidden fire. The air around it hums with power, and I feel drawn to it, as though it's calling to me, waiting.

Damian's hand on my shoulder grounds me, and I glance up to see him watching me, his expression both wary and awed. "This is it," he murmurs. "The Velvet Charm. The true source of the castle's magic."

I reach out, my fingers brushing the edge of the pedestal, and a jolt of energy shoots through me, sharp and exhilarating. The crown pulses in response, its glow intensifying, and I can feel the magic in the air, thick and potent, pressing against my skin.

But before I can take hold of it, a sound echoes through the chamber—a low, menacing laugh that sends a chill down my spine. I turn, my heart pounding, to see the agent standing in the entrance to the chamber, his eyes gleaming with a dark, twisted satisfaction.

"Did you really think you could just take it and walk away?" His voice is a low hiss, filled with a dangerous edge. "That power belongs to the council, and to me. You have no idea what you're dealing with."

Damian steps in front of me, shielding me from the agent's gaze, but I can see the tension in his stance, the way his fists clench at his sides. "You have no claim here," he says, his voice cold and unyielding. "The castle chose us. This power isn't yours to take."

The agent's smile widens, his eyes gleaming with malicious glee. "Oh, but you've made it easy. The two of you have done all the work, and now... all I have to do is take it from you."

With a sudden, fluid motion, he raises his hands, dark energy swirling between his fingers, forming a vortex of shadow and malice that grows, expanding outward. The golden veins in the walls flicker, their light dimming as the energy pulses through the chamber, cold and suffocating.

The air grows heavy, pressing down on us, and I feel the weight of the magic around us, thick and oppressive, like a storm about to break. Damian glances at me, his eyes fierce, and I know he's thinking the same thing—there's no way out. We're trapped, cornered by a force we can't hope to defeat on our own.

Just as the darkness reaches for us, something shifts in the crown, a pulse of light so bright it sears the air, blinding us both. I feel a surge of power, raw and wild, pulling me forward, and before I can stop myself, my hand closes around the crown.

The light explodes outward, a blinding flash that consumes everything, and I'm left standing in the darkness, holding my breath, waiting for whatever comes next.

Chapter 16: The Crimson Heir

The glint in Ethan's eyes catches the sliver of moonlight streaming through the abandoned building's cracked windows, lending him an air of eerie grandeur. His hair falls around his face in loose, dark waves, slick with rain that's dripped from the battered roof and somehow making him look like some dark prince from a gothic nightmare. There's a flash of nostalgia—a memory from years past, when he'd been little more than a boy with ambition, laughing under the same rain-soaked skies that now cast shadows over his twisted expression.

He steps forward, his lips pulling into a cruel smile that seems to carve lines into his face. "I knew you'd come here eventually, Tessa," he says, his voice like velvet over steel. "Did you think you could hide from me? From what you and I both know we are destined to become?"

Behind me, I feel Damian's hand tense, his fingers flexing as if itching to reach for his weapon. His presence is a balm and a warning all at once, grounding me in the surreal, twisted nightmare that's somehow turned so vividly real. But I can't afford to look away from Ethan, not now, not after he's bared his secrets in such a horrific, confident manner. The weight of the revelation—Ethan as the Crimson Heir—settles over me, a shroud as suffocating as the mist that clings to the air. It's a role he's coveted for years, though I'd never have believed he'd pursue it at the cost of his humanity.

"You lied to me," I say, my voice sharper than I feel, defiance chipping through my shock. "All those years, you pretended to be something else, something... good." The word feels like sandpaper against my tongue. I doubt he even remembers what it means. "Or was that always just a mask?"

His smile deepens, as if my anger feeds him, as if he's delighted by the game he's played with my heart. "You're oversimplifying things,

Tessa." He shrugs with a casualness that makes my stomach turn. "I was both. A mask and the real thing. You should know better than anyone how easy it is to wear both."

That stings, mostly because there's a grain of truth in it. I've worn my own masks, been both hero and antihero depending on the company I kept. But this... this is a different betrayal altogether. Ethan didn't just lie. He orchestrated a decade of deception, building layers upon layers of misdirection until the truth barely resembles what I thought I knew. The past feels as if it's crumbling beneath me, leaving only shards I'm reluctant to touch, lest they cut me even more deeply.

"What do you even want, Ethan?" I ask, forcing myself to meet his gaze head-on. His eyes, a shade darker than the crimson crest stitched onto his cloak, hold a gleam of something unhinged, something that makes him both familiar and utterly foreign. "What was the point of all this? To get the throne? To control the Velvet Charm? Was it worth destroying everything between us?"

"Oh, Tessa," he says, a mocking lilt in his voice that chills me. "It was never about the throne. That's just a seat—a crown to wear while I reshape this miserable world. The Velvet Charm is a tool, a means to end suffering in ways you could never comprehend." He reaches for me, his hand extending as if to cup my face, to draw me in as he once did so easily. "And I wanted you by my side to see it. To rule it."

His fingers brush my cheek, and the sensation jolts through me, a mix of revulsion and the remnants of something that once was. His touch, once warm and familiar, now feels as foreign as poison. I take a step back, my body instinctively moving toward Damian. I don't look at him, but I feel his steady presence like a fortress at my back.

"Don't," I whisper, low and fierce. "Don't you dare touch me. You're not the man I thought you were."

He sighs, a weary sound, as if I'm the one being unreasonable. "You and I are the same, Tessa," he murmurs. "We both have blood on our hands, more than either of us cares to admit. And that blood binds us, whether you like it or not. I'm offering you a way out. A chance to be more than you are. To matter."

I laugh, a harsh, bitter sound that surprises even me. "Matter? You think betraying everything we stood for is the path to significance?" I can feel the anger simmering beneath my skin, hot and volatile. I turn to Damian, finally meeting his gaze, and the resolve in his eyes steadies me.

"Whatever plans you've twisted up in your mind, Ethan, I want no part of them. You don't get to rewrite history and drag me into your version of it," I say, my voice sharp, almost cutting. "Not after what you've done."

Ethan's face flickers, a crack in his mask. There's anger there, disappointment even, though it's wrapped up in that cold exterior of his. For a moment, I almost see the boy I once trusted, the one who'd stayed up all night devising plans and dreaming of a better future, a future where we were both free from the chains of power that bound us. But that boy is gone, if he ever existed at all.

"Very well," he says, his tone resigned but calculating. He glances at Damian, dismissing him with a flick of his gaze before turning his attention back to me. "I suppose it's fitting that you've chosen him. He's simple, straightforward, predictable. Not unlike a pet."

A muscle in Damian's jaw twitches, but he doesn't rise to the bait. Instead, he steps forward, placing himself firmly between me and Ethan, his hand resting lightly on his weapon—a reminder of the distance, the irrevocable choice I've made.

"You'd do well to watch your words," Damian says, his voice low, dangerous. "The throne may be yours, but the respect of those around you is earned."

Ethan's smile turns icy. "Respect is overrated. Fear, now that's a language everyone understands."

And with that, he turns on his heel, his cloak swirling around him like a shroud as he disappears into the shadows, leaving behind an emptiness that presses against my chest, sharp and suffocating. I let out a breath I didn't realize I was holding, the weight of his betrayal settling into the pit of my stomach. Damian reaches for my hand, his touch grounding me in a world that still holds fragments of hope.

In that moment, I know the battle isn't over. It's only just begun.

The silence that follows is almost tangible, thick and taut, stretching between us like a live wire. Ethan's back is still turned, his figure rigid with a barely contained fury, though I can tell he's lingering just to test my resolve. Damian's hand remains on mine, steady and firm, his touch a reminder that I am no longer swayed by whispered promises or glances that once spoke of something shared. That connection, whatever it had been, is a bridge I'd willingly burned, and watching the last of its embers die in Ethan's departing form is somehow both liberating and laced with regret.

Ethan turns, only halfway, the edge of his profile illuminated by a thin, slanting ray of moonlight. His face is a mask, revealing nothing of the emotions that must be stirring underneath, but there's an intensity in his gaze that makes me pause. "This isn't over, Tessa," he says, his voice low and venomous, a whisper that slices through the silence. "You've chosen your side, but sides are... fickle things. When the time comes, I wonder if your loyalty will stand as strong as you think."

With that, he strides out of the shadows and into the mist, leaving the faint scent of leather and something metallic—a hint of blood, perhaps—in his wake. My heart is pounding, the reality of what just transpired settling heavily in my chest. Ethan isn't simply a rogue figure within the Crimson Society; he is the Crimson Society, or at least the inheritor of its darkest secrets. And by choosing Damian, I've made myself the enemy of everything Ethan now stands for. I can feel the weight of it pressing down on me, a reminder that loyalty isn't just a declaration; it's a choice with consequences that ripple outward, affecting everything and everyone.

Damian's hand shifts, pulling me gently but insistently back toward the main street. "Let's get out of here," he murmurs, his tone soft but resolute. There's no judgment in his eyes, only understanding, and it's a comfort I hadn't realized I needed until now. He doesn't ask if I'm all right, because he knows I'm not. He doesn't tell me that everything will be fine, because he knows it won't—not yet, maybe not ever.

We make our way through the narrow, winding streets, each step echoing against the cobblestones like a reminder of the path we're choosing. It's late, and the town is quiet, an eerie kind of stillness settling over the old stone buildings and crumbling archways that seem to watch us pass with silent judgment. I can feel the tension still humming in the air between us, but it's different now—more a shared determination than anything else. I glance up at Damian, his profile lit by the faint glow of distant streetlamps, and for the first time, I allow myself to imagine a future that doesn't involve Ethan, a future that doesn't hinge on some twisted loyalty to a man I thought I knew.

As we turn onto a quieter street, Damian finally speaks, his voice barely more than a whisper. "He's dangerous, you know. More dangerous than we even realized. It's not just about power for him—it's about control, about reshaping everything in his image." He looks at me, his expression shadowed but resolute. "You need to be ready for that, Tessa. He won't stop just because you walked away."

I nod, the truth of his words settling over me like a cold cloak. I know Damian's right. Ethan isn't the type to simply accept rejection. For him, this isn't about losing someone he cared for; it's about betrayal, about a threat to his carefully constructed plans. In his mind, I was supposed to be part of that, and by stepping away, I've become the very thing he despises—a variable he can't control.

"He thinks I'll come back," I say softly, a bitter smile tugging at the corner of my mouth. "He thinks that eventually, I'll realize he's the only choice that makes sense." The words taste sour, like poison on my tongue, because there's a small, quiet part of me that still remembers the way things used to be—the way I used to be—and wonders if he's right. But I bury that thought, knowing that giving it any ground would only lead me down a path I'm not willing to take.

Damian squeezes my hand, his expression softening as he looks at me. "He doesn't know you as well as he thinks he does. People like Ethan only see what they want to see. They build versions of us in their minds, versions that serve their needs. But that's not you, Tessa. You're stronger than he'll ever understand."

The words sink in, soothing a part of me I didn't realize was so raw. I lean into Damian, grateful for his presence, for the unwavering steadiness that seems to radiate from him like a lifeline. Together, we walk in silence, each lost in our own thoughts, but bound by the shared resolve to see this through, no matter what Ethan throws at us.

As we reach the edge of the town, where the quiet gives way to the bustling outskirts and the distant glow of neon signs, Damian pulls me aside, his gaze suddenly intense. "Tessa," he says, his voice low but urgent. "You need to know... this isn't just about us. Ethan's plans—whatever he's scheming—go deeper than anything we've seen before. There are whispers, rumors about alliances he's forming, people he's recruiting. And these aren't just regular followers; they're people who believe in his vision. People willing to do whatever it takes to make it a reality."

The weight of his words sinks into me, a cold reminder that this isn't just some personal feud between me and Ethan. This is bigger, darker—a battle not just for power, but for the very soul of everything we've fought to protect. I can feel the chill of it seeping into my bones, a reminder that Ethan isn't simply an old lover turned enemy; he's something far more dangerous, a shadow lurking on the edges of a world that's already teetering on the brink.

"I won't let him win," I say, the words slipping from my lips with a fierceness that surprises even me. "Whatever he's planning, whoever he's trying to control—I won't let him have it. Not without a fight."

Damian's eyes soften, and he nods, a hint of a smile tugging at his mouth. "I never doubted you for a second," he says quietly, and there's something in his tone—a mixture of pride and something deeper, something that makes my heart skip a beat.

For the first time, I feel the faint stirrings of hope. It's fragile, like the first light of dawn after a long, brutal night, but it's there, glowing steadily in the darkness. And as Damian and I stand together, our resolve renewed, I realize that this is what Ethan will never understand. He may have the Crimson Throne, the loyalty of his twisted followers, but he'll never have this. He'll never know the power of standing beside someone who believes in you, someone who sees you for who you truly are, not who they want you to be.

And in that moment, I know that whatever comes next, I won't be facing it alone.

The morning sun spills over the edge of the rooftops, casting sharp, clean lines of light across the cobblestones as Damian and I step into the square. It feels surreal, standing here in the ordinary daylight after the shadowed turmoil of the night. I've always loved this square with its mismatched paving stones and crooked benches, a gathering place filled with laughter and gossip. But today, the familiarity of it feels like a thin layer stretched over a well of unknowns, the echoes of Ethan's parting words still vibrating in my mind.

Damian's fingers brush against my arm as he steps closer, his face somber but resolute. "We're not safe here," he says, his voice low, scanning the streets as if half-expecting Ethan's shadow to reappear in broad daylight. "If he's really as far gone as we suspect... Tessa, he'll stop at nothing."

I let out a breath, watching the world bustle around us, people going about their lives, blissfully unaware that the Crimson Heir has claimed his throne. The thought clenches in my chest, the weight of it impossible to ignore. The Velvet Charm's allure was never just its wealth or influence. No, its pull is deeper, more insidious, drawing on people's desires, their ambitions, the things they'd rather keep hidden. Ethan's mastery over it means he has access to their secrets, a leash on every soul who's ever dared to indulge in the Charm's promises. I'd always known he was ruthless, but this—this power could warp even the best intentions into something grotesque.

"We'll go somewhere he can't reach us," I say, sounding braver than I feel. "At least until we figure out what his next move is."

Damian's lips press together in a thin line, his eyes flicking back toward the direction of the Crimson Society's headquarters. "He has resources, Tessa. Connections we can only guess at. And with the Charm under his control, he doesn't need to follow us. He can have others do the work for him, people who'd never question his motives." His hand finds mine, gripping it as if trying to anchor us both to some fleeting semblance of safety. "Running won't be enough."

I sigh, the weariness creeping into my bones, heavier with every word. "Then what, Damian? We don't have the numbers, or the funds, or the... the influence he does. We can't just waltz into his lair and demand he step down."

He smiles, a rare spark of humor breaking through the grim set of his jaw. "Actually, I'd pay to see you try that. Just march in there with all your fire and tell him he's being unreasonable. Might be the first time anyone's ever dared."

"Only if you'd be there to back me up," I say, trying to match his smirk, but my heart isn't in it. I glance around, the buildings around us suddenly feeling too close, the walls too high. The reality is harsh: we're outnumbered, outsmarted, and out of options. My mind races, grasping for something—anything—that might give us a fighting chance.

As we turn down a quieter street, Damian pulls me into a small alleyway, his expression turning serious again. "There might be one way," he says, his voice barely above a whisper. "Someone who could help us. Someone who knows Ethan, maybe better than you or I ever could."

A flicker of hope sparks in my chest. "Who?"

He hesitates, glancing around as if even the walls might betray us. "His sister," he says at last. "Eleanor."

The name hangs in the air like a threat, an unspoken warning wrapped in potential. Eleanor had been the black sheep, exiled from the Crimson Society years ago for reasons that were never fully clear to anyone outside their circle. I remember the whispers, the rumors of her defiance, her reckless disregard for the Society's rules. She'd been a legend in her own right—a force that had burned too bright for the confines of the Crimson Society's carefully manicured image.

"Eleanor?" I repeat, trying to keep the skepticism out of my voice. "If she's even alive... wouldn't she want nothing to do with him? With any of this?"

Damian's gaze hardens. "Maybe. But she's the only one with enough insight into Ethan's mind. She knows his weaknesses, knows what he's afraid of. If anyone has a chance of helping us, it's her."

The possibility dangles before me, a lifeline I hadn't dared hope for. But it's also a risk, one that could easily turn on us if Eleanor isn't who we think she is—or worse, if she's even more dangerous than Ethan himself. "Where is she?" I ask, a thrill of determination threading through my exhaustion.

Damian glances down, his thumb tracing idle circles on my hand. "Last I heard, she was living on the fringes of society, keeping a low profile in the Southern District. But that was months ago, and people like her... they don't stay in one place for long."

I swallow, trying to ignore the sinking feeling in my stomach. The Southern District is a place of shadows, a labyrinth of narrow alleys and dimly lit taverns where people trade in secrets and whispers. If Eleanor's hiding there, it's because she doesn't want to be found—and that doesn't bode well for us.

"Then we'll go," I say, the decision settling over me with a strange calm. "We'll find her, and we'll make her see reason. She might hate Ethan, but if there's any part of her that still cares about stopping him, then we have to try."

Damian nods, his face shadowed by an expression I can't quite read. There's something in his eyes, a flicker of worry, maybe even fear, but he masks it quickly. "Then let's not waste time. The longer we wait, the stronger he becomes."

We set off toward the Southern District, weaving through the streets as the city begins to wake around us. The square gives way to narrower, darker streets, the sounds of clinking glass and hushed voices drifting from the doorways of unmarked taverns and dimly lit shops. The Southern District isn't a place of order or control; it's a place where rules dissolve into whispers and danger waits around every corner.

As we make our way deeper into the shadows, I feel the prickling sensation of eyes on us, hidden figures watching from the periphery, their attention keen and predatory. Damian's pace quickens, his hand never leaving the hilt of his weapon. "Stay close," he murmurs, his voice tight with tension.

Suddenly, a figure steps out from an alleyway, blocking our path. A woman, tall and slender, wrapped in a dark cloak that obscures most of her face, save for the glint of sharp, calculating eyes. She tilts her head, regarding us with a smirk that's equal parts curiosity and amusement.

"Well, well," she says, her voice smooth and unhurried. "A couple of lost souls, wandering so far from home." Her gaze shifts to me, sharp and probing, as if she can see right through me. "You don't belong here, darling. People like you don't last long in places like this."

"We're looking for someone," Damian says, his tone guarded but firm. "Eleanor. We were told she might be… nearby."

The woman's smirk widens, a glint of something predatory in her gaze. "Eleanor, you say? Now that's a name I haven't heard in some time." She studies us, her eyes lingering on my face as if assessing my worth, my motives. "But people don't come looking for Eleanor unless they're desperate. Are you desperate?"

"Yes," I say, surprising even myself with the raw honesty of the word. "We need her help."

The woman's expression shifts, something unreadable flashing across her face. "Desperation is a powerful motivator, but it's also dangerous. You should be careful what you wish for."

She steps aside, gesturing for us to follow. A chill runs down my spine, a warning I can't shake. But Damian and I exchange a glance, silent understanding passing between us. We don't have a choice.

As we step into the darkened alleyway behind her, the shadows close in, swallowing us whole.

Chapter 17: Chains of Fate

Ethan's smug smile is the first thing I see as I open my eyes, the hazy remnants of a dream slipping away like smoke. The familiar chill of the castle's stone walls presses in around me, and my wrists ache, encircled by silver cuffs that pulse faintly with an eerie, magical light. I glance down, and my heart sinks as I see the delicate but unbreakable chains that anchor me to the wall. They hum with power, drawing energy from me in a slow, insidious drain that leaves me feeling as though I'm trying to walk through water—every movement heavy, every breath labored. The sensation is invasive, a steady pull at my strength, as if it's tearing away pieces of me, bit by bit.

Damian is beside me, bound in much the same way, though he's glaring at Ethan with a venom that could probably kill if it had any real power behind it. "Ethan, this is a new low," Damian spits, his voice taut with fury and an edge of something raw that I can't quite name. Maybe fear. Maybe helplessness. It makes my chest hurt to see him like this, his eyes wild, like a caged animal's, every muscle straining against the chains as though he believes, just for a moment, that he might be able to break them. But of course, he can't. That would be too easy, and if there's one thing I've learned, it's that nothing with Ethan is ever easy.

Ethan just shrugs, tilting his head to one side as he regards us both with an air of polite, detached amusement. "It's a necessary precaution," he says, his voice infuriatingly calm. "You two have proven yourselves... unpredictable. And I can't have you interfering in my plans. Besides," he adds, a glint of malice sparking in his eyes, "you belong to me now. Both of you."

I almost laugh, but the sound catches in my throat, twisting into something darker, more bitter. "You think chaining us up will make us loyal?" I manage, my voice a shaky imitation of defiance. It's all I have left. "You can't control us, Ethan. Not like this."

His smile widens, sharklike, as though he's been waiting for me to say that. "Oh, but I don't need to control you, my dear. I just need you to stay right here, nice and quiet, until I decide what to do with you." He reaches out and taps one of the chains lightly, and I feel a surge of energy leech out of me, as though I've been drained of a piece of myself. "In the meantime," he says, his voice as smooth as velvet, "why don't you two... bond? It might be your last chance."

He strides out of the room, the echo of his footsteps fading down the stone corridor, leaving only the faint hum of the chains and the heavy, oppressive silence between Damian and me. I don't dare look at him, not right away. Instead, I focus on the cold stone floor, trying to ground myself, to remember that I am more than this room, these chains, this awful feeling of helplessness that's threatening to swallow me whole. But it's difficult, and I feel something tighten in my chest as the reality of our situation sinks in.

After a long, tense silence, Damian's voice cuts through the stillness, low and rough. "I should have seen this coming," he says, his tone laced with bitterness. "I thought I could protect you. I thought... I was different from him."

My heart aches at his words, and I finally look up, meeting his gaze. There's a vulnerability in his eyes that I've rarely seen, a kind of desperate honesty that feels almost sacred in this bleak, miserable place. "You're nothing like him," I say softly, my voice firm despite the exhaustion dragging at me. "You've risked everything for me, for us. Ethan would never do that. He only takes."

Damian shakes his head, and there's a haunted look in his eyes, like he's wrestling with demons I can't see. "But what if I'm just like him? What if... what if this is my fate? To be trapped, to become someone I hate?" His voice cracks slightly, and the sound slices through me, sharp and painful.

I reach out as far as the chains will allow, my fingers brushing against his. The contact is slight, barely there, but it's enough to anchor me, to remind me that we're in this together, no matter how bleak it seems. "Damian, listen to me," I say, and I can hear the fierceness in my own voice, a fierce protectiveness that surprises even me. "You are nothing like him. You're here because you care, because you fight for the people you love. That's what makes you different. That's what makes you... you."

For a long moment, he just stares at me, as though he's searching for something in my eyes, something that will convince him that what I'm saying is true. And then, slowly, the tension in his face softens, and his hand tightens around mine, his fingers warm and solid, grounding me in a way that I didn't know I needed.

"I don't deserve you," he murmurs, almost too softly to hear, and there's a raw honesty in his voice that makes my throat tighten.

I want to tell him that he's wrong, that he deserves everything good in this world and more, but the words catch in my throat, tangled up with emotions that I'm not sure I'm ready to face. Instead, I lean in, closing the distance between us, and our lips meet in a kiss that's gentle at first, hesitant, as though we're both afraid of breaking the fragile moment between us. But then, slowly, the kiss deepens, and I feel the weight of our fear, our anger, our desperation melting away, replaced by a fierce, unbreakable bond that transcends the chains holding us captive.

In that moment, it doesn't matter that we're trapped, that the odds are stacked against us. All that matters is the warmth of his touch, the steady rhythm of his heartbeat against mine, a reminder that as long as we're together, we are stronger than any prison Ethan can build.

When we finally pull away, the faint glow of hope in Damian's eyes mirrors my own, and I know, without a doubt, that we will find a way out of this. We will break free—not just from these chains, but from the twisted fate that Ethan has tried to impose on us. Together, we are unstoppable.

The kiss leaves us both breathless, and when we finally pull apart, there's a new, fierce determination in Damian's eyes. It's a look I've seen only rarely, usually when he's facing something insurmountable with the quiet resolve of someone who has no intention of losing. It fills me with a spark of hope that refuses to die, even in this dim, dungeon-like room, with the chains draining our strength minute by minute. My hand is still entwined in his, and I give it a squeeze, not wanting to break the moment.

"We're getting out of here," he says, voice a low, steady promise. The strength in his tone makes me want to believe it with every cell in my body. I feel his thumb tracing a gentle line across my knuckles, an absentminded gesture that sends warmth through me, despite everything.

"Any grand plan I should know about?" I murmur, half-joking, though I can't deny the little glimmer of hope sparking in my chest. If anyone could conjure a miracle from the scraps of a broken plan, it would be Damian.

He shakes his head, a rueful smile playing at his lips. "Working on that part. I've been told I'm annoyingly persistent. Just trying to live up to the reputation." His tone is light, but I can feel the tension in his grip, the way his eyes dart around, searching for anything that might give us a sliver of advantage. He's calculating, strategizing, clinging to any thread of control in a situation that's designed to strip us of every last shred of it.

Ethan's voice echoes down the corridor, interrupting the quiet, and my entire body tenses. Even when he isn't in the room, his presence hangs over us like a specter, the embodiment of everything that's wrong, everything that's twisted and cruel in this place. I feel Damian's hand tighten around mine as the footsteps grow louder, and a familiar weight settles over my heart, a mixture of dread and fury. Ethan has always had a way of making me feel small, powerless, but now there's something else. A defiance, raw and stubborn, bubbling up despite the chains, despite the pain.

Ethan's figure appears in the doorway, framed by the flickering torchlight, casting strange shadows across his face. There's that glint in his eyes, a predatory satisfaction that makes my skin crawl. He takes a leisurely step into the room, crossing his arms as he surveys us, his gaze lingering on Damian for a second longer than necessary.

"Comfortable, are we?" he drawls, raising a brow. "I'd hate for you two to be uncomfortable. After all, you've both worked so hard to get here." His words drip with mockery, and I can feel my hands curl into fists, though it takes everything in me to keep my expression calm, unflinching.

"Ethan," Damian says, his voice steady, calm in a way that only makes his anger more chilling. "What exactly is your plan here? Keeping us tied up until we agree to play along with your delusions?"

Ethan laughs, and the sound is almost pleasant, almost friendly. He has this uncanny ability to make cruelty look charming, to slip barbed words into honeyed tones, and somehow it only makes him more insidious. "Oh, Damian, I don't expect either of you to agree. That would be far too easy. No, I'm quite content to let you both suffer a little. A lesson in humility, perhaps. A reminder of where loyalty truly lies."

I feel Damian shift beside me, his posture taut, like a spring ready to snap. "Funny," he says, his voice a soft, dangerous murmur. "I was under the impression that loyalty had something to do with choice. Not chains and cages."

Ethan's smile sharpens. "Oh, but choice is an illusion, isn't it?" His gaze flicks over to me, and there's something in his eyes that makes my stomach twist. "Some of us realize that sooner than others. Some of us learn the hard way."

I meet his gaze, refusing to flinch, refusing to give him the satisfaction of seeing me cower. "Then maybe you should have chosen differently," I say, my voice steady, laced with the barest edge of defiance. It's reckless, and I know it, but there's something about being so thoroughly trapped that makes courage feel like the only weapon left.

Ethan's eyes flash, just for an instant, and I see a flicker of something there—a crack in his composed façade. It's gone as quickly as it appeared, replaced by a look of cold amusement. "Oh, I did choose, my dear. And I chose power. Something the two of you clearly lack."

With that, he turns, his cloak sweeping behind him as he strides back down the corridor, leaving us once again in silence, the chill of his presence lingering like a bad taste in the air. As soon as he's gone, I feel a rush of relief, mingled with a simmering anger that makes my blood pound in my ears. I glance over at Damian, and I can see the same fury mirrored in his face, a silent, shared understanding between us.

"We're going to make him regret that," I say, my voice low, fierce.

Damian meets my gaze, a spark of something dark and determined flickering in his eyes. "Yes," he says, and there's a grim satisfaction in his tone, a promise that makes my pulse quicken. "But first, we have to get out of these damn chains."

He shifts, testing the bonds around his wrists, his expression sharpening as he examines the silver links. "The enchantment," he mutters, his brow furrowing. "It's draining us, but... it's not invincible." He glances at me, his gaze intense. "If we can disrupt the magic somehow, just for a moment..."

The flicker of hope in his voice makes my heart race, and I nod, focusing on the chains with renewed determination. The links are smooth, deceptively delicate-looking, glimmering faintly with a light that pulses in time with our breathing. I can feel the energy slipping away, like a slow leak, weakening us with every passing second.

"Disrupt the magic?" I murmur, frowning. "Do you think we have enough strength left to manage that?"

Damian hesitates, and I can see the doubt in his eyes, a hesitation that he quickly masks with a forced confidence. "We don't need much," he says, more to himself than to me. "Just one good moment. A crack in the enchantment."

He looks at me, his expression resolute. "It'll be risky. But we've got nothing left to lose, right?"

I hold his gaze, and for a heartbeat, I forget about the chains, the castle, even Ethan. All I see is Damian, and the unspoken promise between us, the silent vow that whatever happens, we'll face it together.

"Right," I say, my voice soft but firm. "Nothing left to lose."

We shift closer, our hands finding each other, fingers intertwining as we brace ourselves, gathering what little strength we have left. I can feel the magic crackling between us, a fragile, tenuous thread of power that feels like it could snap at any moment. But it's enough. It has to be enough.

With a deep breath, we focus, channeling every ounce of defiance, every shred of hope, into one last desperate attempt. The chains hum with energy, and I feel the faintest tremor, a tiny, almost imperceptible shift in the magic holding us captive.

Just one moment, I think, holding my breath. Just one.

The tremor in the chains deepens, a faint vibration that feels like hope stirring from its long slumber. Damian's grip tightens, his thumb tracing a reassuring line along the back of my hand, a quiet promise that he won't let go. Every nerve is focused on that one fragile connection we share, a thread of power between us, woven from sheer defiance. We hold on, pushing against the current of magic draining our strength, fighting the pull with a determination that borders on desperation.

"Come on," Damian whispers, as if coaxing the chains themselves, his voice laced with grit and something that sounds suspiciously like fear. I hear the strain in his tone, and I wonder if he's as close to breaking as I am. But there's something else in his voice too—a fierce protectiveness that sends a spark of warmth through me, lighting up the darkness that presses down from all sides.

For a moment, the air shifts. It's subtle, almost imperceptible, but I feel a tiny fissure in the magic, a crack that might just be big enough to slip through if we're quick, if we're willing to risk everything. I don't have time to second-guess myself. I meet Damian's gaze, a silent question in my eyes, and he gives a single, determined nod. We're doing this.

With a sudden surge of energy, I pull, yanking against the chains with all the strength I have left. The metal is cold and unyielding under my hands, biting into my skin, but I don't care. I feel Damian's hand tighten around mine, and together, we throw everything we have at the enchantment, channeling our defiance, our anger, our hope into one last, desperate push.

The chains shudder, and for a brief, beautiful moment, they loosen, the magic faltering, just enough for us to slip free. I gasp, the sensation like a weight being lifted, a rush of adrenaline and disbelief flooding through me. But there's no time to celebrate. I tug Damian forward, and he stumbles after me, both of us moving in a wild, chaotic scramble, our hands still linked, as if letting go would somehow break the fragile spell holding us together.

The corridor outside the cell is empty, dark and silent, the air thick with the scent of damp stone and something faintly metallic. I glance around, my heart pounding, half-expecting Ethan to appear out of the shadows, that mocking smile back on his face. But there's nothing. Only the eerie quiet, broken by the soft, hurried sound of our footsteps as we make our way down the hall, clinging to the shadows.

"Do you have any idea where we're going?" I whisper, my voice barely more than a breath. The walls seem to press in on us, and I can feel the weight of the castle around us, ancient and watchful, like it's aware of our every move.

"Not exactly," Damian admits, though there's a trace of a grin in his voice, as if the thrill of escaping is enough to override the terror of not knowing what comes next. "But I'd say anywhere that isn't a dungeon is a step in the right direction."

I roll my eyes, but a reluctant smile tugs at my lips. Even here, even now, with the threat of capture looming, he manages to make me feel like maybe, just maybe, we'll be okay. It's infuriating and comforting all at once.

We make our way through the winding corridors, every turn an exercise in holding our breath, in bracing for the possibility of running straight into Ethan or one of his guards. The castle seems endless, a maze of identical stone passages and narrow, twisting staircases that all look disturbingly alike. I start to wonder if this is all some sick game, if Ethan has designed it to trap anyone foolish enough to try to escape.

After what feels like an eternity, we reach a narrow stairway that spirals up into darkness. Damian pauses, his gaze flicking upward, a frown creasing his brow. "This should lead to the main hall," he says, though he sounds more like he's convincing himself than me.

"Then what?" I ask, trying to ignore the flutter of anxiety gnawing at my stomach. "You think we can just waltz out the front door?"

He gives a low chuckle, and the sound is strangely reassuring. "Let's not rule it out just yet. I've got a few ideas up my sleeve."

I bite back a retort, swallowing down the urge to ask if those ideas involve a magic carpet or a teleportation spell, because we're going to need something pretty spectacular to get out of here alive. But I keep the thought to myself, because right now, Damian's confidence is the only thing keeping me from completely losing it.

We climb the stairs in silence, each step echoing faintly, a reminder of just how precarious our situation is. The air grows colder the higher we go, a chill that seeps into my bones, making me shiver. I can feel the magic pulsing in the walls, a reminder that this place is as much a fortress of enchantment as it is of stone. But I refuse to let it intimidate me. Not now.

Finally, we reach the top of the staircase, emerging into a grand hall lined with tall, narrow windows. The moonlight filters through the glass, casting silvery patterns on the floor, illuminating the emptiness of the space. It's beautiful, in a bleak, haunting sort of way, but there's no time to admire it. We need to find a way out, and fast.

Damian pulls me forward, his hand warm and steady in mine, and for a moment, I allow myself to believe that maybe we'll make it. Maybe we'll find a way through this, find a way to escape the chains of fate that Ethan has tried to bind us with.

But as we cross the hall, a cold voice echoes from the shadows, freezing us in our tracks. "Leaving so soon?"

Ethan steps forward, his figure silhouetted against the moonlit windows, his eyes gleaming with a dangerous amusement. There's no sign of surprise in his expression, no indication that he's the slightest bit perturbed by our attempted escape. If anything, he looks... pleased.

My heart sinks, the weight of his gaze pressing down on me, and I feel Damian's hand tighten around mine, a silent reassurance that he won't let go, no matter what.

"Ah, you're both so predictable," Ethan murmurs, his voice dripping with mockery. "You really thought you could escape? That I wouldn't see this coming?"

I open my mouth to retort, but Damian cuts in, his voice hard and unyielding. "We're not yours to control, Ethan. Not now, not ever."

Ethan's smile widens, a sharp, predatory grin that sends a shiver down my spine. "Oh, but you are," he says, his tone laced with a chilling certainty. "You're both exactly where I want you. And you're going to learn, one way or another, that fate isn't something you can outrun."

With a flick of his wrist, Ethan raises his hand, and the air around us shifts, thickening with a dark, ominous energy. I feel the chains again, invisible this time, tightening around my chest, binding me to the spot, and a surge of panic rises in my throat as I struggle to breathe, to move, to do anything but stand there, helpless.

Damian's hand slips from mine, his fingers reaching out to grasp me, but it's too late. Ethan's magic pulls us apart, separating us with an invisible wall of force that feels like cold iron, and I watch in horror as he's forced back, his expression twisted in a mixture of rage and desperation.

Ethan's smile is the last thing I see before the darkness closes in, his voice echoing in my mind as everything fades to black.

"Welcome to your fate."

Chapter 18: Fire and Glass

The night air is thick, heavy as I hold the shard in my hand, a jagged piece of the Velvet Charm still humming with power. Its edges glint, sharp and almost sentient, as though eager to taste magic again. I catch Damian's eye, his face half-hidden in shadows, the flicker of torchlight dancing over his jawline, fierce and determined. We don't need words anymore; there's a rhythm between us now, a pulsing heartbeat that guides our movements. He nods once, his eyes hard, and in a swift motion, we bring the shard down on the enchanted chains binding our wrists. Sparks erupt, a surge of power like lightning through my veins, but I barely flinch.

The Crimson Society—loyal and fierce, even in disarray—scrambles around us, their crimson robes fluttering in panic as they try to regroup. Some of them notice us, eyes wide as they witness the breaking of the unbreakable. But Damian is already moving, pulling me close, weaving through the panicked crowd, his hand a firm anchor in the chaos.

He doesn't look back; neither do I. We've given enough to this place, to the people who would control us, bind us, break us. I catch a glimpse of the intricate tapestries on the stone walls, the rich scarlet and gold threads that once felt like symbols of honor, loyalty, purpose. Now they're just colors in a dark place, bleeding into each other like secrets hidden too long. We pass a mirror, the glass fractured and grimy, and for a second, I see my own reflection: fierce eyes, tangled hair, a face I barely recognize as my own. It doesn't matter. Tonight, I am something else—a force, an element, an answer.

We make it to the main hall, the heart of the castle. It's a grand room, or it would be, if the power didn't feel so twisted here, as if the walls themselves absorbed years of betrayal and lies. And in the center of it all, standing beneath the chandelier with that damned self-satisfied grin, is Ethan. His eyes glint with a feral intensity as he cradles the full Velvet Charm, the last piece we need to end this, to be free. I almost laugh at the theatricality of it—of course he would choose this moment, this room, to make his final stand.

"So you made it this far," he says, voice dripping with mock surprise. "I suppose I underestimated you...again." His gaze slides to where Damian stands beside me, and his lip curls. "And you, my friend. How low you've fallen."

Damian doesn't respond immediately. He stands tall, steady, his hand still entwined with mine, like a silent vow he doesn't need to say aloud. "You call it falling," he finally says, his voice cool, deadly. "I call it waking up."

Ethan's face twists, his confidence cracking just slightly, though his grip on the Velvet Charm tightens. "Waking up to what? To her?" He laughs, a cruel sound that echoes through the empty hall. "She's your weakness, Damian. She always was. And now, look at you—a traitor, a fool, all for a girl who will ruin you."

I feel Damian's hand tense in mine, the anger simmering just below the surface, but I squeeze his fingers before he can say a word. I take a step forward, my voice calm, though I feel anything but. "Funny, Ethan, I thought loyalty was supposed to mean something to you. Or is that just another lie you tell yourself to justify every terrible thing you've done?"

He scowls, and there's a flicker of doubt in his eyes, gone almost as quickly as it appears. "You know nothing," he sneers. "Loyalty is power, control. It's not some childish promise to be kept or broken at whim. You don't have the strength to understand that."

"Strength?" I echo, a bitter smile tugging at my lips. "You don't know the first thing about strength. You only know fear. That's what this is about, isn't it? You're afraid of us, of what we could be together. You're terrified because we chose each other over your precious rules, your precious control."

The air between us crackles, thick with unspoken words and old wounds. Ethan glares, the Velvet Charm pulsing in his hand, casting a strange, eerie glow that flickers over his face. His mouth twists, a hint of desperation slipping through his composed facade. "You want to be free?" he spits. "Fine. But freedom comes with a cost. Let's see if you're willing to pay it."

In a heartbeat, he raises the Velvet Charm, and the room darkens, shadows stretching and twisting as the magic within the stone flares. I can feel it, the pull of power like a magnetic force, raw and consuming. My heart pounds, fear skittering down my spine, but I stand my ground, meeting his gaze, unyielding.

Damian steps forward, and his voice is like steel. "You're not the only one who understands power, Ethan." He raises his free hand, and with a flick of his wrist, a blaze of light erupts between us, fire roaring to life, bright and fierce. It curls around him, around us both, a barrier of flame that shimmers, casting the room in golden hues. "And you're not the only one willing to fight for it."

For a moment, Ethan hesitates, his expression faltering as he looks between us, the fire and the bond that holds us together, stronger than anything he could break. But then he snarls, his face contorted with fury. "You think you're strong? Then prove it," he hisses, thrusting the Velvet Charm forward, unleashing a torrent of dark energy that collides with the flames, sending shockwaves through the air.

The ground trembles beneath us, and I tighten my grip on Damian's hand, my other clutching the shard of the Velvet Charm, still pulsing faintly. I channel everything I have into that shard, pouring my will, my love, my defiance into it, feeling it grow warm, then hot, as it connects with Damian's power, the two forces merging into something new, something greater.

Together, we step forward, a united front against the darkness, our combined strength radiating outward in waves that push Ethan back, his own power struggling against the sheer force of our will. I can see the fear in his eyes now, real and raw, as he realizes that he's not as invincible as he thought. We press on, unwavering, and with a final, blinding burst of light, our magic collides with his, shattering the hold he once had over us.

Ethan's words linger, poisonous in the silence. His mocking sneer twists my stomach, but I can't let it show. Not now, not when we're so close. Damian's hand in mine is steady, grounding me, a reminder that despite every twisted corner and every wall of fire, he's here. We're here. Together. I take a deep breath, feeling the sharp sting of magic in the air, the volatile hum of our powers locked in this tense dance, waiting to collide.

"So, what's it like, Ethan?" I ask, my voice loud in the eerie stillness. "Being this desperate, this... afraid?" My words come out sharp, deliberate, a calculated challenge I hope will prick his vanity just enough to distract him. "You, the fearless leader of the Crimson Society. Shaking in your boots."

He narrows his eyes, the muscles in his jaw flexing as he laughs, a low, dangerous sound. "Afraid? Oh, please." He holds the Velvet Charm aloft, its dark energy swirling around him, seeping into his skin, making his features look carved from shadow. "I hold the most powerful artifact in existence," he sneers. "You two are nothing but sparks dancing in my flames."

"Flames burn out, you know," Damian says, his voice calm, though his fingers tighten just slightly around mine. He knows as well as I do that this is a gamble, a reckless one at that. The power emanating from Ethan is unlike anything we've ever faced—vicious, ravenous, as though the Charm itself has a will, a hunger for more than just magic.

"Cute," Ethan replies with a sneer, his gaze sliding from Damian to me, dismissive, almost bored. "And what exactly do you two plan to do? Talk me into submission?"

VEIL DAWN 197

"No," I say, a hint of a smile tugging at my lips. "We just plan to beat you."

For the briefest moment, I see something flash in his eyes—hesitation, maybe even fear—but he masks it quickly, his posture shifting as he raises the Velvet Charm. The air around him shimmers, distorts, and I feel a rush of power surging toward us. Instinctively, I brace myself, grounding my energy, feeling Damian's presence beside me like a steady drumbeat in my veins.

But then something happens, something neither of us expected. Just as the wave of dark energy crashes toward us, the shard of the Velvet Charm in my hand begins to glow, faint at first, then brighter, until it's pulsing with a fierce, defiant light. It's as though it's answering Ethan's power, a rebellious spark against the oppressive darkness.

"What is this?" Ethan snarls, his expression shifting from confidence to something more uncertain. "How are you—?"

I don't give him time to finish. Channeling everything I have into the shard, I thrust it forward, meeting his energy head-on. There's a blinding flash, a force so intense it sends shockwaves through the room, rattling the chandeliers, cracking the walls. I hear Damian shout something, his voice lost in the roar of energy as our combined powers clash with Ethan's.

For a moment, I think we might have overestimated ourselves. The weight of Ethan's magic presses down, suffocating, like a tidal wave swallowing us whole. My knees buckle, and I feel Damian's arm around my waist, steadying me, his own power flickering, struggling to hold back the dark flood. But then, just when it seems like we're about to be overwhelmed, the shard in my hand pulses again, stronger this time, a surge of warmth that fills me, pushes back against the darkness.

It's then that I realize something Ethan doesn't—something he could never understand. This isn't just about power. It's about connection, trust, the raw, unyielding force of two people who would risk everything for each other. He may have the full Velvet Charm, but he's alone, consumed by his own greed and fear. And that, I realize, is his greatest weakness.

Ethan's face contorts as he realizes he's losing ground. His grip on the Velvet Charm tightens, his expression growing wild, desperate. "You think this changes anything?" he shouts, voice raw with fury. "You're fools if you believe you can beat me!"

"Maybe," Damian replies, his voice a low, steady challenge. "But I'd rather be a fool with her than a coward with power."

The words hang in the air, potent, laced with a kind of defiance that makes something in Ethan snap. He lets out a roar, unleashing a torrent of energy that slams into us with the force of a hurricane. I grit my teeth, the shard in my hand blazing, meeting his power with our own. The energy twists, writhes, until I can barely see through the swirling maelstrom of light and shadow.

And then, suddenly, it's over.

The light fades, the darkness recedes, and for a moment, there's only silence, a strange, echoing stillness that fills the shattered hall. I look around, disoriented, trying to catch my breath. Ethan is standing a few feet away, his chest heaving, his expression one of shock and disbelief. The Velvet Charm in his hand has dimmed, its power diminished, the once-brilliant stone now a dull, lifeless gray.

"You...you did this," he stammers, his voice shaking as he stares at the Charm, as though it's betrayed him. "How did you—"

"It's over, Ethan," I say, my voice quiet but firm, the finality of it settling over us like a weight. "You lost."

He looks at me, his eyes wide, panicked, like a cornered animal. For a moment, I almost feel sorry for him. Almost. But then he bares his teeth in a snarl, clutching the Velvet Charm like a lifeline. "This isn't over," he hisses. "You'll regret this. I'll make sure of it."

Without warning, he turns, his form blurring as he vanishes into the shadows, leaving behind only the echo of his threat, a chilling reminder that this victory, though hard-won, may not be the end.

I let out a shaky breath, the weight of exhaustion settling over me. I turn to Damian, his face a mixture of relief and something else, something softer. He opens his mouth to say something, but I beat him to it, offering a wry smile as I tuck the shard into my pocket.

"Well," I say, trying to sound nonchalant despite the lingering adrenaline coursing through me. "That was... fun."

Damian lets out a low chuckle, shaking his head as he pulls me into a hug, his arms warm and solid around me. "You really are something else," he murmurs, his voice filled with a kind of awe that makes my cheeks flush.

"Yeah, well, I had a good teacher," I reply, my voice muffled against his chest. I pull back, meeting his gaze, the intensity in his eyes making my heart skip a beat.

For the first time in a long time, I feel a glimmer of hope, a sense that maybe—just maybe—we can leave this nightmare behind and find something worth fighting for. And with Damian by my side, I know that whatever comes next, we'll face it together.

The hall feels empty without Ethan's presence, but the silence is deceptive, coiled tight like a snake about to strike. I feel the reverberations of our struggle in the stone walls, the floor cracked and smoking where his dark magic collided with our light. Damian and I stand there, just the two of us in the aftermath, breaths shallow, the adrenaline fading, leaving only the exhaustion and the sting of half-healed bruises. My hand slips from his as I brace myself against the wall, and he watches me, a mixture of pride and worry etched across his face.

"You really should stop doing that," he says, his voice soft yet tinged with exasperation. "Saving us both by sheer willpower alone."

I manage a tired smile, looking up at him through a few loose strands of hair plastered to my forehead. "Well, someone has to be the reckless one," I reply, only half-joking. "It's practically my job description by now."

He lets out a low chuckle, though his eyes are still shadowed with concern. But before he can respond, a faint sound catches my attention, a distant rumbling that makes my heart skip. It's faint, like an echo, yet unmistakably there, a reminder that Ethan's parting words were more than empty threats. A cold dread settles over me, and I feel Damian tense beside me, his gaze shifting toward the door.

We barely have time to exchange a look before the floor beneath us trembles, the cracks deepening, spreading like veins through stone. Somewhere in the distance, I hear the faint, rhythmic thud of boots. Lots of them. I straighten, the exhaustion slipping away as my instincts sharpen, my pulse quickening.

"Reinforcements?" I murmur, glancing at Damian.

He nods, his jaw tightening. "Looks like he had a backup plan." His voice is grim, but there's a spark of determination in his eyes, a familiar fire that reignites my own resolve. "We need to move."

With a final glance at the ruined hall, I grab his hand, and we take off, weaving through corridors and half-collapsed archways, our footsteps echoing in the silence. I can feel the weight of every second pressing down on us, each turn we take fraught with the danger of running straight into a trap. But we keep going, moving through the shadows, relying on the faint, distant glow of moonlight through cracked windows to guide us.

As we near the outer courtyard, the rumbling intensifies, a steady, oppressive force that shakes the ground and rattles the doors we pass. I cast a worried glance at Damian, whose expression has turned steely, a flicker of frustration flashing in his eyes. He stops abruptly, pulling me into an alcove just as a group of Crimson

Society guards rounds the corner, their dark cloaks billowing as they march past, oblivious to our presence.

He looks at me, his voice barely a whisper. "They're searching the grounds. We don't have much time."

"Then let's not waste it," I reply, my voice equally quiet, though my heart pounds louder than I'd like. I feel the fragment of the Velvet Charm in my pocket, the comforting pulse of its residual magic against my fingers, and an idea begins to form, reckless and desperate but possibly our only chance.

I pull it out, meeting Damian's questioning gaze. "I think there's still enough power in this shard to create a diversion," I say, carefully holding it between us. "If I can channel it—just enough to make them think we're going one way while we slip out another…"

His brows knit in concern. "Are you sure? That thing nearly burned you alive last time."

"I'll be careful," I say, though I'm not entirely certain it's possible to be "careful" when dealing with volatile magic. But he doesn't protest, his hand coming up to cover mine, steadying me as I close my eyes and focus on the shard's warmth, feeling its magic prickling under my skin.

The power flares to life, brighter and hotter than I anticipated, and I bite back a gasp as it courses through me, like holding onto lightning. But I grit my teeth, channeling the energy, letting it flow outward, creating a pulsing illusion of light and sound that radiates down the hallway in the opposite direction.

It works. The guards stop, their attention snapping to the false trail as they take off in the wrong direction, weapons drawn, their voices a chaotic blur in the distance. I open my eyes, releasing the shard, which dims, its energy spent, leaving my fingers tingling and my breath shaky.

Damian squeezes my hand, a mixture of admiration and exasperation on his face. "Remind me to never doubt your ability to make a scene."

I manage a grin, though the effort leaves me weak, and he slips an arm around me, guiding us forward as we hurry toward the exit. But as we reach the edge of the courtyard, a figure steps out of the shadows, blocking our path. My heart sinks as I recognize him—one of Ethan's closest advisors, a man I'd hoped never to see again.

"Leaving so soon?" His voice is oily, his smile cold and calculated. He leans against the doorway, his arms crossed, watching us with an unsettling gleam in his eyes. "Ethan warned me about you two. Said you'd try something foolish like this."

Damian steps in front of me, his body tense, a wall of defiance between me and this new threat. "We're done taking orders from Ethan. Step aside, and we won't make this any uglier than it has to be."

The advisor laughs, low and mocking. "Oh, I don't think you're in any position to make demands. In fact, I think you'll find that your little act of rebellion ends here." With a flick of his wrist, he conjures a barrier, a shimmering wall of energy that hums with power, trapping us in the courtyard.

I feel a surge of frustration, my hands clenching as I stare at the barrier, at the advisor's smug face. Every nerve in my body screams to fight, to break through, but the faint ache from the Velvet Charm's residual power warns me that I'm not fully recovered. Damian, however, steps forward, his expression hardening, and I can see the resolve in his eyes, a promise of retribution.

"We don't have to do this," he says, his voice cold. "But if you insist—"

"Oh, I insist," the advisor sneers, his fingers curling as he prepares another spell. The energy around him darkens, crackling with a menacing intensity that makes my stomach twist. I can feel the threat in the air, thick and electric, and every instinct in me is shouting to run, but there's nowhere to go.

Damian shifts, positioning himself defensively, and I know that whatever happens next, we're going to have to fight our way out. I reach for the last reserves of strength I have, feeling the faint flicker of the Velvet Charm's magic, ready to use whatever's left.

But before I can act, a sound cuts through the tense silence—a low, rumbling groan, like the earth itself is waking up. The ground shudders, stones shifting underfoot, and a crack snakes through the courtyard, widening with each second, as though something buried deep within the castle is trying to break free.

The advisor's smug expression falters, his eyes darting to the ground, panic flickering across his face. Damian and I exchange a look, both of us poised, uncertain, as the crack expands, a yawning chasm splitting the courtyard in two.

And then, with a deafening roar, the ground gives way.

Chapter 19: Shattered Crowns

Ethan's laugh echoes down the hall, a low, venomous sound that crawls up my spine. There's nothing left of the boy I once knew—just this creature with hollow eyes, wielding the Velvet Charm as though it's an extension of his very soul. I watch as the dark energy coils around his fingers, twisting and writhing like a thousand snakes, ready to strike. Damian stands beside me, his grip tightening on my hand as we face Ethan together, his steady presence grounding me in a moment that threatens to sweep me away. Every nerve in my body is on high alert, every instinct screaming at me to run, to hide, but I force myself to stand tall.

"Give it up, Ethan," I say, my voice stronger than I feel. "There's nothing left for you here."

Ethan's smirk deepens, and the dark magic intensifies, flooding the room with a sickly, suffocating heat. "Oh, but there is. You'll see." He lifts his hand, and the Velvet Charm blazes to life, a roiling mass of shadow that pulses with a heartbeat I can feel vibrating through the air. The walls tremble, cracks spidering out from where his power hits, jagged lines spreading like veins through the stone.

Damian squeezes my hand, a silent reminder of the bond we share. We move as one, a seamless rhythm born of countless battles fought side by side. He draws his sword, and I can feel the familiar hum of my own magic rising within me, a warmth that drowns out the chill of Ethan's darkness. Together, we are unstoppable. Or at least, we were—until today.

Ethan's laughter fades, replaced by a look of grim determination as he launches forward, the Velvet Charm swirling around him like a cloak of shadows. His movements are erratic, unpredictable, and it takes every ounce of focus I have to keep up, to block each attack with magic that feels weaker against his relentless onslaught. Damian is beside me, striking at the shadows that dart in from every angle, but for every blow we land, Ethan's darkness grows thicker, more consuming.

"Stay close," Damian murmurs, his voice rough and urgent. His eyes flash with an intensity I've only seen once before, and I know he's willing to do whatever it takes to stop Ethan, even if it means risking everything. I swallow hard, the weight of his words sinking in as I brace myself for whatever comes next.

Ethan's gaze flickers over us, his smirk twisting into something colder, harder. "You think you can fight me? With that little spark you call magic?" He raises his hand, and the Velvet Charm lashes out like a living thing, a torrent of shadow that crashes against us with the force of a tidal wave. I feel myself being thrown back, my body slamming into the wall with a force that rattles my bones.

Damian's hand slips from mine, and for a terrifying moment, I'm alone, gasping for air as the darkness closes in around me. I can hear his voice somewhere in the distance, calling my name, but the shadows are thick, oppressive, pressing down on me with a weight that feels insurmountable. I close my eyes, reaching deep within myself for the warmth of my magic, for anything that can push back against the crushing darkness.

And then, just as I think I'm lost, I feel it—a spark, a faint flicker of light that pulses with a warmth I know is Damian's. I cling to it, letting it anchor me as I force myself to stand, my body trembling but unbroken. I reach out, feeling the connection between us strengthening, our bond a tether that pulls me back from the edge.

Damian's voice is closer now, steady and unyielding. "We can do this. Together."

I nod, the words sinking into me like a lifeline. We close the distance between us, our hands finding each other once more, and I can feel his magic mingling with mine, a power that feels stronger than anything I've ever known. Together, we face Ethan, our combined strength a wall of light against his darkness.

But Ethan is relentless. He lashes out again, the Velvet Charm a storm of shadows that slams into us, testing the limits of our bond. I feel Damian falter beside me, his strength wavering, and for a brief, heart-stopping moment, I think he's going to fall. But then he turns to me, his eyes blazing with a fierce determination that sends a shiver down my spine.

"Take it," he says, his voice barely a whisper, but there's a weight to his words that makes my heart skip a beat. "Take my power. Use it."

I shake my head, fear clawing at me. "I can't—"

"You can," he insists, his grip tightening on my hand. "Together, we're stronger than he is. But you have to trust me."

I swallow hard, the gravity of his words settling over me. I close my eyes, reaching out with my magic, and I feel Damian's power flowing into me, a steady pulse that fills me with a warmth that drowns out Ethan's darkness. It's overwhelming, a flood of energy that feels like it's going to tear me apart, but I hold on, focusing on the bond between us, letting it ground me.

Ethan watches, his smirk fading as he realizes what we're doing. "No," he snarls, his voice thick with desperation. He raises the Velvet Charm, but it's too late. I can feel the power building within me, a force stronger than anything I've ever felt, and with a final, desperate surge, I release it, a blinding wave of light that crashes into Ethan with the force of a thousand storms.

The Velvet Charm shatters, fragments scattering across the floor like shards of glass, and for a moment, there is nothing but silence, a heavy stillness that settles over the room like a shroud. I feel Damian's hand in mine, his warmth grounding me as I try to catch my breath, my heart pounding in my chest.

When I finally look up, I see Ethan on the ground, his form crumpled and defeated, the darkness that once surrounded him fading into nothingness. The curse that has haunted us for so long is broken, the weight of it lifting from my shoulders like a heavy cloak.

Damian squeezes my hand, and I turn to him, a smile breaking through the exhaustion. We've fought for so long, but in this moment, I know it was worth every sacrifice, every struggle. The future we've dreamed of is finally within reach, a future free from the shadows that once threatened to consume us.

The air crackles with the remnants of magic, and silence settles over us, thick and heavy. My hand still clings to Damian's, his fingers warm against mine, grounding me in the surreal quiet that follows a battle that felt like it might never end. I can hardly believe that Ethan is really gone, that the Velvet Charm—the instrument of so much pain, betrayal, and ruin—lies in shattered fragments around us. I pull my hand free from Damian's, kneeling to pick up one of the pieces. It's cold, unnervingly so, the jagged edges biting into my palm as if it holds a grudge, even in pieces. I let it slip back to the ground, unwilling to hold on to even a fragment of its malice.

Damian stands beside me, his eyes still wary, a shadow of fatigue etched across his face, but he looks at me with something I haven't seen in what feels like a lifetime: hope. His face softens, and despite the bruises and weariness lining his features, he gives me a crooked smile.

"That's the last time we let a centuries-old cursed artifact anywhere near our family," he says, his tone light but his eyes heavy. It's the kind of joke he makes to cover the weight of what we've done, what we've survived, and I can't help but laugh, even as I feel my heart twist in my chest.

"Agreed," I reply, shaking my head. "Next time, we'll keep our curses under lock and key. Preferably buried at the bottom of the ocean."

He lets out a dry chuckle, but the sound is clipped, as if he's holding something back. There's a flicker in his eyes, a darkness I've come to recognize as regret, or perhaps guilt, though he would never admit it aloud. Damian has always carried more than his share of burdens, and I know that what we did today will only add to that weight.

"Hey," I say, reaching out to touch his arm, grounding him in the same way he's done for me countless times. "We did what we had to. It's over now."

For a moment, he just looks at me, his eyes searching mine, as if looking for something he's afraid he won't find. Then, he nods, a barely-there dip of his head, but it's enough. He takes a breath, and some of the tension melts from his shoulders. The battle may be over, but I can tell he's still holding on to the remnants of the fear that gripped him, the fear that we might not survive this, that he might lose me or himself in the process.

Just as I think we might be able to leave this room, to walk away from the broken crown and the dark memories it holds, I hear a low rumble. The sound is faint at first, like the distant roll of thunder, but it grows louder, the floor beneath us trembling. I look at Damian, panic flaring in my chest.

"Please tell me that's just the castle settling," I murmur, though we both know better.

He grabs my hand, pulling me toward the door. "Run," he says, his voice a sharp command that brooks no argument.

We sprint down the corridor, the ground shaking beneath our feet as the castle seems to groan in protest, as if the very stones are rebelling against what we've done. The Velvet Charm's power was woven into the fabric of this place, and now that it's been destroyed, the foundation itself is crumbling, unraveling the ancient spellwork that held it together.

"Damian, what's happening?" I shout over the deafening roar of collapsing walls.

"We broke the curse," he replies, his voice strained. "But we also broke the magic that held this place together. We need to get out before—"

A beam crashes down in front of us, cutting off his words and our path. Dust billows up around us, thick and choking, and I cough, blinking through the haze to find another way forward. I can feel Damian's hand on my arm, steadying me as we stumble through the chaos, dodging falling debris and gaping holes that open up in the floor.

We make it to the grand staircase, but half of it has collapsed, the stone steps crumbled into a pile of rubble. Damian glances at me, and I can see the wheels turning in his mind, calculating our options. There's a determination in his eyes, a refusal to let this place claim us, and I feel a spark of that same fire ignite in me. We've come too far to be defeated by this castle's last act of vengeance.

Without a word, he pulls me toward a narrow passageway, one of the hidden corridors that wind through the walls of the castle. It's dark and cramped, the air thick with dust, but it's our only chance. We squeeze through, the walls pressing in on either side, and I have to fight the urge to panic as the sound of collapsing stone echoes around us.

"Just a little further," Damian says, his voice a reassuring murmur in the darkness. I cling to the sound, letting it guide me as we navigate the twisting passage, the weight of the castle bearing down on us with every step.

Finally, we emerge into the open air, stumbling out onto the edge of the cliff where the castle sits, towering over the valley below. I take a deep breath, filling my lungs with the crisp night air, the cool breeze a stark contrast to the oppressive heat of the castle's collapse. I look back at the ruins, the once-grand fortress now reduced to rubble, and a strange mixture of relief and sadness washes over me.

Damian is beside me, his gaze fixed on the remains of the castle, and I can see the weight of everything we've lost reflected in his eyes. This place held memories, both good and terrible, and now it's gone, buried beneath the rubble of its own making.

"It's strange," he murmurs, his voice barely audible over the wind. "I thought I'd feel... more relieved. But all I feel is—"

"Empty?" I finish, and he nods, a small, sad smile tugging at the corners of his mouth.

We stand there in silence, watching as the last remnants of the castle settle into the earth, a tomb for the secrets it held, for the curses we've broken and the lives we've left behind. There's a finality to it, a sense that we're leaving more than just stones and memories behind. We're leaving a part of ourselves, a part of the story that brought us here, and I don't know if we'll ever truly be free of it.

But as Damian's hand finds mine once more, I feel a spark of something new—a glimmer of hope, fragile and flickering, but real. We've survived this, and whatever comes next, we'll face it together.

The cliff stretches out beneath us, the wind whipping through my hair, biting at the edges of my torn cloak. I can feel Damian's eyes on me, but I can't look at him, not yet. The silence between us feels both charged and oddly empty, like the aftermath of a storm that hasn't quite ended. We've escaped the castle, escaped Ethan, but something tells me we're not done yet, that there's still a thread left untied, a shadow lurking in the corners of this quiet night.

I take a shaky breath, forcing my gaze down toward the valley below, where the mist curls along the riverbank, silver and ghostly in the moonlight. It should look peaceful, but I know better. Magic rarely lets go that easily. There's always a price, always a toll that demands to be paid in full, and I can't shake the feeling that we've only paid the down payment on this particular deal.

Damian shifts beside me, his hand brushing against mine. "Penny for your thoughts?" His voice is soft, too soft, and it makes my skin prickle with unease.

"Maybe they're worth more than that," I murmur, trying to inject a note of levity into my voice. But he sees right through it, his mouth quirking up in that infuriatingly knowing way that always makes me feel like he's one step ahead, even when he's just as clueless as I am.

"Probably," he replies, his smile fading as he studies me with a seriousness that's all too rare. "But I don't think either of us can afford the price right now."

I laugh, a hollow sound that feels strange in the open air. "No, probably not," I admit, glancing at him from the corner of my eye. His face is cast in shadows, but I can see the hard set of his jaw, the tension still coiled in his shoulders, and it hits me that he's just as uneasy as I am.

The wind picks up, and I shiver, pulling my cloak tighter around me. Damian notices, stepping closer so that our shoulders touch, his warmth seeping into me despite the chill in the air. For a moment, I let myself lean into him, taking comfort in the solidness of his presence, in the steadiness he exudes even when I know he's just as lost as I am.

But the moment doesn't last. A faint rustle in the trees below catches my attention, a flicker of movement in the shadows, and I stiffen, my hand instinctively going to the dagger at my belt. Damian notices, his gaze following mine to the dark line of trees along the edge of the clearing.

"Did you see that?" I whisper, my voice barely audible over the wind.

He nods, his body tensing as he shifts into a defensive stance, his hand going to the hilt of his sword. "Stay close," he murmurs, his tone low and deadly serious.

We move as one, stepping quietly along the edge of the cliff, our eyes trained on the shadows below. I strain to see, to catch any sign of movement, but the darkness is thick, impenetrable, and I can feel the hairs on the back of my neck standing on end. Whoever—or whatever—is out there, they're hiding well.

And then I hear it—a low, guttural growl, barely more than a whisper but enough to send a jolt of adrenaline through me. I tighten my grip on my dagger, my pulse racing as I glance at Damian, his expression grim but resolute.

The growl grows louder, closer, and I catch a glimpse of something in the shadows—a pair of eyes, glowing faintly in the darkness, watching us with a predatory intensity that makes my blood run cold. I swallow hard, forcing myself to breathe, to stay calm, but every instinct in my body is screaming at me to run.

Damian takes a step forward, positioning himself between me and the creature, his sword drawn and ready. "Stay behind me," he says, his voice a low command that leaves no room for argument.

I grit my teeth, resisting the urge to protest. I may not be as strong as Damian, but I'm not helpless, and the thought of standing idly by while he faces whatever horror lurks in the shadows doesn't sit well with me. But I know better than to argue, not now, not when every second could mean the difference between life and death.

The creature steps forward, emerging from the shadows, and I feel my heart drop. It's massive, its body covered in thick, matted fur, its eyes glowing with a malevolent intelligence that sends a shiver down my spine. Its mouth is twisted into a snarl, rows of razor-sharp teeth glinting in the moonlight, and I realize with a sickening jolt that this is no ordinary beast. This is something darker, something twisted by magic, and I can feel the remnants of the Velvet Charm's curse lingering around it, a dark aura that clings to it like a second skin.

"Damian," I whisper, my voice barely audible over the pounding of my heart. "That thing... it's part of the curse. It's not over. Not yet."

He doesn't respond, his focus entirely on the creature as it circles us, its movements slow and deliberate, as if savoring the moment, drawing out the tension. I can feel the magic coiled within me, a flickering ember that I know I'll need to use, but I'm afraid—afraid of what it might cost, of what piece of myself I might lose in the process.

The creature lunges, and everything happens in a blur. Damian moves in a flash, his sword slicing through the air as he steps between me and the beast, but it's fast—faster than anything that size has any right to be. It dodges his attack, its claws raking across his arm, and I hear him grunt in pain, blood staining his sleeve as he stumbles back.

A surge of anger flares within me, hot and fierce, and I feel the magic rise, unbidden, a wave of power that pulses through me, demanding to be unleashed. I don't think, don't hesitate—I just act, thrusting my hand forward as a burst of light erupts from my palm, slamming into the creature with a force that sends it reeling.

But it's not enough. The creature recovers, snarling as it lunges at me, its eyes blazing with fury. I brace myself, my heart pounding as I prepare for the impact, but before it can reach me, Damian is there, his sword plunging into its side with a brutal efficiency that leaves no room for mercy.

The creature lets out a final, agonized roar before collapsing to the ground, its body shuddering as it takes its last breath. I stand there, panting, my hand still outstretched, the remnants of my magic flickering in the air around me.

But before I can fully process what's happened, I hear another growl—this time from behind us. I whirl around, my heart sinking as I see another pair of eyes gleaming in the darkness, followed by another, and then another, until a whole pack of creatures emerges from the shadows, their eyes fixed on us with a hunger that sends a chill down my spine.

"Damian," I whisper, my voice trembling as I back up, my gaze darting between the creatures. "There's... there's more of them."

He glances at me, his face pale but determined, his jaw set as he raises his sword, his eyes meeting mine with a fierce resolve that makes my heart clench. We're outnumbered, outmatched, but I know one thing for certain: we're not going down without a fight.

The creatures close in, their growls filling the air, and I take a deep breath, preparing myself for the battle to come, for whatever price we might have to pay to survive. The night stretches out before us, dark and endless, and as the first creature lunges, I raise my dagger, ready to face whatever fate awaits us.

Chapter 20: Embers and Echoes

The early morning light filters through the soot-streaked windows, casting an eerie glow over the abandoned theater. Dust floats in beams of sunlight, and the silence feels thick, almost like a held breath. Every sound, every small creak from the worn floorboards, seems amplified. Damian's grip on my hand tightens, and it's the only thing grounding me as we pick our way through the remnants of the Velvet Charm. Shards of its glass-like structure litter the floor, glistening in the dawn light, taunting us with the fragility of our victory.

A low chuckle rumbles from Damian, humorless and tinged with exhaustion. "Can't believe we made it out," he mutters, his voice barely more than a whisper, as if he's afraid to shatter the brittle calm surrounding us.

I manage a grim smile. "Me either. We're supposed to be the ones who survive by the skin of our teeth, aren't we?" I'm not sure if I'm asking him or myself. I don't know if we're survivors or just two reckless people lucky enough to still be standing.

We reach the exit, the large brass doors swinging open with a groan. The air outside feels lighter, fresher, as if the city itself is breathing a sigh of relief that one more piece of the Crimson Society's dark influence has crumbled. But as I take a deep inhale, savoring the cool morning breeze, a bitter realization settles over me.

"They're not done with us, are they?" My voice sounds hollow, even to my own ears. "The Crimson Society isn't the kind to let something like this go."

Damian's jaw clenches, a muscle in his cheek twitching as he looks away, his gaze sweeping over the cityscape stretching before us. His silence is answer enough, and I feel the weight of it pressing down, settling like stones in my stomach. I want to shake him, make him promise that we're done, that we can walk away and find some semblance of peace. But I know better than that by now. In our world, peace is an illusion, a soft dream in a world of sharp edges and cold shadows.

He turns back to me, his eyes shadowed but resolute. "We might have taken out the Velvet Charm, but there are more weapons where that came from. They won't stop until they either own us or destroy us."

"Then they'll be sorely disappointed." I force a smile, but my heart feels tight. The Crimson Society has never been disappointed in their lives, and I have no reason to believe they'll start now. Still, there's a sliver of satisfaction in knowing we've dealt them a blow, even if it's temporary. I cling to it, knowing I'll need every ounce of courage for what's coming.

Damian's hand finds mine again, and this time, his grip is firmer, steady. "Whatever comes next, we face it together. I meant that."

My chest aches with a mixture of relief and dread. The warmth of his hand, the sureness in his eyes—it's a balm, a promise, a reckless vow in the face of impossible odds. And, somehow, it's enough to make me take that first step forward, down the cracked stone steps, away from the wreckage of our battle and into the unknown.

We walk through the quiet streets, our footsteps echoing in the early morning stillness. The city feels strange in this light, washed clean but somehow unreal, as if the battle we just survived has shifted everything slightly out of place. It's a lull, a calm that I know won't last. The Crimson Society will come for us, and when they do, they'll come with everything they have. But in this moment, as Damian and I move through the empty streets, I let myself pretend that we're just two people walking home after a long night. No vendettas, no life-or-death struggles, just us.

As we turn a corner, Damian tugs me to a stop, his gaze locked on something up ahead. I follow his line of sight, my breath catching as I realize what he's staring at. A small group of figures stands silhouetted in the street, cloaked and motionless, watching us with an unnerving stillness. They're far enough away that I can't make out their faces, but the insignia on their cloaks gleams in the early light—a twisted, thorny rose, dripping with crimson.

The Crimson Society.

I freeze, every nerve in my body on high alert. Beside me, Damian shifts subtly, his posture tensing, his hand slipping from mine as he takes a step forward, positioning himself protectively in front of me. My heart pounds in my chest, a frantic rhythm that feels all too loud in the silent street.

One of the figures steps forward, his movements slow and deliberate, as if he's savoring every second of our fear. His face is hidden in the shadows of his hood, but I can feel his gaze on us, cold and calculating, a predator eyeing its prey.

"Well, well," he drawls, his voice a slick, oily sound that makes my skin crawl. "I was beginning to wonder if you two would make it out of that little theater. I must say, you've exceeded our expectations."

My fists clench at my sides, the anger rising up to burn away the fear. "Sorry to disappoint," I snap, my voice sharp and defiant. "Guess you underestimated us."

The figure chuckles, a low, mocking sound that sets my teeth on edge. "Oh, not at all. In fact, we were rather counting on it. You've proven to be... most entertaining." He pauses, tilting his head slightly, and I get the distinct impression he's smiling beneath his hood. "But playtime is over. The Society has given you enough leeway. It's time to bring this little rebellion of yours to a close."

Damian shifts beside me, his voice a low, dangerous murmur. "We're not going anywhere with you."

The man sighs, as if he's disappointed, but there's an unmistakable gleam of satisfaction in his tone. "Oh, I think you'll find you don't have much choice. The Society is quite determined when it comes to matters of... loyalty."

He lifts a hand, and the other cloaked figures take a step forward, their movements synchronized and menacing. My heart races, my mind scrambling for a plan, an escape, anything that will get us out of this. But we're cornered, outnumbered, and I can feel the weight of our earlier fight dragging at me, the exhaustion seeping into my bones.

Damian's hand brushes against mine, a brief, grounding touch that steadies me, reminds me of the promise we made. Whatever comes next, we face it together.

Damian doesn't move, his shoulders squared, his gaze steely. It's as if he's daring the Crimson Society to come closer, to test the patience of someone who has nothing left to lose. The defiance in his stance sends a jolt through me, steadying my heartbeat and igniting something fierce and reckless within me. I step forward, standing by his side, ignoring the dull ache in my legs and the sting of the cuts on my hands. We're battered, bruised, but still here, still standing.

The figure watching us chuckles again, a low, mocking sound that feels like sandpaper against my nerves. He doesn't speak right away, letting the silence settle, thick and heavy. I know this game; I know he's trying to unnerve us, make us feel small. And I hate that it's working, even a little.

Damian's voice slices through the silence, smooth and unyielding. "If you wanted us, you should have sent someone better than a lackey."

There's a flicker of surprise in the figure's stance, a slight shift of weight that betrays his confidence. I hide a smirk, resisting the urge to nudge Damian's arm in approval. It's a risky tactic, goading them like this, but it's the only one we have left. If we show any hint of weakness, they'll pounce, and we'll be back in chains before the sun finishes rising.

The figure steps forward, his footsteps echoing against the cracked pavement, and I can feel his gaze shift between us, assessing, calculating. "Bravado is charming," he drawls, "but ultimately, futile. The Society will always be a step ahead. Surely you've realized that by now."

"I've realized something," I say, my voice sharper than I intended, the words spilling out before I can stop them. "I've realized that your precious Society is afraid. Afraid of people who know too much, who see through the polished façade."

I know I've hit a nerve when his head tilts, just slightly, a flash of something dark crossing his face. He takes a deliberate step closer, and Damian's arm shifts, moving protectively in front of me. I want to tell him I don't need protecting, but I know it's instinct for him—an instinct I've grown to depend on, even if I hate admitting it.

"We're not afraid," the figure sneers, his voice dripping with contempt. "We're patient. There's a difference."

"Maybe," Damian replies, his tone carefully controlled, "but patience can run thin. And right now, it seems like the Society is out of time."

The figure's hand twitches, the faintest hint of a reaction, and for a brief, electrifying moment, I think we've rattled him. But then he regains his composure, his face smoothing into a mask of indifference.

"It doesn't matter what you think," he says, each word slow and deliberate, like he's savoring his own superiority. "The Society has been watching you since the beginning. Every choice you've made, every path you've taken—it was all part of the plan. And now, you're exactly where we wanted you."

A chill races down my spine. I've heard enough of the Society's self-assured monologues to know that they rarely lie outright. They manipulate, twist truths until they're unrecognizable, but outright lies? Those are beneath them. And that thought alone makes my stomach lurch.

"You think you've cornered us?" I force a laugh, hoping it sounds more confident than I feel. "All you've done is give us a reason to fight harder."

Damian's hand brushes against mine, a silent reminder of our promise to face this together. And even though every logical part of me is screaming that we're outmatched, that we're playing a dangerous game with an opponent who has more resources, more influence, I feel a spark of defiance.

The figure sighs, like he's bored with the conversation, and waves a hand toward his cloaked followers. "Enough of this. Take them."

The group behind him moves as one, a shadowy wave converging on us. My body tenses, every instinct on high alert. Beside me, Damian shifts into a fighting stance, his posture calm, poised, like he's done this a thousand times before. And maybe he has. The thought of what he must have endured, what he must have sacrificed to get to this moment, fuels my own resolve.

The first of them lunges, and I sidestep, my instincts kicking in, the adrenaline sharp and unforgiving. I feel Damian at my back, his movements fluid and precise, like a dancer in a deadly ballet. Together, we weave through the onslaught, each movement calculated, each strike deliberate.

But they keep coming, relentless, their faces obscured, their intentions unmistakable. My heart races, my breaths coming in short, ragged gasps. I throw a punch, my fist connecting with the solid weight of an attacker's shoulder, and he stumbles back, momentarily disoriented. But there's no time to revel in the small victory; another one takes his place, moving in with eerie precision.

Damian's voice cuts through the chaos, low and urgent. "We need to get out of here."

I glance around, my mind racing as I search for an escape route, any way out of this mess. The street is narrow, boxed in by tall buildings on either side, the walls casting long shadows that stretch toward us like greedy fingers. We're trapped, hemmed in on all sides.

But then I see it—a narrow alleyway branching off to our left, half-hidden by debris and shadows. It's a slim chance, but it's better than nothing.

"Over there!" I shout, nodding toward the alley. Damian's eyes follow my gaze, and he gives a sharp nod.

We break away, darting toward the alley, our footsteps pounding against the pavement. Behind us, the Society's followers give chase, their footsteps echoing in a chilling rhythm that matches the frantic beating of my heart.

As we reach the alley, I can feel their presence closing in, a relentless force determined to snuff out any hope of escape. But we don't stop. Damian grabs my hand, pulling me forward, urging me to move faster. The world narrows down to the sound of our breaths, the slap of our feet against the ground, and the distant shouts of our pursuers.

We twist through the labyrinthine alleyways, the city a maze of narrow passages and dark corners. Every turn feels like a gamble, every step a risk, but we push forward, fueled by the sheer will to survive.

Finally, we burst into an open space—a quiet courtyard, hidden from the main streets, surrounded by tall, ivy-covered walls. The sound of our pursuers fades, their footsteps growing distant, until there's nothing but the quiet hum of the city in the early morning.

We collapse against the wall, gasping for air, our bodies pressed close in the small, dark space. My heart pounds, adrenaline still coursing through my veins, and I realize that, somehow, we've done it. We've escaped. For now, at least.

Damian looks at me, his face streaked with sweat and grime, a wild light in his eyes. "You alright?" His voice is rough, breathless, but there's a spark of triumph there, too.

I nod, barely able to speak, my chest heaving. But then a grin breaks across my face, unexpected and fierce. "Yeah. I'm more than alright."

I lean against the wall, the coolness of the stone seeping through my jacket and grounding me in the present. The city around us feels quiet, almost serene, like the calm before a storm. Damian's hand lingers on my shoulder, his fingers grazing my collarbone with a touch that feels both comforting and electric. I meet his gaze, and for a brief, disorienting second, I forget about the Crimson Society, our pursuers, the world beyond this tiny courtyard. All I see is him, fierce and unbreakable, his expression a mix of triumph and something else, something softer.

"You know," he says, his voice low and teasing, "this wasn't exactly how I pictured our morning going."

"Oh? And what did you picture?" I arch an eyebrow, my voice coming out more breathless than I'd like. "A quiet coffee, perhaps? Maybe a leisurely stroll without an ambush?"

A smirk tugs at the corner of his mouth. "Something like that. Though I admit, the company is just as good as I imagined." His words are light, but there's a shadow in his eyes, a flicker of vulnerability he tries to mask with humor.

I feel the tension in my shoulders ease, just a fraction. There's a comfort in his banter, a familiar rhythm that's kept us going through all the darkness. It's the only normal thing in this abnormal world, and I cling to it, savoring every second.

"Come on," he says finally, pulling back, his expression shifting to something more guarded. "We need to keep moving. They might have lost us for now, but it won't take them long to figure out where we went."

I nod, swallowing back the urge to argue, to insist we stay here a little longer, let ourselves breathe. But I know he's right. The Crimson Society isn't known for giving up, and they certainly won't start with us. I push off the wall, straightening my shoulders, and fall in step beside him as we slip back into the maze of alleyways.

The streets seem even narrower now, the shadows stretching long and dark, concealing hidden threats in every corner. I can feel the weight of the Velvet Charm's destruction pressing down on us, a silent reminder of the cost of defiance. My senses are on high alert, every sound amplified, every flicker of movement making my pulse race.

Damian glances at me, his expression unreadable. "You're awfully quiet," he murmurs, his voice barely above a whisper.

"Just thinking," I reply, keeping my tone light. "Wondering if we're ever going to get a day that doesn't end with someone trying to kill us."

He chuckles softly, though there's no real humor in it. "If that day ever comes, I'll buy you a drink. Or ten."

"Oh, it'll take at least twenty after all this," I say, flashing him a grin. But the smile doesn't reach my eyes, and I can see the same weariness in his.

The conversation fades as we navigate the twisting streets, and soon we find ourselves in a quieter part of the city, far from the crowded alleys where the Society's spies lurk. It's a part of town I barely recognize, with narrow buildings that lean in toward each other, their facades cracked and faded, a forgotten corner where no one cares to look twice.

"We can hide here for a bit," Damian murmurs, gesturing to an old, boarded-up shop with peeling paint and broken windows. It looks abandoned, forgotten—a perfect hiding spot.

We slip inside, the air stale and thick with dust. The floor creaks beneath our feet, and I resist the urge to cough as the musty scent of old wood fills my lungs. Damian checks the windows, peering through the cracks to make sure we haven't been followed, while I explore the small, cramped space. Shelves line the walls, filled with remnants of a life long abandoned: chipped teacups, yellowed paperbacks, a broken vase with a faded rose still clinging to the bottom.

"It's strange, isn't it?" I say softly, running my fingers along the edge of an old picture frame. "How people just... leave, and all that's left are these little pieces of them, scattered and forgotten."

Damian watches me, his expression unreadable. "Maybe they didn't have a choice. Sometimes leaving is the only way to survive."

I meet his gaze, searching for the meaning behind his words. There's a haunted look in his eyes, a flicker of something painful and raw. I want to ask him what he means, what ghosts he's carrying, but I hold back, sensing that some things are better left unspoken.

Instead, I change the subject, trying to keep my voice steady. "Think we're safe here for a while?"

"For now," he replies, though I can see the doubt in his eyes. "But we'll need a plan if we're going to get out of this city. The Society's reach extends farther than we thought."

I swallow, the weight of our situation settling over me like a cold shroud. "So, what's the plan?"

He hesitates, his gaze shifting to the cracked ceiling as if searching for answers in the crumbling plaster. "There's a contact," he says finally. "Someone who might be able to help. But it's risky."

"Risky?" I snort, crossing my arms. "Have you met us? Risk is practically our middle name."

A ghost of a smile tugs at his lips, but it quickly fades. "This is different. This contact... she's not exactly trustworthy. But she has connections, access to safe routes, ways to get out without the Society tracking us."

I raise an eyebrow. "And why, exactly, would she help us?"

"That's the tricky part," he admits, running a hand through his hair. "She's... let's just say she has her own reasons for wanting to see the Society fall. But she'll demand something in return. She always does."

I let out a low whistle. "Great. So we're going to trust a potentially backstabbing contact with our lives. Sounds like a solid plan."

"Do you have a better one?" He gives me a pointed look, and I bite back a retort, knowing he's right. We're out of options, backed into a corner with nowhere else to turn.

A heavy silence settles between us, filled with unspoken fears and the weight of what lies ahead. I glance around the dim, dusty room, feeling the walls close in on us, the sense of entrapment pressing down like a vice. There's no running from this, no easy escape. The only way out is through, and that thought chills me to the bone.

But before I can voice my doubts, the sound of footsteps outside makes us both freeze. Damian's hand goes to his side, reaching for a weapon he's no longer carrying, and I feel my own pulse spike, a jolt of adrenaline shooting through me.

We exchange a look, and he presses a finger to his lips, signaling for silence. My heart pounds as the footsteps draw closer, each step echoing ominously in the stillness. I barely dare to breathe, my mind racing with possibilities—have they found us? Are we trapped already?

The footsteps stop just outside, and for one agonizing moment, there's nothing but silence. I strain to hear, my nerves stretched taut, every muscle coiled and ready to spring.

Then, a low, familiar voice drifts through the door, and my blood turns to ice.

"Come out, come out, wherever you are," the voice taunts, dripping with menace. "You didn't think it would be that easy, did you?"

Damian's face pales, and I feel my own heart drop. I know that voice all too well. It belongs to the one person I'd hoped we'd never see again. The one person who knows us better than anyone.

The door rattles, the handle twisting, and I feel Damian's hand grip mine, a silent plea for courage.

Chapter 21: Return to Shadows

Damian's jaw is set like granite, his hand wrapped protectively around my wrist as he steers me down a narrow alley that reeks of stale beer and something faintly metallic. I can feel the tightness of his grip; it's not meant to hurt, but the urgency burns hot between us, something fierce and unspoken. I yank my hand free, refusing to be dragged like a child through the backstreets of my own city. I can almost see him grit his teeth, the tension gathering in his shoulders as he glances at me, a sharp look in his dark, unreadable eyes.

"You don't need to hold onto me like I'm going to bolt, Damian. If I wanted to leave, I would've done it already." My voice is steady, though I can't deny that there's a tremor of something I can't name, a quiet, coiling fear, but not fear of him. No, it's something else entirely—something as inevitable as a storm on the horizon.

Damian's gaze softens for just a moment, a flicker of something almost tender slipping through. "You're right," he admits, and it's almost funny how much he hates it, how the words seem to taste bitter on his tongue. "But you're not exactly known for playing it safe, are you?"

I lift my chin, a defiant smirk tugging at my lips. "And you are? Remind me who single-handedly incinerated Ethan's lair without a backward glance?"

His eyes narrow, but there's the smallest hint of a smile lurking there, something unbidden, almost reluctant. "Touché," he says, a word like a murmur, and then he's back to scanning the alley, back to that razor-sharp focus that both unsettles and reassures me.

The city is quieter than it should be. Even this deep into the shadows, you'd expect noise—cars rumbling, someone laughing from a window above, the hum of a television. Instead, it's as if the world itself has pulled back, watching, waiting for what we'll do next. It makes my skin crawl, that weighty silence pressing in on us like a living thing, and I find myself walking closer to Damian, though I'd never admit it. He notices, of course, and his hand hovers near mine, not quite touching but close enough to let me know he's there. I find myself strangely grateful for it.

We weave our way through the labyrinth of alleyways, slipping past the more populated streets, the neon lights of bars and nightclubs casting lurid colors on the walls. There's a strange kind of beauty here, in the stark shadows and splashes of neon, like something out of a dream that's only half-remembered. For all its flaws, this city is my home, and the idea that I'm now a fugitive in it gnaws at me.

As we turn a corner, I notice Damian tense, his gaze fixed ahead, sharp and unyielding. I follow his line of sight and see them—two figures lingering near the entrance of a run-down shop, their faces shadowed, but I recognize the crimson insignia stitched onto their jackets. Crimson Society scouts. Just the sight of that color, bold and defiant, makes my pulse quicken, and I press myself closer to the wall, hoping the darkness will swallow me whole.

Damian gestures subtly, a silent command to stay hidden, and for once, I don't argue. He's watching them like a hawk, his body poised to strike, every inch of him exuding a dangerous energy I can almost feel buzzing through the air. I realize then that this isn't the Damian I'd known before, the one who had always seemed detached, as if he were observing everything from a distance. This is someone else, someone who has every intention of walking into hell if it means he can protect what's his.

And somehow, in some way I still don't fully understand, that includes me.

The scouts linger for a moment longer, muttering something to each other, and then they move on, disappearing into the night like shadows themselves. Damian lets out a breath, and I hadn't even realized he was holding it. He glances at me, his expression unreadable, and I feel a pang of guilt for whatever price he's paying for keeping me safe.

"They're getting closer," he says quietly, his voice low and steady, but I can sense the tension beneath it. "It's only a matter of time before they find us."

"And then what?" I ask, trying to keep the edge of fear out of my voice. "What happens when they do?"

He doesn't answer right away. Instead, he looks at me, really looks at me, as if he's searching for something he's afraid to find. "Then we fight," he says finally, the words heavy, almost resigned. "But not here. We need to get somewhere safe first."

I scoff, a bitter laugh escaping before I can stop it. "Safe? Damian, look around. The Crimson Society has eyes everywhere. There's no 'safe' left in this city, not for us."

He shrugs, unbothered by my sarcasm. "Maybe not, but there are places they wouldn't think to look. Places they don't even know exist."

I raise an eyebrow, skeptical. "And you just happen to know about these places because...?"

For the first time, he allows himself a small, secretive smile, one that's equal parts charming and infuriating. "Let's just say I've been hiding from people long before you came along."

Something about his tone gives me pause, a flicker of doubt threading through my anger. It's easy to forget, in moments like these, that Damian has his own shadows, his own ghosts that he never talks about. And maybe that's why we're drawn to each other—two people who can never quite escape the things that haunt them, but who, for some strange, inexplicable reason, find solace in each other's presence.

Without another word, he takes my hand, his touch surprisingly gentle, and together we slip further into the night, leaving the familiar streets behind. The city fades away, replaced by something darker, something older, as if we're stepping back into a place that time forgot. I feel a chill run down my spine, but Damian's hand in mine steadies me, grounding me in a way I can't explain.

As we move deeper into the shadows, I can't shake the feeling that we're being watched, that the city itself is holding its breath, waiting to see what we'll do next. I glance at Damian, and for a brief, fleeting moment, I see something in his eyes—fear, maybe, or regret, though it's gone as quickly as it appeared. But it's enough to remind me that we're not invincible, that we're two people against a world that wants to consume us.

Damian's steps slow, just enough for me to catch a glimpse of something unfamiliar in his gaze—a flicker of uncertainty, quickly masked by the familiar veneer of cold control. He pauses at a narrow doorway, its paint peeling like old bark, half-hidden between two crumbling buildings. The faded lettering above reads "Sable and Sons Antiques," but the shop windows are thick with dust, displaying nothing but relics of a life long abandoned. He raises an eyebrow at me, an unspoken question, and without waiting for my response, slips inside.

The air within is stale, heavy with the scent of wood polish and mildew, and yet, somehow, it feels oddly comforting. The shop is cluttered, filled with shelves of forgotten treasures—old clocks with cracked faces, tarnished silverware, and stacks of faded books that look as if they haven't felt a human touch in decades. Damian moves through it all with a quiet reverence, his fingers trailing along the edge of a carved cabinet, his shoulders relaxing ever so slightly. It's a rare glimpse of him at ease, and I find myself watching him, caught off guard by the softness in his expression.

He catches my stare, of course, because Damian doesn't miss a thing. His mouth quirks up in that maddening, lopsided grin of his. "Like what you see?" His voice is low, almost a whisper, as if he's afraid of disturbing the stillness of the shop.

I scoff, rolling my eyes in a way I hope hides the warmth creeping up my cheeks. "I was just wondering if you actually collect this junk or if you just have a penchant for hiding in depressing places."

Damian chuckles, a sound that surprises me—rich and warm, with none of his usual bite. "You think this is depressing?" He gestures around, as if presenting a royal palace instead of a dusty hole-in-the-wall. "I'd call it... character. Every piece here has a story, a history. You'd be surprised what you can find if you just look hard enough."

I raise an eyebrow, glancing pointedly at a particularly ghastly porcelain doll with cracked cheeks and a half-bald head, its eyes staring lifelessly back at me. "I think I'll pass on uncovering that one's backstory, thanks."

He laughs again, and it's so genuine, so unguarded, that I can't help but smile too. It's moments like this that throw me off balance, make me forget that we're fugitives, that there are people out there who would gladly see us dead for what we've done. But the reminder is never far away, as sharp and cold as a blade against my skin.

The laughter fades, and he shifts, turning serious once more. "This place has been a safe house for... people like us, for years," he says, his tone dropping. "The owner's long gone, but the hiding spots, the escape routes—they're still here." He pulls back a dusty rug, revealing a trapdoor set into the floorboards, just wide enough for a person to slip through. "In case things go south."

My stomach twists, a reminder of how precarious our situation truly is. "Always the optimist, aren't you?" I murmur, though there's no real venom in my voice. Truthfully, the thought of an escape route gives me a strange sense of security, even if I hate admitting it.

Damian gives me a level look, his eyes softening in a way that makes my chest ache. "I'd rather be ready than regretful."

There's a finality to his words that I don't challenge, and we stand there in a strange silence, suspended between what we were and whatever we're becoming. Before I can think too deeply about it, Damian steps back, motioning for me to follow him further into the shop.

As we move, he points out a few hidden compartments in the walls, hollowed-out sections of wood that contain supplies—a couple of water bottles, a flashlight, a rusty but serviceable pocketknife. "In case we're here longer than expected," he explains, his tone casual, but there's a shadow behind his words that I don't miss. For all his bravado, there's a part of Damian that expects the worst, that knows just how easily things can go wrong.

I watch him as he tucks the supplies back into place, marveling at how carefully he moves, how meticulous he is with every motion. "You really have done this before, haven't you?" I ask, my voice softer than I intended. "Running, hiding... it's not just a backup plan for you. It's your way of life."

For a moment, I think he might brush off my question with one of his usual deflections. But then he sighs, running a hand through his hair in a rare display of vulnerability. "Let's just say I've spent a lot of time learning the art of disappearing. It's kept me alive more times than I can count."

There's a sadness there, one I recognize all too well—the kind of sorrow that only comes from a life spent on the edge, from too many losses and too few victories. It hits me then, how much I still don't know about him, how many secrets he's buried beneath that carefully constructed exterior.

"You don't have to do this alone, you know," I say, surprising even myself with the softness in my tone. "Whatever happens... we're in this together. I won't leave you."

He looks at me, something unreadable flickering in his gaze, and for a moment, I think he might let down his guard. But then he straightens, the mask slipping back into place, and he offers me a tight smile, one that doesn't quite reach his eyes. "I'll hold you to that," he says, his voice light, but I can hear the strain beneath it.

We settle into a rhythm, moving through the shop in silence, checking the doors, securing the windows. It's strange, this dance of preparation, like we're setting up camp in a battlefield. But I can feel the tension coiling beneath the surface, the quiet understanding that this might be our last stand.

Just as I'm about to voice my concerns, there's a faint noise from outside—a shuffle, barely audible, but enough to make my blood run cold. Damian freezes beside me, his entire body going taut, his eyes sharp and focused. Without a word, he presses a finger to his lips, signaling me to stay silent.

We wait, breath held, listening to the sound of footsteps approaching the door. I feel my heart hammering in my chest, my pulse pounding so loudly I'm certain they'll hear it. Damian inches closer to me, his hand brushing mine, a silent reassurance that we're in this together, no matter what.

The footsteps pause, just outside the door, and I can feel the tension radiating from Damian, a palpable, electric charge that crackles through the air. I grip the edge of a nearby shelf, steadying myself, ready for whatever comes next.

The silence stretches, each second an eternity, until finally, the footsteps recede, fading into the distance. We wait a moment longer, neither of us daring to breathe, until Damian lets out a slow, measured exhale, his shoulders sagging in relief.

"They're not giving up, are they?" I whisper, more to myself than to him.

He shakes his head, his gaze distant. "No. They won't stop until they have us, one way or another."

The words hang between us, heavy and unspoken, a reminder of the stakes we're playing for. I glance at Damian, and for the first time, I see a hint of fear in his eyes—real, raw, and undisguised. It's enough to make my own resolve harden, to remind me that no matter what happens, I won't let him face this alone.

Whatever lies ahead, we'll face it together. And somehow, against all odds, that thought gives me strength.

The hours crawl by in uneasy silence, broken only by the occasional groan of the building settling around us. Damian and I make ourselves scarce, crouching low, hiding in the corners where the shadows press thickest, our ears straining for the faintest sound of movement outside. I can feel the tightness in my own chest, a dull, unrelenting weight that presses down, leaving little room to breathe.

Damian's eyes are unfocused, his expression drawn tight, and for once, I wonder what exactly he's thinking. It's rare that I catch him off guard like this, stripped of his usual steady confidence. But even now, with danger encircling us like a wolf pack, he's still doing that thing—guarding me with a kind of fierce, silent loyalty that tugs at something deep inside me. The very thing that has, without question, bound us together.

At some point, he pulls out a small notebook, well-worn and frayed at the edges. It's nothing special, just a plain black cover with no distinguishing marks, but the way he holds it, the reverence in his hands, makes me look closer. He opens it to a page filled with slanted, hurried writing—lists, names, places crossed out in dark, deliberate strokes. He studies it like a map, a blueprint to some hidden part of his past, and I catch a glimpse of one name before he flips the page quickly, shielding it from view.

"Who's Adrian?" I ask, letting the question slip before I think better of it. His reaction is instant, a flicker of surprise, quickly hidden behind a wall of practiced indifference.

He doesn't look up, but his jaw tightens almost imperceptibly. "No one you'd know," he replies, too quickly, too defensively. And that's when I know he's lying.

I arch an eyebrow, crossing my arms. "Try again, Damian. I know that look. You don't go all tight-lipped and cagey for 'no one.'"

He closes the notebook, slips it into his pocket, and gives me a look that's half warning, half reluctant resignation. "Adrian was someone... important. A friend. Someone who got tangled up in this mess because of me."

He doesn't elaborate, but the weight in his voice is enough. Whoever Adrian was, he's long gone, and from the way Damian stares at the floor, his absence is a wound that hasn't healed. I don't push him further, but something tells me that name—and whatever it means to Damian—won't stay buried forever.

Before I can dwell on it, there's a sudden crash outside, sharp and jarring, echoing down the narrow street. My heart leaps into my throat, and I instinctively reach for the rusty pocketknife Damian had shown me earlier, gripping it so tightly the edge bites into my palm. Damian is already at the window, his body tense, his eyes narrowed as he peers through a gap in the curtains.

He swears under his breath. "They're here. Crimson Society scouts. At least three of them, maybe more."

My pulse races, each beat loud and frantic. "Do they know we're here?"

"Not yet. But they're getting closer. We have two options," he says, voice clipped and focused. "We stay hidden and hope they pass, or we go out the back and take our chances in the open."

The idea of running through the streets again, of slipping like shadows through alleyways, dodging enemies at every corner, sends a chill down my spine. But staying here feels equally dangerous, like a trap waiting to spring. I swallow hard, glancing at him. "What's your call?"

For a moment, he hesitates, his gaze flickering over me, assessing, calculating. And then he nods, his decision made. "We leave. I'll cover you, but we need to move fast. Stay close, and whatever you do, don't look back."

There's no time to argue. He takes my hand—briefly, just enough to steady me, to pull me out of my own fear—and then he's moving, guiding me toward the back door, each step a quiet promise that he'll see me through this. The alley beyond is narrow, barely wide enough for us to slip through side by side, and every inch is filled with the heavy, stagnant smell of the city. I can't help but glance over my shoulder, heart pounding, expecting to see shadows flickering behind us.

But the alley is empty. For now.

We move quickly, Damian leading the way, his every movement precise, controlled. I follow close behind, my nerves strung so tight I'm certain I'll snap at the slightest provocation. The night feels colder, sharper somehow, each gust of wind cutting through me like ice. My breaths come shallow and rapid, each one a silent mantra of don't stop, don't look back.

After what feels like hours but must only be minutes, Damian stops, pressing himself against a wall, his gaze scanning the street beyond. He holds up a hand, a silent signal to stay hidden, and I obey, ducking down beside him, straining to listen. The street is silent, but there's a tension in the air, an oppressive stillness that makes my skin prickle.

And then, faintly, I hear it—the sound of footsteps, deliberate and slow, echoing down the street. I risk a glance around the corner and freeze. There, not more than a hundred yards away, is a figure dressed in the deep crimson of our enemies, their face obscured by the shadows but their posture unmistakable. They're looking, searching, and it's only a matter of time before they find us.

Damian grabs my hand, his grip tight, grounding me in the moment. "When I say go, we run," he whispers, his voice barely audible but filled with a fierce determination that sends a thrill of fear and exhilaration through me. I nod, my pulse pounding, every nerve in my body screaming to move, to get away.

He counts down, his voice a steady beat that drowns out everything else. "Three... two... one..."

We bolt from the alley, slipping through the darkness like ghosts, our footsteps barely audible against the pavement. The figure doesn't react immediately, but I know it won't be long before they notice us, before the chase begins. I don't dare look back, don't even breathe as we sprint down the street, the night air biting at my skin, filling my lungs with a cold, burning fire.

Just when I think we might make it, might actually outrun them, I hear it—the sound of voices, close, too close, and the heavy thud of footsteps pounding after us. Damian pulls me around a corner, and we duck into a side street, pressed against the wall, holding our breath as our pursuers draw nearer. The footsteps are almost on top of us now, and I feel Damian's hand tighten around mine, a silent promise, a last line of defense.

The figures round the corner, their silhouettes sharp and menacing against the dim streetlight. I catch a glimpse of crimson, of hard, unyielding eyes, and I know that hiding is no longer an option. Damian shifts beside me, his stance tense, poised, ready to fight if it comes to that.

But then something unexpected happens. One of the figures—the one in front, a man with a scar cutting across his cheek—pauses, his gaze falling directly on us. He raises his hand, and for a heart-stopping moment, I think he's about to give the order to attack. But instead, he does something that leaves me reeling.

He lowers his hand, a signal for the others to stop, and then he speaks, his voice low, edged with a strange mix of regret and resignation.

"I don't want to hurt you," he says, his eyes fixed on Damian, and there's something in his gaze that's almost... familiar.

Damian's jaw clenches, his eyes narrowing as he takes a step forward, shielding me with his body. But the man shakes his head, his expression somber.

"Damian, it's me. Adrian."

Chapter 22: Ghosts of Yesterday

The room was dark, steeped in shadows that writhed and whispered as though the walls themselves were alive. I forced myself to keep a steady breath, ignoring the way my hands tingled with anticipation and fear. It had been years since I'd come to this part of the city—this forgotten corner where the streets were nothing more than twisted veins, pulsing with secrets and danger. But desperation, like a sudden storm, had pushed me here. And so, I waited for him, knowing he would appear like a ghost summoned from the deepest parts of my past.

He used to go by the name of Larkin. Back then, he'd been untouchable, a master in every sense of the word, his reputation thick with tales of impossible escapes and legendary thefts. To me, though, he was simply my teacher, a man who saw something in me worth molding, worth sharpening to a fine, dangerous point. But now? Now, as he emerged from the shadowed alcove, there was a hollow in his eyes—a void where once, I'd believed, burned the fire of invincibility. His steps were slow, measured, almost limping, as though the very ground resisted his presence.

"Larkin," I said, the name feeling foreign on my tongue, like trying to resurrect a language I hadn't spoken in years. He looked at me, his gaze piercing yet somehow faded, as if he were seeing me through a layer of dust.

"So," he murmured, voice rough like sandpaper, "the girl who swore she'd never come back."

"I didn't have a choice." My voice sounded small, even to my own ears. I hated that. Hated that he could still reduce me to that uncertain, raw version of myself. "I need your help."

He laughed—a sound that held no warmth, no trace of the man I'd once known. "Of course you do. They always come back, don't they? When they've run out of options."

Behind me, Damian shifted uncomfortably, his presence a reminder that I wasn't alone in this, though it didn't feel that way. Damian had been my anchor, my partner, my... well, my everything these past months. But Larkin didn't know him, didn't care to know him. To Larkin, we were just another set of desperate souls seeking his favor, nothing more.

"And what exactly do you think I can do for you?" he sneered, leaning against the wall, his arms crossed, shadows pooling around him like an aura of menace. "You know I'm not the man I used to be."

"I know," I replied, forcing my voice to remain steady. "But you still have the contacts, the resources. I need to find a way out of this city, unnoticed."

Larkin's gaze flickered to Damian, lingering, assessing, and then back to me, his expression unreadable. "And what's in it for me?"

I'd expected that question, braced myself for it. The city had taken its toll on him, and even a legend needed something to live off. I reached into my bag, pulling out a small pouch of coins, its weight a bitter reminder of just how much we'd already lost. I tossed it to him, watching as he caught it, his face expressionless as he felt the weight.

He opened the pouch, looked inside, and then laughed, a humorless, dead sound. "You think this is enough? I thought I taught you better." His eyes slid to Damian again, sharp and calculating, his smile curving into something dark. "I want something... else."

My stomach twisted, but I kept my expression neutral, barely glancing at Damian, who was now watching Larkin with a mixture of disdain and defiance. "What do you want?" I asked, though I already knew I wouldn't like the answer.

Larkin's smile widened, predatory and cold. "Your friend here, he has something... rare, doesn't he? That magic he's got—there's power in it. Power I could use."

I tensed, feeling Damian's sharp intake of breath beside me. This was exactly what I'd feared, why I'd hesitated even coming here. Damian's abilities, his connection to the old magic, were what made him invaluable. And Larkin, of course, would sense that. He always did have a nose for advantage.

"No," I said, my voice firmer than I felt. "That's not an option."

"Oh, isn't it?" Larkin's voice was a low, mocking drawl, his gaze shifting between us like a predator toying with prey. "You come crawling back to me, begging for help, and then dictate the terms? If you want my assistance, you'll pay my price."

Damian placed a hand on my shoulder, a reassuring weight that steadied me even as my mind spun with options, with exit strategies that all ended in dead ends. "I'm willing," he said softly.

I turned to him, shaking my head before he could even finish. "No. We don't trade pieces of ourselves for this."

His eyes softened, a warmth there that broke my heart even as it fueled my resolve. "You've been risking yourself for me since the day we met. Let me do this for you, for us. It's the only way."

My throat tightened, anger and desperation mingling in a bitter concoction that I couldn't swallow. But Damian's hand didn't leave my shoulder, his steady gaze anchoring me, reminding me that sometimes sacrifices had to be made. Still, I wasn't ready to give in. I wasn't ready to lose any part of him, not after everything we'd been through.

"Larkin," I said, my voice carrying an edge even I hadn't expected. "There has to be another way. Don't make me regret trusting you again."

He arched a brow, looking almost amused. "Trust? Oh, little sparrow, I don't recall you ever truly trusting me. You just had nowhere else to turn."

I clenched my fists, biting back the sharp retort that burned my tongue. He was right, of course. Larkin had always been the one you turned to when you were out of options, the devil at the end of the road.

"Take it or leave it," he said, finally dropping the smugness for a flicker of genuine impatience. "I don't have all night, and I doubt you have the luxury of time either."

Time. The one thing we never seemed to have enough of. I glanced at Damian, my heart aching, torn between loyalty to the life we'd built together and the cold reality that this was our last, desperate shot. He gave me a slight nod, resigned but determined.

I didn't want to lose him.

The room seemed to tighten around me as I faced Larkin. His eyes glittered, catching the meager light that filtered in through cracked windows, making him look like a wolf caught just outside the glow of a campfire, waiting to pounce. Damian shifted beside me, his fingers brushing mine in the faintest reassurance. I could feel the unspoken question in his touch, the silent strength that he offered even now, even here, when every logical thought in my mind told me to turn and run.

Larkin leaned back, his arms crossing as though he were lounging in a parlor rather than in this forgotten wreck of a building. "You always were stubborn," he drawled, each word slow and deliberate, like he was savoring the taste of them. "But you're wasting precious time, sweetheart. How much longer do you think you can play the hero before reality bites?"

His words were needles, barbed with truths I didn't want to admit. I wanted to retort, to tell him that he was wrong, that I could figure this out without compromising what Damian had worked so hard to protect. But all my retorts felt hollow in the face of his unyielding stare. Larkin had always been good at stripping people down to the bone, peeling back the layers until you were left raw and exposed, questioning every choice you'd ever made.

Damian, to his credit, didn't flinch under Larkin's scrutiny. He met the older man's gaze with a calm, steady resilience that I envied in that moment. "I'm willing to do whatever it takes to keep her safe," he said, his voice low but clear.

Larkin let out a bark of laughter, shaking his head. "Ah, lovebirds. Sweet, but misguided." His gaze settled on me, narrowing. "What you need to ask yourself, little sparrow, is if you're willing to let him do this for you."

I hated how well he knew me, hated the way his words wormed their way under my skin. Larkin had trained me to survive in this city, to fight, to steal, to protect myself at any cost. But now, with Damian beside me, I felt the weight of those lessons in a different way, a burden pressing down on choices I wasn't sure I could make. I glanced at Damian, and he offered me a soft, reassuring smile that only made my heart ache more.

"No," I said, shaking my head. "There has to be another way. I'm not—"

"Not what?" Larkin interrupted, his voice as sharp as a knife's edge. "Not willing to make a hard choice? Not willing to use what's at your disposal?" He took a step closer, his face darkening. "You came to me, girl. Don't play saint now."

I felt Damian's grip tighten slightly on my hand, grounding me, holding me in place when I wanted to lash out. Larkin's words were cutting, meant to pierce my armor, but Damian's presence reminded me why I was here, why I couldn't let Larkin push me into decisions that would break us.

Before I could speak, Damian stepped forward, his voice calm, resolute. "If my magic is what you want, fine. I'll give it to you. But you give her safe passage out of the city, no questions asked."

I stared at him, disbelief and dread flooding my veins. "Damian—"

He turned to me, silencing me with a look, one that held both affection and a fierceness I'd only seen once before, back when he'd saved me from a mess I'd never meant to drag him into. "This is my choice. You don't have to protect me from it."

I felt my resolve waver, cracking under the weight of his gaze. Larkin's cold smile told me he knew he'd won, that he'd found the chink in my armor, the one thing that could make me bend.

"Well, then," Larkin said, clapping his hands with exaggerated cheer. "I do love a good deal. Magic for safe passage. Let's seal it, shall we?"

My instincts screamed at me to stop this, to find another way, but Damian's hand remained firm, his resolve unshakeable. He looked at Larkin, his face set, his eyes dark with determination. "What do you need me to do?"

Larkin grinned, a smile as sharp and merciless as a blade. "It's a simple enough exchange. I take what I need, and in return, you get what you want." He paused, savoring the tension between us, letting it stretch thin and taut. "But you'll need to come with me. This isn't something we can do here."

He turned on his heel, heading for the door without waiting for our response. I hesitated, glancing at Damian, searching his face for any sign of fear, of regret. But he just squeezed my hand, his expression calm.

"Trust me," he murmured, so softly I could barely hear him.

I wanted to argue, to fight, to tell him that this was madness. But there was something in his eyes that told me he'd already made up his mind, and that nothing I said would change it. With a heavy heart, I nodded, falling into step beside him as we followed Larkin into the darkened hallway.

The silence was oppressive as we walked, each step echoing like a heartbeat, steady and inevitable. Larkin led us through twisting corridors, down narrow staircases that spiraled into the depths of the building, into spaces that smelled of damp and decay, places where light had been banished long ago. At last, we arrived in a small, windowless room, lit only by the faint glow of a single, guttering candle.

"Stand there," Larkin instructed, gesturing to the center of the room. Damian complied, moving into place without hesitation. I stayed by the wall, my back pressed against the cold stone, every instinct telling me to run, to pull Damian out of here before it was too late.

Larkin approached him, a predatory gleam in his eyes. "Hold still," he said, his voice low and rough, like gravel scraping against metal. He lifted a hand, and I saw a faint shimmer in the air around his fingers, a glimmer of magic that made my skin crawl.

As he began to murmur words in a language I didn't understand, I felt the air grow thick and heavy, pressing down on me, filling my lungs with a suffocating weight. I could see the strain in Damian's face, the effort it took for him to keep still, to let Larkin draw the magic from him bit by bit. His jaw clenched, his hands fisted at his sides, but he didn't flinch, didn't pull away.

My heart pounded, every fiber of my being screaming at me to do something, to stop this. But I was frozen, helpless, watching as the man I loved was stripped of the very thing that made him who he was.

Finally, after what felt like an eternity, Larkin stepped back, his face flushed with triumph, his eyes gleaming with a hunger that made my stomach churn. He looked at me, his grin wide and terrible.

"There," he said, his voice thick with satisfaction. "Your friend paid the price. You're free to go."

I didn't wait for him to say anything more. I rushed to Damian's side, my hands shaking as I reached for him, desperate to reassure myself that he was still there, still whole. He gave me a faint smile, his eyes dim but steady.

"It's done," he murmured, his voice weak but certain. "We're free."

But as I looked into his eyes, a cold dread settled in my chest. We were free, yes. But at what cost?

The old warehouse loomed ahead like a forgotten relic, its rusted metal exterior blending seamlessly with the overcast sky. Inside, the air was thick with the scent of damp concrete and memories best left undisturbed. My heart raced as we approached, each step echoing the desperate rhythm of my thoughts. Would the man I once called mentor even recognize me? Would he remember the hope I once saw in his eyes, before the world had turned its back on him?

As we entered, a faint light flickered from a solitary bulb hanging by a frayed wire, illuminating a disheveled room filled with remnants of a life long abandoned. Shadows danced across the walls, twisting into grotesque forms that hinted at the darkness lingering within. There he stood, hunched over a makeshift workbench, surrounded by an array of arcane artifacts—things that whispered of power, of danger, and of debts yet unpaid.

"Lila?" His voice was gravelly, each word laced with disbelief and resentment. "Is that really you?"

"Hi, Gregory." I forced a smile, my heart sinking at the sight of him. The man who once exuded confidence now wore the weight of regret etched into every line on his face. "I need your help."

He looked me up and down, eyes narrowing. "Help? What's so important that you'd come crawling back after all these years?"

I could feel Damian shift beside me, his silent strength a steadying force. "We're in trouble," I said, my voice steady despite the turmoil roiling within. "It's... it's bigger than I imagined. I need your connections, your expertise. We need to find something, and I can't do it alone."

A bitter laugh escaped him, and I braced myself. "You want my help? After you turned your back on this life? What's changed?"

"Everything has changed!" I snapped, frustration boiling over. "I've lost people, I've been hunted, and now... now it's my turn to fight back. You taught me how to survive, Gregory. I need to tap into that knowledge, to protect what's mine."

He studied me for a long moment, his gaze flickering with something resembling admiration before hardening once more. "You don't understand the cost of this game, Lila. You think you can just waltz back in and claim a seat at the table? The stakes are higher than ever."

Damian stepped forward, his voice low but firm. "We're not looking for a seat, Gregory. We're looking for a way out. Just tell us what you need, and we'll make it happen."

I held my breath as the tension hung between us, the weight of unspoken truths lingering like smoke in the air. Gregory's expression shifted, and I could see the internal struggle etched on his face. He was wrestling with ghosts of his own—a past he couldn't shake, a future he no longer believed in.

"Fine," he said finally, a hint of resignation in his tone. "I can help you, but there's a price. I need something from you, something very specific."

"What do you need?" I asked, hope flickering in my chest.

"A piece of magic," he replied, eyes gleaming with a predatory light. "And I mean true magic, the kind that only the rarest of souls possess. I want Damian's essence."

The air in the room shifted, an electric pulse of danger coursing through me. "You can't be serious." My voice was barely a whisper, the reality of his request hitting me like a punch to the gut. "That's not just a trinket, Gregory. That's a part of him."

"Exactly," he said, his tone matter-of-fact. "Without it, he'll never be able to access the depths of power you seek. And with it, I can ensure your safety from those who hunt you. It's the only way I'll help."

I felt the ground beneath me shift, the world spinning in a way that threatened to send me tumbling into darkness. "You're asking me to sacrifice him?" The words felt foreign, lodged in my throat like a thorn.

"I'm asking you to weigh your options," he shot back, his eyes hardening. "You want to save your little world, but it comes with a price. Damian's power is your key to survival. Without it, you'll lose everything you care about."

Damian took my hand, his grip a silent promise. "I'd do anything for you, Lila. You know that."

I could see the resolve in his eyes, the unwavering strength that had drawn me to him in the first place. But at what cost? Could I really allow him to give up a part of himself, knowing it could change him forever? The uncertainty gnawed at my insides, a relentless whisper that told me I was about to make a decision that could shatter everything we'd built.

"Think it through," Gregory continued, sensing the turmoil in the room. "Time is running out. You'll need to act fast if you want to keep your enemies at bay."

As I stood there, torn between love and the weight of my own past, the shadows in the room began to shift. A chill swept through, making the hair on my arms stand on end. Something was coming, something dark and relentless, and I could feel it creeping closer.

"Lila," Damian said softly, his voice grounding me. "Whatever you decide, I trust you. But we need to make a choice, and we need to make it now."

Just then, the sound of shattering glass echoed from the far side of the warehouse, sending a jolt of fear through my veins. A figure emerged from the shadows, cloaked in darkness, their eyes glowing with an unsettling light. "You think you can bargain with a ghost?" the figure sneered, voice dripping with malice. "You have no idea what you're up against."

The atmosphere crackled with tension, and in that moment, I realized the true stakes were far more than I had ever anticipated. The ground beneath us shifted again, and I knew—whatever decision I made would send ripples through the fabric of our world, setting us on a path from which there was no return.

Chapter 23: Veiled Allegiances

The city hummed with a restless energy as twilight descended, casting shadows that stretched like fingers across the cobblestone streets. A cool breeze stirred the remnants of the day's warmth, weaving through alleys thick with the scent of spices and sweat, carrying with it the echoes of distant laughter and the clinking of glasses from hidden taverns. In this moment of dusk, the air crackled with an anticipation that sent a shiver down my spine. We were on the precipice of something monumental, but beneath that thrill lay an undercurrent of anxiety that I couldn't shake.

Damian stood beside me, his silhouette a striking contrast against the dimming light. The sharp angles of his jaw and the way his dark hair caught the last glimmers of sunlight ignited something within me—an urgency wrapped in uncertainty. We had fought so hard to forge our path through the chaos that was the Crimson Society, and yet, here we were, entangled with a faction that had their own agenda and their own fears.

"Just try to stay close," he murmured, his voice low and rough like gravel. There was a tension in his tone, a seriousness that pulled at me. I nodded, though I could feel my heart thumping in my chest, the adrenaline racing through me.

We made our way through the back streets toward a dilapidated warehouse that the rebels had claimed as their meeting ground. It loomed ahead, an ancient structure draped in shadows and memories of a time when it served a purpose far less grim than plotting rebellion. A flickering sign creaked above the entrance, its neon glow fighting against the encroaching night. Inside, the air was thick with a palpable energy, charged with a mix of fear and resolve that filled the room as we stepped through the heavy door.

Livia stood at the center, surrounded by a group of fierce-looking rebels. The sharp lines of her face were softened by the light, but her eyes burned with a ferocity that commanded attention. I felt a rush of unease wash over me as she turned, locking her gaze on Damian. There was an intimacy in the way they regarded one another, a shared history that I could feel prickling at the back of my mind.

"Damian," she said, her voice smooth yet edged with something I couldn't quite place. "You finally decided to show up."

"Had to find a way to keep myself entertained," he replied, his tone light but the tension between them was unmistakable. I shifted my weight, suddenly hyper-aware of how out of place I felt amidst their banter.

Livia crossed her arms, her posture confident and assertive. "And you brought a friend. How quaint." The way she smiled didn't reach her eyes, a sharp edge lingering beneath her words. I felt her scrutiny, a laser-like focus that made my skin crawl, yet I squared my shoulders and returned her gaze, unwilling to show any signs of insecurity.

"Livia, this is—" Damian began, but she waved a hand dismissively.

"Don't bother. I've heard about you, the girl who thinks she can bring down the Crimson Society. Ambitious." The word was laced with a challenge, as if she was daring me to prove my worth.

"Ambition is often a necessity in our line of work," I retorted, matching her tone. "Besides, I'm not here to impress anyone. I just want to end this nightmare."

A flicker of surprise crossed her face, quickly masked by a look of amusement. "You're feistier than I expected. That might serve you well."

I bristled at her condescension but held my ground. Damian's presence was a steadying force beside me, yet the more I saw of Livia, the more I felt the walls closing in around me, tightening the grip of doubt in my chest. We had come too far to turn back now, but could I really trust these rebels?

"Let's get to it, shall we?" Damian said, cutting through the tension like a blade. He turned to the group, his demeanor shifting from casual to commanding. "We need to discuss our next steps if we're going to have any chance against the Society."

Livia nodded, her expression turning serious as she motioned for everyone to gather closer. "We've been gathering intelligence on their operations. They're planning something big, and if we don't act fast, it could be the end of us."

As she spoke, I found myself studying the faces around the room. There was a mix of determination and fear, a collective understanding that we were teetering on the edge of a precipice. I felt the weight of their expectations pressing down on me, and I swallowed hard, reminding myself of my own resolve.

"Damian, you have inside knowledge. You know their tactics, their leaders," Livia said, her voice steady, almost pleading. "We need your insight if we're going to make this work."

I watched as Damian's expression hardened, a flicker of something unrecognizable passing through his eyes. "I'll help, but it's going to require trust. Trust I'm not sure we have yet."

"Then we'll earn it," Livia replied, her tone clipped but firm. "All of us."

As the discussion unfolded, I couldn't shake the feeling that beneath the surface of this alliance, hidden agendas swirled like dark clouds overhead. Each rebel brought their own burdens, their own stories, and the uncertainty of our success loomed larger than the warehouse's rafters. But if we wanted to bring down the Society, we had no choice but to work together—no matter how uncomfortable it felt.

Suddenly, the door creaked open behind us, and a chill swept through the room. The atmosphere shifted, a tension so thick it could be cut with a knife. I turned, my heart racing, half-expecting the shadows to materialize into a threat. The city outside had not forgotten us, and I knew that danger lurked just beyond those walls, waiting to strike.

"Who goes there?" a voice barked, and all eyes snapped toward the entrance. In that moment, I realized that our fragile alliance was about to be tested, and the true nature of our veiled allegiances would soon be revealed.

The tension hung heavy in the air, thick enough to make each breath feel like a laborious effort. I shifted my weight from foot to foot, acutely aware of the whispered conversations among the rebels as they regarded the intruder who had just walked through the door. It was a woman, her silhouette framed by the fading light, with a presence that commanded attention without uttering a single word. She stepped fully into the room, and the conversations hushed to a whisper, all eyes trained on her as if she were a candle in the dark, illuminating the uncertainty that loomed over us.

"Who's this?" she demanded, her voice sharp and cool as winter air. She had an air of authority about her, the kind that made me both intrigued and wary. Her gaze landed on Livia, and for a brief moment, an unspoken challenge passed between them. The atmosphere crackled with an intensity that felt personal, as if the very air was charged with their history.

"This is important," Livia replied, her tone now steady, almost icy. "We have allies here. We're making plans." The way she said "allies" felt like a quiet admission that perhaps she hadn't fully expected this interruption.

The newcomer crossed her arms, her eyes flaring with skepticism. "Plans? Or are we just throwing darts at a board in the hopes of hitting something useful? I didn't come here to waste my time."

The rebuff hung in the air, thickening the atmosphere further. Damian took a step forward, his protective instinct kicking in. "What do you want, Claire?" His voice held a warning, an undercurrent of frustration that I hadn't heard before.

"Isn't it obvious?" she retorted, her expression unwavering. "I want to know what you're planning. If we're to take down the Society, we can't afford to lose our heads over sentimental attachments."

The air shifted as Claire's words sank in. I could feel the weight of every unspoken thought, each rebellious spirit calculating the risks involved. This wasn't just about alliances; it was about trust, and trust was a commodity in short supply. I was an outsider, and they all knew it, which made me wonder how much sway I actually had in this increasingly volatile situation.

"Sentimental attachments?" I shot back, my voice unexpectedly steady despite the tumult inside me. "Is that what you think this is about? You think we're here playing house while the Society runs rampant? You have no idea what we've been through."

"Watch your tone," Claire snapped, but there was a flicker of surprise in her eyes that told me I'd struck a chord. "This isn't about you, or Damian. This is about survival. If you want to fight, you have to be willing to lose everything."

"And yet, here we are," I said, crossing my arms defiantly. "Ready to lose it all. What's your excuse?"

Damian's hand brushed my arm, a gesture that sent a jolt of reassurance through me. "Enough," he said, his voice firm but tempered. "We need to focus on the real enemy. Claire, if you're here to help, then stop wasting time on petty rivalries. We need every hand we can get."

Claire studied him, the skepticism in her gaze softening just a fraction. "Fine," she relented, the tension in her stance easing. "But if we're going to work together, I need to know that you're not here for a stroll through the garden. We need a plan, a real one."

The rebels began murmuring among themselves, weighing their options, but my attention was drawn back to Damian. He was watching me with a mix of concern and admiration, as if I had just passed some kind of test. I felt my cheeks warm under his gaze, a flurry of emotions stirring within me. Here we were, surrounded by potential allies, and yet it felt as if we were teetering on the edge of a cliff, each breath threatening to send us tumbling into chaos.

"We can't just react," Damian said, bringing the focus back to the matter at hand. "We need to anticipate their moves. The Society is planning something—something big. We need to figure out what it is before it's too late."

Livia nodded, a renewed determination brightening her expression. "We've been tracking their movements. There's chatter about a gathering of their high-ranking members, something they're calling the 'Conclave of Shadows.' If we can infiltrate that, we might learn everything we need."

"What's the catch?" Claire interjected, her gaze sharp as a blade.

"Security will be tighter than a locked vault," Livia replied, her confidence unwavering. "But we've got a few ideas on how to get inside."

"What kind of ideas?" I asked, my mind racing.

Livia hesitated, her brow furrowing slightly. "We can create a distraction—something that draws attention away from the gathering. With the right diversion, we can slip in and out unnoticed."

"Like what?" I pressed, the gears in my mind turning.

"Something loud, something big," Livia said, her voice dropping to a conspiratorial whisper. "A raid on one of their supply lines, perhaps. It would divert their attention, create chaos."

"Except chaos isn't just the absence of order. It's a breeding ground for mistakes," Claire countered, her tone skeptical. "And if we make one wrong move, we're done for."

"Exactly," Damian said, nodding in agreement with Claire. "We need a plan that minimizes risk. If we go in guns blazing, we'll be dead before we even get to the meeting."

The discussion flowed around us, a whirlwind of ideas and counterarguments. I found myself caught between the factions, absorbing their strategies and fears like a sponge. As their plans crystallized, I felt a sense of urgency pulse through me. This wasn't just about strategy; it was about survival and loyalty, about finding my place within this volatile mix of ambition and desperation.

"I'll lead the distraction," I finally declared, surprising even myself with my boldness. "I'm more than just a pretty face. If you can get me close enough, I can create enough of a stir to draw their eyes away from the Conclave."

Damian turned to me, his brow arched in surprise, and I could see the admiration shining through his skepticism. "Are you sure? It could be dangerous."

"Of course it's dangerous," I shot back, my heart racing. "But what isn't these days? Besides, someone has to take the risk. I'm tired of waiting on the sidelines."

A silence enveloped the room, the weight of my words sinking in. Livia glanced at Claire, who looked like she was wrestling with her own doubts. Finally, Livia spoke, her voice steady. "If you're willing to take that risk, then I'm willing to support it. We'll need everyone on board, though. This isn't a one-person show."

"Then let's make sure we're all on the same page," Damian said, his gaze shifting between us. "We've got a lot to lose, but we've also got everything to gain. The Society has taken enough from us."

As plans took shape around me, I could feel the tension simmering beneath the surface, an unspoken agreement binding us together. This wasn't just an alliance forged in necessity; it was a bond of shared purpose, however tenuous. We were stepping into the unknown together, a motley crew of rebels ready to challenge the very foundations of the world we lived in.

And as the shadows deepened outside, I couldn't help but feel a flicker of hope igniting within me. Maybe, just maybe, we were about to ignite a spark that would change everything.

As the plans unfurled like the wings of a phoenix, I felt a mix of exhilaration and trepidation. The air was charged with purpose as we prepared to strike a blow against the Crimson Society. My heart raced at the thought of stepping into the belly of the beast, yet beneath that thrill was the gnawing realization of just how little we really knew about the enemy we were about to face.

The rebels gathered in a loose circle, exchanging ideas and strategies with the kind of fervor typically reserved for a team on the brink of victory. Livia assumed command, her authoritative demeanor eclipsing any lingering doubt. "We'll need to split into two teams. One will create the diversion, while the other infiltrates the Conclave. I want everyone to be ready by dawn."

"Dawn?" I echoed, the gravity of the timeline hitting me. "That's hardly enough time to prepare."

Claire shot me a sidelong glance, her expression unreadable. "Preparation is overrated. It's about execution. You either have the guts to do this or you don't."

"Maybe we can strike a balance," Damian suggested, his tone level. "Planning is just as crucial as bravery. If we're going to pull this off, we need to think through every possible outcome."

"Or we could just charge in and hope for the best," I quipped, a nervous laugh escaping my lips. The tension was still thick, but humor had always been my coping mechanism, a shield against the uncertainty that loomed over us.

Livia gave me a faint smile, a hint of appreciation mingling with her steely resolve. "We're all in this together. Everyone has a role to play, and it's vital that we stick to the plan."

I took a deep breath, feeling the weight of responsibility settle on my shoulders. "I can handle the distraction," I affirmed, forcing confidence into my voice. "Just tell me what I need to do."

Livia nodded, and as we brainstormed ideas, I found myself gravitating toward the fringes of the group, listening and absorbing every detail. There was a thrill in the air, an electric buzz that ignited something deep within me. I had always been the girl who stayed in the background, but now, standing among these fierce souls, I felt a spark of purpose.

With a plan slowly taking shape, we began to divide tasks. Livia and Damian would lead the infiltration team, and I would coordinate the distraction. "We'll need to create something loud enough to pull their attention," I mused aloud, pacing as ideas flitted through my mind. "Something big... a fire, maybe? Or perhaps a staged fight?"

"Explosions work well," Claire interjected, her tone dry but with an unmistakable glimmer of mischief in her eyes. "But I wouldn't recommend that unless you're willing to set the whole city ablaze."

I chuckled, the nerves dancing in my stomach easing just a little. "How about a good old-fashioned brawl? The kind that brings the whole neighborhood out to see the action?"

"Not a bad idea," Livia said, her eyes brightening. "If we can make it look authentic enough, it might just do the trick. A little chaos to cover our real intentions."

As the details began to crystallize, I found myself immersed in the excitement, almost forgetting the reality of our situation. We were working together as a unit, weaving our individual threads into a larger tapestry of rebellion. It was intoxicating, and the more we strategized, the more I felt a part of something bigger than myself.

But amid the exhilaration, shadows lurked. I couldn't shake the feeling that we were being watched, that the city itself held its breath, waiting for our next move. I stole a glance at Damian, whose focus remained unyielding, but I could see the weight of his thoughts etched across his features. We were bound by this cause, yet a tension lingered between us, a thread of unspoken words woven tightly beneath the surface.

"Hey," I said softly, stepping closer to him as the meeting wound down. "You okay?"

His eyes flickered toward me, a hint of vulnerability breaking through the steely exterior. "Yeah. Just thinking about what's at stake. If we fail..." He didn't finish the thought, but the implication hung heavily in the air.

"Hey, we're not going to fail. We're going to do this together," I reassured him, placing a hand on his arm. The warmth of his skin ignited a spark of courage within me.

"I know," he replied, his gaze holding mine a moment longer than necessary. "Just... be careful out there."

The intensity of his words sent a shiver through me, and I nodded, my pulse quickening. "You too."

As night descended, the group dispersed, each member slipping into the shadows like ghosts, preparing for the confrontation that would come at dawn. I lingered a moment longer, staring out into the darkened city, where the flickering lights of taverns and homes created a constellation of warmth amidst the cold uncertainty of our mission.

I turned to leave, but then a movement caught my eye—a shadow darting through the alley across the street. My heart skipped a beat, the air suddenly thick with an ominous feeling. I squinted into the darkness, but the figure vanished before I could register anything more than a fleeting silhouette.

"Just my imagination," I muttered to myself, but unease curled in my gut. I stepped away from the meeting place, thoughts racing. What if someone was watching us? What if the Society already knew our plans?

As dawn approached, I felt a whirlwind of anticipation and dread swirling within me. We were on the brink of something significant, but the specter of failure loomed over us, threatening to engulf everything we had fought for.

My mind buzzed with possibilities as I hurried back to my temporary refuge, weaving through the labyrinthine streets, now cloaked in a blanket of shadows. I reached for my keys, fumbling them in the dim light, the weight of our impending mission heavy on my shoulders. The plan was bold, reckless even, but sometimes, recklessness was a necessity in a world filled with danger.

Just as I finally managed to unlock the door, a noise echoed behind me—a low growl, almost primal, vibrating in the air. I froze, heart hammering in my chest. My instincts kicked in, and I turned, ready to face whatever was lurking in the darkness.

The moment stretched, the tension suffocating, and then the shadows shifted. A figure emerged, cloaked in black, the contours of their face obscured. My breath caught in my throat, and before I could react, they lunged forward, the glint of a weapon catching the faint light.

"Stop right there!" I shouted, my voice trembling but defiant.

But my command fell on deaf ears as the figure closed the distance between us, and in that instant, I realized the truth—I was not as alone as I had thought, and the stakes had just been raised higher than I could have ever imagined.

Chapter 24: Hearts and Lies

The air crackled with tension, a palpable electric charge that coursed through the rebel camp like a brewing storm. Shadows danced in the flickering firelight, the silhouettes of my comrades swaying with uncertainty as the weight of the evening pressed down upon us. I could sense the murmurs around me, the hushed whispers of doubt threading through our ranks, but I pushed them away, focusing instead on the flickering flames that seemed to ignite the very air with hope. We had fought too long and too hard to let fear creep in now.

But then came the shattering sound—a distant crack, a splintering of trust that shattered the night. Before I could even process it, shouts erupted from the periphery, voices distorted by panic. The scent of smoke and burnt magic filled my lungs, thick and acrid, as chaos unfurled in a heartbeat. They had found us. We had been betrayed.

"Stay close!" Damian's voice cut through the cacophony, a fierce command wrapped in the urgency of survival. He was at my side in an instant, his presence a steadying force in the swirling tempest of bodies and chaos. I had always admired his strength, but in that moment, it was something deeper—an unyielding resolve that anchored me amidst the rising tide of fear. I looked into his stormy eyes, and for a fleeting moment, everything else faded. Here, in the heart of chaos, I felt a surge of something unmistakable—a fierce, unbidden affection that clawed at my insides, making me want to scream and cry all at once.

The night exploded with blinding light as a blast of magic rocketed past us, its fiery arc painting the sky in streaks of orange and gold. I ducked instinctively, the thrill of danger igniting a wild adrenaline within me. I felt Damian's hand grasp mine, his grip firm as he pulled me deeper into the heart of the camp, the chaos swirling around us like a storm threatening to consume us whole. "We need to move, now!" His voice was a low growl, urgency laced with something more, something primal.

Together, we navigated through the shifting sea of bodies, my heart racing not only from fear but from the unshakeable realization of how much he mattered to me. In the midst of this swirling tempest, I was acutely aware of his every movement, his every breath, as if he were a lifeline pulling me away from the brink of despair.

Then, amid the madness, we stumbled into an alley—a narrow escape shrouded in darkness, the air thick with the scent of damp earth and decay. The distant shouts faded slightly, muffled by the encroaching shadows. I turned to Damian, my heart pounding not just from the chase but from an overwhelming urge to understand this connection that had grown between us. "What now?" I gasped, desperation threading through my voice.

"We find a safe place," he replied, his gaze fierce, scanning the surroundings with a predator's awareness. "There's an abandoned factory just outside the city. We can regroup there." His confidence ignited a flicker of hope in me, but beneath that hope lay an undercurrent of dread. I knew as well as he did that every second we lingered was a risk—a chance for the darkness to swallow us whole.

We fled, darting through the remnants of what had once been a vibrant community, now reduced to echoes of life. The shadows swallowed us, the silence pressing in, broken only by the echo of our hurried footsteps. It wasn't until we reached the crumbling façade of the factory that we paused, breathless and battered, our bodies slick with the remnants of fear and adrenaline.

Inside, the factory loomed like a forgotten giant, its once-mighty walls now draped in shadows and layers of dust. The smell of rust and disuse surrounded us, but I welcomed it; it felt like a sanctuary, a reprieve from the chaos outside. As we leaned against the cold metal walls, our breath mingled in the stillness, I stole a glance at him. His features were sharp in the dim light, eyes glimmering with determination but tinged with something softer, something that made my heart race in a way I hadn't thought possible.

"Damian," I began, my voice barely above a whisper, but he cut me off with a quick shake of his head, a fierce intensity radiating from him.

"Not now. We need to—"

But I couldn't hold it in any longer. "No, we need to talk. About us." The words spilled out, raw and unfiltered, tumbling into the space between us, filling the air with tension. "I can't keep pretending I don't feel this. This connection. This... whatever it is that's happening between us."

His gaze softened, and for a moment, the world outside faded away. "You don't know what you're saying," he replied, but the way he breathed my name made it sound more like a plea than a rejection.

"Maybe I do," I countered, stepping closer, the space between us shrinking until I could feel the heat radiating from him, a palpable force that made my pulse quicken. "I never thought I could feel so strongly, not after everything, but with you—"

Before I could finish, he closed the distance, capturing my lips with his in a kiss that felt like a promise, fierce and desperate. It was a melding of our souls, a declaration wrapped in uncertainty and fear, as if he knew that our time was fragile and fleeting. The kiss deepened, igniting something within me—a spark that illuminated the dark corners of my heart, revealing fears and desires I hadn't known I harbored.

But then reality crashed back in, the weight of our circumstances pressing down upon us. Pulling away, I searched his eyes, breathless and longing. "Damian, we can't ignore this. Not anymore."

He ran a hand through his hair, the gesture laced with frustration and something else, something more tender. "I know, but what if this is all we have? What if we lose everything, and all that's left is regret?"

I took a step back, his words striking a chord deep within me. "I'd rather have this, however brief, than nothing at all."

The tension hung in the air, thick and suffocating, as we faced the reality of our situation. The world outside was still shrouded in chaos, but within the walls of the factory, we stood on the precipice of something beautiful and terrifying. I reached for him, our fingers intertwining, a silent promise that even in the face of uncertainty, we would fight for what we had found in the darkness.

The remnants of chaos clung to us like a second skin, the tension still taut in the air as we stood together in the shadows of the abandoned factory. My heart raced, the weight of unspoken words lingering between us, heavy and electric. I could feel the pulse of the night reverberating through my veins, each beat a reminder of the fragility of our situation. Out there, the storm still raged, and in here, in this sanctuary of rusted metal and forgotten memories, we faced the truth of our uncharted territory.

"Are we safe here?" I asked, my voice a low murmur as I glanced toward the fractured windows, their jagged edges resembling sharp teeth ready to bite. The thought of being discovered sent a chill down my spine, but I clung to the warmth radiating from Damian, the way he stood close enough that I could feel the heat of his body, a comforting presence in the gloom.

"For now," he replied, his brow furrowed in thought. "But we can't stay long. They'll be looking for us." His eyes darted toward the entrance, a mix of determination and concern etched across his face. There was something noble about him, something that made my heart swell with admiration. He had a way of bearing the weight of the world on his shoulders, and in that moment, I wanted nothing more than to shoulder it with him.

I stepped closer, drawn by the gravity of the moment, and touched his arm lightly. "What if we don't have to fight this battle alone?" I ventured, my voice imbued with a mix of hope and fear.

"We have allies. We can gather them, plan our next move. We don't have to face this darkness by ourselves."

He turned to me, his gaze piercing through the shadows, and I could see the flicker of uncertainty in his eyes. "That's the thing, isn't it? We thought we could trust them. But betrayal runs deeper than we ever imagined." The intensity of his words struck me like a blow, and for a moment, I felt the ground shift beneath my feet. The implications of his statement weighed heavily on my heart, the realization that our closest allies might not be as loyal as we had believed.

I took a deep breath, forcing myself to remain steady. "We can't let one traitor define us. If we give in to fear, we lose everything we've fought for." My words hung in the air, a plea laced with fervor, and I could see Damian's resolve waver slightly. He looked at me, really looked, and in that gaze, I felt the walls he had built around himself begin to crack.

"Maybe you're right," he conceded, his voice softening. "But trust is a delicate thing, and once it's broken..." He trailed off, shaking his head as if to dismiss the weight of his thoughts. I knew the battle within him—he wanted to believe, but the shadows of betrayal had cast a long pall over his heart.

"Then let's rebuild it," I said, my voice gaining strength. "We start with what we have. We gather our loyalists, regroup, and come up with a plan. Together." I could see the flicker of something in his eyes, a spark of hope igniting amidst the shadows. It was just enough to propel me forward.

Damian nodded slowly, the weight of my words sinking in. "Alright. We'll do this. Together." The promise hung between us, a fragile thread woven with possibility. I felt a rush of warmth, the kind that seeped into my bones, and in that moment, the darkness outside felt a little less daunting.

Before we could delve deeper into our plans, a distant sound shattered the fragile calm—a low rumble that sent vibrations through the ground beneath us. My heart raced as I turned to Damian, our eyes locking in a moment of shared trepidation. "What was that?" I whispered, the quiet urgency of my voice lost amid the echoes of the factory.

He held up a hand, signaling for silence. "I don't know, but we should check it out. It could be more of our people." His determination was palpable, and I felt a fierce swell of admiration for his courage. Together, we moved cautiously through the factory, the silence thick and stifling, each creak of the old metal echoing like a warning in the dark.

As we rounded a corner, we were met with an unexpected sight—a group of figures huddled together, their silhouettes illuminated by the flickering glow of a makeshift lantern. I felt a rush of relief as I recognized them—our loyal allies, faces taut with worry but alive with determination. They turned as we approached, and the tension in the air shifted, replaced by a flicker of hope.

"Damian! You made it!" one of them, a wiry young woman named Elara, exclaimed, her voice tinged with disbelief. She rushed forward, her eyes scanning my face before settling on Damian. "We thought you were caught in the ambush."

"We were, but we managed to escape," he replied, his voice steady. "What about you all? Are you alright?"

Elara exchanged glances with the others, her expression grave. "We're holding up, but we've lost many. They're hunting for us. We need to regroup and get out of the city while we still can."

I stepped forward, the weight of responsibility settling over me like a heavy cloak. "We can't just run. We need a plan. We need to figure out who we can trust and how to turn this around." The eyes of our allies turned toward me, a mix of skepticism and curiosity flashing in their expressions.

Damian's gaze met mine, a flicker of admiration sparking in his eyes as if he saw something within me he hadn't before. "She's right," he said, his voice strong and unwavering. "We can't let them dictate our moves. We have to strike first."

A murmur of agreement rippled through the group, and I felt the tide turning in our favor. It was time to reclaim our narrative, to stand together against the rising tide of darkness threatening to engulf us. "Let's gather intel. We need to know who's still with us and who's working against us," I suggested, my heart pounding with the thrill of possibility.

As plans began to form, the weight of the night seemed to lighten, and amid the shadows of uncertainty, I caught Damian's eye once more. In that fleeting moment, I understood that whatever lay ahead, we would face it together. And no matter how the tides shifted, I would fight for him as fiercely as he fought for me. Our connection, forged in fire and turmoil, would be our greatest strength, and together, we would rise from the ashes of betrayal, ready to reclaim our destiny.

The atmosphere within the factory buzzed with a tense energy, our group now animated by a newfound sense of purpose. As the shadows played tricks on our minds, we gathered around the flickering lantern, each face illuminated by its dim glow, revealing the determination and resilience etched into their features. I could see the remnants of fear mingling with hope, and I felt the weight of leadership settle more comfortably on my shoulders.

"Let's split into pairs," I suggested, my voice steady despite the racing thoughts in my mind. "We can cover more ground that way. Find out who's left and where they're hiding. Gather any information on the ambushers. If we know who betrayed us, we can use that knowledge to our advantage."

Damian nodded in agreement, his fierce gaze roving over our companions. "Elara, you and Finn take the east side of the factory.

Check the old storage units. I'll head west with—" He turned to me, a spark of mischief in his eyes. "—my favorite partner in crime."

I couldn't suppress a grin at his words, even as the reality of our situation pressed against us. "Let's just hope we don't end up as crime scene evidence." A chuckle rippled through our small group, tension easing for a moment, the camaraderie a fragile thread binding us together.

As we moved out, the factory loomed around us, its decaying walls filled with echoes of long-gone workers and dreams now collected as dust. The scent of rust and damp metal hung thick in the air, mingling with the adrenaline thrumming in my veins. I could hear whispers of conversation behind closed doors, the scuff of feet on the gritty concrete floor, the distant drip of water from a corroded pipe. Each sound heightened my senses, wrapping me in an uneasy cocoon of anticipation.

We made our way deeper into the labyrinthine corridors, and I caught a glimpse of Damian's profile, his brow furrowed in concentration as we scoured the shadows for signs of our allies. I felt an undeniable warmth in my chest at the sight of him, his fierce spirit urging me to keep pushing forward. The factory was a maze of hidden corners and potential ambushes, but I welcomed the challenge. It was exhilarating to be moving with purpose, a sense of agency in a world that had felt so uncontrollable for far too long.

"Over here," Damian whispered suddenly, his voice low but urgent. He gestured toward a narrow hallway that seemed darker than the others. My heart quickened, the fear of the unknown clawing at my insides. "Let's check it out."

With a nod, I followed him into the dimness, the air growing colder as we ventured farther from the safety of our group. The hallway was lined with old machinery, their hulking forms looming like sentinels guarding secrets best left undisturbed. As we moved cautiously forward, I could feel the tension tightening in the air, a coiled spring ready to snap.

"Do you think they'll come for us here?" I asked, keeping my voice low, though the fear gnawed at the edges of my resolve.

"They might," Damian replied, his gaze scanning our surroundings, sharp and alert. "But if they do, we'll be ready."

Just as the words left his lips, a loud crash echoed from behind us, a thunderous sound that sent my heart racing. We exchanged a panicked glance, and before we could react, the ground beneath us trembled violently. It felt as if the factory itself were alive, groaning in protest as the walls shuddered and dust fell from the rafters like confetti from a funeral.

"What the hell was that?" I yelled, struggling to keep my footing.

Damian's expression turned grave, and without a word, he grabbed my arm and pulled me toward a nearby door, its surface pocked and peeling. We burst through just as another tremor shook the foundation, and the door slammed shut behind us. Inside, the room was dim, lit only by the ghostly glow of old windows smeared with grime, but the air was thick with something else—a palpable tension that prickled the back of my neck.

"Stay close," he murmured, his voice a protective growl that sent warmth blooming through me. We moved cautiously, our footsteps muted against the worn floorboards, each creak reverberating in the stillness.

Suddenly, a low voice broke through the silence. "You really thought you could hide forever?"

I froze, my heart leaping into my throat. The voice was familiar, laced with malice. My skin prickled as I turned slowly, and there, emerging from the shadows, was one of our former allies—Lysander, a man I had once trusted with my life.

"What are you doing here?" I demanded, a mix of disbelief and anger flooding through me. "I thought you were on our side!"

His smile was a serpent's grin, chilling and false. "Oh, darling, you're mistaken. I was never on your side. I've always played both ends against the middle."

My breath caught in my throat as realization washed over me. He had been the traitor, the one who had sold us out. Anger bubbled beneath my skin, igniting a fire within me that I could no longer contain. "You sold us out?"

"Of course!" he laughed, the sound harsh and mocking. "Why align myself with a group destined for failure when I could stand at the top of the winning side? I'm afraid your little rebellion is about to come to an end, my dear."

As he spoke, the ground beneath us trembled again, but this time it was accompanied by a low, rumbling growl that seemed to resonate from within the very bones of the factory. The air thickened, a strange energy swirling around us, and I glanced at Damian, who stood rigid beside me, his expression a mix of rage and determination.

"Get ready," he whispered, eyes locked on Lysander. "We're not backing down."

But before we could react, the walls around us seemed to tremble more violently, the very foundation quaking as if responding to some dark, unseen force. Lysander's grin faltered, uncertainty creeping into his eyes as he realized something was wrong.

"What's happening?" he shouted, but the question was swallowed by the resounding roar that echoed through the building. The lights flickered, casting erratic shadows across the room, and a sudden rush of wind swept through, knocking over crates and sending debris flying.

"Get out!" I screamed, grabbing Damian's arm, and we bolted toward the door, but as we turned, we were met by a figure emerging from the chaos—tall and cloaked, a presence that exuded power and malice.

"Leave them!" the figure commanded, and just like that, everything stopped. The chaos, the trembling earth, all of it froze under the weight of their voice, and I felt my heart drop.

"Who are you?" I demanded, but my voice trembled, uncertainty clawing at my resolve.

The cloaked figure stepped closer, the shadows wrapping around them like a living shroud. "You've meddled in things far beyond your understanding. It's time to face the consequences."

Damian moved in front of me, an instinctive barrier against the unknown, but I could see the realization dawning in his eyes—the sense of impending doom swirling around us like smoke.

In that moment, the darkness closed in, the atmosphere charged with an ominous energy. I felt the air grow thick, each breath a struggle as the figure's presence loomed larger, and my heart raced with the terrifying knowledge that we were no longer in control.

And then, just as quickly, the world erupted into chaos again, the ground shaking violently as the cloaked figure raised a hand, a flash of dark magic illuminating the room.

Everything spiraled into an explosion of light and shadow, the ground beneath us giving way to the unknown, and I could only grasp Damian's hand tightly as we were engulfed in darkness.

Chapter 25: The Hunter's Game

The moon hung low in the inky sky, casting a silvery glow over the cobblestone streets of Greystone, a once-thriving town now draped in shadows and silence. Each building loomed like a specter, windows like darkened eyes watching as Damian and I sprinted through the deserted alleys, our breath coming in frantic bursts. The air was thick with the scent of damp earth and fading autumn leaves, a perfume that mingled with the adrenaline coursing through my veins. We had only each other, and the hunter, an ominous figure sent by the Crimson Society, lurked somewhere behind us, tracking our every move with ruthless precision.

"Do you think we lost him?" I panted, glancing over my shoulder, the cool night air brushing against my flushed cheeks. My heart raced, not just from the chase but from the way Damian's fingers entwined with mine, a lifeline amidst the chaos.

"Not yet," he replied, his voice steady despite the urgency of our flight. His gaze was sharp, scanning the street ahead, taking in every potential hiding spot, every alley that could offer refuge. "We need to keep moving. There's no time to lose."

We ducked into a narrow passageway, its walls damp and covered in a mossy green that seemed to cling to the stone as if trying to escape the dark. I could hear the echo of footsteps behind us, an unsettling reminder that we weren't alone. It ignited a spark of fear in my chest, one that was not entirely unwelcome. Fear kept us alert, kept our senses heightened, but it also served as a harsh contrast to the warmth spreading between us. With every glance shared, every breath taken in sync, I felt something deeper brewing, a connection that transcended the night's peril.

The passage opened up into a small courtyard, overgrown with weeds that clawed at the cracks in the stone. Moonlight pooled in the center, illuminating a weathered stone fountain that had long since ceased to flow. I stopped, drawing in a shaky breath. "What's the plan?" I asked, urgency tinging my voice.

Damian ran a hand through his dark hair, the moonlight catching the silver flecks in his eyes. "We need to create a distraction," he said, his mind working faster than my own. "If we can lure him away from our trail, we might stand a chance."

My pulse quickened with a mix of fear and excitement. "And how do we do that? We're not exactly equipped for a battle here."

"Leave that to me," he said, a hint of mischief flashing across his features. It was the same spark that drew me to him, the way his confidence mingled with the danger that surrounded us. "You trust me, right?"

"More than I should," I replied, unable to suppress a small smile. The moment felt electric, our laughter ringing out into the night, a brief reprieve from the tension that clung to us like the mist rising from the ground.

In a swift motion, Damian slipped away, his silhouette disappearing into the shadows, leaving me momentarily alone. I strained to listen, the sounds of the night wrapping around me—the rustle of leaves, the distant hoot of an owl, and the faint thud of my own heartbeat echoing in my ears. Every second stretched into eternity as I waited, an unrelenting knot of worry forming in my stomach. I could feel the hunter getting closer, could sense the darkness encroaching upon us, but I clung to the hope that Damian would execute his plan flawlessly.

The silence shattered like glass when a loud crash echoed through the alley to my left. My heart leaped as I turned, spotting Damian darting into the courtyard, followed closely by a figure cloaked in shadows. The hunter. My instincts kicked in, and I dashed toward the nearest exit, calling out to Damian.

"Now!" he shouted, his voice slicing through the tension. I caught a glimpse of his determined expression, the resolve etched in the lines of his face. The hunter was close, dangerously so, but I could see the trap unfolding.

I threw myself into the shadows of a nearby alcove, pressing against the cold stone as the hunter lunged for Damian, who deftly sidestepped, leading the assailant into a narrow alleyway. The sounds of a struggle filled the air, harsh grunts and the thud of bodies colliding. My heart raced as I debated my next move. Should I stay hidden and trust Damian's instincts, or should I intervene?

With a deep breath, I chose action. Emerging from my hiding spot, I spotted a loose cobblestone on the ground. Grabbing it, I hurled it into the darkness of the alley, the sound reverberating off the walls. The hunter turned, momentarily distracted, just long enough for Damian to gain the upper hand.

"Now!" he barked, and I rushed to his side, adrenaline fueling my movements. Together, we pressed forward, forcing the hunter deeper into the maze of streets, our minds racing as we searched for a way to outsmart our relentless pursuer. Each turn was a gamble, each corner a potential trap, but we pressed on, driven by a singular desire—to escape and survive.

As we turned yet another corner, I felt the weight of our shared fear but also the exhilaration of our bond, forged in the crucible of danger. I was no longer just running for my life; I was fighting for our future, for the promise of something more than survival. And as long as we faced this together, I felt an unshakeable belief that we would find a way to emerge from the darkness.

We weaved through the labyrinth of alleys, each corner presenting a new puzzle, a chance for evasion. Damian's energy was palpable, a potent mix of adrenaline and fierce determination that drew me in. We were a storm on the brink of breaking, and as we dashed past remnants of a once-vibrant town, I couldn't help but feel the thrill of danger wrapping around us like an intoxicating cloak.

"Are you sure you know where you're going?" I teased, though my voice was tinged with urgency. The last thing I wanted was to sound anxious, but with the hunter on our tail, I felt the weight of every second.

"Of course," he replied, a grin breaking across his face despite the circumstances. "I just have a thing for taking the scenic route when I'm being chased."

"Scenic? This place looks like a set for a horror film," I shot back, but laughter bubbled up, easing the tightness in my chest. There was something about his unfaltering confidence that made me believe we could outsmart even the darkest of foes.

We ducked into another narrow passage, the air growing cooler as we ventured deeper into the heart of Greystone's forgotten paths. The walls were damp and slick with moss, and the ground beneath our feet was littered with crumbling bricks and shards of glass, remnants of a world that had once thrived. Each step was a reminder of the fragility of our surroundings, yet somehow, it felt as though we were stepping into the unknown together, and that made the fear bearable.

Damian paused, his hand gripping my arm as we approached a dead end. "We need to find a way up," he said, scanning the area. His gaze landed on a fire escape ladder partially hidden behind an overgrown vine. "That could work."

Without hesitation, he hoisted me up, his hands steadying my waist. I scrambled to reach the first rung, the rough metal cold against my palms. "You know, I never thought I'd be climbing a fire escape in the middle of a deadly game of tag," I remarked breathlessly, my heart racing for more reasons than one.

"Life's full of surprises," he shot back, a playful glint in his eyes. "Just think of it as a really twisted date."

"Great. Next time, I'd prefer dinner and a movie," I laughed, the sound breaking the tension between us, infusing the moment with warmth despite the chilling circumstances.

As we ascended, the world below faded into a distant murmur, and for a moment, it felt as if we were suspended in time. The stars twinkled above, their brilliance overshadowed by the lurking darkness of our pursuer. Once on the roof, we crouched behind a chimney, our breaths synchronized as we listened for any sign of the hunter.

"Do you think he'll follow us up here?" I whispered, feeling the heat of Damian's body beside mine.

"If he does, he'll wish he hadn't," Damian replied, his expression fierce, the kind of determination that made him all the more alluring. I could sense the edge of his frustration, the desire to protect me and to take control of a situation spiraling into chaos.

A sudden clang echoed from below, and we both froze, hearts pounding in tandem. The hunter had found the fire escape, and I could almost feel the weight of his presence, a shadow stretching across the roof, searching. I stifled a gasp, and Damian squeezed my hand, grounding me as we waited, hearts thundering like war drums.

"Let's create a distraction," he whispered, a plan forming behind his piercing gaze. "If I can lure him away, you can slip down the other side and find an exit."

"Are you out of your mind?" I hissed. "I'm not letting you take that risk alone."

He chuckled softly, the sound both reassuring and maddening. "I'm a risk-taker by nature. Plus, I can't let you out of my sight when it's this dangerous."

"Who's the one that almost got us killed in the first place?" I countered, trying to keep my tone light, but beneath the playful banter, a wave of worry crashed over me. I was terrified of losing him.

"Touché," he admitted, eyes glinting with mischief. "But it's my turn to be reckless. Just trust me. I'll find you."

With that, he slipped away, a ghost in the night, leaving me trembling behind the chimney. My heart raced, caught between admiration for his bravery and fear for his safety. I felt utterly exposed up here, the roof no longer a sanctuary but a perch from which I could see all the dangers creeping closer.

I peered over the edge, catching sight of the hunter now making his way onto the roof, a dark silhouette moving with predatory grace. His cloak fluttered like wings in the wind, and I could feel the dread knotting my stomach. I needed to keep my wits about me, to remember why we were in this together.

Damian's laughter suddenly rang out from the far side of the roof, a deliberate invitation that tugged at the hunter's focus. "Catch me if you can!" he called, his voice buoyant and carefree, a stark contrast to the danger lurking just beneath the surface.

The hunter turned, a snarl twisting his lips as he lunged toward the sound, and in that instant, I felt the primal urge to protect Damian rise within me. With a decision made, I crouched low and made my way toward the edge of the roof, searching for a route that would allow me to follow them without being seen.

As I reached the far side, I spotted a rusty vent leading down to the alleyway. It wasn't ideal, but it was my only chance to rejoin Damian and help him. Climbing down felt like sliding into the depths of a well, but I had no time to second-guess myself. I slipped into the vent, pulling myself through the narrow space, the cool metal pressing against my skin like the sharp edge of fear.

The sound of struggle echoed in the distance, and I crawled faster, urgency driving me forward. The smell of damp earth and old metal filled my lungs as I maneuvered through the vent, the world above me a cacophony of chaos. I could almost hear Damian's voice, commanding and confident, urging me onward.

With one final push, I tumbled out of the vent and into the alleyway, my heart racing not just with exertion but with a fierce determination to find him. The hunt was on, and I wouldn't let him face the darkness alone. I might have entered this game as a mere player, but now I was ready to rewrite the rules.

The night draped over the city like a heavy velvet curtain, muffling the usual sounds and replacing them with a tense silence that thrummed in the air. Every shadow felt alive, every corner could conceal the threat that trailed us—an unknown hunter with a singular intent: our demise. Damian and I moved with a desperate urgency, weaving through the remnants of a long-abandoned marketplace, where once-vibrant stalls now stood as silent witnesses to our plight. The smell of decay mingled with the faint hint of spices, remnants of a time when laughter and bargaining filled the streets.

"Do you think they're watching us?" I whispered, glancing over my shoulder, half-expecting to see a glint of steel or the flicker of a cruel smile. My heart raced, thumping in my chest like a drum, a reminder of the peril we faced.

Damian's expression was set, his jaw tight. "They always are. The Crimson Society never lets its targets slip away easily." He pulled me closer, our bodies brushing, a simple act that sent sparks of warmth coursing through my veins despite the chill of the night. "We need to keep moving. Head toward the river; the docks have a maze of old warehouses that might give us some cover."

I nodded, adrenaline sharpening my senses. The river had always held a peculiar allure for me, the way its waters reflected the moonlight, creating a shimmering path that seemed to beckon with secrets. But now it felt more like a dark abyss, a vast expanse filled with potential dangers. As we sprinted forward, I felt a pull towards him that went beyond mere survival; it was a connection, forged in the crucible of fear. I had known Damian only briefly, but every shared glance and hurried touch was cementing a bond that felt inexplicably profound.

"Let's split up," he suggested suddenly, halting in a narrow alley where the buildings leaned in like conspirators. "If we can confuse them, it might buy us some time. Meet me at the old boathouse in an hour."

"No way," I shot back, my voice firm. "I'm not leaving you. Not now." The thought of facing this predator alone sent a chill deeper than the night air. "We'll figure it out together. We're stronger that way."

He hesitated, his dark eyes searching mine as if weighing the merits of my argument against the instinct to protect me. "I can't lose you, not like this. If I get caught, you—"

"If you get caught, then I'm next. I'm not hiding while you fight this alone." My words hung in the air, a fragile promise between us, and I watched as the storm of conflicting emotions played out on his face.

Finally, he relented, a reluctant grin breaking through the tension. "Alright, but you follow my lead. If I say run, you run."

"Deal," I agreed, matching his grin with a fierce determination. Together, we stepped back into the fray, our footsteps a silent pact against the encroaching darkness.

The streets twisted and turned like a snake, leading us deeper into the heart of the city's forgotten veins. Each time I caught a glimpse of a movement in the periphery, a surge of adrenaline coursed through me. We navigated through the remnants of a once-bustling community, dodging piles of debris and the occasional flickering streetlamp that seemed to pulse like a heartbeat. Just when I thought we'd found our rhythm, a sound cut through the air—a low, mocking laugh that echoed from the shadows.

"Do you think you can outrun me?" The voice was smooth, dripping with a chilling confidence that sent a shiver down my spine. "You're just prolonging the inevitable."

Damian's grip on my hand tightened, a silent reassurance that we were in this together. "Ignore them," he hissed, leading us into a narrow passageway that smelled of mildew and rust. "They're just trying to get in our heads."

But as we pressed on, I could feel my resolve slipping, gnawed away by the darkness that surrounded us. I could almost hear the hunter's footsteps trailing behind, relentless and steady, a countdown to our capture. "Damian," I breathed, my voice barely above a whisper, "what if they know our every move? What if this is just a game to them?"

He shot me a sidelong glance, a flicker of uncertainty crossing his features. "Then we have to change the rules," he replied, his tone steely yet laced with that familiar warmth. "Let's give them a show."

As we rounded a corner, the silhouette of an old warehouse loomed ahead, its rusty exterior a stark contrast against the night sky. "In there," I urged, pointing toward the entrance, a yawning black mouth that promised temporary refuge. The heavy door creaked ominously as we pushed inside, the air thick with dust and the weight of secrets long forgotten.

Inside, the warehouse was a cavern of shadows, each sound amplified in the silence. We found ourselves surrounded by forgotten crates and broken machinery, remnants of a time when this place was alive with purpose. "We can hide here for a moment," I suggested, glancing at the scattered debris that could serve as a makeshift barricade.

Damian nodded, moving to help me shift a heavy crate against the door. Just as we settled into a wary silence, a sound echoed through the stillness—a subtle scrape followed by a low thud that sent my heart into a frenzied race. "They're close," I breathed, my chest tightening with dread.

Suddenly, the door rattled violently, and a cruel voice called from the other side, "Game over, lovebirds. You can't hide forever."

Damian's gaze met mine, a shared understanding of our precarious situation igniting between us. The hunter was no longer just a shadow; they were a tangible threat, and our time was running out. In that instant, I realized the truth: love might bind us, but it was our cunning and resourcefulness that would determine our fate. And as the door shuddered beneath the weight of the impending confrontation, I steeled myself for whatever came next, knowing that the game had only just begun.

Chapter 26: Beneath a Fractured Sky

The wind swept through the crumbling remnants of the watchtower, a hollow whisper against the stone walls, as if the past itself was cautioning us. I could feel the chill creeping into my bones, intertwining with the electric tension crackling in the air. Rain was imminent, its promise heavy with the scent of impending storms, mingling with the distant smell of earth after a long drought. Damian stood beside me, his presence a sturdy anchor amidst the chaos that swirled around us. Our fingers were intertwined, a small, fierce declaration of defiance against the gathering darkness.

Thunder rolled in the distance, a low growl that matched the pounding of my heart. I was acutely aware of the weight of the moment; this was it. The confrontation we had been dreading since we first learned of the hunter's relentless pursuit. My mind flickered back to the days when my biggest concern was whether I'd have enough time to bake another batch of lemon tarts for the café. Now, standing on this precipice, I was teetering on the edge of something far more dangerous and thrilling than any sweet confection.

"Do you remember the first time we came up here?" Damian's voice broke through the tension, pulling me from the whirlwind of my thoughts. His eyes glinted with a mix of nostalgia and determination, as if he was drawing strength from our shared memories.

I chuckled softly, the sound feeling foreign in the weighty silence. "You mean the time you nearly fell off the edge trying to impress me with that ridiculous balancing act?" The memory of him, arms flailing comically as he lost his footing on the moss-covered stones, was a welcome reprieve from the grim present. "You were lucky I was there to save you."

"Or perhaps it was your baking that saved me," he replied, a playful grin breaking the tension etched across his features. "Who knew a chocolate chip cookie could pack such a punch?"

The sound of our laughter echoed eerily against the stones, a stark contrast to the ominous rumble of thunder overhead. Yet, in that moment, it felt like a shield against the encroaching fear. We were here together, as we always had been, and we would face whatever came next with the same determination that had seen us through so many challenges.

But the laughter faded as the shadows lengthened, coiling around us like serpents ready to strike. The hunter was near, his presence a palpable darkness that clawed at the edges of my consciousness. I could feel the air grow heavier, charged with a sinister energy that sent shivers racing down my spine.

Damian squeezed my hand tighter, grounding me. "Whatever happens, stay close," he murmured, his voice low and steady. I nodded, my throat suddenly dry, the gravity of his words sinking in deeper than the threat looming ahead.

As the storm clouds gathered, swirling ominously above us, the first drops of rain began to fall, tapping against the stone like the anxious heartbeat of the world. The patter quickly escalated into a downpour, drenching us in a matter of moments. The sky cracked open, pouring its fury upon the watchtower, each droplet amplifying the impending conflict, transforming the air into a slick, charged battlefield.

The hunter emerged from the shadows, a wraith-like figure cloaked in darkness, his eyes burning with malevolence. His presence sent a shockwave through the air, a chill that turned my blood to ice. I could feel my breath hitch in my throat, the sheer terror of his gaze piercing through me. "You think you can escape your fate?" he spat, voice a low, cruel snarl. "You're nothing but prey, and I will enjoy feasting on your fear."

Damian stepped forward, positioning himself protectively in front of me. "We're not afraid of you," he declared, his voice steady despite the fear clawing at his insides.

"Really? That's rich," the hunter laughed, a harsh sound that grated against my ears. He moved with a fluidity that was terrifying, circling us like a predator sizing up its prey. "You're a fool to stand against me."

As he lunged forward, darkness swirling around him like a living thing, I felt an unexpected surge of power crackling through me. It was as if the very storm itself was awakening something dormant within, a strength that had been buried beneath layers of doubt and fear. I focused, channeling that energy into my fingertips, and unleashed a burst of light—a dazzling flare that illuminated the darkness, momentarily blinding the hunter.

He staggered back, the shock rippling through him, and in that brief moment of chaos, Damian and I moved in tandem. Every lesson we had learned together surged forward, igniting a fire within me. We were a team forged in trials, and this was our chance to finally end this nightmare.

With every spell we conjured, every strike we launched, we pushed him closer to the edge of the tower, our movements synchronized like a perfectly choreographed dance. The air crackled with energy as the storm raged above, a furious backdrop to our battle. Each moment stretched like an eternity, the stakes higher than they had ever been. And yet, with each clash, each defiant stance, I felt an unexpected clarity.

As the hunter fell, his body teetering on the precipice, I felt a strange, serene calm wash over me. It was as if, in that chaotic whirlwind of conflict, I had finally found my place in this fractured world. I looked up at the sky, now split with flashes of lightning, and understood that survival was only the beginning. I would no longer allow fear to dictate my choices or chain me to the shadows of my past.

Together, we had faced the storm and emerged stronger. The world stretched before us, filled with possibilities that shimmered like the first light of dawn breaking through the clouds. I grasped Damian's hand tightly, my heart swelling with a fierce determination. This was not the end; it was merely the dawn of something new, something that would change the course of our lives forever.

The storm roared around us, a wild tempest of rain and wind that mirrored the turmoil surging in my heart. As the echoes of the hunter's fall faded into the distance, the reality of our survival began to seep in, heavy and suffocating. I turned to Damian, who was still catching his breath, his expression a mix of triumph and disbelief. The light from the remnants of our spells danced across his features, casting shadows that seemed to hold their own secrets.

"We did it," I breathed, the words barely escaping my lips, drenched in the aftermath of adrenaline. "I can't believe we actually did it."

"Don't get cocky," he replied, his voice laced with a teasing tone that belied the intensity of our recent encounter. "One battle down, and now we need to figure out how to get home without becoming a lightning rod." He flashed a grin that lit up his face, momentarily chasing away the lingering darkness.

I couldn't help but smile back, the warmth spreading through me despite the chill that clung to our skin. "Right, because getting struck by lightning is definitely on my bucket list," I quipped, scanning the clouds above. They churned ominously, a swirling mass that seemed almost alive, as if protesting our victory.

Damian's laughter faded as he looked into the distance, the vast expanse of the city sprawling beneath us, a patchwork quilt of light and shadow. "We should go before the storm worsens. I'd rather not test my luck any further tonight." His grip tightened around my hand, a reassuring tether to reality.

We began our descent down the weathered steps of the watchtower, each footfall echoing like a drumbeat of finality. As the rain poured, washing away the remnants of the battle, I felt a sense of clarity settling over me. The air, thick with the scent of wet stone and earth, revitalized my spirit, sharpening my senses. This was more than just survival; it was a turning point. I would no longer let fear dictate my actions.

Halfway down, a crack of thunder split the sky, reverberating through the air like a warning. I stumbled, nearly losing my footing, but Damian caught me, his grip firm and unyielding. "Easy there, hero," he teased, his voice soothing amidst the storm's fury. "We wouldn't want to add an injury to our victory lap."

I rolled my eyes but couldn't suppress a laugh. "Just trying to make sure I don't slip back into the abyss, you know. Can't have me falling back in love with danger."

With each step, I felt more grounded, the weight of our confrontation settling into the past where it belonged. But the sense of victory was soon tainted by the creeping uncertainty of what lay ahead. The city below us was a vibrant tapestry of life, yet it felt fractured, as if the shadows of the hunter had woven their darkness into every corner.

As we reached the ground level, the streets glistened under the persistent rain, reflections shimmering like the remnants of our battle. The world felt transformed, as if the storm had washed away not only the grime of the city but also the fears that had held me captive for so long. Yet I could not ignore the questions that loomed in my mind. What would we find once we returned home? Would the peace we had fought for endure, or would new threats emerge from the shadows?

Damian nudged me, drawing me from my reverie. "What's brewing in that brilliant mind of yours?" he asked, a playful smirk tugging at his lips.

"Just thinking about our next adventure. I have a feeling that we're not quite done with the hunter's legacy." I paused, biting my lip as I glanced around the dampened streets. "And if there are others like him lurking in the shadows, we need to be prepared."

"Prepared? Or should I be worried about your baking again?" he replied, raising an eyebrow in mock seriousness. "You know, the last time you made cookies for our 'preparations,' they almost caused a riot."

I couldn't help but laugh, the tension easing as I recalled the chaos that had erupted in the café when I had experimented with a new recipe. "Well, maybe I'll stick to spells instead of sweets this time around," I said, "but only if you promise not to burn the cookies again."

"Deal." His eyes sparkled with mischief. "But I think we should plan a little differently. Maybe this time we bring the cookies as bait instead of distraction."

I felt the warmth in my chest spread into a full-blown laugh. As we strolled through the rain-soaked streets, our banter wrapped around us like a warm cloak, a stark contrast to the looming darkness. I knew the threat wasn't truly over, yet in that moment, I felt invincible.

Suddenly, a figure appeared in the distance, half-hidden beneath the shadows of a crumbling building. I instinctively pulled closer to Damian, the laughter dying in my throat as a sense of foreboding settled in. "Do you see that?" I whispered, my heart racing once more.

"Yeah," he replied, his demeanor shifting as he took a cautious step forward. "Stay behind me."

As we approached, the figure stepped into the dim light, revealing a familiar face, worn and tired yet unmistakably strong. It was Lila, an ally we had thought lost in the chaos. Her eyes, however, held a wild gleam, a hint of desperation mixed with determination. "You two are in grave danger," she said, her voice urgent, slicing through the tension like a knife.

"Lila?" I stammered, shock coursing through me. "What happened? We thought you were..."

"Dead? No, but I might as well have been," she interrupted, her gaze darting around us as if expecting enemies to emerge from the shadows at any moment. "There's much you don't know. The hunter was just a pawn in a much larger game, and if we don't act quickly, everything we fought for will be in jeopardy."

The air thickened with uncertainty, and my heart plummeted. Just when I thought we had emerged from the darkness, the shadows were closing in once more, wrapping around us like a shroud. I exchanged a look with Damian, his expression mirroring my concern. Our battle might have been won, but the war was far from over.

Lila's urgency electrified the air around us, a stark contrast to the calm that had just settled after the chaos. The world felt charged with anticipation, and I sensed that every word she spoke carried the weight of hidden truths. Her usually vibrant eyes were shadowed with the burden of knowledge, and the tension radiating from her made it impossible to ignore the gravity of the situation.

"What do you mean a pawn?" I asked, my voice barely above a whisper, as if saying it aloud might summon whatever darkness she hinted at.

Lila took a step closer, her expression intense, as if she were searching our faces for some sign of understanding. "The hunter was just one piece in a much larger game. He was sent to retrieve something—something powerful that's been hidden for centuries."

She paused, glancing over her shoulder, wary of the shadows that clung to the alleyways. "And now that he's gone, others will come for it. They'll stop at nothing to reclaim what they believe is theirs."

Damian leaned in, his brow furrowed. "What is it? What are they after?"

"The Heart of the City," Lila replied, the name slipping from her lips like a secret meant for only the bravest of souls. "An ancient artifact believed to have the power to control the very essence of our world. Whoever possesses it can bend reality to their will."

The implications of her words sent a shiver racing down my spine. This wasn't just about us anymore; it was about the balance of everything we held dear. "And you know where it is?" I asked, my heart pounding with a mix of hope and fear.

She shook her head, frustration etching lines on her forehead. "Not exactly. I have a lead, but it's dangerous. We'd have to venture into the Hollow—an old district that's been forgotten by time, full of secrets and traps." Her voice dropped to a conspiratorial tone, laced with trepidation. "And the last time anyone went looking for the Heart, they never came back."

"Well, that sounds cheerful," I muttered, glancing at Damian, who was lost in thought, his jaw set.

"We don't have a choice," he said finally, breaking the tension. "If there's even a chance we can find it before they do, we have to try."

Lila nodded, the flicker of determination igniting in her gaze. "I'll lead the way. But we need to move quickly. The storm isn't just a natural occurrence; it's a signal. They're coming."

As we plunged deeper into the heart of the city, the rain continued to pour down, drenching the streets and sending rivulets coursing along the cobblestones like tiny rivers. The familiar sights of our world were distorted by the downpour, and the lights from the storefronts flickered like will-o'-the-wisps, beckoning us into the unknown.

"Do you think we'll really find the Heart?" I asked, needing reassurance as much as I sought clarity. "What if it's all just a myth?"

Lila glanced over her shoulder, her expression unreadable. "Legends are often rooted in truth. And truth can be stranger than fiction."

Damian, always the pragmatist, added, "Myths don't scare people into hiding, do they? Someone believes in this enough to send a hunter after it."

A shiver of apprehension slithered up my spine as we moved through the slick, darkened streets. Each shadow seemed to hold a whisper of danger, and I felt the weight of every step we took, as if the ground itself was a reminder of how precarious our situation had become.

The Hollow loomed ahead, a labyrinth of decaying buildings and tangled vines that had long since reclaimed their territory. It felt like stepping into another world—one where time stood still and forgotten echoes lingered in the air. The architecture was a chaotic jumble, old stone mingling with iron and brick, a once-vibrant neighborhood now reduced to mere shadows of its former self.

"This is it," Lila said, halting at the entrance to a narrow alley, her voice a mix of reverence and dread. "We have to be careful. The Heart is said to be hidden within the ruins of the old library. If we can get there first, we might have a chance."

I could feel the pulse of the city thundering in my ears as I scanned the surroundings. The rain had eased, but a thick fog began to creep in, swirling around us like a living entity, distorting our vision and heightening the eerie atmosphere. "What kind of defenses are we talking about?" I asked, trying to steel myself for whatever might be waiting.

"Traps, illusions, maybe even guardians," Lila warned. "We need to stay close, trust each other. This place has a way of playing tricks on your mind."

As we advanced, every creak of the old structures and whisper of the wind seemed to amplify the danger, wrapping around us like a shroud. I felt the urge to turn back clawing at my insides, but a deeper resolve propelled me forward.

Suddenly, the ground shifted beneath us, a low rumble echoing through the alley. I exchanged worried glances with Damian and Lila, our hearts pounding in sync. "What was that?" I asked, dread pooling in my stomach.

Before anyone could answer, a figure emerged from the mist, tall and cloaked, features obscured by shadows. "You shouldn't have come here," it intoned, voice smooth like silk yet laced with menace. "You're trespassing in a domain that should remain undisturbed."

"Who are you?" Damian stepped forward, hands clenched at his sides, ready to defend.

The figure shifted, revealing a glint of silver at its waist. "I am the Keeper of the Hollow, and you have awakened forces beyond your comprehension."

The air crackled with tension, and as the Keeper's gaze met mine, I felt a jolt of recognition, a flicker of something ancient swirling in the depths of my memory. "What do you want?" I demanded, forcing my voice to remain steady.

"To protect what is sacred," the Keeper replied, voice low and resonant, "and to keep the Heart from those who seek to misuse its power."

My heart raced as I took a step back, realization dawning. "You're here to stop us."

"Indeed," the Keeper said, raising a hand that shimmered with an ethereal light. "And I will do whatever it takes to prevent you from entering."

With that, a blinding flash erupted from their fingertips, illuminating the alley in a blare of white-hot energy. I barely had time to react before the world around us shifted, the shadows twisting and warping, as if the very fabric of reality was tearing apart.

"Run!" Damian shouted, grabbing my arm as we stumbled backward, the Keeper's power enveloping us in a whirlwind of light and darkness. I could hear Lila's voice echoing in my ears, blending with the chaotic sounds of the storm, a cacophony that threatened to swallow us whole.

As the ground quaked beneath our feet, I felt the last vestiges of hope slipping away, uncertainty clawing at my mind. We had come so far, but were we about to lose everything?

And just as the darkness threatened to close in, the light consumed us, plunging us into an abyss where reality blurred into chaos. In that moment, I realized our fight was only just beginning, and the true test of our courage lay ahead.

Chapter 27: Cracks in the Glass

The air crackled with tension, thick as smoke, as I weaved through the debris-laden streets of Aleron. I could hear the distant roar of flames, the sound a mournful howl, yet it felt unreal, like something torn from the pages of a nightmare. Each footfall was punctuated by the thud of my heart, echoing in my chest as I gripped the hilt of my dagger, the cool metal a comforting reminder of my resolve. I was acutely aware of the chaos swirling around me; the streets, usually a tapestry of laughter and life, were now a chaotic blend of desperation and fury, with shadows of the Crimson Society flitting through the carnage like phantoms.

It was hard to breathe, harder still to push aside the suffocating fear that clawed at my throat. I had fought so hard for peace, yet here we were, right back in the throes of a conflict that threatened to consume us all. The flickering flames from a nearby building cast a warm glow on the faces of those fleeing, illuminating their expressions—some twisted in terror, others set in grim determination. I had seen the best and worst of humanity during these dark times, and at that moment, the worst seemed to be winning.

Racing through the throng, my gaze darted from one crumbling facade to another, searching for the familiar form of Damian. The thought of him, vulnerable amidst this chaos, sent a jolt of urgency coursing through me. I had to find him. Just as I rounded the corner of a burned-out storefront, the unmistakable sight of Livia stepped into my path. She stood there, tall and fierce, her dark hair whipping in the wind like a banner of rebellion. Her eyes, usually so full of mischief, were now filled with something darker—a determination that sent a chill down my spine.

"Livia!" I gasped, half-relieved, half-terrified. "What are you doing here?"

"Saving you from your foolishness," she replied, her voice sharp as glass. "You think you can protect him? That you can hold back the tide? You're only making it worse."

Her words hit me like a slap, the sting reverberating in my mind. "I can't just stand by while he faces this alone! You don't understand!"

"Understand? I understand all too well." Livia stepped closer, lowering her voice, her intensity almost palpable. "Damian's past is a storm, and you're the eye of it. If he stays with you, he'll drown. You need to let him go before it's too late."

Doubt crept in, insidious and unwelcome, gnawing at the edges of my resolve. I had fought so hard to keep my heart open to Damian, to trust in the bond we had forged. Yet Livia's words clung to me like a fog. "What do you know about his past?" I shot back, my voice trembling with a mix of anger and fear. "What do you know about love?"

"Love? Is that what you think this is?" Livia's laugh was bitter, cutting through the air like a blade. "Love is not enough to protect you from the darkness that surrounds him. You're not seeing the whole picture. You're too close to the flame to see the smoke."

The heat from the fires nearby seemed to intensify, wrapping around us like a warning. I felt trapped in her gaze, unable to look away from the fierce passion igniting her features. "And what do you propose I do?" I challenged, my voice rising above the din of destruction. "Turn my back on him? Abandon him to this chaos?"

Livia's expression softened for a fleeting moment, revealing a flicker of vulnerability before her walls came crashing back down. "I'm not saying to abandon him. I'm saying to protect yourself. You can't save him if you're lost too."

Her words hung heavy in the air, and the truth in them struck me like a punch to the gut. The roar of the flames and the cries of the city became a distant murmur as I grappled with her meaning. Livia had faced her own battles, fought against her own demons. She was trying to warn me, but the walls I had built around my heart made it hard to see her perspective. I had lost so much already. Was I willing to risk everything again?

Suddenly, the ground beneath us trembled—a shuddering reminder of the chaos erupting all around. We exchanged a glance, a fleeting moment of understanding amidst the chaos. I wanted to scream, to argue, but deep down, I sensed the truth in her words, an undercurrent of dread weaving through my thoughts.

"I have to find him," I declared, more to convince myself than her. I turned away, the heat from the flames urging me forward. Each step felt like a small rebellion against the fear that threatened to overwhelm me. "He needs me. We need each other."

Livia's voice trailed behind me, laced with urgency. "Then go! But remember, you're not just fighting for him. You're fighting for yourself too. Don't lose sight of that."

Her words echoed in my mind as I pushed through the throng, adrenaline propelling me forward. The world around me was a blur of chaos, yet I focused on the singular thought of finding Damian. Each face I passed was a reminder of what was at stake—lives shattered by the war, dreams turned to ash.

I plunged deeper into the fray, each shadow a possible threat, each echo a reminder of the ticking clock. The city was unraveling, and somewhere within the wreckage lay the man I cared for, a piece of my heart entangled in his fate. I could no longer afford the luxury of doubt; I had to believe that love, fierce and resilient, would be enough to shield us from the encroaching darkness. As I rounded a corner, the familiar silhouette of Damian emerged from the chaos, and in that moment, the world narrowed to just him and me, standing on the precipice of everything we had fought for.

The moment I spotted Damian, my heart surged with a mix of relief and trepidation. He stood near the remnants of a once-majestic fountain, its waters now choked with ash and debris, a grim testament to the chaos surrounding us. His face was smeared with soot, eyes narrowed against the smoke that choked the sky, yet there was a fierce determination etched into his features that drew me closer. I rushed towards him, weaving through the frantic crowd that swirled like a tempest, every scream and shout punctuating the air with desperation.

"Damian!" I called out, my voice barely rising above the cacophony. He turned, and for a brief moment, time stilled. Our gazes locked, and in that instant, the world around us faded. I took in the way his hair fell across his forehead, tousled and wild, and how the shadows accentuated the sharp lines of his jaw. Despite the carnage, he remained a beacon of strength, his presence both grounding and exhilarating.

"Get back!" he shouted, a hint of urgency breaking through the steadfastness in his tone. His gaze flickered over my shoulder, and I felt a surge of fear as I turned to see a group of masked figures advancing toward us, the crimson emblem of their society gleaming ominously in the dim light. The realization hit me like a splash of cold water; they were coming for him, and I was caught in the crossfire.

"Damian, we have to move!" I urged, grasping his arm. The heat from the fires enveloped us, mingling with the palpable tension as we fell into step, each of us instinctively knowing that survival was our only goal. As we dashed down the narrow alleyways, the sounds of destruction echoed behind us—a relentless reminder of the city's perilous fate.

"Where's Livia?" he asked, glancing back, concern threading through his voice.

"Trying to save me from myself," I said with a wry smile that felt more like a mask than a true reflection of my emotions. "You know how she is. Very dramatic."

"Dramatic or not, we need to stay together," he replied, his tone sharp as a blade. "If they catch us alone, it'll be over before we even know it."

I nodded, the gravity of his words weighing heavily on my heart. I had come to understand the depths of his past, the shadows that haunted him, but facing the specter of those who would drag him back into darkness was a different battle altogether. The city, once a tapestry of vibrant life, now felt like a crumbling husk, threatening to swallow us whole.

We darted through a narrow passageway, the scent of smoke and fear clinging to the air. Suddenly, Damian stopped, his body tensing as he pressed me against the wall, hidden from view. My breath quickened, the thrill of danger intertwining with a pulse of adrenaline that surged through my veins.

"What are we doing?" I whispered, trying to peer around him.

"Waiting. We can't rush headlong into this. They'll be looking for us." His voice was a low murmur, just above a whisper, and I could feel the warmth of his body radiating against mine. It was a strange comfort amidst the chaos, one that made my heart race for reasons I dared not explore.

"Right, because hiding in the shadows is always the best strategy," I quipped, attempting to inject some levity into the dire situation. "I suppose next we'll be waiting for the cavalry to arrive."

Damian smirked, a flicker of humor breaking through his tense demeanor. "You know, in some stories, the hero does wait for the cavalry."

"Ah, yes, but this isn't one of those stories. This is our reality, where the hero is perpetually late."

Before he could respond, a loud crash reverberated through the alley, followed by the unmistakable sound of shattering glass. My heart dropped. "They're close," I murmured, panic rising like bile in my throat.

"Stay behind me," he instructed, his voice firm but low, a command that ignited my instinct to resist. I had fought too hard to be a passive participant, but as I caught a glimpse of the shadowy figures advancing, my resolve wavered.

With a swift movement, he pulled out his dagger, its blade glinting ominously in the dim light. "We'll fight if we have to. But first, we need to know what we're up against."

As the footsteps drew nearer, I sensed the urgency coiling around us like a tightening noose. The muffled voices of the approaching adversaries became clearer, each word laced with menace. "Find them! They can't have gone far!"

My stomach twisted, the reality of the situation settling in. They were hunting for us, and I couldn't shake the feeling that they knew more than we did about what lay ahead. "Damian, what if we—"

"No. We stick to the plan. If we can flank them, we might stand a chance." His gaze was fierce, a fire igniting within him that mirrored my own desperation. "Trust me."

Trust. The word hung in the air between us, heavy with implication. I wanted to believe in him, in us, but the shadows of doubt that Livia had cast loomed large. What if trusting him meant leading us both to ruin?

As the voices drew closer, I swallowed my fears and nodded, determination replacing my uncertainty. "Let's do this then. Together."

He shot me a look that felt like a promise, a silent vow that we would face whatever came next side by side. Just as we prepared to spring from our hiding place, a figure stumbled into view—a young woman, face streaked with dirt and tears, fear etched across her features. She looked like a ghost, and my heart clenched at the sight of her anguish.

"Please, help me!" she cried, her voice barely rising above the din.

Damian and I exchanged glances, a silent conversation passing between us. I saw the hesitation in his eyes, the instinct to protect ourselves battling against the desire to help. "We can't leave her," I whispered, a plea that felt like a weight pressing down on my chest.

"I know," he replied, jaw tightening. "But if we expose ourselves..."

"Then let's be quick," I urged, stepping out from behind him, determined to act. "We can't abandon anyone to this nightmare."

Without waiting for his agreement, I rushed toward the girl, my heart pounding with each step. The fire of determination blazed in me, driving out the doubt. In that moment, I realized I would fight for those who couldn't fight for themselves, no matter the cost.

I moved toward the young woman, who was trembling in the shadow of a collapsed wall, her eyes wide with terror. "It's okay," I said, forcing my voice to remain steady even as my heart raced. "We're here to help. What happened?"

"They... they're coming!" she stammered, glancing over her shoulder as if expecting the worst to appear at any moment. "They took my brother. He was just trying to get to safety—"

Before she could finish, a loud crash echoed through the alley, shaking the very ground beneath our feet. I felt the air thrum with impending danger. "We need to move," I urged, taking her hand. Her grip was small and fragile, and I could feel her fear radiating through the contact. "Can you walk? We'll get you somewhere safe."

Damian stepped forward, his brow furrowed with concern. "We can't just run into the open. We need a plan."

"The only plan is to get her out of here," I shot back, my impatience flaring. "Those men will be upon us any second!"

He hesitated, torn between instinct and strategy. I could see the wheels turning in his mind, each one heavier than the last. "Fine. But we need to be quick and quiet," he finally conceded. "Stick close to us."

We began to move, the girl squeezed between us, her breaths coming in shallow gasps. Each footfall echoed like a drumbeat, and I could feel my own heartbeat pounding in my ears as we navigated the wreckage of the alley, the remnants of our city hanging precariously around us. The fear of being discovered turned the air electric, but the urgency propelled us forward.

We reached the end of the alley and stepped out into the open street, where chaos reigned supreme. The once-bustling thoroughfare was now a graveyard of rubble and despair. I scanned the area, searching for an escape route, when I noticed a group of cloaked figures moving swiftly along the periphery, their intentions as sinister as the night itself.

"There!" I pointed, my voice low but urgent. "We can head toward that shop. It looks intact."

Damian nodded, and without hesitation, we began to sprint toward the building, the girl gasping as we pulled her along. The shop's entrance loomed closer, a faint hope flickering within its shattered windows. Just as we reached the threshold, a cry erupted from behind us—a voice that pierced through the chaos, sending a jolt of dread down my spine.

"Stop them!" It was a voice I recognized—a chilling command that belonged to one of the Society's enforcers. My blood ran cold as I glanced back, spotting the unmistakable figure of a man, cloaked in the crimson garb that marked him as one of their own.

"Go!" Damian shouted, his grip tightening on my arm. We burst through the doorway, the interior dim and laden with the scent of mildew and old wood. My heart raced as we ducked behind a row of wooden shelves, my mind spinning with the realization that we had just entered a new level of danger.

The girl clung to my side, her fear palpable as we crouched low, listening to the thundering footsteps that approached. I could hear Damian's breaths, steady yet charged with an unspoken tension. "We can't stay here long," he whispered, his voice barely above a murmur. "They'll search the place."

I nodded, my eyes scanning the room. It was a small shop, likely once filled with trinkets and charms, now a graveyard of forgotten treasures. Dust motes danced in the dim light, and the faded posters on the walls told stories of better days. But none of that mattered now; we needed a way out.

Suddenly, the front door swung open with a loud crash, and the enforcer stepped inside, his figure casting a long shadow over the floor. "They can't have gone far!" he barked, voice booming in the empty space. My heart raced as I held my breath, the very air around us charged with tension.

Damian's eyes darted around the shop, seeking an escape route. "Back here," he whispered, pointing toward a door at the rear of the shop. It looked like it led to a storage area, possibly another way out.

With a silent nod, we began to inch toward the door, moving as quietly as possible, each creak of the floor beneath us feeling like a death knell. I felt the girl tremble beside me, and I squeezed her hand reassuringly, hoping my presence would bolster her courage.

The enforcer, seemingly oblivious to our movements, began rummaging through the shelves, sending items crashing to the floor. "They must have taken shelter in here," he muttered, frustration lacing his voice. "Find them!"

"Now!" Damian urged, propelling us forward. We slipped through the door just as the enforcer turned his attention back toward the front, the creaking of the hinges barely audible over the din.

The storage room was dark and cluttered, filled with old crates and dust-laden furniture. I could feel the claustrophobia closing in as we navigated through the maze, but there was no time to dwell on that. I glanced back to make sure the girl was still with us, her eyes wide and filled with a mixture of fear and determination.

"Stay close," I whispered. "We'll find a way out."

Damian led the way, his movements precise and careful, and I followed closely behind, my heart pounding in time with the rhythm of our escape. We stumbled upon a narrow window at the far end of the room, its glass cracked and filthy, but a glimmer of daylight seeped through. "We can fit through here," he said, urgency lacing his voice.

I nodded, my breath catching as I hoisted the girl onto my hip. "You first," I instructed Damian, shoving him toward the window. He nodded, his expression a mixture of resolve and concern, and he scrambled up, pushing himself through the opening with surprising agility.

"Now you," he called, his voice muffled.

I turned to the girl, her small frame trembling with uncertainty. "You can do this. Just climb up to me," I encouraged, lifting her gently and guiding her toward the window. She hesitated, fear evident in her eyes, but desperation quickly overcame her trepidation.

"Okay," she finally murmured, her voice trembling as she gripped the edge of the sill and began to climb. I held my breath, praying she wouldn't falter. Just as she was about to hoist herself through, the door behind us crashed open, the enforcer's furious voice ringing out, "They're here somewhere!"

"Go!" I shouted, urgency igniting my voice as I helped her up. She scrambled through, her small frame disappearing beyond the window just as the man stormed into the room.

"Damn it!" he roared, spotting me as I turned to face him, heart racing with a mix of fear and defiance. I backed away, my dagger instinctively raised, ready to fight if necessary. The shadows around me felt alive, thrumming with tension as I stood my ground, adrenaline surging through my veins.

The enforcer's eyes gleamed with malevolence as he advanced. "You're outnumbered, girl. You can't hope to fight me."

"I'm not outnumbered yet," I shot back, my voice steadier than I felt. But as I prepared to make my stand, I heard the sound of shuffling behind me—the girl, now at the window's edge, struggling to pull herself up.

"Help!" she cried, her voice a mixture of fear and urgency.

In that fleeting moment, I made a decision. I had to buy her time. "Damian!" I yelled, my voice cracking. "Get her to safety!"

I could see the conflict in his eyes, a battle between loyalty and survival, but then he nodded and turned back to the window. The enforcer lunged at me, and I sidestepped, narrowly avoiding the grasp of his outstretched hand.

"Go!" I shouted again, adrenaline fueling my fight.

Damian helped the girl through the window, and I felt a flicker of hope surge within me. But as I turned to face the enforcer, the shadows around us shifted, and I knew this would be a fight for my life, one that would determine not only my fate but also the fate of everyone I loved.

With a fierce determination, I prepared to face him, the weight of the world resting squarely on my shoulders. The clash of our destinies hung in the air, the darkness closing in as I steeled myself for the confrontation that would change everything.

Chapter 28: Bound by Blood

The air hung heavy with the scent of rain-soaked earth, a dampness that clung to my skin as I stepped into the hollowed remains of the once-grand hall. Crumbling stone walls loomed around us, decorated with the remnants of forgotten glory—faded tapestries that once told tales of triumph, now frayed and dust-covered. It felt like a mausoleum, a fitting backdrop for the ghosts of our pasts, both personal and collective. Damian stood across the room, his silhouette outlined by the last light of a dying sun, a beacon of hope even as shadows threatened to consume us.

He turned, eyes blazing with the ferocity of a storm. "We don't have much time, Ariadne. They're coming." His voice was a mix of urgency and despair, a melody that struck a chord deep within me, stirring the chaos of emotions I had fought to contain. I could see it—the strain of his hidden truth, the weight of a legacy that threatened to drown him, and by extension, us.

"Damian," I stepped closer, heart pounding in sync with the thunder rumbling outside, "whatever it is, we can face it together. We've done everything together." My words felt like a flimsy bridge over a chasm of uncertainty, but I meant them with every fiber of my being. We had endured so much—the betrayals, the relentless battles against the Crimson Society's dark machinations—and yet here we were, on the cusp of what could be our final confrontation.

He raked a hand through his disheveled hair, the strands glistening with moisture from the air. "This isn't just about us anymore. It's bigger than that." The vulnerability in his gaze pierced through my bravado, sending a shiver down my spine. I knew that look too well—it was the same expression I had worn when I first uncovered the truth of my own past, the fractured pieces of my identity that had been ripped apart and sewn together again by the hands of fate.

"What do you mean?" I pressed, determination bolstering my courage even as dread gnawed at my insides.

His sigh was a storm, heavy with the burden he carried. "My bloodline, Ariadne. It's cursed, bound to the Velvet Charm in ways I never understood until now. The power that flows through me—it's both a gift and a scourge. The deeper I delve into it, the more it claims me." His eyes bore into mine, filled with an anguish that felt like ice against my heart. "I can't let it destroy you too."

"Then let's find a way to break it!" I insisted, my voice rising in fervor. "We've faced monsters before. Why can't we face this one together?" The desperation clawed at my throat, a raw plea for him to understand that leaving was not an option, not now when we were so close to victory. The world outside this crumbling sanctuary was a tempest of chaos and uncertainty, but within these walls, our resolve forged an unyielding connection.

"You don't understand," he said, stepping back as if the weight of my presence was too much for him to bear. "Every moment I remain here, I risk unleashing a darkness that could swallow everything we've fought for. I have to sever the tie—cut it clean. I can't let you bear the burden of my lineage."

Anguish twisted in my chest, clawing at the edges of my hope. "Damian, please." I took another step forward, reaching for him. "You're not alone in this. You never have to be. We've built something—something worth fighting for."

But he shook his head, resolute and heart-wrenching in his finality. "It's not just about us. It's about everyone in this city. The charm—it's calling to me, and the more I resist, the stronger its grip becomes. I won't let it take me."

As I looked into his eyes, I felt the surge of emotion—the love, the fear, the shared history that bound us tighter than any blood oath. "You don't get to decide that alone, Damian. We made promises to each other. I won't let you throw that away." My voice trembled with the weight of my conviction, desperation lacing each syllable.

He flinched at my words, a moment of vulnerability breaking through his steely facade. "What if I can't control it? What if I become the monster I've fought against?"

"Then we'll fight it together," I insisted, my voice softening. "We can find a way to break this curse—there has to be something in the lore, something we can use."

The silence that followed was thick with unspoken fears and lingering doubts. I watched as the storm outside brewed, dark clouds roiling and churning, mirroring the turmoil within us. His expression shifted, and for a fleeting moment, I glimpsed a flicker of hope. "You really believe we can?"

"I have to believe," I replied, willing myself to bridge the gap between our hearts. "I believe in us. In what we can create, in what we've already built. You're not just a bloodline, Damian. You're so much more than that."

As thunder cracked in the distance, a deep rumble that echoed the urgency of our situation, he stepped closer again, the air between us charged with unspoken promises and the desperate flicker of hope. "Then let's find that way." His resolve ignited something within me, a flame that refused to be extinguished. "Together."

The weight of the world still pressed down on us, but with every shared breath, I felt the chains of despair begin to weaken. The Velvet Charm may have woven itself into the fabric of his existence, but we were more than its threads. We were the fire that could unravel its hold, one strand at a time.

A soft patter of rain began to drum against the cracked windowpanes, each drop a reminder of the tempest brewing outside, a fitting backdrop to the turmoil within. The sound wrapped around us like an old, familiar melody, a signal that our time was running thin. I turned to Damian, heart thundering like the storm as I contemplated the weight of his words. We were on the precipice of something monumental, the shadows of our fears stretching longer than the fading daylight.

"Let's start by looking into the lore," I suggested, my voice steadier than I felt. "There has to be a way to sever this link. You mentioned the Velvet Charm calling to you, right? Maybe we can turn that against it."

Damian's eyes sparkled with a mixture of admiration and trepidation. "You always have a plan, don't you? How did I get so lucky?" His wry smile cut through the tension, igniting a warmth in my chest that chased away some of the cold fear lingering there.

"It's a gift," I quipped, a playful smirk creeping onto my lips. "But it often involves a fair amount of reckless abandon."

With a shared chuckle that felt like a fragile thread pulling us back from the edge, we turned our focus to the ancient tomes lining the shelves, their spines cracked and faded, echoing the secrets they held. Dust motes danced in the low light as I reached for a thick volume, its cover embossed with symbols I recognized from our earlier confrontations with the Crimson Society. "This one looks promising," I said, flipping it open with a flourish that felt far more confident than my heart.

As I scanned the yellowed pages, words leaped out at me—my pulse quickened at the mention of a ritual, something that could potentially unravel the ties binding Damian to the Velvet Charm. "Listen to this," I said, reading aloud, "The Bond of Blood can be severed through the cleansing of the soul, an act of selfless sacrifice."

He leaned closer, his warmth brushing against my shoulder, a grounding presence amid the storm of possibilities. "Sacrifice?" he echoed, the gravity of the word hanging heavily in the air. "What does that mean? Are we talking about a symbolic gesture, or are we about to enter the realm of melodrama?"

I rolled my eyes playfully. "Oh please, it can't be that theatrical. I refuse to believe that severing a bloodline involves dramatic monologues and sacrificial pyres. We're not in some over-the-top fantasy novel."

"Fingers crossed," he muttered, flipping through the pages until his brow furrowed. "Aha! Here it is—an ancient rite called the Cleansing of the Bound. It requires two willing participants, but there's a catch."

"What's the catch?" I asked, my pulse quickening again.

"It demands the binding of a shared essence." He looked at me, his gaze intense and unwavering. "We'd have to connect our blood, Ariadne. It would link us, momentarily. And if one of us falters, the other could be lost in the process."

A shiver ran down my spine, but I squared my shoulders, determination surging. "We've faced worse odds, and we're still standing. Besides, it's a risk I'm willing to take. We can't let fear dictate our choices."

"I admire your spirit, but it's not just fear I'm concerned about." His voice was a mix of concern and admiration, like he was both proud and wary of my resolve. "If we fail—if I fail—it could mean losing you forever."

"Hey, let's not get morbid. We'll find a way through this. Together." The word felt powerful, resonating between us like a vow.

He nodded slowly, a flicker of hope igniting in his eyes. "Together."

With renewed purpose, we delved deeper into the lore, the pages whispering secrets as we turned them eagerly. The storm outside intensified, a cacophony of nature that mirrored the tempest in our hearts. It felt surreal, as if the universe was both urging us forward and reminding us of the stakes.

Hours passed in a blur of discovery, and the world outside faded into a distant echo. My fingers ached from flipping through the pages, but I was unwilling to relent. Each passage was a thread pulling us closer to a solution, a way to break the chains that bound Damian to his cursed bloodline.

Finally, a passage caught my eye—"Only through the truest of connections can the essence of blood be shared." My heart raced as I read on. "When the moon is at its zenith, the participants must exchange a drop of blood, invoking their deepest desires."

"Romantic, isn't it?" Damian quipped, leaning back against the wall, arms crossed. "An invocation under the moon. Maybe we should light some candles and put on some mood music."

"Very funny," I shot back, laughter bubbling up to the surface despite the gravity of our situation. "I'll bring the wine if you bring the spontaneous poetry."

"Deal. Though I'm more of a 'staring into the abyss' kind of guy than a romantic poet."

"Then we'll see if we can't convert you," I retorted, but my heart was racing for different reasons. The reality of what we were proposing settled heavily between us.

As we continued our search, a sense of urgency began to crystallize. The moon would soon reach its zenith, and with it, our opportunity to confront this legacy once and for all. The thought sent a thrill of fear and excitement coursing through me.

Damian's gaze turned serious again, the weight of his resolve shining through. "We need to gather everything we can. The components for the ritual, the right location—this isn't something we can wing."

"Then we'll make a list and check it twice," I replied, determination threading through my words. "We'll turn this place upside down if we have to."

"Just promise me one thing," he said, a rare intensity in his voice. "Whatever happens, if we start to lose control, you promise you'll run."

"Absolutely not," I shot back, my heart racing. "I'm not leaving you, Damian. Not now. Not ever."

The air crackled with unspoken words and unyielding promises as we set about our preparations. I could feel the storm outside echoing the tumult within me, a prelude to the challenges ahead. But one thing was certain: we were bound by more than blood, more than a shared curse. We were entwined in a destiny forged by our choices, and together, we would find a way to rewrite our story.

The moon hung high, a ghostly sentinel in the velvet sky, casting an ethereal glow over the remnants of our makeshift sanctuary. The air was electric, charged with the weight of possibility and the impending storm of our choices. We had gathered our supplies—an assortment of crystals, herbs, and ancient texts spread across the table like a haphazard map of our desperate quest. Each item gleamed under the soft light, symbols of our determination to break the chains binding Damian to his cursed bloodline.

As I adjusted a cluster of flickering candles, their flames dancing like mischievous spirits, I glanced over at Damian. He was deep in thought, his brows furrowed in concentration as he meticulously arranged the components we had chosen for the ritual. I caught the way his fingers brushed over the materials, and for a fleeting moment, I was reminded of how the simplest of touches could hold so much power.

"What are you thinking about?" I asked, breaking the silence that had wrapped around us like a shroud.

He looked up, a shadow of uncertainty lurking in his gaze. "Just wondering if we've got everything we need. You know how these things are—if you miss one little detail, it could all go sideways."

"Or it could go gloriously right," I countered, attempting to infuse some optimism into the heavy atmosphere. "We're due for a bit of luck, don't you think?"

"Luck is a fickle companion," he replied, a wry smile twitching at the corners of his mouth. "But I like your optimism."

"Consider it my personal brand," I said, mimicking a playful, exaggerated inflection as I waved my hands theatrically. "Ariadne's Unwavering Optimism! Guaranteed to defy the odds."

He chuckled, and the sound sent a warm rush through me, dissipating some of the tension that had woven itself around our plans. "If that's the case, we should bottle it and sell it. I'm sure we could fund our future adventures."

"Only if we promise to use it sparingly. Can't let the universe catch on to our schemes." I leaned closer, studying the preparations laid out before us. "So, how does this all work?"

"According to the text, once we've gathered everything, we'll have to stand together at the moon's zenith. The connection will need to be forged during that moment. I'll invoke the bloodline while you—"

"While I do what?"

He hesitated, and the light in his eyes dimmed slightly. "While you offer your own essence in exchange. It's a symbiotic act."

"Symbiotic?" I repeated, feeling a pang of apprehension. "Isn't that just a fancy way of saying I'm about to be a part of your cursed bloodline?"

"In a sense." His voice softened, a soothing balm against my growing unease. "But it's more than that. It's about creating a new bond, one that can break the old curse. If we can merge our essences at the right moment, we could sever the ties binding me to the Velvet Charm."

"And if something goes wrong?"

"Then we adapt," he said, resolve hardening his features. "We've made it through worse, haven't we?"

"True," I conceded, though my heart was a restless bird flapping against its cage. "Still, I'd prefer to avoid any near-death experiences tonight."

"Agreed. But let's not dwell on that. We've got a moon to invoke." He shot me a grin that filled my chest with warmth, grounding me amidst the uncertainty.

The hour approached, and I could feel the air thickening with tension as we set the last of the candles. Each flickering flame mirrored the heartbeat of the moment, a soft reminder that everything hinged on what we were about to do. The world outside seemed to hold its breath, a silence descending as if it understood the gravity of our endeavor.

"Ready?" Damian asked, stepping closer, his presence a comforting weight beside me.

"Ready as I'll ever be," I replied, forcing a smile even as my insides twisted with anxiety. The wind howled outside, a mournful sound that resonated with the uncertainty lurking in the shadows.

As the moon reached its zenith, casting its silver light across our small sanctuary, we positioned ourselves at the center of our carefully arranged circle. I could feel the energy swirling around us, a palpable force that thrummed with potential. "Now what?" I whispered, glancing at the ritual text, the words swimming in my mind.

"Now we begin," he said, taking my hand. His grip was firm, grounding, and I could feel the warmth radiating from him, igniting a spark of courage within me.

With a steadying breath, he recited the first incantation, the ancient words flowing from his lips like water from a spring. The air around us shimmered, the candles flickering wildly as if responding to his voice. I felt the vibrations of the words deep in my bones, resonating with something primal and powerful.

"Now," he urged, a spark of intensity in his gaze. "We share our blood."

I nodded, adrenaline surging through me as I produced a small dagger, its blade glinting ominously in the moonlight. My heart raced as I pressed the cold metal against my palm, a shiver running down my spine. "Here goes nothing," I murmured, before making a quick cut, wincing as the sharp pain sliced through me.

Crimson droplets fell into the center of our circle, each drop a testament to my resolve. Damian followed suit, his blood mingling with mine, creating a vivid swirl of color that seemed to pulse with life. The moment our essences connected, the world around us shifted, a whirl of sensations igniting our surroundings.

"Now the incantation," he instructed, his voice a fervent whisper as he pulled me closer.

"Together," I said, intertwining my fingers with his, feeling the heat of our blood merging beneath the light of the moon.

"By blood and bone, we summon thee," he intoned, our voices weaving together in a haunting harmony. The air crackled with energy, a tangible force that swirled around us like a tempest. I could feel the power rising, wrapping us in its embrace, but it was more than just the magic of the ritual—it was the depth of our connection.

With each passing moment, I could sense the presence of something ancient stirring in response to our call, a force both alluring and terrifying. "What is happening?" I breathed, a shiver of exhilaration and fear racing down my spine.

"I don't know!" he shouted over the growing winds, his face alight with a mixture of wonder and dread. "Stay focused!"

As the final words spilled from our lips, the room erupted in a brilliant flash of light, blinding and overwhelming. The air grew thick, heavy with a sense of impending change, and I could feel the very fabric of reality shifting around us. But then, in the blink of an eye, the light extinguished, plunging us into an eerie silence.

I blinked, disoriented, and as my vision cleared, I found myself staring into the depths of a churning darkness, the shadows pooling around us like ink. "Damian?" I called, fear creeping into my voice.

But he didn't respond. In that heartbeat, as the air thickened with tension, I realized the truth—I was standing alone in the encroaching darkness, and the bond we had forged was suddenly being tested in ways I couldn't comprehend.

Just then, a chilling laughter echoed through the void, a sound both familiar and haunting, resonating in the very marrow of my bones. "Welcome back to the fold, my dear."

Panic surged within me as I turned, and my heart dropped at the sight that greeted me. A figure cloaked in shadows stepped forward, a smile curving their lips in a way that chilled me to my core. "You've come a long way, but it seems the night is just beginning."

Chapter 29: The Last Ember

The air crackled with energy as we stood in the dim light of the abandoned warehouse, the scent of damp concrete mingling with something sweet and metallic, a remnant of magic long since faded. I could feel the weight of history pressing down around us, ancient and unyielding, each dust mote a silent witness to the power that had once thrived in this forgotten place. The flickering of candlelight cast jagged shadows on the walls, flickering like the remnants of dreams we dared to hope for.

Damian's hand felt warm and steady in mine, a grounding presence amidst the swirling chaos of my thoughts. He looked at me, his eyes deep pools of uncertainty mingled with fierce determination. It was a strange juxtaposition, but then again, everything about our lives had become an exquisite contradiction. He was the embodiment of darkness—both the one who wore it and the one fighting to break free. I could almost feel the remnants of the Velvet Charm still clinging to him, a whisper of its insidious touch.

"Are you sure about this?" he asked, his voice a low rumble that vibrated through the stillness of the room. I caught the glimmer of doubt in his gaze, and it echoed the trepidation in my chest.

"More than ever," I replied, the words tumbling out with an urgency that surprised even me. "We've come too far to turn back now. This is our only chance." The ritual was a dance with destiny, and I was ready to take the lead.

We stepped forward into the circle marked by salt and herbs, the faint aroma of sage and rosemary wrapping around us like a protective cocoon. I glanced at the intricate symbols etched into the floor, their meanings ancient and lost to time, yet pulsing with a familiar resonance. I could feel the magic thrumming in my veins, a heady rush of potential and peril.

As we joined hands, a brilliant light exploded around us, a kaleidoscope of colors swirling in a dizzying dance. The warmth enveloped me, seeping into my skin, igniting every cell in my body. I could see the threads of magic weaving together, connecting us in ways I couldn't yet comprehend. "Stay focused," I reminded him, squeezing his hand tighter. I could feel his heartbeat syncing with mine, a rhythmic reminder that we were in this together.

"Always," he murmured, his voice steady as the light intensified. I looked at him, the shadows that had clung to him for so long beginning to dissipate, revealing a man I had fought for, a man I had come to love.

With a breath that felt like a promise, I chanted the words of the ritual, my voice weaving through the luminescence like a song, wrapping around us in tendrils of sound. The world outside faded, and for a moment, it was just us and the power we summoned. Each syllable poured from my lips, rising in crescendo, echoing off the walls until it felt as though the very foundation of the warehouse shook beneath us.

"Let the light break the shadows," I implored, feeling the magic pulse in time with my heartbeat. The air thickened, each breath a struggle as I felt the tether of Damian's curse unravel, thread by delicate thread. "Let it sever the bond and free the soul!"

The energy exploded in a burst of white, blinding me for an instant. I could feel Damian's presence shift, the weight of his darkness evaporating like mist in the morning sun. A heart-stopping moment passed where time itself seemed to freeze, and then suddenly, it was over.

As the last echoes of magic faded, I blinked against the afterglow, my senses reorienting. I turned to him, my heart racing. There he stood—truly free, bathed in light, a fierce and beautiful spirit no longer shackled by the shadows. Relief surged through me, a wave of euphoria that left me breathless.

But that joy was short-lived, replaced by a gnawing uncertainty. The world outside had changed. As we stepped out of the circle, the remnants of our victory crashed around us like the debris of a shattered dream. The warehouse, once a sanctuary, now lay in ruins, the crumbling walls a testament to the cost of our battle.

"What happened?" Damian's voice was low, edged with disbelief as he surveyed the destruction. I followed his gaze, my heart sinking.

"The city..." I whispered, the realization hitting me like a cold wave. The magic we had unleashed to save him had come at a steep price. The vibrant heart of the city we loved had been left in tatters, the echoes of laughter and life now replaced by an eerie silence.

We stepped outside, the air heavy with the scent of ash and smoke. The streets were littered with remnants of what had once been—a playground swing swaying in the wind, a storefront window shattered, the glass glinting like fallen stars. Our allies, those brave souls who had fought alongside us, were scattered like leaves caught in a storm.

"We'll find them," I said, turning to Damian, my resolve hardening as I looked into his eyes. "We have to. They sacrificed so much for us."

He nodded, a flicker of determination igniting in his gaze. "Together," he affirmed, the word hanging in the air between us, laden with promise.

As we walked through the remnants of our home, my hand clasped in his, I felt an unshakeable bond between us—a connection forged in fire and fear, tempered by love. The darkness had tried to tear us apart, but we were still standing, still fighting. It was a new beginning amidst the ruins, and as long as we faced whatever came next together, I knew we would reclaim not just our city, but also the pieces of our lives that still sparkled like embers in the aftermath.

The streets lay in disarray, a cacophony of shattered glass and smoldering debris underfoot, each crunch a reminder of what we had fought to protect. The air was thick with the acrid scent of smoke, mingling with the faintest hint of rain that threatened to fall, as if the heavens themselves were mourning for the city we once knew. We moved cautiously, hand in hand, the warmth of Damian's touch grounding me amidst the chaos.

"Maybe we should start at the café," I suggested, glancing at the skeletal remains of what had once been our favorite haunt, where laughter had spilled into the streets like sunlight. "If anyone survived, they'd head there."

Damian's lips curled into a wry smile, the kind that hinted at his unyielding spirit. "Or they're busy hoarding all the pastries," he replied, his tone light but laced with an underlying tension. I knew he felt the weight of our loss, and yet here he was, ready to find humor where none seemed to exist.

We pressed on, the distance between each step feeling like a countdown. My heart raced not only from the devastation around us but also from the thrill of uncertainty that hung in the air like the promise of a summer storm. As we approached the café, my mind raced with thoughts of our friends—Rhea, with her fiery spirit and fierce loyalty, and Eli, whose quick wit and charm could light up any room.

"Do you think they're okay?" I asked, biting my lip, the anxiety clawing at me. I wasn't sure if I was seeking comfort or reassurance, but the uncertainty of it all felt like a storm gathering at the horizon.

"We'll find them," Damian said with quiet conviction. "They're tougher than they look." He paused, glancing around at the desolation that surrounded us. "And they know how to run when things get messy."

The café stood before us, its doors ajar like an invitation, or perhaps a warning. We stepped inside, the sound of our footsteps echoing in the empty space, the once-bustling atmosphere replaced by an eerie silence. The familiar aroma of fresh coffee hung in the air, now tinged with a bitter aftertaste that spoke of loss and abandonment. I shivered, the chill of reality seeping into my bones.

"Is that coffee?" I murmured, momentarily distracted by the scent, my stomach betraying me with a growl. "Or am I just imagining it?"

"Definitely coffee," Damian said, a hint of amusement in his voice. "We might just need to break into the espresso machine if we want to survive this apocalypse."

I couldn't help but chuckle, the absurdity of the situation sparking a flicker of hope within me. "Let's just find our friends first before we start an impromptu barista competition."

Moving deeper into the café, I pushed through the chaos of overturned tables and scattered chairs, my heart pounding not just from fear but from a surge of adrenaline. Each corner we turned held the potential for either reunion or heartbreak, and I steeled myself against the latter.

As we reached the back room, the door creaked open slightly, revealing a flicker of light. My breath caught in my throat, a mixture of dread and excitement bubbling to the surface. "Do you hear that?" I whispered, my eyes locked on the sliver of warmth illuminating the darkness.

"Yeah, and it doesn't sound like a horror movie," Damian said, his voice low but steady. "Let's check it out."

With a nod, I pushed the door open, the hinges groaning in protest. The sight before us took my breath away—a small group huddled together, their faces illuminated by the flickering light of a makeshift lantern. Rhea sat cross-legged on the floor, her fierce red hair a beacon of defiance against the shadows. Eli leaned against the wall, his trademark grin just visible in the dim light, a sight that filled me with relief.

"Look who decided to crash the party," Rhea exclaimed, her eyes lighting up with a mixture of surprise and joy. "We thought you two were toast."

"We're tougher than we look," I shot back, unable to suppress my smile. "Though the ruins outside are a bit dramatic, don't you think?"

Eli chuckled, pushing himself upright. "What can we say? We wanted to keep things interesting." He glanced around the makeshift refuge, his expression sobering. "But we need to figure out our next move. The city's in chaos, and we can't just sit here."

Rhea's brow furrowed, her usual spark dimmed by the weight of our situation. "The Velvet Charm is still out there. We can't let it regroup or regain its strength."

Damian exchanged a look with me, a silent understanding passing between us. "We just broke its hold on me," he said, his voice steady. "But it's clear we need to finish what we started. We need to find the source of its power and end this once and for all."

"Where do we even begin?" Rhea asked, her fingers tapping nervously against her knee. "It's like chasing shadows in the dark."

"There's an old library on the outskirts of the city," I suggested, my mind racing back to the stories I had heard. "It was said to house the original texts on the Velvet Charm, things the current keepers don't even know about."

Eli perked up at this, his curiosity piqued. "The one that's been abandoned for years? I thought it was just a rumor."

"Rumor or not, we need to check it out. It might give us the answers we're looking for," I replied, the sense of urgency igniting a fire within me.

Damian nodded, his grip tightening around my hand. "Then we leave at first light. We'll gather supplies and be ready to face whatever waits for us out there."

As we began to plan our next steps, I felt a surge of hope mingling with the uncertainty. The road ahead was fraught with danger, but I knew with Damian, Rhea, and Eli by my side, we could face whatever darkness loomed in our future. The weight of our past would not define us; we were carving our own destiny, one filled with light, laughter, and the unbreakable bonds of friendship.

The sun rose timidly over the shattered skyline, casting a warm golden hue on the remnants of our city, the light filtering through the ruins like a gentle sigh. It felt surreal, as if the world were holding its breath, waiting for something to shift. I stood at the edge of our makeshift camp, watching the flickering flames of the small fire we had built to ward off the morning chill, each crackle a promise of resilience. The scent of smoke mingled with the earthy aroma of damp leaves, grounding me in this moment, even as my mind raced with thoughts of what lay ahead.

Damian emerged from the shadows, his silhouette framed by the light, and I couldn't help but admire the way it danced around him. "You know, if we keep surviving like this, we might as well start charging for admission," he quipped, a teasing smile on his lips that sent warmth flooding through me.

"Or we could just write a best-selling survival guide," I replied, arching an eyebrow. "How to Navigate a Post-Apocalyptic Café: Tips and Tricks for Sipping Coffee Among the Ruins."

He chuckled, the sound a balm against the backdrop of our grim reality. "I'll add in a chapter about the best pastries to stockpile during a magical crisis. You know, the essentials."

Our banter was a welcome distraction from the gravity of our mission, but as I looked around at the faces of my friends—each of them weary yet determined—I felt the weight of our task settle over us like a heavy fog. We had one goal: to reach that old library, rumored to hold the secrets of the Velvet Charm. With every step we took toward that destination, the stakes grew higher, and the dread coiled tighter in my stomach.

"Ready?" I asked, gathering the courage that felt like a fragile thread in my chest.

"Let's do this," Damian replied, his voice steady, drawing strength from our shared resolve. The fire crackled behind us, a flicker of warmth as we packed up our few supplies and prepared to face whatever awaited us beyond the threshold of the familiar ruins.

As we navigated through the remnants of the city, the streets were a graveyard of memories, each building a testament to a life lived and loved. We moved in silence, the sounds of our footsteps muted against the debris of what once thrived. The air was thick with the scent of ash and forgotten dreams, mingling with the whispers of our own fears.

It wasn't long before we reached the outskirts, where the library stood shrouded in vines and neglect, a looming giant that had once housed knowledge and wisdom. Its stone façade was weathered, crumbling under the weight of time and neglect, but to us, it was a beacon of hope, a promise of answers waiting to be uncovered.

"I always imagined libraries to be more inviting," Eli remarked, eyeing the cracked windows with a mix of trepidation and excitement. "Maybe with a nice coffee shop on the side?"

"First, we'll need to survive the journey inside," Rhea countered, her voice low, betraying the tension that hung in the air. "Then we can consider opening a franchise."

With a shared glance, we stepped into the shadowy entrance. The air was cooler inside, thick with the musty scent of ancient paper and dust motes dancing lazily in the filtered light. The silence was almost deafening, broken only by the soft creaking of the old building settling. I shivered, feeling the weight of the library's history pressing down on us.

"Stick together," Damian whispered, his tone serious. "We don't know what we're up against."

As we moved deeper into the labyrinth of shelves, the light dwindled, the shadows creeping closer, wrapping around us like a shroud. I ran my fingers along the spines of the books, their titles faded and forgotten. Each one held a story, a piece of history that could either save us or condemn us.

Suddenly, a sound broke through the silence—a low rumble that resonated through the floor beneath us. My heart raced as I turned to the group, eyes wide with alarm. "What was that?"

"Probably just the building settling," Eli suggested, though his voice lacked conviction.

"Or something else," Rhea added, her gaze darting toward the far corner of the room where shadows flickered like whispers.

Without warning, a loud crash echoed through the aisles, sending a cascade of dust raining down from the shelves. We jumped apart, instinctively forming a defensive circle, hearts pounding in unison.

"Stay sharp!" Damian ordered, his stance wide, ready for anything that might come at us from the darkness.

I strained my ears, listening intently. The silence was thick, palpable, punctuated only by the distant sound of something heavy scraping against the stone floor. "It's not just the building," I whispered, the realization sinking in like a stone in my stomach.

As if in response to my fear, a shadow shifted at the edge of the room, a figure emerging from the depths of the darkness. My breath caught in my throat as I squinted, trying to discern its form.

"Who goes there?" I called out, trying to sound brave, but my voice trembled.

The figure stepped forward, illuminated by a beam of light that spilled through a broken window. My heart sank as recognition washed over me, a mixture of disbelief and horror. It was a familiar face, twisted by something darker, a reflection of the man I once knew.

"Ah, the fearless heroes return," he sneered, his eyes glinting with malice. "I was wondering when you'd find your way back to me."

"Marcus," Damian growled, stepping protectively in front of me. "What are you doing here?"

"Oh, just cleaning up the mess you left behind," he said, the words dripping with contempt. "You think you can just waltz in here and undo everything I've worked for? The Velvet Charm belongs to me now."

Before I could react, Marcus raised his hand, and the air crackled with energy, the remnants of dark magic swirling around him like a tempest. I felt the ground shift beneath my feet, a powerful force rising that threatened to pull us into a void of shadows.

"Get back!" I shouted, instinctively pulling Rhea and Eli closer as I felt the air grow heavy with tension. "Damian, we need to—"

But before I could finish, the floor trembled violently, and with a deafening roar, the library began to collapse around us. Dust and debris rained down, and in that heart-stopping moment, everything I thought I knew hung in the balance, teetering on the edge of oblivion.

As the world blurred into chaos, I reached for Damian's hand, desperation clawing at my heart. "We can't let him win!"

The ground shook, and I felt the pull of darkness beckoning, the shadows eager to swallow us whole. And just as the world around us began to shatter, I realized with a jolt that this was only the beginning of our fight—a battle that would either break us or forge us anew.

In that instant, with the walls crumbling and the shadows closing in, I knew we had to face Marcus, but whether we would emerge victorious or be consumed by the very darkness we sought to defeat remained uncertain.